TETHERED

REMNANANTS

By:

Page Parker

Acknowledgments

As always, I owe my family every ounce of gratitude for encouraging and having faith in me. My husband has never once failed to support whatever endeavor I've wanted to achieve. I would especially like to thank my daughter for her contributions to this particular book. She has been my sounding board for ideas throughout this whole process, and I'm so thankful for her.

One

Walking down the jet bridge is miserable. There's no air circulating and I can feel the heat of a hundred bodies filling the small space. My head is already pounding and I can't wait to shed my zip-up hoodie as soon as I get on the plane. The couple in front of me are in their seventies, and they're clearly struggling with their carry-on luggage, bags, and neck pillows. I assume they are husband and wife and they appear to be stressed. The husband is holding their passports and boarding passes and trying to help his wife move toward the door of the plane with all of their belongings. I can tell they're frustrated and they're snapping at each other. The wife gives him an irritated glance and he seems to be able to read her facial expression without even looking at her or a single word being uttered. Then, just as quickly as the irritation reared its head, the husband leans into her and whispers something in her ear. It's brief, and he nudged her with his arm while speaking. I couldn't catch what he said, but it must have been something wonderful because I saw her shoulders relax and she tilted her head down toward the floor. I could see a slight smile on her face from her side profile. Then she looks up at him and chuckles. Her smile clearly brings him joy as he returns her smile with his own. It was such a fleeting exchange between the two of them, but it obviously changes their dynamic in an instant. She leaned into him and he brought one arm around her shoulders for an embrace. Whatever the irritation and frustration had been, it was gone in a flash. Watching it brings on a wave of emotion and envy for me. I'm envious of the fact that they have each other to snap at, share the frustration, and laugh in joy at everyday things. That built-in companion who can anticipate what you're thinking and needing without a single word spoken. I'm missing my partner. The emptiness is crushing me and I'm struggling to keep moving. Part of me just wants to lie down right here and give up, but I keep moving because the line I'm in is naturally propelling me forward.

I step across the small gap that separates the jet bridge and the plane. The small sliver of daylight that I feel the need to cautiously step across. I wonder to myself if anyone has ever fallen through that crack. I'm immediately greeted by a smiling flight attendant who is wearing a very large smile with lots of white teeth. She's gorgeous and seems very kind, but I'm just not in the mood for pleasantries. I decided to be nice in return, though, because I'm going to need her help during this flight. It's going to be a struggle. I briefly glance at her nametag and notice her name is Kate. She says, "good evening, what's your seat number?"

I responded, "3 A please." Kate graciously smiles and points me to my left toward the front of the plane. I've never been able to go left before. This is my first time sitting in first class. I walk through the narrow doorway that has a curtain hanging to the side. I recall sitting in the main cabin and always thinking how pretentious it seemed that first-class passengers had to be curtained off from the rest of us peasants. Like they just couldn't be bothered to even have to look at the likes of us commoners sitting in the back. I realize now that probably wasn't a fair assumption and feel a pang of guilt. Partly because I don't deserve to be in first class and partly that I judged people that I didn't even know. I guess that's what happens when you section people off based on how much money they can afford to pay for something.

I reach my seat on the left-hand side. It's a single window seat and I'm overjoyed that I'm not in the middle where I would have to be beside another person in their pod. The idea of having to talk to someone and be social makes my head pound harder. I immediately unzip and remove my hoodie because the plane is hotter than that stupid jet bridge was and I'm about to melt. I place my crossbody bag, hoodie, book and backpack in my seat and then hoist my carry-on up into the compartment overhead.It's a struggle to even get it up there; and then getting it turned in the compartment so that others can fit their bags up there is such a pain. It's just another reminder of the help I no longer have at my side for these small tasks in life. I plop down into my seat and get my things situated. My first goal is to dig out my ibuprofen from my backpack. I find my Sam's Club industrial sized bottle of ibuprofen and toss three pills into my mouth promptly. Thankfully there is a small bottle of water waiting for me on my side tray. I gulp down the pills and the water, lean my head back against the seat and close my eyes. I take a deep breath to try to calm my nerves now that I'm settled. A rush of relief comes over me, but it's instantly followed by a searing hurt in my heart. The grief is raw and often ebbs and flows weirdly. It sometimes comes over me at the most unusual times, and it doesn't seem to care where I am.

I squeeze my eyes and I can feel the burn of tears behind my eyelids. My mind flashes to a couple of months ago when I was dressed in my mid-length black dress and heels. They were some of my favorite heels with a pointed toe and a 2 inch height. They were surprisingly comfortable considering they were heels. I watched them as I struggled to put one foot in front of the other. They were clicking on the pavement annoyingly and alerting everyone around me of my presence. All I wanted to do was disappear and blend in, but my shoes were like an alarm giving away my location. Walking into the gymnasium and seeing a sea of sad faces staring at me as if my world had ended. It had. There were so many people and I tried so hard to recognize and acknowledge each one, but they seemed to meld together forming one big smear of grief-stricken looks. It was like looking at an impressionistic painting of sad faces. Each one looking the same as the next. I couldn't tell if it was my mind playing tricks on me or because my eyes were blurry and cloudy, but I couldn't focus no matter how hard I tried.

"Ms. …can I get you a glass of champagne?" I jolted at the sound of her voice and opened my eyes in shock. Kate stood there looking at me with a questioning look and she seemed somewhat concerned. I probably looked terrible and was wearing the hurt on my face.

"Yes, please. That would be great. Also, Kate…" I said in a whispered voice, "this is my first time flying first class. Can you kind of give me a run-down on how my seat works and what to expect?" Kate looked at me with a smirk followed quickly by compassion and said she would give me my very own first-class tutorial as soon as she returned with my champagne. She made her way to the attendants 'station and I glanced around to see if anyone had overheard or was looking at me. Thankfully, the other first class passengers seemed to be distracted and most already had earbuds in. They were not concerned with my inexperience with this end of the airplane.

Kate returned promptly with my champagne and she proceeded to give me a quick and dirty run down of all things first class. She helped me navigate the technical components of selecting something to watch, where to connect my earbuds, and how my seat worked for when I am ready to sleep. It really was the epitome of class and elegance. After take off, the meal was served. It was a lovely mix of yummy cheeses, bread, and savory vegetables with pasta. However, I took about four or five bites and was done. I just don't have an appetite and forcing myself to eat the last few weeks has been torture. All I wanted to do was sleep. Sleep helped the time to pass and I didn't have to feel anything while I was asleep. Although, it was always devastating to wake up and remember the reality all over again. It was probably around 5:00pm and we would fly overnight. We were scheduled to land in Edinburgh at about 8:00am. I polished off my champagne and covered up with my blanket. I reclined my seat to the flat position and slid my privacy screen up. I turned off my reading light and decided that slumber was the best choice I could make right now. I needed to turn my brain off and just get through the next few hours.

I awoke to the sound of the seatbelt sign dinging and the muffled voice of the captain. For a brief second I wasn't exactly sure where I was. Then I heard the male flight attendant asking another passenger if she would like anything else to drink. I looked at my phone and saw that I had been asleep for about three hours. I was disappointed that it hadn't been longer. The flight indicator on the screen in my pod showed that we were near Canada. Somehow the thought of Canada made me sad. It's one of the places we had dreamed of traveling to and never made it. There was suddenly a pit in my stomach and instant anxiety about the thought of completing my travel bucket list on my own now. I decided I needed to get up and stretch my legs and go to the restroom. Kate happened to be coming down the aisle just at that time and asked me if I needed anything. I told her I was fine and was heading to the bathroom. She said,"you should head upstairs. There's a bar and restroom up there. You can get a little walking in that way." My response was, "there's stairs?" I was stunned. I had never been on a plane this big. I thought that was only in movies. Kate chuckled and seemed appreciative of my naivety and inexperience. I think she was eager to show someone something new and exciting. She walked me to the curtain and sure enough there was a set of winding stairs leading up. For some reason this was thrilling to me and I began my ascent up the stairs to investigate the bar area.

I quickly located the bathroom and took care of that business. I really didn't want to go back to my seat yet so I approached the bar. It was bigger than I had expected. It was laid out in a semi-circle design with about 8 barstools positioned around it. The bartender was a gentleman that appeared to be in his late 50's or early 60's. He had salt and pepper hair and a well groomed short beard. He wore a navy-blue uniform similar to the other flight attendants, only he had a bow tie instead of a regular necktie. His vest was stretched to the limit around his protruding belly, and the buttons on his vest looked as though they might not make it through the duration of this flight. As I approached the bar, he was drying a glass with a dishcloth and chatting with one of the passengers who was sitting at the bar. He appeared very friendly and gave me a quick nod and smile as I bellied up to the bar. There were three other guests at the bar. The gentleman who was talking to the bartender appeared to be in late 30's or early 40's. He had dark hair and features with just a slight amount of gray trimming the edges of his sideburns near his ears. The other two guests were a young man and woman who were cuddled up to each other and clearly in their own little world. They seemingly had no idea any of the rest of us were on this plane.

As I sat on the barstool, the bartender quickly put down the glass he had been drying and excused himself from the chat he was having. He approached me with kindness and greeted me with "good evening ma'am. What can I get for you?" I replied with a quick hello and said, "I'll have Crown on the rocks please." "Coming right up," he says with a grin. I glance at his nametag and quickly try to commit the name Randy to memory. Crown straight is not something I typically drink, but I'm currently desperate to numb my mind and in search of something to help me sleep through this flight. I could take one of the sleeping pills the doctor gave me, but I was afraid that it would knock me out for a week. I can just picture the flight attendant trying to wake me at the end of the flight. The mental image of them trying to lug me off the plane in a sleeping pill coma flashed through my head. No, let's avoid that. Maybe some Crown will do the trick. Randy places the square-rimmed rocks glass in front of me. I thank him and then, as if he could read the expression on my face, he says, "drinks are included with the flight" and glances quickly toward a tip jar. The jar has a few bills in it. Some are pounds, and some are dollars. I look back to Randy and smile. At first I panicked because I didn't bring my purse or wallet with me to the bar, but then I remembered the ten dollar bill in my pocket. It was my change from buying a Starbucks hazelnut iced latte in the airport earlier today. I slipped it out of my pants pocket and got up to walk over to the tip jar. As I placed the bill in the jar, Randy gave me a wink with a crooked smile and returned to drying glasses behind the bar.

The man Randy had been talking to glanced at me and gave me a nod with a brief smile as I returned to my barstool. He was an attractive man with dark, short hair that was sprinkled with a small amount of grey. He had a shadow of dark stubble growing where a beard would stand if allowed more time. It appeared that his eyes were a light color, but it was difficult to tell with such a brief look. His dark eyelashes and brows seemed to be masking the color of his eyes. He returned to his conversation with the bartender as I slid back onto my barstool and picked up my drink for another numbing dose. As they continued their conversation, my mind wandered over the events of the last few weeks. My thoughts immediately brought on a heartache that I couldn't begin to describe. The loss and devastation engulfed me every time I allowed my thoughts to return. I was able to recall with shockingly good detail the pain and grief on my family members 'faces. My in-laws were absolutely shattered and almost inconsolable. I remember thinking that I wanted to take that pain away from them, and I wanted to protect them and make them feel better. But then again, I just didn't have the energy or the strength to console anyone. I was using every ounce of my strength just to keep myself upright and going.

I remember looking down at my leg during the service and noticing a run in my off-black pantyhose. I remember thinking to myself, "who even wears pantyhose anymore?" I think I had reached a point of so much devastation that I couldn't even keep my thoughts on track anymore. It was like I was losing my mind, I knew it in real time, and there was nothing I could do about it. The rest of the service was an absolute blur. I faintly recalled looking over a blanket of grieving faces; many family, friends, and co-workers. They all looked solemn and sad. I dreaded the condolences and the social exchanges I was going to have to endure after the service. I just wanted them to all go home and not say a word to me, but I knew that wasn't going to happen so I braced myself for the hugs and offerings of "thoughts and prayers."

"Would you like another?" Randy asked as I snapped back to the present moment. Somehow, I had sipped until my whole drink was gone. I wondered if I was going to be able to walk back to my pod without playing bumper body. I replied, "no thank you. I think I've had enough for now" and gave him a shy smile. I eased off my bar stool and steadied myself for what might be a wobbly stroll back downstairs and to my seat. Thankfully, I navigated the stairs relatively well and descended to the lower level without incident. Once back in my seat, I decided that some time watching a movie might help ease me back into slumber. I grabbed the small retractable remote attached to the screen in front of me and began my search. I definitely needed something light-hearted. I've never been one to watch movies that are scary or dark in nature, but I really didn't need anything bringing me down right now. I was barely keeping myself above water as it is. After a couple of minutes scrolling, I finally settled on an oldie but goodie rom-com. I've probably watched "Maid of Honor" a dozen times, but it's a good one to occupy my headspace for a while. About 45 minutes into the movie I could feel my eyelids betraying me and I decided to take advantage of the sweet peace that sleep could bring. I reclined my seat to the flat position once again and eagerly drifted off to dream land.

"Mrs. Andrews.... Mrs. Andrews?" I awakened in a haze and struggled to peel my eyes open to look up. Standing over me was Kate smiling down sweetly. I immediately tried to sit up and pay attention to her, but I was having trouble coming out of my sleep fog. I was moving in slow motion and having a hard time adjusting my eyes to the overhead light of the cabin. Once I appeared somewhat with it, Kate let me know that we had landed in Edinburgh. I couldn't believe it! I slept through the whole rest of the flight. I was grateful, but stunned because I normally can't sleep for long stretches of time on a plane. I guess that Crown did the trick. I stored that little tidbit away in my memory bank. I wasn't really one to drink alcohol much, but every once in a great while I might have something. This was one of those times and it did me right. Instantly, I began collecting my things and trying to get organized. I had kicked off my shoes at some point, so I put them and my hoodie back on. I quickly slipped my crossbody bag strap over my head and unzipped it to find my powder compact and tinted lip gloss. I'm sure I looked a mess and just needed to get myself together a bit before getting off the plane. I looked in my small little round mirror to investigate the hot mess I was sure was going to be staring back at me. I was right. I looked exactly like I had drank some alcohol and slept on a plane all night. Oooof. Oh well, I quickly swiped some powder on my face and added some color to my lips and cheeks. I then ran my comb through my tangled hair. I decided to pop a stick of gum in my mouth to kill what was sure to be a foul-smelling disaster. Besides, my mouth felt fuzzy and I couldn't take that for very long. I decided that my first stop after deboarding would be to find an airport bathroom and brush my teeth asap.

I then stood up and took a moment to stretch and twist to pop my back. It felt so good to move. The overhead compartment was already open and mine was the only bag remaining. I reached up to grab it, but it had slid all the way to the back of the compartment and was just out of my reach. I quickly glanced around me to survey how I might solve this problem and decided that stepping onto my seat to get the boost I needed to reach it was the best option. But before I could make that happen, a voice beside me said, "Here, let me get that for you." I glanced over and it was the same gentleman that had been upstairs at the bar talking to Randy earlier in the night. He gave me a quick look of acknowledgement and reached up for my bag before I even had time to respond. He had it down on the aisle floor and slid the handle up in one fluid motion. I looked up and said "thank you so much."

He replied, "no problem.... any time." His voice was deep and his eyes crinkled at the corners when he half smiled. Somehow, that act of kindness and his reassuring voice eased my nerves. I smiled back at him, thanked him again, then grabbed my rolling bag and turned to walk toward the exit.

I walked as quickly as I could to keep pace with the rest of the passengers on the walkway. We were all clearly anxious to get to our next destination, which for me was baggage claim. I followed the crowd somewhat while watching and reading the signs to navigate to the baggage area. We refer to it as Baggage Claim in the U.S., but here the airport signs say "Baggage Reclaim." I guess that really does make more sense since you are reclaiming bags you already gave them to take care of before the flight. I found the "merry go round" as I call it that's linked with our flight number and came to a stop with all the rest of my fellow travelers. It hadn't started yet and I figured it's going to take a minute so I took the opportunity to go to the restroom to potty and brush my teeth.

When I re-emerged from the restroom, I could see that the baggage was on the trolley and everyone was smushed up beside it to fight for their luggage. I squeezed into a space just as another couple had retrieved their luggage and were leaving. I only had one large suitcase to grab and I spotted it right away. However, I knew it was heavy and would require both of my hands to hoist off of the trolley. I set my backpack and rolling carry-on aside and prepared myself. I grabbed it quickly and lifted it off pretty easily. Once I had everything collected, I set off toward the exit to find a cab. I knew getting a cab was going to be pricey, but I didn't care. It was going to be easier and less hassle than trying to catch a bus or train. As luck would have it, there were several cabs lined up waiting for their prey just outside the door. I approached a cab driver that looked as close to an old trustworthy grandpa as I could possibly find and asked him if he could give me a ride. He agreed immediately and gave me a big Scottish smile that put me right at ease. His accent was thick, but I understood him well. He made short work of putting all my luggage into the "boot" of the car (as they say) while I slid into the back seat and buckled my seatbelt. He asked me, "what's your destination my dear?" and I showed him the address I had pulled up on my phone. And we were off. The cab driver initially asked me a few questions and we shared some back-and-forth chit chat, but eventually he let me just rest and enjoy the view out my window. He could probably tell I had had a long journey and was exhausted.

The streets of Edinburgh were just as I remembered. The old buildings and charming architecture had always fascinated me, and somehow made me feel at home in a place I had never lived. It was currently June and probably about as warm as it was ever going to get. You could tell the locals from the tourists as they walked along the sidewalks. The locals were in summer clothing with short-sleeve shirts and shorts, but the tourists who weren't used to this climate were wearing jeans or pants with jackets or long-sleeve shirts. It was kind of comical to see such differing attire. The skies were a sort of mix of overcast cloud cover, and moments of sunshine peeking through. When the sun peeked through, it instantly warmed my face through the window of the cab. I briefly closed my eyes to take it in and enjoy the warmth and feeling of comfort it provided. After about a twenty-minute drive, the driver announced that we had arrived at my apartment. I had rented an AirB&B apartment for a mid-term stay of 3 months. I had worked out a deal with the owner of the apartment to stay for three months with a provision of extending the term to longer depending on my circumstances.

The sweet old grandpa driver collected my luggage out of the back and flashed me a huge smile. He said, "I hope you enjoy your stay." I thanked him and did my best to return a smile that matched his. I handed him a $20 bill and apologized that I only had American currency on me. He didn't seem bothered by that nuisance at all and thanked me before he was on his way. I approached the steps of the apartment building and found the digital lockbox on the front facade. The owner had left detailed instructions on how to get into the apartment and I had saved a screenshot of the instructions as a picture on my phone. I quickly read the instructions and entered the code. The box clicked open and I found a set of keys. One key opened the door to the building and the other key was meant for the apartment door. The apartment was located on the third floor. Well, it's called the 2nd floor in the UK. They consider the first floor the ground floor and everything else gets numbered accordingly. Nevertheless, I had to climb three flights of stairs with my luggage.This was going to be a workout for sure. About 10 minutes later, I reached my apartment door with all my luggage in tow. I was huffing and puffing though. I clearly needed to put "finding a gym to join" on the top of my to-do list.

I opened the door to the apartment and fumbled my way inside with all my belongings. It was a cute little place with a decent sized-kitchen that opened to the living area just off to the right of the front door. It had one bedroom and attached bath to the left of the door, and a small hallway with a closet that housed a washer and dryer. Well, the washer and dryer are really one in the same. You wash your clothes in it and then turn it on "dryer" mode. I don't know how great that's going to work, but I'm just grateful to have the option. Most of the time, these apartments only have a washing machine in the kitchen and no dryer at all. You usually have to hang your clothes on a drying rack and let them dry the old fashion way.

In the living area, shoved up against the wall, there were several of my boxes that had been shipped over ahead of me. The apartment was furnished, but I had to bring some things to make it feel like home. Luckily, the owners were so kind and sweet and agreed to let me send my things ahead of time. They were there to let the delivery guys in when the shipment arrived. I made a mental note to do something nice for them in return.

I glanced at my phone to see that the time was 9:24 a.m. I was so exhausted. I looked into the bedroom and saw the big queen-sized bed and could just imagine myself crawling in it and sinking into a long nap. But my OCD tendencies wouldn't let that happen. I had too much to do to get organized and I wouldn't be able to rest until my stuff was unpacked and put away. First, though, I had to call my parents and text some friends to let them know I had made it safely. They were all worried sick about me and thought I was an absolute nut job for moving across the world to live by myself in a new place where I knew no one. Especially given the amount of grief and mourning I had been in for the last several weeks. I know they all thought I was being impulsive and crazy….and they were probably right. I just had to do it. I had to get away from the normal where all the memories and reminders of what I had lost were.

My mind flashed to images of my husband. Every time I thought of him, he was smiling. That's pretty much who he was; always happy and bringing joy to everyone around him. My heart squeezed in my chest and the grief washed over me. I sat down on the edge of the couch and buried my face in my hands. Tears slipped out around my fingers as I sobbed quietly. I eventually tried to take a deep breath and wipe my face with my hands. I hated the crying. It made me so tired and I was so tired of doing it. I'm sure the current moment was part grief and part exhaustion, and overwhelmed from traveling, but I wondered when I would be able to move into a phase of grief that didn't result in crying every time. I was ready to get this grief process over with because it hurt so badly. I just wanted to fast forward to a time that everyone promised would come. I still thought of it, but it didn't wound me so much.

After several minutes on the couch, a few texts, and a phone call to my parents, I felt a little better and decided it was time to get to work. Staying busy with putting my stuff away would help me pass the time so I could try to get on UK time and go to bed at a normal time tonight. I spent the next several hours unpacking my luggage, hanging up clothes, folding clothes and unpacking boxes. Around 2:00 I took a short break and remembered that I hadn't drunk or eaten anything since last night on the plane for dinner. Yikes…that's probably not good. I went into the kitchen and opened the fridge. To my surprise, there was a loaf of bread, six eggs, butter, and two liters of flat water. I loved these owners. They were really taking care of me. I quickly scrambled up a couple of eggs and made some toast. I scarfed those down in no time and was kind of surprised at myself. I hadn't been that hungry or eaten that well in weeks.

I drank one of the liters of water and then made a mental note that I probably needed to find a store nearby and get more essentials. I found a notepad in one of my boxes and began making a running list of items I was going to need.

Once I had eaten and taken a break, I returned to my organizing and worked for about three more hours until it was all done. By this time it was around 5:30 and I figured I'd better go out and find a store, or dinner, or both. I grabbed my jacket, purse, phone, and keys and headed out the door. I was intimidated once I was out on the street. I didn't know this area at all, but I had looked at the map to see what was around. There was a Tesco located what appeared to be about four blocks from me so I headed in that direction. Google said it was open until midnight so I had plenty of time. On the way there, I ran across a small pub that smelled heavenly as I passed by. I decided to stop in there and grab dinner because the thought of cooking or making my own dinner by that point was out of the question.

I stepped inside and was immediately greeted by the girl behind the bar. She smiled and told me to sit wherever I liked. So, I sat at the bar. She seemed nice and welcoming. She asked me what I would like to drink and I replied, "just a flat water please." She said, "oh American! Where are you from?" I told her I had just moved, today actually, from the state of Texas in America. She smiled broadly and nearly squealed with delight. She then proceeded to ask me about cowboys and horses. This is always hysterical to me. The perception that's how all Texans live…it's pretty funny. She gave me some recommendations on menu items and once I had ordered we continued our chit chat about America vs the UK. She actually gave me lots of recommendations on places to shop, coffee shops nearby, and the immediate surroundings. She was so sweet. Rachel is her name and I tried to file that away in my brain for the next time I saw her. I was sure I was going to be back here soon.

By about 7:30 I had stumbled up the three flights of stairs once again carrying as many bags of groceries as I could. I was loaded down and my arms and hands were burning from all the bags I was toting. Once inside the apartment, I put them away quickly and then headed straight for the shower. I hadn't showered in well over 30 hours and I was starting to smell pretty rank. After I showered, I watched a few videos on social media and caught up with what friends and family were doing. Then, finally, I crawled into bed and closed my eyes. The exhaustion of the last few weeks and the last 2 days was pulling me under quickly. I could hear the faint sounds of the streets of Edinburgh. It was just enough to make me feel less lonely, but not loud enough to bother me. I drifted off to sleep in the hopes that I would have sweet dreams and wake up feeling a little less grief than the day before. That's what I hoped for each night.

Two

The smell of the coffee in the cafe is just the jolt I need to tackle the day ahead of me. Rachel gave me the recommendation of coming to Black Sheep Coffee and she was spot on. Their coffee is amazing and the service is even better. There's a sweet fella working here named Hamish who's always friendly and welcoming. Each morning I'm greeted with a "hiya" and a broad, cheeky smile that makes me feel like I'm part of the barista family. I'm starting to think I come here too much though because he's already memorized my order. He says, "yer usual latte?" and I nod in agreement. Luckily, my favorite spot in the cafe with a seat near the window overlooking the busy street is available, so I slide into the chair and pull out my laptop. I get situated with my computer and my notepad of to-dos, but ultimately I find myself staring out the window fascinated by the goings-on outside. In true Scotland fashion, it's overcast with a light mist falling this morning. I watch as people walk past the window on their way to work or wherever they're going and I'm struck by the fact that none of them seem to care about the misting rain. They all have umbrellas or rain jackets with hoods, but they're not exactly rushing to get away from the rain. They're walking as they would if it were sunny and dry outside; not like we walk in the rain back home. We'd be walking quickly or half-running with our heads down trying to escape the rain and get indoors as fast as possible. But they seem to be oblivious and are not annoyed by the rain at all. Something about that observation shows me it's all about perspective and how you view something. You can either choose to let it annoy you and rush through it, or you can settle in and accept it for what it is.

I'm startled back into reality when Hamish brings my latte to me. He sets it down on the table in front of me with a slight rattle of the spoon on the saucer and says, "I put an extra spot of tablet for you" and gives me a warm smile. He clearly knows that I like the tablet. You're supposed to put it in your coffee to sweeten it, but I often just pick it up and eat it. It's kind of like fudge back home. I'm a little bit embarrassed that he noticed I eat it and gave me extra, but not so embarrassed that I'm going to stop eating it.

Immediately I think of Michael. He would have loved this place and we would definitely have had to purchase extra tablet for him. He loved all things sweet. I made him fudge at Christmas time every year for the last twelve years. The thought that I'll no longer need to do that is suffocating to me. I'm instantly remorseful for the times that I dreaded making the fudge because it took time or I was tired and didn't want to. I'd give anything now to be able to continue something that simple to make him happy. I'll never get that chance again. The grief beginning to wash over me makes my heart seize and I squelch those thoughts at once. I'm in a public place and I don't want to lose control of my emotions in the middle of my new favorite coffee shop, so I pick up my latte for a sip and swallow down the warm, rich flavors along with my sadness.

At this point, I've been in Scotland for about two weeks. I've spent most of my days doing a mix of some touristy things and some everyday things in an effort to stay busy and start to create a routine. Rachel gave me some other recommendations for places to shop, coffee of course, fun things to do, restaurants, and a gym. I really wanted to get started with my exercise routine and I knew that walking the streets in the rain wasn't going to cut it for me. She pointed me in the direction of a gym that's about 7 blocks from my apartment so I can get a little walk or jog in on the way there and back each day. It's a quaint gym that's locally owned. It's not one of those huge meat-market type gyms where everyone is already perfect and trying to impress each other. It's fairly small but has everything I could possibly want. I get up at 5:00 each morning; mainly because that's been my routine for years and partly because the sun is fully out at that time and it wakes me up.I haven't quite gotten used to the extended daylight of summertime. The sun doesn't set until about 10:30pm and then comes up again around 4:30am. I get up and have some coffee at home and then I head to the gym. By the time I get there, it's about 6:30 and still early enough that there's not a ton of people to battle for equipment and space. This morning there were only two people there. It was what appeared to be a man and wife, or girlfriend and boyfriend perhaps. They were working out together and seemed to spend an equal amount of time working out and flirting with one another. It wasn't in a "gross, get a room" kind of way, but a cute "they're smitten with each other" kind of way. Watching them made me long for that kind of comfort again.

Michael and I were similar in that way. We genuinely enjoyed being together all the time. I never felt the desire to have time away from him like other women said about their husbands. I have girlfriends that would talk about getting some peace and quiet away from their husbands as if they just needed a break from them. But, I never felt that way about Michael. I couldn't relate to that feeling at all, and I'm pretty sure he felt the same way. We truly liked each other and were the best of friends. We could talk to each other about anything. Or, we could sit in silence with one another and be completely comfortable about it. He was absolutely one of the funniest people I know. Knew. Having to adjust my thinking to the past tense destroys me. I can't believe he's gone and this is my new reality. The heaviness of that sets in on me and weighs me down. It's like a huge boulder sitting on my chest and I struggle to breathe each time it occurs to me that he's no longer here.

The rain outside the cafe window has stopped for the moment. It's still gray out, but the streets and buildings look renewed from their soaking. My latte is almost gone and I feel like I didn't even get to enjoy it because I was absent-mindedly drinking it while lost in thought and memories. I put my cup down and slide it to the edge of the table. Opening my laptop, I begin my online search for a job. I've decided that a part time job is something I need. I don't really need to work. The settlement from Michael's life insurance and the rental of our house back home are more than enough to sustain me, but I just need to stay busy. I need to have something else to focus on and also a way to meet people. My job has always kind of been a big part of my social life. I've always generally liked the people I work with and have formed some great, life-long friendships from my jobs. I need to have some purpose each day; a commitment to show up, be productive, and accountable. I know myself too well to think I will be sucked into the depths of depression if I don't busy myself with ordinary life. My heart wants to just go to bed and sleep away the pain. My brain, however, knows that will lead to more heartache and despair.

For the last fifteen years, I've been in pharmaceutical sales. That's how I met Michael. He was a physician's assistant at one of the hospitals I repped for in Texas. I remember the day we met so clearly. I was visiting the hospital that day to approach a specific group of physicians to sell them on the idea of a new drug on the market. The main doctor of the group, who was ultimately in charge of making those kinds of decisions, was a particularly grumpy old codger whose favorite word was "no." Everyone knew he was a grouch and was so hard to crack. I dreaded having to approach him, but there was a part of me that was just plain stubborn and determined to nail him. So, there I was, in the physicians 'lounge trying to corner him to discuss this new drug. He was always flitting around acting like he was too busy to be bothered by a peon like me, so I had to follow him around the lounge while he fixed his plate of lunch. The physicians were being treated that day by the hospital admin to a buffet lunch, so the room was full of doctors sitting around shooting the breeze and indulging on their prime rib. Dr. Grumpy pants was doing a great job of eluding me as I chased after him. He was completely annoyed with me and I with him. He finally stopped, turned to me and said, "I don't have time for this today and I probably don't want what you're offering anyway." I just stood there and stared at him with no emotion on my face. I knew that's what he wanted. He was just a bully and was trying to get a reaction out of me. I was stoic and our stare-off was becoming ridiculous. He finally just walked off and out the door. I rolled my eyes and huffed in exasperation. As I turned to gather my things, his PA was standing there and looking at me apologetically.

He stepped up to me and said, "I'm sorry….I'll talk to him about the product you're proposing. It sounds like it might be a really good option. Sometimes it takes some time to sort of wear him down about something and make him think it was his idea. I'm Michael by the way. I don't think we've met."

"It's nice to meet you", I replied. "I'm Krista, " I said as we shook hands. "And thank you for your help. He can be rather difficult to……..well…..to do anything with" I said as I sarcastically smiled. Michael gave me a huge grin followed by a knowing look. He was young and sexy to be honest. He was about 6 feet tall with broad shoulders and very fit. His hair was a sandy blonde color cropped into a tight military style crew cut. His eyes were dark brown and he had the longest, darkest eye lashes I had ever seen on a man. They were long enough to make most women jealous. His skin was noticeably tan with an olive tint. He immediately struck me as a humble, unassuming type of person. Even though I didn't know him, I sensed that he was genuine and kind. There was something about the way he held himself that exuded confidence, but with good ol 'boy manners and politeness. If I'm being honest, I was pretty much enamored with him from that day on. I have always considered that day to be one of the best days of my life. It was the beginning of a love affair that continued for thirteen years.

My online search begins with a quick Google search of "administrative assistant jobs near me." I had absolutely no desire to return to pharmaceutical sales. At least not now anyway. I wanted something easy. I didn't really need the money, so I was looking for something that requires basic computer skills, phone answering, organization, etc. I was probably going to be WAY overqualified for jobs like that, but it's all I wanted. I didn't want something super stressful. My degree in business administration was going to be under-utilized in my near future if I had anything to do with it. Instantly, my search popped up more than 30 jobs in and around the Edinburgh area. After about an hour of sifting through job descriptions, I finally narrowed it down to about five that I felt like I should apply for. I began the process of submitting my applications online and once I had finished, I decided it was time for another latte. I get up and head to the counter to place my order. This time I got another latte but I also added a scone with jam and clotted cream to my order. It's nearly 10:30am by this point and my stomach is starting to rumble a little bit. By the time I returned to my table, I noticed that I had a message in my email inbox. To my surprise, it was from one of the companies I had just applied to. The subject line read, "Schedule Interview" and I quickly clicked into the email.

It read, "Mrs. Andrews, We appreciate your interest in our company and based upon your application, we would like to schedule an interview at once. Best regards, Erick Eden." I was shocked to have received a response this quickly. I really thought it would take a week or more to get any responses, so I had just a smidgeon of hesitation in replying. That was probably just my anxiety talking. This company was one I thought was especially intriguing when reading the job description. This position was listed as "Administrative Assistant and Personal Assistant" with Eden and Associates. I did a quick search just to see what kind of company this was and it seemed to be some type of structural engineering company from what I can tell. This was fairly overwhelming to me because I know nothing about this field. Maybe even less than nothing. Is this really a company I can be an assistant for? I quickly dismissed my trepidation as my own anxiety and decided that it'll probably be ok since they reached out to me so fast. It seemed like they were desperate. So, I took a deep breath and squelched my apprehensions.

"Dear Mr. Eden, I'm very interested in the position and am available for an interview at your earliest convenience. Best, Krista Andrews." I hit send and held my breath. I immediately received a response.

"Ms. Andrews, Please be at our offices on Thursday morning at 9:00am. Our address is 107 George Street. We look forward to speaking with you. Best, Erick Eden."

Whoa! That's in two days. I'd better go shopping for a new pantsuit.

"Mr. Eden, Thank you for the opportunity. I will be there on Thursday morning at 9:00am. Sincerely, Krista Andrews." Well, no going back now. I'd better brush up on my interview skills. It's been more than a few years since I've had to sit in that hot seat. I was suddenly struck with a severe case of nerves. My latte and scone were placed on the table by a smiley young woman. "Thank you" I say and she nods sweetly and walks back to the kitchen. I proceed to sip my hot coffee and enjoy the scone, but I'm struggling to completely relax. My nervous energy was getting the best of me and I'm eager to get prepared for this interview. I finish my late morning brunch and pack up my backpack.

Once outside the cafe, it dawns on me that the sun has somehow gotten confused and decided to peek out. It felt wonderful on my face and I took a moment to close my eyes and tilt my head up toward the sky to soak it in. Despite the fact that I've been feeling pretty lonely and lost in this new place, I was also grateful to have the freedom not to be in a rush for anything. I could just take it all in without any pressure to do anything specific. I have no goals or anything I feel I have to achieve on a timeline. That was a deviation from how I've always led my life. It had always been full of goals and milestones to reach. I've never taken the time to just breathe and take it all in. Now, even though I'd been forced into it, I have the capacity to just exist and try to be observant and thankful for the small things in life. I opened my eyes and looked ahead down the street. The noise of the busy, bustling street whooshes back into existence and I set out toward my apartment.

Over the next 24 hours I've managed to find a few local shops, thanks to Rachel, and beefed up my professional wardrobe a little. I've found the perfect black pantsuit for my interview tomorrow morning. I sat at Rachel's bar for dinner again last night and she was able to spend some time with me asking interview questions. I asked her how she knew all those questions, and she told me she used to work in the corporate world. I was kind of shocked to learn that and apparently it was written all over my face. She said, "what? I don't look like a corporate girlie to you?"

I said, "no, it's not that. I just….." She laughed and winked at me to let me off the hook. Rachel told me she worked in the corporate world for about ten years, but then one day she just got fed up with the stress and the rat race. She lived in London at the time and decided to give it up and move back here to Edinburgh. When she moved back, her uncle offered her a job bartending in this pub. It was supposed to be a short-term gig until she figured out her next move, but it's turned into two years. She said it's the happiest she's been in a long time, so for now she's sticking with it. I currently identify with that sentiment. Right now, happiness is my pursuit. Most days I feel like I'm failing miserably at being happy because my grief takes over with almost every thought. There are other days, or moments really, where I find myself feeling happy and then I feel incredibly guilty for it. This makes me think of Michael. How would he want me to feel right now? What would he be saying to me? Would he be encouraging me to find all the joy I can and move on? Probably so. That's who he was. He wouldn't want me to be hurting and sinking into despair. He'd be saying, "K, you gotta move forward. That's the only direction to go."

Move forward. That was the whole point of me moving to the UK. I thought I might be able to do that if I went somewhere new and got away from all the familiar things, places and people that would constantly remind me of Michael. Some people want to stay surrounded by the things that remind them of someone they've lost, but I felt like I might suffocate if I stayed. I didn't want the constant condolences, the looks of sorrow and pity, and the flood of memories in my home every single day. I know that's probably weird to some people. Like I was trying to forget him. But, forgetting him would be impossible. I'll never forget him and I don't want to, but I wouldn't have survived the crushing pain if I had stayed.

My mind flashes to that phone call. The one we're all afraid of receiving. The kind of phone call you hope you never get. It was a Thursday evening around 6:00 if I remember correctly. The timeline is still fuzzy even though I've been over it in my head a million times. I had been home from work for maybe about thirty minutes and was working on getting some dinner ready. I had talked to Michael earlier in the afternoon. He had been traveling back from Dallas where he had attended a conference that day at UT Southwestern Medical Center. We lived out in a rural area in North Texas so he had about an hour drive. I was expecting him home at any minute but wasn't really worried because I knew that getting out of Dallas in five o'clock traffic would take longer.

As I popped some dinner into the oven, my phone rang. I picked it up off the kitchen island as I turned the tv volume down. I looked at my cell screen and saw "Denton County Sheriff." Immediate panic set in. I answered the phone with a worried hello. "Is this Krista Andrews?" I heard on the other end of the line.

"Yes, this is she," I responded. My heart was pounding and I felt a rush of heat come up my neck and face. A sweat broke out and my breathing quickened. I knew. I knew I was about to hear the worst kind of news I could possibly hear and there wasn't any way for me to stop it. I held my breath hoping I was wrong, or that he had been in an accident and was hurt, but would be ok. No such luck.

"Ma'am, is your husband Michael Andrews?" he asked.

I said, "yes, why? What's going on?"

The sheriff's deputy said, "Ma'am, I'm sorry to have to tell you this, but your husband has been critically injured. He was at the scene of a wreck and was pulled from the water. The EMTs just loaded him into the ambulance to take him to the hospital. But ma'am, he's non-responsive. They lost a pulse and they're doing CPR right now. You need to get to Denton Regional as soon as possible."

I don't even remember responding to the sheriff's deputy. I think I might have just hung up on him. I'm not sure. All I could think was I have to get out the door. Somehow, I thought to turn the oven off. Why I thought of that I don't know. I put on my shoes, grabbed my phone, keys and purse, and jumped into my car. Our house was about twenty minutes away from the hospital. It was the longest twenty minutes of my entire life. I remember crying and my eyesight was getting blurry, so I wiped the tears away and gave myself a pep talk. I didn't have time for tears. I had to focus on getting there and keeping it together. I'm sure I drove way too fast. All I could think of was picturing them doing CPR on Michael. For some reason I was trying to picture his wet, lifeless body and the trauma of resuscitation. I don't know why I was thinking of that, but maybe I was just trying to prepare myself for seeing him in a way I feared most. It was so hard for me to imagine him hurt, helpless, or lifeless. He'd always been so strong. Never helpless.

I finally arrived at the hospital and quickly found my way to the ER parking area. I ran inside and went straight to the triage desk. I told the nurse at the station, "My name is Krista Andrews. I think they brought my husband, Michael, here." I knew instantly by the look the nurse gave me. It was one of sorrow and devastation. He was gone.

Three

I woke up early the morning of my interview. Even earlier than usual at around 4:30. I don't know if it was the sun coming up, or my anticipation of the day that woke me, but I seemed to wake up with my body humming. Like I had an energy that I hadn't had in several months. I jogged to the gym and got in a really great workout. I walked back home and quickly showered. I hung my already pressed new pantsuit in the bathroom, and got to work on doing my makeup and hair. I hadn't really put a lot of effort into my looks in the last several months, but today I felt inspired to look my best. I was nervous, but it was a good kind of nervous. I dressed and put on the finishing touches with jewelry. I decided not to wear my wedding ring simply because I didn't want to have to explain my situation if someone happened to ask. I took one last glance in my floor-length mirror to give myself a final inspection. I looked good. I didn't look tired and drawn like I had for the last several weeks. I had color in my cheeks and my eyes were bright. This was going to be a good day.

The facade to Eden and Associates on the outside appeared to be nothing fancy. It looked like every other door front down the street. There was a relatively small black placard on the outside wall next to the door to show their business name and address. But, once I walked inside, it was pretty amazing. It was elegantly furnished and the design appeared to be a mix of old 19th century charm and modern-day finishings. The woodwork was elaborate and the ceilings were designed with elegant, ornate ceiling tiles. However, the flooring and light fixtures were more modern and chic. Just inside the door, there was a long, wide staircase leading to the second floor. To the left of the staircase were plush chairs, a couch, and a coffee table arranged around a beautiful fireplace. Toward the back of the room, there was a large desk with floor-to-ceiling bookcases lining the whole back wall of the front room. There was a small door to the right of the door that I assume led to a back room. To the right, under the stairs, was a small powder room for guests. I approached the desk where a young woman was seated and she had just hung up the phone. As she hung up the phone, she looked up and smiled warmly.

"Good morning," she said. "Do you have an appointment?"

"Yes, my name is Krista Andrews. I have an interview scheduled for 9:00am with Mr. Eden."

"Oh yes, of course. I'll let Mr. Eden know you are here. Please feel free to take a seat." the woman replied.

The waiting area was empty which I found rather comforting as that probably meant that there weren't a ton of contenders for this position. At least not any scheduled back to back. I chose to sit in one of the large, wing back chairs facing the stairs and to the open room so I could see when someone approached me. I sat taking in the details of the room and nervously trying not to wring my hands the whole time. I kept wiping my hands on my pants in an effort to make sure they weren't clammy and gross when Mr. Eden came to shake my hand. After about 5 minutes, the young woman came over and said, "They are ready for you in the conference room. I'll walk you up." I smiled and got to my feet quickly. I followed her up the stairs and as we topped this flight of stairs, I could now see there were more flights of stairs leading up to at least one or two more levels.

The young assistant led me to a set of french doors with small panes of glass that were frosted so you couldn't see inside. She rolled one of the doors to the side and directed me inside. As I stepped into the room, I was pretty surprised at how large it was. It probably took up at least two-thirds of this level if I had to guess. There was a large conference table with what had to be at least twenty-five chairs. Maybe more. To my right, at the far end of the table, sat two gentlemen. I walked toward them as the young assistant smiled and dismissed herself from the room quietly. One of the gentlemen stood up first and approached me with an outstretched arm to shake hands. He took a couple of steps toward me with his hand extended and was smiling. "Good morning, I'm Erick Eden. It's nice to meet you." he said as we shook hands.

I replied, "Hello, I'm Krista Andrews. It's nice to meet you as well." During this exchange, the other gentleman stood up and stepped around the end of the table to introduce himself as well. As he approached, I immediately noticed he looked familiar, but I couldn't quite place where I had seen him. Mr. Eden quickly took a step back and began to introduce the other man.

"This is my colleague, Sam Strickland." The man reached out to shake my hand and I could tell that he had the same realization that I had because it came across his face.

"Hi, it's nice to meet you," I responded.

"Likewise," he said. It hit me. This was the guy on the plane. The one sitting at the bar talking to the bartender. And, the same guy that had helped me get my luggage down from the overhead bin at the end of the flight. I gave him a knowing and quizzical look and said "you were on my flight, right?" "You helped me with my luggage."

I could see his facial expression change from confused to resolved in the matter of a second. He said, 'oh yes, that's right. I knew I had seen you before, but I couldn't place it."

Mr. Eden interrupted and said, "So you two know each other?"

I said, "no, not really. We were just on the same flight a few weeks ago from Dallas to Edinburgh. Mr. Strickland was kind enough to help me with my bag as we were deboarding the plane."

Mr. Eden said, "Oh, what a small world it is, eh?" We all agreed as we chuckled. Mr. Eden then motioned for me to take a seat at the end of the table and pulled the chair out for me. As I sat, both men sat on the sides of the table opposite each other. Mr. Eden began by explaining that they are a small structural engineering company in that they don't have a huge number of employees. However, it seems they handle some huge clients and broker very large deals. Mr. Eden goes on to explain that they oversee the design and construction of multiple large projects across the UK. They specifically target reconstruction and reinforcement of old structures such as bridges, buildings, and archways to make them safe and structurally sound for modern-day use. It all sounds really interesting and impressive, but at the same time, it's overwhelming because it's an area totally outside my field of knowledge. I try to reassure myself by giving a little internal pep talk. They have your resume. They know you're not from this field, so it must be okay.

After telling about the company, Mr. Eden indicates that my primary responsibilities, if I were to accept this position, would be as an administrative and personal assistant to Mr. Strickland. I don't know why, but this was a little bit surprising to me and I glanced over at Mr. Strickland. He gave a half smile at me and then looked down at his notepad on the table in front of him. It was almost as if he was embarrassed to need an assistant. I looked back to Mr. Eden and he continued to list out the specifics of the job.

"You will be responsible for secretarial duties such as answering his phone, keeping his appointments and calendar organized, drafting basic letters or email correspondence, keeping track of his receipts and expenditures and submitting to our accounting person, etc. In addition to all that, you'll also be responsible for any personal assistance he needs such as picking up his dry cleaning, running errands, making sure he has lunch here at the office or on a job site, getting coffee, etc." Mr. Eden continued, "you should know that there will be travel involved. Whenever Mr. Strickland needs to go to a job site for several days or even weeks at a time, you will be expected to travel along with him. The company will, of course, pay for your private lodging, food, and other travel expenses, so you wouldn't need to worry about any of that. The role may also involve you coordinating business dinner meetings or small events that need to take place. It will be a very time-consuming job, Mrs. Andrews."

I'm guessing at this point I may have looked a little overwhelmed because Mr. Eden stopped and asked if I had any questions. I replied, "well, yes actually…. I have a few." "Will I receive some type of formal training to help understand the day-to-day processes of the company? "And also, will the travel requirements be international or based solely in the UK?"

Mr. Eden let me know there would be no international travel and all jobs are based here in the UK. He reported that most of them are in Scotland, but they do have several in England and Wales as well. As for the training, his personal assistant would be training me for the first 6 weeks. I would shadow her and just simply observe for the first week, and then I would begin handling Mr. Strickland's affairs with his assistant there to answer any and all questions or to help as needed.

Mr. Strickland spoke up to interject at this point and said, "You should know that I'm not new to the world of structural engineering. I have about 13 years of experience, but I am new to this company as well. So, we will be learning together." That definitely helped me feel more at ease.

Mr. Eden then asked, "Mrs. Andrews, your resume is very impressive. You have a bachelor's in business administration and spent the last 15 years in pharmaceutical sales, is that correct."

"Yes, that's correct." I said.

"May I ask why you are leaving that field and not pursuing pharmaceutical sales here in the UK?"

And there it was. I knew this was going to be asked. I mean, that's what I would be thinking if I were interviewing me. I knew this was going to be awkward, but I felt that I just needed to explain the whole thing. It wasn't going to make sense to them if they didn't know the whole story. So, I decided that I was going to tell them in as short a summary as physically possible.

"Mr. Eden, I feel that I need to explain my situation so you can see where I'm coming from if you'll allow me a little time?" He nodded in agreement and I began. "I lost my husband about 5 months ago. He was killed in a tragic accident. To make a long story very punctuated, I decided to move to the UK for a fresh start. We did not have children, so I didn't really have any other ties. I just needed something different, so I packed up and moved to the UK. I've been here for almost 5 weeks" I said as I looked to Mr. Strickland. "I want a job that will keep me busy and make me feel productive, but I didn't want to go back to the pharmaceutical industry. I've had enough of it and I want something less stressful. I'm certain that I can do a great job here. I'm a very organized, Type A, kind of person. I'm good at the clerical details and I have a good memory....which I suspect might be an asset in this position." Both men laughed and nodded in agreement. I continued, "Having been in sales, I will be good at making things happen that are generally difficult for other people. I'm not one to take "no" for an answer. I know you may have some reservations about hiring someone with my credentials for an assistant position, but I assure you I seek this role based on my personal circumstances. It's not related to my limitations."

Mr. Eden sat for a moment and looked at me with both admiration and the slightest hint of sadness. He then said, "Mrs. Andrews, your determination and sheer will to take on such a change in your life after tragedy is quite astonishing." He then proceeded to give me the standard closing interview rote speech about how they have a couple more interviews to conduct, and then they would make their decision, and I'd be hearing from them by the end of next week. They politely stood and shook my hand again with all the nice salutations that one would expect. Mr. Eden then ushered me from the room and walked me to the top of the stairs where he said, "please check in with Allison again on your way out to make sure we have your correct phone number." I agreed politely and we said goodbye. As I headed down the stairs, I was a little bummed. I think maybe they were overwhelmed and caught off guard with my sob story. That probably wasn't the right move and I maybe should have kept that to myself. I noted that in my head for the next interview.

I reached the bottom of the stairs and headed over to Allison's desk. She looked up and smiled sweetly. "Mr. Eden wanted me to make sure you have my correct phone number on file before I leave." Allison checked the copy of my resume that she had on her computer and read my number to me. She assured me that she had all my contact information. I nodded and said, "Great, thank you. It's nice to meet you. Have a good day." She replied the same and I walked to the door.

Behind me I heard footsteps descending the stairs very quickly. It sounded like an army trampling down the stairs. so I turned to see what the commotion was. To my surprise, it was only one person. Mr. Strickland. He basically landed full throttle at the base of the stairs and smiled as I turned to look at him. He said, "Mrs. Andrews, I'm sorry to startle you, but I wanted to catch you before you left." I couldn't imagine why he wanted to catch me. I thought maybe I had left my purse in the conference room or something. He then said, "We've made our decision. Well, my decision really. I would like to offer you the position." I think I stood there a little speechless and blank-faced for a second because Mr. Strickland started to look as if something was wrong. He said, "You don't have to decide right now if you would like to take some time to think about it."

I finally snapped with it and responded, "No...no, I don't need time to think about it. I accept" as I smiled bigger than I meant to. I was genuinely excited. Almost giddy to be honest. I hadn't felt this much excitement or eagerness in months. I felt like I was coming out of this long, hazy coma where I had been aware that life was going on around me, but I hadn't been a part of it; only a spectator. I felt that tinge of enthusiasm for the future and something to look forward to.

Mr. Strickland responded with a broad smile and a look of relief. He said, "That's great! When can you start?"

I said, "How about Monday morning?"

"I'll see you at 8:00am on Monday then." and he shook my hand one last time.

I headed straight for Rachel's pub. By this time, it was only 10:00 in the morning and I knew they wouldn't be open yet, but I knew Rachel would be there already getting the bar set up for the day. Hopefully, she would let me in so I could squeal in delight as I shared my news with the only friend I have right now. I reached the pub in no time and tried to open the door. It was locked, so I knocked multiple times in the hopes that Rachel was there. Sure enough, she opened the door with an annoyed look on her face until she realized it was me. She said, "Are you okay?"

I said, 'Yes, I'm great actually" and I smiled, squeaked, and bounced up and down multiple times to show my excitement.

Her eyes went wide and she said, "You got the job, didn't ya?"

"Yes!!" came out of me a little louder than I intended and she chuckled while giving me a congratulatory hug.

"So, when do you start?" Rachel asked.

"Monday morning at 8:00am" I replied.

"Great, that means you have three days to have fun and rest up. You want to take a little two-day trip to Aberdeen with me tomorrow? I have the whole weekend off." said Rachel.

"Oh my gosh….yes, absolutely. That sounds so fun." I said. This day was turning out to be one of the best I've had in a long time.

Rachel responded, "Awesome! We'll leave around 10:00 tomorrow morning. I'll pick you up at your apartment. We should get to Aberdeen about 12:30 just in time for lunch. My uncle has an Airbnb flat in Aberdeen that's not being rented this weekend, so he said we could use it. It's a two-bed, one-bath flat right in the heart of the city. You'll love it and we can explore as much as we want. We'll get back home late Saturday night, so you'll still have the whole day on Sunday to rest and get ready for your first day."

The absolute surge of energy I was feeling at this moment was refreshing. I had lived in an alternate universe of existence for the last 6 months, and having something to look forward to was promising for my sanity. There was a small part of me that felt just a hint of guilt for feeling this way, but I quickly tampered that down. My thoughts always go back to what Michael would say or think. I know, without a shadow of a doubt, that he would say moving on is required. He would encourage this excitement and would probably be disappointed in me if I dwelled on the sadness and grief. So, I allowed myself to feel good about what was happening in my life. That was the point, after all, of moving to a new place and starting anew. There was hope in the future even though it wasn't the future I had planned.

Rachel and I had the best weekend ever. It was such a laid back experience and traveling with Rachel was even more fun than I had expected. She picked me up Friday morning and we made a quick stop for coffee before hitting the road. She really knew a lot about the surrounding area along the way to Aberdeen. It was like having my own personal tour guide. I also got to know her much better during the car ride. We had time to sort of talk about ourselves. Her last name is Cameron, which she explained means "crooked nose." I thought that was hilarious. Like, the thought of how names came into existence by naming people's features or their actions is just comical to me. Rachel is only about three years younger than me as she turned 34 in January. She is typically pretty reserved when I talk to her, but she's also usually at work so I imagine she tries to keep her personal life quiet at the pub. But, during this road trip, she was much more open and talked about her personal life quite a bit. Apparently, she was in a long term relationship when she lived and worked in London. By the sound of things, she had a bad break up with her longtime boyfriend and that was a big reason for her moving from London back to Edinburgh. She told me that her boyfriend had promised marriage and led her on for many years, but always kicked the can down the road each time a new work promotion came around. He always blamed his delay in getting married and settling down on his job circumstances, but Rachel said those were just excuses. She figured that out the hard way when she caught him cheating on her. Red-handed. She said she got off work early one day and went to his apartment to surprise him with an early take-out dinner of his favorite Chinese food. Instead, she found him disheveled when he opened the door. She said she knew immediately that he was up to no good. He was acting strange and not really wanting to let her inside. She kind of forced her way into the apartment and found a naked young woman on the couch half covered with a blanket. A quick survey of the room revealed items of clothing strewn about. Rachel said she stood there stunned for what felt like several minutes, but was really only a few seconds. Then, without saying a word, she walked out of that apartment and went home. Her boyfriend tried to call and texted her several times over the next week, but she didn't respond. After about two weeks of work and life after that day, Rachel was fed up. With all of it. She walked into work the next morning and gave her notice. She called her uncle and told him the whole story and said she was moving home. He was there the very next day to help her pack up her things and make the move. She never talked to her ex again. He eventually stopped trying to call her.

Rachel's parents were alive; although I was starting to wonder because she never talked about them. They owned a successful online tech business building applications for a variety of uses. Because that business could be done remotely from virtually anywhere in the world, Rachel's parents traveled all over the world and were rarely ever home. She indicated she wasn't very close with them and had always felt a closer connection to her uncle; which is her dad's brother.

Driving through the countryside and getting to tell each other about our history and viewpoints on the world was very cathartic for me. It was like therapy that I hadn't had. I hadn't really been able to talk to anyone since Michael died. It wasn't so much that I didn't have the opportunity. I had many friends and family attempt to talk to me, but I just wasn't able to talk during that time. But now, I feel ready to talk and open up. I think it helps to tell it all to a new person that's not close to the situation.

The next two days were so good. We talked, ate way too much, walked around Aberdeen to see the sights, relaxed at the flat, and went out to a nice dinner in the heart of the city Friday night. On Saturday, we rented bikes and rode along the streets nearest the port. We stopped at shops and just took our time checking things out with no real plan or schedule. After grabbing a late lunch, we went back to the flat and packed up our things. The drive back was peaceful and remarkably we weren't sick of each other. We talked almost the whole way back. Rachel was so easy to talk to. She's a good listener, never gives the impression she's judging, and doesn't give unsolicited advice. She just takes it all in and makes you feel validated. I think this is the beginning of a great friendship.

We got back into Edinburgh and pulled up to my apartment around 8:00 pm. I said good night to Rachel and thanked her profusely for the much needed excursion. I climbed the three flights of stairs to my door and realized that I was exhausted. But, it was a good kind of exhaustion.

I ordered some takeout and jumped in the shower while I waited. My food delivery arrived just as I had combed out my wet hair and put on my pjs. I was ready to settle down and watch a little tv, chow down on some dinner, and call it a night.

For the first time in months, I slept really well without the use of the sleeping pills my doctor had given me after Michael's death. I vividly remember getting a phone call from my doctor's office two days after he died. I saw the number come through on my cell and I almost didn't answer it because I figured it was just one of those appointment reminders they send out. For some reason, I was compelled to answer and it was actually my doctor on the line. I wasn't expecting her; I thought it would be the scheduler or her nurse. She said, "Krista, this is Dr. Davis."

I was kind of surprised so I think I took a couple of seconds to respond. "Hi Dr. Davis."

She said, "Hi Krista" and there was a small regretful pause. "Krista, I heard about your husband, Michael. I'm so sorry for your loss." I really didn't know what to say. My mind was both confused about how she knew, and why she would be calling to offer her condolences. I mean, we weren't close friends or anything; it was strictly business between the two of us usually. I think she could hear the confusion over the phone and proceeded to explain her call.

"I'm calling not only to say how sorry I am, but I also want to know if there's anything I can do for you?" She continued, "you know… many people in your situation, in grief, struggle to function in general in the first several days or weeks. Many have trouble sleeping and I just want to help you with that in case you have trouble. Krista, I'm going to prescribe a sleep aid for you. It's not anything terribly strong. I know how you feel about taking medicine. But, I think it's something you need to consider taking for the short term. You're going to need sleep to get through the days to come. I'm sending it to your pharmacy now. Promise me you'll go pick it up and consider taking it to give yourself the rest you're going to need."

I took what seemed like several minutes to even respond. I was so stunned that she would reach out and be proactive like this for my benefit. "Yes, yes I'll go pick it up. Thank you so much for calling and thinking of me." But there was more that I needed to know. "If you don't mind me asking, how did you know my husband had passed?"

She said, "Well, I cover in the ER of Denton Regional a couple of weekends a month. I wasn't there when the incident happened, but several of my coworkers told me about it. I figured out that he was your husband after recognizing the name. I went into your chart at the clinic and saw that he was your emergency contact and listed as your spouse."

My heart squeezed at that moment. I was so incredibly sad and heartbroken, but I was so thankful for the people around me taking care of what I didn't even know I needed. I thanked her again and again, and promised to call if I needed anything else. Later that day, I had just left the funeral home for the second time in two days. I was exhausted, both physically and emotionally. I headed straight for the pharmacy to get that prescription. I knew I was going to need it that night. My doctor was right, I typically hate taking medications. But this was different. This was for survival.

I woke up Sunday morning after our trip to Aberdeen, feeling refreshed and well-rested. And I didn't have to take my sleeping pills. It was encouraging to me that I was finally starting to heal and move forward. I was starting to feel some joy and normalcy again. I didn't want to forget about Michael at all, but I knew for my own sanity that I needed to start healing my heart and moving on. One can't live in that kind of grief for very long. It will suck you under and there's a chance you won't recover if you don't try to get on with your life. I didn't want to live in that state of depression and sadness forever. Michael wouldn't have wanted that for me either.

I spent the day doing all the normal things. I had coffee on my small little balcony, then walked to the gym to get in a good workout. After the gym, I decided to just walk around the city a little today. The sun was actually out and shining bright today. The temperature was perfect at about seventy-five degrees and it just felt so glorious outside. I couldn't let the opportunity to be outside pass me by. I wanted to rest up today, but I also wanted to stay busy and prep for the week ahead of me. I was filled with excitement and nerves about my new job, so I felt like I needed to get some of that nervous energy out by filling my day.

I walked around and tried to just stick to the main areas that I knew fairly well. I wandered a little into new areas and onto new streets to explore, but for the most part I stuck to the heavy traffic, popular areas. The last thing I needed today was to get lost or wind up somewhere I didn't know. As I strolled along and took in the sights, I stopped in several small shops. I came across a bookstore that was so cute. It was tiny in area, but made up for its small area with its height. They had very tall ceilings and shelves went up to the tops with ladders available. I don't know how you would peruse for books up there on the ladder. I guess you would just have to request a specific book and the shopkeepers would climb up there and get them. I did manage to find a fiction romance book that I thought I might like. I had seen some people recommend it on social media.

Before I knew it, it was about 11:30 and I was starving. I stopped into a small cafe and found a table at the back. I would have preferred to sit by the window, but this place was pretty packed. A sweet old lady who worked there approached me and asked what I would like to drink. I ordered a coffee and a flat water. She had a kind face and a warmness about her. She didn't sound Scottish though. I was guessing maybe Armenian by the sound of her accent and her color. She had very dark hair, olive skin, and hazel colored eyes with specks of brown. I bet she was gorgeous in her younger years. She returned quickly with my drinks and asked if I was ready to order. I gave her my order and she returned to the open window of the kitchen to hand in my order. The other waitress was a young girl and there were two middle-aged men also working there. They all looked similar and in my head I decided they were probably related. It was probably a family business.

About an hour later, I decided it was time to head back home and get things ready for the week. I stopped at the grocery on the way and picked up things for lunch and meal prep for the week. This time I loaded down with groceries and there were too many bags to walk home with so I caught an Uber back to my apartment. My driver's name was James and he insisted on helping me carry all those bags up to my apartment. To be honest, I was a little hesitant about a stranger coming up to my apartment door, but he turned out to just be a kind-hearted person who wanted to help. I was still getting used to the kindness and sincerity of the people in this country. Back home, you had to be much more on guard and alert about that kind of thing. I was glad James helped me though, because it would have taken me three or four trips to carry all that upstairs by myself. I don't know why I got so much. I tipped James an extra ten pounds on top of my fee and he was very grateful.

I spent the afternoon cleaning the apartment, washing my sheets, doing laundry, and meal prepping for the week. I knew my first week on the job was probably going to be exhausting, so I figured getting my meals prepared and the apartment cleaned would be helpful. By 6 pm I pretty much had everything done so I settled down to eat dinner and watch some tv. I crawled into bed by 8:30 and did a little reading of my new book. I turned on my 5 am alarm and turned out the light. My mind raced; as I knew it would. I thought about what my job would be like tomorrow, what we might do and go over. I worried about whether I would learn things quickly and what they would think of me. And then I thought of Michael. I wondered what he would think of my life right now. What would he say? I think he would be proud of me, but I couldn't help but wonder if he would agree with how I had chosen to handle life without him so far. I could still see him in my mind's eye. Thankfully, I had not lost the ability to visualize him and remember what his hugs felt like. I chose to pretend that he was sleeping in bed with me and I could almost smell his scent as I drifted off to sleep.

My alarm went off and my eyes popped open immediately. I don't normally get up to the first alarm. I usually hit snooze a couple of times, but this morning I could feel the excitement and exhilaration of a new job. I climbed out of bed instantly and went straight to the coffee pot to make a cup. I quickly drank my cup of coffee, which was like warmth to my soul. I ran to the gym this morning and did a quick 40 minute interval workout with weights and high intensity cardio. I didn't have as much time this morning so I needed to get the most bang for my buck. Then I quickly ran back home and jumped in the shower. I put on my charcoal grey suit and black sling-back block heels. Then

I did a full face of makeup; complete with a dark ruby red lip color that made my blue eyes pop. I curled my hair, but it'll probably fall out by the time I get to work because it's misting rain outside. My suit looked sharp as I glanced at my final results in the full length mirror on the back of the bedroom door. I was ready to tackle this new adventure. I grabbed my lunch bag and tote and headed out the door. My uber ride arrived just as I was walking out the door to the sidewalk. I hopped in and off we went. I took a deep breath and tried to calm my nerves. The driver apparently took notice of my nerves and asked if everything was ok. I said, "yes, I'm starting a new job this morning and I'm just a little nervous."

He smiled and said, "ah, well, I'm sure yer gonna do well lass." That Scottish twang thrilled me and I smiled in return. He was right. It was going to be a good day and I was going to enjoy every moment.

Four

I stepped out of the Uber car and onto the rain-soaked sidewalk in front of 107 George Street. I hurriedly skipped up the steps and into the front door. Allison looked up from her desk and smiled heartily. She quickly rose from her desk and walked toward me while greeting me with a sweet "good morning." She said, "I'll walk you upstairs and show you your office." She began heading up the stairs and I followed. I was curious to see what my office looked like. I had just kind of assumed that I would have a cubicle or desk in the hallway in front of Mr. Strickland's office. I guess that's what most assistants have in tv shows so that's what I had envisioned in my head. We reached the top of the stairs on the third floor and I was really glad that I exercised daily because climbing several flights of stairs each day requires you to be in decent shape without sucking wind. I would be so embarrassed if I were huffing and puffing by the time I climbed those each morning.

At the top of the stairs we turned to our left and walked along a long, wide corridor that followed what appeared to be several offices. They each had glass fronts so I could see the people sitting behind their desks. It seemed that some had not arrived yet as some of the offices were empty. We approached the end of the corridor and Allison opened the door to a large corner office. It was huge. Mr. Strickland was there sitting behind his desk working on his computer. He turned as we entered the room and Allison greeted him. She said, "Mr. Strickland, Mrs. Andrews is here." He rose from his chair promptly and came around his desk to greet me.

"Good morning, Mrs. Andrews. It's nice to see you again." he said.

I replied, "Good morning, it's nice to see you as well" as I reached out my hand to shake his. I tried to shake his hand firmly and with confidence. I think I pulled it off, but inside my head I was a bundle of nerves. I don't know why. I shouldn't feel pressured because I didn't really need this job, but I wanted to make a good impression and do a good job. I think the professional, formal vibe of the office was getting to me as well. Mr. Strickland then asked Allison to show me my office and give me a quick lay of the land, and then he was going to give me a full tour of the whole office building and make introductions.

Allison led me to my office which was connected to Mr. Strickland's by a sliding french door. It was bigger than I had expected. Honestly, it was the size of what I would expect a corporate office for someone important to be. I was shocked at the amount of space. It had a large wrap-around desk with three sides. There were two wing-back chairs facing one side of the desk. On the side of the desk against the wall, it had shelves that went nearly all the way up to the ceiling with storage space galore. There was a desktop computer on that side of the desk with probably the biggest monitor I had ever seen. It was more like a small flatscreen tv. Behind the desk, there was a wall of windows overlooking George street with a pretty great view of the city from the third floor. I was mesmerized at what I got to look at everyday. Many people would kill for a set up like this. Across the room from the desk, there was a small sofa and coffee table. Across from that, on the opposite wall, there was a small table set up with a coffee maker, coffee pods, tea, and all the fixings. As I was inspecting the coffee table, Mr. Strickland walked in and leaned against the doorframe of the door connecting our two spaces. I think he was amused at my obvious wonderment of the coffee table. He said, "you must be really special. I didn't even get a coffee table" and chuckled. I grinned and felt slightly embarrassed that he must have been reading my thoughts.

Meanwhile, Allison spoke up and said, "there are restrooms right across the hall when you need them. And I'm sure Mr. Strickland will show you to the break room so you can put your lunch in the refrigerator."

He jumped in and said, "oh yes, of course. In fact, if you want to put your things away, then we can get started on our orientation of the office." I noticed a large pull-out drawer in the bottom of my desk, so I put my tote and my purse in there for safe-keeping. I grabbed my lunch bag and followed Mr. Strickland out of the glass door of my office and into the corridor. He quickly pointed to the restrooms that Allison had spoken of so that I would know where they were. We walked the length of the third floor first and he pointed to each office and told me who they belonged to and each person's role. The whole third floor essentially belonged to Mr. Eden and the associates. All of the associates 'offices were large and had connecting offices for their assistants. Mr. Strickland introduced me to two assistants right away. We quickly said hello to each other and then headed for Mr. Eden's office. He was not in the office today and Mr. Strickland explained that he would be out of the office all this week. He was on a job site, but his assistant would be here and I would be spending most of the week with her to get trained. The thought of this made me so nervous. I was so anxious about doing a good job and learning fast. I didn't want them to regret hiring me, but I knew it would be a ton of new information in an area that I had no previous knowledge in.

We walked into the assistant's office and behind the desk I saw an older woman who was probably in her 60's if I had to guess. She stood up from her chair immediately and smiled the sweetest smile I had ever seen. It instantly put me at ease. It was like being greeted by my mom or favorite aunt. She couldn't have been more than about five feet tall and was a little on the heavier side of life. She had short curled hair that looked like she had it rolled and styled once a week like my grandma used to do. I could just imagine her sitting under a heat lamp, in curlers, in an old beauty salon. Her hair was a light brown with a hint of red and not a grey hair to be found. I felt pretty certain she paid for that color. She had on reading glasses that were attached to a gold chain to keep them around her neck. She was dressed in a nice blouse that tied in a bow at the neck, a cardigan over her blouse, and a mid-length full skirt. She was wearing neutral colored pantyhose and black low profile, old lady comfort shoes. You know…like the SAS brand that your grandma would wear. She was cute as a button. Classic working granny.

Mr. Strickland said, "Ms. Graham, I'd like to introduce you to my new assistant. This is Krista Andrews." She approached me with her arms outstretched and wrapped me into a hug. "Oh my, I've been looking forward to meeting you, lass. We're blessed to have ye as part of our Eden family."

My heart melted and the instant relief I felt was beyond what I could describe. The warmth of her face and that Scottish granny voice made me feel right at home. I felt my shoulders relax and had an overwhelming feeling of calm. Not to mention I was thinking to myself, if she can do this job….surely I can. I replied with, "it's so nice to meet you too. Thank you so much for being willing to train and teach me. I'll do my best to keep up with you."

At that, she giggled and patted me on the arm. She said, "I'm sure yer gonna do just fine, lass." Then she said, "well, once Mr. Strickland is done giving ye the grand tour, then you and I will get started."

I turned toward Mr. Strickland and he smiled at me with a knowing smile like he understood how she made me feel, and he also knew what a gem she was. We walked out of her office and began the rest of our stroll through the building. We made a quick stop in the break room where I put my lunch bag in the fridge. I noticed that there was also a sink, coffee machine, microwave, cabinets, and a small table and chairs. There was also a large ice machine that dispensed water as well. One of the other assistants had stepped in quickly to refill her large water cup, so I marked that in my head for future reference.

The rest of our tour was spent on each of the four floors of the building. The fourth floor was essentially storage for office supplies, rows of filing cabinets and various other office furniture. Mr. Strickland joked that he thought this is probably where old computers and office desks went to die. The second floor was of course the conference room where I had my interview with a couple more offices at each end of the floor. He introduced me to the other associates and staff as we went along, and then he tried to reassure me that I didn't need to feel pressured to remember all their names right away. It's like he could tell what I was thinking. That made me feel both on edge and relieved all at the same time. We headed downstairs to the first floor. I felt pretty sure I knew what this floor was about, but I was intrigued at what he might show me. We turned off the stairs and walked toward the back of the building past Allison's desk. Then we went through a door which led into a large, open room. It was a full-sized kitchen with a dining table big enough to seat at least ten people. On the other end of the room was basically a living room. There were sofas and chairs surrounding a large fireplace with a huge flatscreen tv mounted above the fireplace. It was very nicely done and homey. It literally felt like we had just walked into someone's home. One of the associates and his assistant were in the kitchen making a breakfast of eggs, bacon, and toast. Another assistant was sitting at the kitchen island drinking her tea and chatting as the other assistant cooked. It all felt very relaxed, and I could see why they felt like a family. They had intentionally set up this workspace to make sure everyone was comfortable and well taken care of. It struck me that this was such a great idea, and definitely not the kind of work culture you find in the States for the most part.

We stayed and chatted for probably about 45 minutes. The other two assistants made me feel right at home. One of them, Ginger, asked me how I took my coffee and then proceeded to make it for me. It was funny to me…she didn't even ask me if I wanted some coffee. She just assumed that I would sit and chat and drink some coffee. It was like she was just welcoming me and accepting me as part of their Eden family right away. As if I had been there forever. I also marveled slightly that most of them were drinking tea, but Ginger offered me and Mr. Strickland coffee. Probably because we're both American and not likely to prefer tea. Her initiative to make me feel welcome and comfortable was very much appreciated. I kept a close eye on Mr. Strickland so I could read his cues for when he wanted to head back upstairs. I thanked Ginger and the other assistant (I already couldn't remember her name) and then we headed back up to the third floor.

On the way up, I leaned close to Mr. Strickland and asked, "what was the other assistant's name again?" in a whisper.

He replied in the same whisper, "I can't remember either." We both giggled and proceeded up the stairs. By this time it was nearly 10:00 and I spent the next two and a half hours with Ms. Graham getting oriented to the job. Thankfully, she was a good teacher and had the patience of a saint. She was surprisingly organized and I was starting to see what an asset she is to this company. She explained their accounting system and had already gotten me set up with a username. I created a password and she helped me log in and started orienting me to the system. It wasn't too hard. All I really had to do was generate invoices, track and log those that had been paid, and enter any receipts into the system. Someone in accounting then handled the more complex tasks She then introduced me to their files in Microsoft 365 where they kept everything. She helped me navigate through the folders and showed me how they communicate with one another in Teams. I had worked in this system before, so I was pretty familiar with how to navigate; of which I think Ms. Graham was pretty relieved.

By 12:30pm, Mr. Strickland poked his head in the door and asked if we were ready for a lunch break. I couldn't believe it was already time for lunch. I felt like the morning had flown by. Ms. Graham practically was out the door of her office and headed to the kitchen downstairs before I even had time to respond. Mr. Strickland said, "I know you brought your lunch today, but would you be willing to let me take you to lunch? I'd like to get to know you have a working lunch meeting so I can go over my expectations."

I replied, "Oh, yes, of course. That sounds great. Let me grab my purse and maybe stop by the restroom and then I'll be ready." We headed down the stairs and Mr. Strickland held the door open for me as we stepped out onto the front steps. The sun was out by this time and it was quite warm. It felt great to step into the warmth and fresh air. The office, like most, was freezing and I was ready to thaw out a bit. I made a mental note to see if I can find a small space heater to put under my desk. Mr. Strickland said we could walk to a pub that was about 3 blocks away, so we set out at a slow strolling pace. I was grateful because walking three blocks in heels sounded like a good way to end the day with blisters. We chatted and began to share some personal details about ourselves as we walked. We began to find some common ground as we compared our current lives in Scotland with life in the States. We exchanged jokes about the cultural differences and our encounters so far.

When we arrived at the restaurant, we stopped at the hostess station and Mr. Strickland let them know he had called and made a reservation for two. My brain caught that detail. He had planned this before his seemingly impromptu lunch invitation. Once we were seated, our waiter came and took our drink order, and then shortly after that our food order. We spent the lunch hour talking about Mr. Strickland's role at Eden & Associates. He filled me in on his work style, the day-to-day needs, and specifically what he needs from me. It all seemed relatively manageable, and he struck me as a pretty laid-back type of boss. He seemed intent on setting clear expectations, but didn't come across as a micromanager or dictator at all.

On the walk back to the office, he asked me where I was from in the States. I explained that I had lived in a rural area just northwest of Dallas in Texas. He indicated that he was familiar with the Dallas area and actually spent some time there on a job for several months prior to moving to Edinburgh. He indicated he was originally from St. Louis, but had previously worked for a large engineering firm that required him to travel all across the U.S. doing jobs. When I felt brave enough, I asked him how he came to settle in Edinburgh. He said that he had actually experienced something pretty traumatic in his life a few months ago and that caused him to reflect on his life and how he wanted to spend it. He didn't elaborate on that trauma and I didn't want to pry beyond what he was willing to share. He said he decided that he wanted to settle into one place and also wanted to see more of the world so he began a job search with something abroad in mind. He said his search didn't take long and he was contacted by Eden & Associates almost immediately after submitting his resume. He didn't really talk about his family so it was hard to get a read on his personal life. He didn't have a wedding ring on, so I assumed he probably wasn't married. Surely he would have mentioned that when talking about his decision to move across the world.

Soon we were back on the front steps of the office building. I stopped momentarily and said, "Thank you, Mr.

Strickland, for the lunch and for being so kind and welcoming on my first day."

He responded, "You're very welcome. And also....I would really like it if you would just call me Sam. Mr. Strickland sounds like my dad." I smiled and agreed to the request with a nod.

I replied, "Of course. But only if you'll agree to call me Krista. Fair is fair."

He grinned and said "Done deal."

We proceeded into the office and up the stairs to the third floor again. I feared my legs were going to be sore after all these stairs and my workout this morning. Climbing these stairs tomorrow might be even harder. I spent the rest of the afternoon with Ms. Graham. Only this time, we stayed in my office so she could help me get acquainted with my computer, files, and Sam's organizational workflow. Of course, to her, I still referred to him as Mr. Strickland. It just seemed more professional and unassuming. Especially for my first day. I might ease up on that as I got to know everyone in the future, but for now it seemed unprofessional to reference him as Sam. Before I knew it, it was 4:00pm and everyone started coming out of their offices and heading downstairs. I saw them all going downstairs, but I wasn't sure what was going on.

Ms. Graham said, "Oh heavens, it's time for tea. Come on dear… let's head downstairs."

We met Sam coming out of his office as well and headed down the stairs together. Ms. Graham went down before us and she was rather slow going down. Sam and I glanced at each other and smiled, but I think we were both okay with the turtle pace. We all headed into the back kitchen-living space and everyone was there. Allison had prepared multiple kettles of tea and had all the cups and trimmings ready to go. Everyone poured their cup of tea and added whatever they preferred. I added both cream and sugar, but I noticed Sam drank his tea with nothing in it. Yuck. I don't think I'll ever be that kind of tea drinker.

The office chit chat quickly ensued and the conversations became lively. Several of the women took off their shoes and settled onto the sofas and chairs. They made themselves comfortable and started sharing news about their personal lives. The men all took off their suit jackets and rolled up their sleeves. They quickly engaged in a game of darts that was set up on the wall. After I made my tea, I approached the living room area and Ginger looked up and motioned me over. She patted the seat on the couch next to her to encourage me to join them. As soon as I sat down, they launched into a thousand questions. They wanted to know all about me, so I gave them as much information as I could. The one they all wanted to know was how I came to settle in Edinburgh from Texas. Of course the truth to this answer was probably a heavier topic than I needed to share on my first day, so I tried to keep it light. I told them I had had some trauma in my life a few months ago and I just decided I needed a change and a new adventure. They seemed relatively satisfied with that answer for the moment, but I could tell they were gonna want more details in the future. I looked up and saw Sam looking at me and he smiled with a compassionate look. He knew the truth, and it was clear on his face that he felt bad for me at that moment.

Tea time lasted for about an hour and I really enjoyed it. I could tell that I was going to be fast friends with most of my colleagues. They were so warm and welcoming. And they had a ton of questions about American life which I was happy to indulge with answers. At 5:00pm we all went back upstairs and I noticed that Sam returned to his office and back to work at his computer. So, I sat down at my desk and began to sort through some of his receipts and invoices that needed to be logged. Sam stuck his head in my door and said, "it's 5:00, so you can go home. I'm going to stay longer and get some work done, but you don't have to stay. Your day ends at 5:00."

I nodded and said,"Ok, I'm just going to enter these receipts and invoices really quickly and then I'll head out." He nodded in agreement and started to turn to go back into his office.

"Sam?" I called. He turned to me and I said, "thank you for making my first day so good."

He smiled and replied, "I'm glad you're here, Krista. I think this is going to work out well."

After finishing up a few things, I packed up my belongings. I walked out into the corridor and was looking at my phone to order an Uber. Sam walked up with his phone, briefcase, and his keys in his hand. He said, "Do you need a ride home?"

I said, "Oh, no…it's okay. I'm just going to order an Uber."

Sam said, "I have a car and I'm happy to give you a ride. Really. It's no big deal at all. Besides, I could use the driving practice." We both laughed at that and I agreed to getting a lift home. At the bottom of the stairs, instead of going out the front door, we walked to the back and through the kitchen and living space. We went out the back door and there was a small parking lot with several cars. Sam led the way to his car, which was a black 4-door BMW. Very sleek and nice. He opened the door for me and I slid into the front passenger seat. The car had a new car smell to it. He got into the driver's side and started the car. He said, "hold on tight. I'm not very good at driving on the wrong side of the road yet." I flashed a smile and told him I was ready for the ride while holding onto the grab bars.

He actually did a great job driving the streets of Edinburgh as I navigated to help him find my apartment. Well, actually it was British google maps girl that helped him navigate.I just pretended to know where I was going. Once we were parked outside my apartment on the street, Sam said, "this is actually not far from my flat. I'm only about four blocks that way" as he pointed straight ahead.

"Oh that's good to know," I replied. "Thank you so much for the ride" and then I proceed to open my door to step out.

Sam said, "Wait…. Would you like me to pick you up in the morning for work?"

I was a little hesitant and surprised that my boss would offer. I didn't want him to feel like he had to take care of me. "Oh no…that's really not necessary. I can get a cab or an Uber pretty easily. But thank you for offering."

He said, "Krista, I really don't mind. I mean, I'll be going this way anyway. We're going to the same place. It only makes sense that you ride with me. But….only if you feel comfortable with it."

I responded, "Yes, of course I feel comfortable. I just don't want to put you out."

He gave me a look to indicate he thought that was absurd and said, "please let me give you a ride. It would be my pleasure." He was very convincing so I finally agreed and told him I would be ready to meet him on the street tomorrow morning at 7:45.

"Ok, great. I'll see you in the morning. Oh, and Krista….great first day." I smiled and nodded and then closed the car door. I turned to walk to my building entrance and he drove away.

I climbed the three flights of stairs to my apartment and conceded in my head that my legs were in fact going to be sore in the morning. I settled into my apartment by absolutely collapsing on my couch. I was exhausted. I just sat there in silence and reviewed the events of the day in my mind. I don't think I moved for at least 30 minutes. Finally, I stood up, stretched, and decided I would go change and then have some dinner. Thank goodness I had meal prepped. There's no way I would cook right now. I took a quick shower and put on my pajamas. Then I went and heated up my dinner. I sat and binge-watched some Netflix nonsense while I ate. After a couple of hours, I brushed my teeth and did my nightly skincare routine. I crawled into bed and settled in to read my book for a little while. But, I didn't last long with that. My eyelids quickly became heavy, so I set my alarm and turned off my lamp. I rolled over to my side and closed my eyes. It had been a good day. Then, my next thought was of Michael. It occurred to me that I hadn't thought of him all day. That made me feel guilty, sad, and strangely relieved all at the same time. This was the first day since losing him, that I had been happy and engaged in life without thinking of him. That was a relief to some degree because I knew I couldn't continue swimming in grief and stay sane. But at the same time, I felt guilty for moving on in any small way. I heard myself take a deep breath, and I couldn't elude sleep for another minute.

Five

Just as I suspected, my legs were sore this morning. My workout at the gym was good, but I was moving slower this morning for sure. I walked back from the gym and got to my apartment around 6:15. Plenty of time for coffee and to get ready for the day. I took an extra long shower this morning because I knew I had plenty of time. The hot water felt so good. While I was washing my hair, my thoughts flashed to Michael. I was thinking about how he would hate this shower because the shower head is so low. He was tall and was always irritated with how low shower heads were. He would have to dip his head under the water stream or squat down to get under the water. The thought of him complaining about that tickled me. He would get so fired up about some things and was so animated with his complaints. I suddenly felt the guilt and pain of his loss. I missed him so much. I missed watching him tell a story, or about some event, and watching how much he used his hands to act it out. He was quiet with most people, but very expressive with me. He felt comfortable with me and would let loose so to speak. I always felt special that he was that comfortable with me and no one else.

Before I knew it, I was sobbing in the shower. Sometimes, the tiniest thing jars my memory and the tears come like a flood. It's so unpredictable and I never know when it might hit me. The pain of being faced with the idea that I would never see him again was something so hard for my brain to comprehend. It seemed impossible, but the reality of everyday life slapped me with that truth over and over. I just let myself cry for a while. I knew better than to fight it. It just had to get out and I probably should be thankful that I was alone, crying in the shower instead of at work or in public somewhere. That has happened too and it's totally humiliating. After several minutes, I was all cried out and ready to move on. I hop out of the shower, dry off, and look at myself in the mirror. My eyes are red and puffy. Great! That's not how I need to start my day. I get busy getting dressed and ready for the day. Thankfully, I have some eye drops that helped take away the redness and an ice roller to help with the puffiness.

My outfit choice today was bolder than usual. I hoped it wasn't too much. My pants are a deep cranberry red paired with a white mock neck bodysuit. I found some heels that are exactly the same color as my pants in patent leather with a pointed toe. I also found a patent leather belt that matched perfectly. I was pretty excited about my outfit, but a little worried that it was too much. Most of the people at work yesterday were dressed in dark colors and very modestly. I guess I would live up to the American standard and probably stick out like a sore thumb. I looked at my phone and it read 7:42. Oh shoot….I gotta go. I grabbed my things and raced down the stairs to the street. I instantly spotted Sam's car parked on the street directly in front of my building's steps and I felt regret that he had waited on me. I hurried to the car and opened the door apologizing for making him wait. He said, "Good morning. I didn't have to wait. I just pulled in about 30 seconds before you came out the door. Perfect timing." I sighed in relief and piled all my stuff into the car. I probably looked like a tornado had just landed in the car as I tried to get my things settled and get my seat belt on. I clicked it into the slot and took a deep breath. Sam laughed and asked, "are you okay?"

I grinned, knowing how ridiculous I looked, and said, "yes, I think I'll make it." He returned the grin and looked slightly amused at my sarcasm and ability to not take myself too seriously. Sam pulled onto the street and we were on our way. The drive would take about 15 minutes or less, but traffic was pretty thick this morning.

"So, are you exhausted after your first day? I know how tiring starting a new job can be," Sam said.

I said, "Ummm, yes, completely. It's been fifteen years since I've started a new job and I forgot how overwhelming it can be. I think the newness of everything around me is adding to the fatigue. And climbing up and down stairs all day," I joked. I went on to explain that yesterday's workout, jog, and stair climbing had left me really sore.

"Oh, do you workout regularly?" asked Sam.

"Yes, actually. I've been in the habit of getting up early and going to the gym to help me stay in shape and I find that it keeps me sane as well," I replied.

"Did you go to the gym this morning?" he asked.

"Yeah, I got up at 5:00 and walked to the gym. It's only a few blocks from my apartment, so I walk or jog there and back most mornings. I walked....slowly.....this morning," I said as I grimaced and chuckled to emphasize my soreness. "I tried to focus more on my upper body this morning since my lower body is mad at me."

Sam said, "Well, it's great to know someone else gets up early to exercise. I get up every morning to run. I don't go to the gym, but I probably should. I try to get in three to five miles most mornings. And I know what you mean about it keeping you sane."

"Oh that's great. Where do you run? Just on the streets, or is there a trail or something?" I asked.

"Most mornings, I just start out from my flat and take a new and different route to keep it interesting. But, I've managed to find some pretty good trails that I return to frequently. The trails out by Holyrood Palace and Arthur's Seat are pretty good, so I like to go there, but it's kind of far so I have to be in the mood for a longer run. I usually reserve that for the weekends when I have plenty of time," Sam said.

"That's awesome. I'll have to consider doing that too. I've been up Arthur's Seat and it's really a hike, but the views are totally worth it," I added. "So, what made you decide to move to Edinburgh if you don't mind me asking?"

"I just needed a change, but I wanted to go somewhere where I spoke the language. I had heard good things about Scotland from friends who had visited, so I decided to give it a shot. It's been an adjustment, that's for sure. I wanted a change, but moving across the world to a place where you know no one and are unfamiliar with a city and culture is challenging to say the least. To be honest, I'm really grateful to have met a fellow American who's probably experiencing the same thing." Sam glanced at me and smiled and then looked back to the street.

I replied, "Yes, there's something comforting about having a fellow countryman who understands the differences, and with whom you can commiserate." We both nodded in agreement as we approached the alley that turns down to the back of our office building. Sam parked the car and we got out to head inside.

"Thank you for the ride, Sam. I really appreciate it" I said.

"You're welcome. I enjoy the company for sure," Sam said as he held open the door for me. "In fact, Krista, I'm happy to give you a ride to and from work each day. There may be a day here and there when I can't do it because of business meetings or dinners, but most of the time I'm available."

"That's very kind; thank you." I replied. We continued in the building through the kitchen and through to the lobby where Allison was just getting settled at her desk. We all said hello to one another and Sam and I headed up the stairs. I groaned under my breath as we began the ascent up the stairs. My legs were screaming at me in revolt. Tomorrow was probably going to be worse, and I made a mental note to drink some electrolytes today to keep the cramps at bay. We topped the stairs of the third floor and I've never been so glad to go straight to a desk and sit down.

Sam and I both made our way to our desks and got settled in for the day. I resumed getting caught up on entering receipts and invoices. Then I started with creating invoices for upcoming projects. Ms. Graham had shown me how to do that yesterday and there was a pretty sizable stack to go through. In between those, I answered the phone and took messages. With each message, I was to send Sam a TEAMS message to let him know who had called and their information. The plan for today was for me to work alone on these tasks in the morning, and then I would spend the afternoon again with Ms. Graham for more training.

There was also a huge stack of files and loose papers on my desk. Ms. Graham and Sam had said that it all needed to be organized and put in a place that was easily accessible and they would leave that system up to me. I was actually eager to do this task because this is where I excel. Organization is my thing. So, after trudging up to the fourth floor to gather some office supplies like file folders, paper clips, pens, stapler, label maker, and various other items, I returned and set to the task. I don't know how long I had been at it when Sam poked his head in the door and found me sitting on the floor with my legs criss crossed. I was neck deep in papers and had stacks of stuff all over the floor. I was making headway, but it was taking a while because I was having to figure out what all this stuff was just so I could organize it. So much of it was foreign to me.

Sam's face looked a little shocked and he said,"Are you alright in here? It looks like you're getting sucked into the abyss."

"Ha! Maybe so. I know it looks rough, but I think I'm about to turn the corner and have it all organized." I looked up at him and said, "You have to trust the process" as I smiled. "But, I do have some questions if you have time," I asked.

"Sure, what do ya got?" he responded. He sat down in my chair near me and scanned the stacks of papers.

"Well, there are a couple of things I don't understand because I'm not familiar with this business and what you do, so I'm struggling to know how to organize or label them. I thought maybe you could run me through them real quick? ' I responded. "Like this one for instance," and handed the paper to Sam.

He said, "Oh yeah, that's a project proposal for this company here" as he pointed to the name and address of the company. "You're probably going to see a lot of these. They're not invoices or receipts, but we need to keep them so that we'll know what we proposed if or when the company decides to use us for their project. Some of these companies will request a quote or estimate of the project, but won't decide to hire us for months or even sometimes a year or more. So, we have to hang on to these to reference when they call us a year from now and want to move forward."

"Oh, I see….that makes sense now," I said. " I'll file them according to company name so we can find them easily in the future." "I just have one more question," as I handed him another packet of papers that were stapled together. He took it and looked through it quickly.

"This is a post-project report," he said. "After we complete a project, we write up a project report. It's basically a summary of all that occurred throughout the project. It's actually something that I'll need you to help me with on future projects, so you might want to read through a few of these and familiarize yourself with their structure. My goal is for you to do these yourself in the future, but we'll do the first few together until you get the hang of it" Sam said. He continued, "This company has been doing these and filing the paper versions, but I would like to save them digitally, or electronically, in the future. That way we don't have so many filing cabinets to keep up with."

"Yes, that makes sense. Ok….I think I can handle that, and now I know how to get all this organized" I said. I looked at the time on my phone and it read 10:45. "Don't worry. I'll have this all squared away by lunch time."

As Sam stood to go back to his office he said, "I have no doubt." I smiled at him and turned to face the mess before me. Time to shove this project into overdrive before my boss loses faith in me. I worked frantically for the next hour and was just closing the filing cabinet drawer when I heard Sam walk out of the office and down the corridor. I briefly wondered what he was doing for lunch today as I saw him start down the stairs.

I went to the break room and got my lunch out of the fridge. The floor was quiet and there didn't seem to be anyone else around. I refilled my water jug and added my much-needed peach electrolytes. I took out my glass container of ground turkey and sweet potato. I popped those into the microwave and set it for a minute and a half. I then got out my avocado, cheese and hot honey. I added the cheese on top and put it back in for a few more seconds. Once my lunch was ready, I walked back to my office and plopped down in my seat. I pulled out my phone and started watching videos on social media to entertain me while I ate. About 20 minutes later, Sam returned to the third floor with a plastic sack in one hand and a drink in the other. He clearly had gone to pick up take-out for lunch. He smiled at me as he was walking back toward our offices, and I gave a slight wave. I tried to smile back, but I had just stuffed a bite in my mouth and it was full. Sam walked to my glass door and entered my office instead of his office. He said, "Would you mind if I joined you while we eat?"

"No, not at all!" I replied as I cleared off space on the desk. He sat down in one of the wing-back chairs facing my desk. I was sitting cross-legged in my chair with my shoes off.

I realized how relaxed and comfy I probably seemed and I quickly uncrossed my legs and sat upright. I said, "I'm sorry, I just got comfortable for lunch because I thought no one was here. I know that's probably not very professional."

Sam said, "You are fine. I want you to be comfortable. You don't have to worry about that kind of stuff with me. I don't get the impression that you are an unprofessional person. I trust you to know when and when not to be professional."

I relaxed a little and we continued to eat our lunch as we chatted about our day so far. Sam was able to spend the time explaining the ins and outs of the business more to me so I could understand how things work. It was really a good working lunch and I truly felt more at ease and knowledgeable about what we do here. At one o'clock on the dot, Ms. Graham appeared out of nowhere with her bright and sunny disposition.

"Are ye ready to learn, dear?" she asked. I nodded eagerly as I put my lunch bags away.

Sam stood to leave and said, "I'm going to get out of your way before Ms. Graham puts me to work too." Ms. Graham snickered and patted him on the shoulder in appreciation of his humor.

Before leaving, Sam turned and said, "Krista, I'm headed out for the afternoon. I have those two meetings. I'm sure you saw them on my calendar. But, I'll be back in the office by tea time."

I smiled and replied, "Yes, of course. Have a good afternoon and I'll see you later. Call me if you need anything from me." Sam gave a half wave and went to his office to grab his suit jacket and his keys. Then he disappeared down the corridor as Ms. Graham and I got busy with more orientation.

Ms. Graham and I worked hard for the next two and a half hours. We covered a lot of ground and had time for me to actually put some of the things into practice while she was there to guide me. I was really starting to feel much better about the job and the expectations. I enjoy Ms. Graham and I could feel myself becoming attached to her. She has such a great attitude and is so patient. She's very positive and has an affinity for sarcasm and humor. I appreciate anyone that can find humor in everyday tasks. Her Scottish granny exterior is really a misleading facade considering her intelligence and wit. Not much gets past her and you can tell she's extremely smart. I'm pretty sure she runs the whole show, but pretends she's just an assistant. She's very humble.

At some point during our work, we got on the topic of family. We both began to share some personal details about our lives. Ms. Graham told me about her three children. She told me their names, their spouses 'names, and all about her grandchildren. I shared with her about my parents and what life is like in Texas. People are always fascinated with what it's like to live in Texas. She was thrilled to know that I had actually ridden horses as a child. She put me squarely into the "cowboy" category as soon as I told her that. Then Ms. Graham told me about her husband, Ronald. She told me that Ronald had passed away about five years ago. He had had a heart attack in his sleep and never woke up the next morning. Mr. Graham said she got up early that morning as usual and went to the kitchen to start breakfast. She said that was pretty typical. She would get up early and Ronald liked to sleep a little later. She would generally go wake him up when breakfast was ready. But that morning, she went in to wake him up and he had passed. Ms. Graham paused and I could tell she was sad all over again. Her chipper, positive self had faded for a few moments. I had tears welling up in my eyes as she was telling the story and when she looked up at my face she could see the hurt. She put her hand on mine and said, "there, there lass... please don't cry." I dipped my head down and looked at my lap trying to keep my emotions in check. Ms. Graham said, "I know about yer husband, dear. Mr. Eden told me what you said in the yer interview." I looked up and she had an expression of love and understanding in her eyes. I couldn't stop the tears once I looked at her. The compassion and empathy she had for me in that moment was something I needed whether I wanted to cry or not. I tried to keep the tears at bay and not lose full control here at work. That's all I needed was for everyone to think I was overly emotional and going to cry all the time. But, Ms. Graham and I were all alone for the moment and she was comforting me through it. She truly understood the tragic loss and it was nice to be with someone who knew. She didn't ask any questions, and she didn't try to get me to talk about it. She just let me cry silently and kept me company. After a few minutes, I was able to regain my composure, and Ms. Graham patted my hand and said, "Well then….I think it's just about tea time. Let's head downstairs for a cuppa." I pulled out my powder compact and lipstick and tried to freshen up after my cry session. I ran a comb through my hair and then headed to the restroom. Once downstairs, I entered the kitchen and everyone was in the kitchen-living great room. They were already in full swing, comfort and chatting mode. I scanned the room and immediately saw that Sam was back from his afternoon meetings. He was talking to one of the other associates and laughing. He glanced my way with a full smile on his face, but it quickly faded slightly when he saw me. He looked a little puzzled and worried and I realized that I probably still looked like I had been crying despite my make-up efforts upstairs. I glanced away and down to break eye contact and to hide my eyes, and Sam reluctantly returned to his conversation. I walked over to the tea cups and poured myself a cup. I quietly added my sugar and cream while the room was abuzz with the sounds of conversations and laughter. Now, I was directly across from Sam as he continued his conversation, but I could feel his gaze on me. His conversation partner's back was to me, but Sam was looking at me with the same concerned look while he listened. I could tell he was worried, so I smiled sweetly in an effort to reassure him that I was okay. That seemed to encourage him somewhat, but I could tell he was still on alert about what was troubling me. I took my cup and saucer over to the couch and took up my same position as the previous day by Ginger. She was in full-fledged story-telling mode about a date she had gone on a couple of weeks back. In no time, she had all of us laughing at her outlandish dating escapades. The sadness I had felt only a few minutes ago had faded and I was eternally grateful.

After about forty-five minutes of tea time, we all went back to work to wrap up our work days. Back in my office, I finished up a few tasks that Ms. Graham and I had started together. Mainly so I could see if I remembered how to do it by myself. Luckily, I did and was pretty pleased with myself for today. At about half past five, Sam looked in and asked, "Are you about ready to head out?"

"Yes, sounds good. I'll just get my stuff together really quick" I said. I gathered all my belongings and met him in the corridor. We fell in step together and went downstairs, saying goodbye to everyone on our way out. We both slid into the car and buckled in. Sam pulled out of the parking lot, or car park as they say, and turned onto the busy streets of Edinburgh. Traffic was heavy and we soon ran into a traffic jam. We sat idle for several minutes and the silence in the car was deafening. We usually don't have this problem and talk pretty easily with one another, but for some reason the air was thick and heavy. I could sense that Sam was still troubled about what had upset me and he was probably trying to come up with a way to bring it up.

After a few more minutes of silence, Sam finally said, "Krista, I hate to ask, but I just have to know if everything is ok?" "Maybe I misjudged, but it looked like you had been crying earlier." The look on his face was so earnest. He really did care and seemed so concerned about me. It was endearing and to my surprise I was glad to know someone cared about what I was feeling.

"Yes, everything is okay," I responded. "Ms. Graham and I got to talking and she shared about her husband dying suddenly and tragically about five years ago. As you know, I lost my husband several months ago and it just brought up some emotions. I'm sorry, I shouldn't have cried at work and I didn't mean to worry you."

Sam's reaction to that was strong. "Krista, you never need to apologize to me for grieving the loss of your husband. You've obviously been through something awful and I don't want you to think that you can't share that with us. With me." The look in his eyes was powerful. He held my gaze for longer than usual to let me know how much he meant his words. It was almost uncomfortable, but something about that moment wouldn't allow me to look away. I finally looked down and then back to the street in front of us.

"Thank you, Sam. You have no idea how much that means to me," I said. The traffic began to inch forward and Sam followed suit. Fortunately, Sam was able to change the subject easily and within minutes we were chatting effortlessly with our back and forth banter and humor. Thirty minutes later we were parked on the street outside my apartment. As I was collecting my things to get out, we noticed a truck parked right outside my apartment and a couple of workers looking around like they were lost. I opened the car door and instantly one of the men approached the car.

"Excuse me. Are you Mrs. Andrews by chance?" the man asked.

Reluctantly, I said, "Yes, can I help you?

"Well, we have a delivery from your landlord. She said you would be here around this time and might be able to let us in. She said she sent you a message about it," the man explained.

"Oh, I'm sorry I didn't see the message" I said. I looked at my phone and sure enough she had sent me an email explaining that she bought a new stackable washer and dryer for the apartment. "So, those are for my apartment?" I asked.

"Yes, Ma'am. We'll haul them up for you and remove the old unit if you'll let us in."

"Of course, no problem" I said, but I think I might have looked worried about it, or hesitant, because Sam put the car in park and said he would come up too if that would be alright. I sighed in relief and thanked him. I was relieved. I didn't really feel comfortable being alone with two strange men in my apartment. An hour later, the two men were finally finished exchanging the washer and dryer and headed out the door. Sam had stayed the whole time even though I tried to tell him he didn't have to. I hated that he was having to stay here and waste his free time babysitting me, but he insisted that he wanted to stay.

Since it was taking so long for the workers to get it done, I had worked on cooking some dinner. I made a cheesy chicken casserole and salad. Sam seemed eager to have a home-cooked American meal and jumped at the chance to stay for dinner. It was ready just as the workers were leaving so we sat down at my tiny dining table and started chowing down. Sam went back for seconds and was honestly giddy to have this meal. We spent the next half hour eating and talking about all kinds of things…work, exercise, family, places we had been. We covered a lot of topics in a short amount of time. He was pretty easy to talk to and I really felt very comfortable with him. I wondered why he wasn't married, but I didn't dare ask him about that. It just struck me as strange that a man in his late 30's or early 40's, presumably, wasn't married. Especially one that seemed so genuinely nice and well-balanced. Maybe he had been married before and I just didn't know. None of that was my business, so I quickly put that out of my mind.

Sam finished up his meal and helped me carry the dishes to the sink in the kitchen. He wanted to help me wash them, but I insisted that I would take care of them and I shooed him out of the kitchen.

"Well, I guess I better be getting home. Thank you for the meal. It was great" Sam said.

"No, thank you for staying while those workers were here. It made me feel much more at ease to have you here" I replied. "I guess I'll see you in the morning?" I questioned.

"Yes ma'am. I'll be outside at 7:45 in the morning. I'll see you then." Sam answered.

"Thanks again," I said as I closed the door behind him. He waved and started down the stairs.

I finished up the dishes and then went to shower. It had been a long day, but it was a good day. I felt like I was starting to make some connections and find my footing here in this new life. This move had been hard and sometimes I questioned my decision to start this new life, but today made me feel like I had made the right choice. Maybe I could start to heal in this new life with a new job and new people. Sleep came easily tonight. I was exhausted, but also my mind and heart felt at peace.

Six

I woke up in a full sweat with my heart racing. I couldn't quite tell where I was and my mind was swimming. I was having trouble separating reality from a dream. I think it was a dream, but it felt so real and I could have sworn I heard Michael's voice calling to me. I sat up in bed and rubbed my eyes. I looked around on the nightstand to find my phone and touched the screen to see the time. It was 3:43 in the morning. After a long deep breath, I lay back down and rubbed at my temples with my fingers. I felt the throb of a headache coming on. I closed my eyes and listened to myself breath as I tried to slow my breathing and calm down. I guess it must have been a dream, but it felt so real.

My mind wandered to the dream where I was standing on the edge of the bridge looking down into frigid, cold water. The sun was shining late in the day, but the temperature outside was freezing. There were muffled voices all around me. I could detect the panic and urgency in those voices, but I couldn't quite make out what they were saying. I just knew something was serious. Looking down from the side of the bridge, I could see the dark water. Everyone around me seemed to be concerned about what was going on in the water, but I couldn't see anything in it.. I couldn't tell what they were so concerned about. Then, very clearly, I heard Michael screaming "Krista!" It was a blood-chilling scream with a sense of panic in his voice that I had never heard before. Something about it scared me to my core. It was so uncharacteristic of him to scream or be that panicked about anything. That's when I awoke.

Thinking about it again made my heart rate spike. I was so unsettled and.....well....frightened. I knew what I was dreaming about. It's a scene that happened in real life, but I hadn't actually been there. It was my mind recreating what I had heard happened to Michael. I only knew details about Michael's death from what the Sheriff deputies had reported to me. I had asked so many questions and wanted to know every detail of what had happened in that accident. They had told me all they knew and now my brain was inventing my own version of it in my dreams. How odd that it's been nearly seven months since the accident and Michael's death and I'm just now starting to dream about this. It seems ironic that just when I've started to occupy my time, move forward in my life, and experience happiness, my brain decides to go back to that time in such detail.

I remember talking to the sheriff at the hospital. Or him talking to me rather. He told me that the best they could tell, from witnesses and other bystanders that were involved, Michael and several other drivers had stopped to try to help when a car driven by two young teenage girls slid off the road and plunged into the ice cold water. Michael and one other man attempted to jump into the water and swim to the girls to help them get out of the car while other bystanders stood on the bank of the river and called 911. It was early February and about 34 degrees outside. We had just had 3 days of severe weather with freezing rain and ice, but the temperature had finally gotten above freezing and the ice on the roads was starting to melt. Most of the world had returned to normal work and life, but there were still slick spots on the roads. Especially bridges and overpasses.

I remember thinking that I wasn't surprised that Michael had stopped and jumped in to help. That was his nature. He was quiet, kind, and reserved. And he would help anyone and everyone. He would literally give you the shirt off his back if he thought you needed it. I remember seeing that mental image of him stopping and jumping out of his truck and running to the water to help. He would have been the perfect person for that job too. He was fit, in great shape, strong, and he was a physician so he could really help, medically, if needed.

They were able to pull both girls from the car. I remember asking the Sheriff whether the girls had survived. He told me that they had been successfully pulled from the car and river and taken to the hospital. As far as he knew, they were transported to the hospital in stable condition. I later heard on the news that they had both survived. I was told that they had both attended Michael's funeral with their parents, but I didn't see them or meet them. I wasn't really up to it at that time. In fact, to be honest, I wasn't in the right head-space at that time. I was angry. They were the reason that I was laying my husband to rest. My heart wasn't open to them then. I regret that now. It wasn't their fault at all. What happened to them was traumatic and out of their control. They were so young to have to bear the burden of feeling responsible for someone else's death.

My alarm blared and startled me from my thoughts. I had lay in bed for over an hour rehashing Michael's tragic death and the events of that accident. I was exhausted, both mentally and physically. Today was going to be a long day and I dreaded tackling it after the emotions I had already gone through this morning. I slowly and begrudgingly crawled out of bed and headed for the bathroom. A quick glance in the bathroom mirror confirmed how tired I was. Dark circles were fighting with the puffiness under my eyes to see who was more dominant. There was going to be a lot of concealer in my future today. I quickly brushed my teeth, swished with some mouthwash, and brushed my hair. Then I put on some under eye gel patches to try to combat the disaster going on under my eyes. I dressed for the gym and headed out the door. I needed to clear my mind and sweat out my emotions. The other option was to crawl back in bed and drink heavily all day. That seemed an unhealthy option, so I picked up my pace and jogged to the gym.

My workout was good and after a quick shower back at home, I felt like a new woman. On my way back from the gym I received a text from Sam asking if I was available for a business dinner this evening. I confirmed that I was available and he indicated that I would need a cocktail dress for this dinner. He also said that we would head there directly after work, so I wouldn't have time to come home and change. That was his nice way of saying bring your clothes and girly stuff with you to work. I dressed in black slacks and a black blouse today. All black…that was kind of my mood today. I packed a small bag with my dress shoes, makeup, hairspray, brush, etc. Then I pulled out a little black dress that was usually my go-to for these kinds of occasions. I folded it neatly and put it in my bag along with my handheld steamer to help get out the wrinkles that were sure to form today. My phone read 7:38 so I made myself a to-go cup of coffee and went down to wait on the street for Sam.

I only waited for about a minute before Sam pulled into one of the parking spots along the street. There wasn't a close spot available so he had to park a few spaces away, so I started walking toward his car with my coffee, purse, and bag in tow. Sam got out of his car and half-jogged to me to help with my bag. That struck me as so kind. I really didn't need the help, but it just proved again how thoughtful and kind he is. He's one of those people who is always worried about the comfort of others around him. We tossed everything in the car and set off toward the office. On the way, Sam filled me in on the business dinner. He apologized for the short notice, but said that it was put together at the last minute and he had just received confirmation that it was happening just before he texted me this morning. I assured him it was no big deal to me; I certainly didn't have anything going on. In fact, I was glad to have a full day ahead to keep my mind off my dream this morning. That had rattled me deeply and I didn't want any time for that to linger in my thoughts today. Sam also told me that he would be out of the office for pretty much the whole day, but he would be back at 5:00 to pick me up and head to dinner. The dinner was actually in Glasgow so it would take about an hour or so to just get there. It was scheduled for 6:30, so if we left right at 5:00 then we could make it on time easily. That was also his subtle way of telling me to be ready to walk out the door at 5:00.

Sam and I arrived at the office and he walked in with me and insisted on carrying my bag. He went to his office and checked a few emails and messages, and then he said goodbye and left shortly after. I suspected he didn't really need to come to the office this morning, but had to drop me off and help me carry stuff. The rest of my day was very busy. I spent more time with Ms. Graham for training. She seemed very impressed with how quickly I was picking up on things and learning the ropes. I had always been a pretty observant and intuitive type of person. I think my high anxiety makes me really in tune with what's going on around me and I tend to pick up on things that others miss. It's one of the qualities that made me a good pharmaceutical sales representative. I could make connections with people because I was very observant of what made them tick.

We sat in on a meeting that the other associates were having about a specific project. I got to see Ms. Graham's role in that meeting and she tasked me with taking minutes. Then afterward, she had me type up the minutes and a summary of the objectives from that meeting. Once she reviewed what I had written, she said she was just going to have me do it from now on. She said she had never seen such great work and she was floored at how quickly I pumped it out. I think she was just trying to fluff my feathers and make me feel good. It worked. It was a good confidence booster to think that I was really getting the hang of the job.

I looked up at the clock and realized it said 4:04pm. Oh shoot! I gotta get ready. I grabbed my dress out of my bag and plugged in my steamer. I hung the dress on the back of the door and gave it a couple of passes until it looked crisp. Then I grabbed my bag and headed to the restroom. I brought my curling wand too so I gave my hair some spicing up so I could make it big and bold. I was doubtful that my hairspray could overpower the Scottish wet air, but I was going to give it a go. I freshened up my make up and added some more eyeshadow and eyeliner for a more dramatic look. Finally, I carefully applied my deep cherry red lipstick that would be a great contrast with my blue eyes and dark hair. I slipped into my dress and struggled to zip it up in the back. It was a plain dress with no real frills, but it was form fitting midi length. It was an off the shoulder asymmetrical look with long sleeves. It would be perfect for the chilly night air. It was simple, but classic. Then I stepped into my black patent heels with an ankle strap.The small clasp was dressy with a rhinestone, squared-shaped buckle for decoration. I brought dangly earrings that were a similar diamond look with a matching bracelet. They were just enough to elevate the black dress for a dressier look. After I had made my hair as big as possible, I stepped back and evaluated the final outcome in the mirror. It was good. I looked professional, but striking, if I did say so myself.

I went back to my office and packed up all my stuff. I pulled out my small black clutch I had thrown in my bag. It had a little shimmer to it on the fabric so it looked elegant. I quickly transferred the essentials from my purse to the clutch. The typical things like lipstick, powder, wallet, lip gloss, a hair pick, and gum were tossed in. Just as I had packed everything up and turned off my computer, Sam emerged from the top of the stairs. He turned to walk toward our offices and caught my attention. He looked so sharp. He was dressed in a black suit with a white dress shirt and a blue tie. He had clearly gotten a haircut today, and was freshly shaven. He continued to walk toward me and for some reason I couldn't stop looking at him. Subconsciously in my mind I knew I should stop staring and look away, but I couldn't make myself. He was a beautiful man. As he approached it struck me how manly and masculine he was. His shoulders were broad, but his waist was trim. Then I sort of snapped out of it, looked intently at his face and realized something. He was looking at me the same way. His eyes were bright and searing. He quickly looked me up and down, but I don't think I was supposed to see that. It seemed as if he couldn't help looking, but didn't mean to look at me that way. His face was serious and intently trained on me. Once he opened the door of my office and entered I tried to break the tension by greeting him with a big smile and said, "Hey there. You look sharp." I figured that was an appropriate thing to say to compliment your boss and not seem overly stunned by his looks.

" You look amazing! My business associates are going to have a hard time staying focused at dinner," he responded with the most serious look I've ever seen. Then he relaxed into an easy smile.

"I'm glad you approve," I said with a flirty smirk. What was I doing? This was really out of character for me.

" Are you ready to go?" he asked.

"Yes, I'm all set."

He picked up my bag and my work tote and held the glass door open for me. We walked out of the office to the car, and Sam opened my door for me. In my head I knew this was a business meeting, but it was starting to feel like something more than that. And I wasn't mad about it. Maybe I was just lonely, but I was enjoying the attention. I hadn't had someone look at me the way Sam just had in a while. Part of me felt guilty for enjoying it, and another part of me was saying you deserve to feel excited about something.

We set out on the drive and google maps said one hour and five minutes. I was pretty impressed with how well Sam navigated the streets and highways of Scotland considering he hadn't lived here very long. Not to mention driving on the wrong side of the road. The conversation was easy and flowed constantly between us. We both seemed very relaxed with one another. We talked about our day and what all we had accomplished. Sam had heard about how awesome my meeting minutes and written review was. That made me chuckle. Ms. Graham had apparently shared that information with Sam and was bragging on how "clever" I was. It almost embarrassed me because minutes were not a difficult task, but then again I was happy they were pleased with my performance so far.

Sam talked about the meetings he had today and the current projects he was working on. Then he began to explain about the dinner meeting we were attending tonight. He said we were meeting with the CEO of an organization called Historic Environment Scotland. Sam was hoping to secure a major contract for Eden & Associates with this company. He went on to explain that HES is basically in control of the restoration of many historic sites such as castles, landmarks and the like all across Scotland. Sam said they had been corresponding back and forth about the possibility of hiring Eden & Associates to help with the structural engineering of restoring about 4 historic sites. He had submitted proposals and fulfilled multiple levels of what was essentially an application process. The final determination of securing this contract would rest heavily on the conversations that occurred at tonight's dinner. It was basically an interview with Sam to answer all the questions and reassure the HES CEO and his staffers about Eden's qualifications. My role tonight, as Sam explained, was for support and to basically help him keep the conversation on track. I remembered seeing this proposal when I was filing all those documents. Sam had encouraged me to review some of the project proposals to familiarize myself with them and that was the one I chose. I basically chose it because it was the thickest, longest one and I figured it would have the most information.

"Isn't that the project where they're restoring several castles across Scotland that are either in ruins or run down? They were wanting to secure the ruin sites for tourism, and restore a couple of castles for profit or to house government delegates, right?" I asked. Sam looked over at me like I had two heads growing out from my shoulders. "What?" I quipped.

"Nothing....I'm just surprised you know that much about it. Today's only your third day of working at Eden & Associates" he responded. "How do you know all that?" he asked.

"Well, you told me to review some of the documentation I was filing so I would know how to help in the future. It just so happens that I started with that project proposal. It was the longest, so I figured it had the most information for me to learn from," I said.

"Huh.." Sam said with a raise of his brows. "That's pretty impressive, and is probably going to be really helpful tonight." We spent the rest of the drive talking specifically about that project. Sam told me everything. He treated me like I was a structural engineer and told me every detail about what they had proposed, the documentation they had submitted, the reviews of each site they had already completed, and more. I had a ton of questions and he answered every single one of them not only with patience, but some sort of pride that I cared enough to know the ins and outs of the project. The drive seemed to go by fast and before we knew it Google was directing us into the city of Glasgow. We were only about 10 minutes away from the restaurant so I pulled out my hair pick, powder, and lip gloss to reapply. I got busy freshening up in the mirror of the visor and I could see Sam watching me with side-eye glances. I think he was intrigued by my beautification process. I put my stuff away and closed the mirror. I looked over at Sam and grinned.

"I'm ready to do my part, " I said. "Sit there and try to look pretty." I laughed.

"You won't have to try. You're beautiful," he said. "And I think you have more to offer than just your beauty," he added.

I could feel the heat rising on my face. I was blushing at his compliments for sure, but mainly I was flushed with the way he looked at me. It was definitely beyond how a boss would look at his assistant. There was something more behind his eyes. It was admiration and respect mixed with a hint of something else. Desire.

The Google Maps girl let us know that we had arrived at our destination. Thank goodness because I couldn't handle much more heat in this car. We needed something to distract us from the moment. Sam pulled up to the front of the restaurant which appeared to be located at the base of an elegant hotel. The valet quickly opened our doors and I stepped out of the car with my clutch in hand. I looked around and surveyed the surroundings while taking a deep breath to settle my nerves. I don't know why I was so nervous, but for some reason I felt like I was the one in the hot seat. Like I needed to prove my professional worth at this dinner. I had to give myself a little internal pep talk and remind myself that I was not the one responsible for the outcome of this project. I was here for support and I could definitely do that. Sam rounded the car and briefly placed his hand at the small of my back as he walked by my side up the steps to the entrance of the hotel. Sam told the attendant who he was and that we had a reservation. The man motioned us to follow him. He led us through the restaurant to the back where he seated us at a round table with six chairs. He told Sam that no other members of our party had arrived yet. I asked Sam where he would like me to sit and he said, "beside me" as he pulled out my chair.

The waiter came to greet us and fill out water glasses. Sam ordered a bottle of red wine I had never heard of. I wasn't much of a wine drinker, so I wasn't too picky or educated about wine. I'd pretty much drink any of it. Sam said, "I hope that's okay."

I responded, "oh yeah, I'm good with anything." I smiled at him and held his gaze for longer than I meant to. I could see it relax him though. I think I was providing more comfort to him than I knew.

Soon, the CEO of HES arrived with two of his associates. They were all men. Now, I really felt intimidated, but somehow I kind of expected this. Fortunately, the two associates looked like they were about twelve years old and more intimidated by this situation than I was. The anxiety on their faces was nearly comical. I realized that I might not know much about this particular business, but my experience in life and sales was going to do just fine. I settled in and began to enjoy the evening. After introductions, we engaged in typical small talk and chit chat to get to know one another. We all ordered and then the business talk went full tilt. Sam got down to business quickly and was very direct with starting the conversation. The CEO, Mr. Harris, started asking questions about Eden & Associates's previous projects, the specific proposal of this project, and wanted to know specifically how Sam was going to handle the very different needs of the four sites throughout the project. Sam eloquently explained his vision of the project. He was the epitome of calm and confident with his proposals. Mr. Harris seemed to want reassurance that Sam was going to be available and hands-on with each site. He gave the impression that he was confident in Sam's skills, but was wondering how Sam was going to handle the busy schedule of simultaneous projects. Sam explained that they would complete the projects in phases so that only two sites would be simultaneous during any time period. Sam was suggesting that we complete 2 sites nearest to each other within the first six to eight months, and complete the other 2 sites over the course of an additional six to eight-month period. The whole of the project would be completed in two years. The time period was pleasing to Mr. Harris, but he still questioned how Sam would run both sites at the same time. He didn't see how that could be done logistically, and ultimately I think he was questioning the size of our firm to handle such a large project.

I had sat and listened quietly up until this point. I was taking it all in and trying to visualize how this was going to work as Sam explained it. Mr. Harris asked, "How are you going to do the work of an engineer, coordinate your crews, and manage the organization of each site at the same time?"

I couldn't help myself. "Pardon my interruption, Mr. Harris, but I think that's where I come in." He and Sam both looked a little surprised at my interjection. Mr. Harris looked at me with a quizzical look as if encouraging me to continue. "My role at Eden & Associates is to assist Mr. Strickland with the organization and logistics of our projects. He requires the time to plan and implement his plans while overseeing the actual work. My job is to make sure everything else runs smoothly. I'll be in charge of a whole host of tasks such as communicating with the crews, making sure they constantly have the most up-to-date schematics, coordinating on site meals and facilities as needed, organizing accommodations, and communicating progress with you and your staff. I'll be on site, going back and forth between sites on a day to day basis, to solve the problems that arise." I proceeded, "This will help Mr. Strickland and his colleagues focus on their specific tasks related to the structures. I can assure you I'm very good at keeping the cogs turning, and putting out the proverbial fires that inevitably pop up. Problems are constant and I'm really good at solving them."

I looked back and forth between Mr. Harris and Sam. They were silent for a moment and Sam was looking at me. Then, he looked toward Mr. Harris and they made eye contact with one another. I was becoming very uncomfortable and was slightly regretting having spoken up. Maybe I had over-stepped and they were irritated with my interruption? The pause of silence was excruciating. I glanced at the two 12 year olds at the table and they appeared to be holding their breath. But then Mr. Harris's serious face turned into a slow, wide smile and he said, "Mr. Strickland, it seems you have a gold mine sitting beside you." Then he asked me,"How do I know that you can really handle all that?"

I replied, "Well...you don't really. But you can't really know that about anyone you hire for this project, can you? You'll just have to trust me when I tell you I can handle it." I continued, "Mr. Harris, I don't have family here. I don't have any other commitments other than my devotion to Mr. Strickland and Eden & Associates. I will be able to dedicate my full attention to making sure this project is completed to your satisfaction. That's all anyone can really promise you, don't you think?"

Mr. Harris considered that for a brief second and then looked to Sam and said,"Mr. Strickland, I think I'm convinced that you and your team are the right fit for HES and this project. If it's alright with you, I'll have my office manager send the contracts over to you tomorrow."

Sam immediately agreed and the two men shook hands across the table to seal the deal. We all let out a sigh of relief and finished our meal together. The rest of the dinner was really good with casual conversation and Mr. Harris wanted to know all about our American backgrounds. We laughed, talked, and the wine flowed. That part of the dinner was just as essential in my mind so Mr. Harris could make a connection with us and we could gain more of his trust.

At the end of the dinner, as we were wrapping things up, I excused myself to the restroom. Once I returned to the table, the men were standing and getting ready to leave. They let me lead the way out of the restaurant and the valet jumped into action to retrieve our cars. We stood by the street and chatted for a bit longer while we waited. Once the cars were pulled around, we shook hands and said our goodbyes. Sam opened the door for me once again and I slid into my seat and buckled up. Sam got in and away we went. I set the google maps for him so we could navigate out of the city easily. We were fairly quiet for the first few minutes and I was starting to worry that he was angry with me for being so bold during the meeting. As we left the city center and found our way to the highway, I could feel Sam relax a little beside me.

"Krista.." he paused. Oh no. Here it comes. He's mad at me for speaking up and he's about to admonish me. I braced myself for the lecture that was about to ensue. "I can't even tell you how much I appreciate you right now." I was stunned and a little speechless. I looked at him and he exchanged a glance with me. "You were absolutely exceptional tonight and I don't think I could have secured that contract without you. Thank you for being there with me. You spoke so confidently and eloquently. I think Mr. Harris really respected your candor. You sold it and it was very impressive" he said.

"Oh my gosh….I thought you were going to be irritated with me for being so bold," I said.

"On the contrary," he replied. "I was proud."

"Thank you," I said.

We were silent for a couple of minutes while we both reflected on our evening. Then I broke the silence.

"I really would like you to walk me through the specifics of the project phases and show me the plans when you have time. I'd like to wrap my head around what that's going to look like and start getting my thoughts together about how to get us organized."

Sam looked at me again with admiration. I think he was truly thankful to have someone that was eager to make this a successful project. "Sure thing," he said. "We'll get started on that tomorrow."

We spent the remainder of the drive just listening to music. We were tired and all talked out. We arrived back in Edinburgh and pulled up outside my apartment at around 10 pm. Sam parked on the street and I thanked him for a wonderful evening and the opportunity to join him. He jumped out of the car and opened my door. He took my bag and work tote from the back seat and said he'd like to walk me up to my apartment to make sure I got in ok. I nodded in agreement and Sam followed me up the stairs. I unlocked my door and walked inside and he followed me in. He handed me my bags and I took them to my bedroom and threw them in the chair. I walked back into the living room where Sam was standing.

"Thank you again for letting me join you this evening," I said.

"It was my pleasure," he replied. "Thank you for your help. You were spectacular."

We stood there looking at each other for a long moment. He was doing it again. Looking at me with a gaze that held me captive. His look was so intense and he looked as if he wanted to say something more, but was hesitant.

"Well, I better get home," he finally said.

"Yes, it's getting late. I'll see you in the morning," I asked.

"Same time, same place," he joked.

I walked him to the door and watched him as he stepped out onto the landing. We watched each other. I think we were both thinking the same thing, but were waiting for the other to say something or make some gesture. The tension and heat between us was palpable. I couldn't bring myself to initiate, and I assumed he was just as hesitant. Ultimately, he gave me one last look and reluctantly turned to go down the stairs. I was both relieved and disappointed that nothing happened between us.

Once again, I found myself pulled into slumber after an exhaustingly long, but good day. I only hoped my dreams wouldn't haunt me again. I thought of Michael, as I did most nights. And then I thought of Sam. I wondered if there was room in my heart for them both.

Seven

The next couple of months flew by at an unexpected pace. Work was busy and provided the distraction that I needed in my life. I had completed my training at work much sooner than the six weeks we had originally thought it would take. I caught on quickly. Ms. Graham was impressed with how quickly I learned the job and my initiative. I was pretty well independent with the exception of occasional questions. Sometimes I would go ask her questions that I really already knew, but I just wanted an excuse to go talk to her. She was like a mom away from home and I enjoyed her life stories.

I spent my days in the routine of going to the gym, going to work, and sometimes joining work dinners with Sam and Mr. Eden. My weekends were mostly spent relaxing, spending time with Rachel doing fun things around the city, or taking quick weekend trips to see other nearby cities or attractions. Rachel was great about being my own personal tour guide and we had so much fun together. Although, she had recently met someone and was spending more and more time on dates with her new man. I was excited for her and she genuinely seemed to have a spark about her that I hadn't seen before.

We were gearing up to leave town at the beginning of September to start the HES project. The firm had left it to me to coordinate the accommodations for our work crews and for Sam and myself. Eden & Associates actually contracted out the labor through a third party company, so all I really had to do was let that company know our expectations and needs for the labor crews. They took care of everything else based on my requests. I just had to let them know what our budget was, how many people to a room, numbers of meals per day, how many porta-potties on site, and things like that. I was just the decision-maker. Hopefully I made good ones, but the woman at the company assured me that I could make changes at any time should we get there and discover some need wasn't being met. She said people did that all the time and she was certain there would be something we would need to change. Her name was Michelle and she gave me her personal cell number. She told me to feel free to call or text anytime. That was a huge relief because I was really worried about making those decisions and screwing it up.

She even gave me some recommendations for AirB&B's to reserve for Sam and me. Which reminded me… I needed to renew my own Airbnb lease agreement to extend. I quickly messaged the owner of my unit in Edinburgh and let her know that I'd like to extend for at least six months. She agreed and sent over the contract for me to sign electronically. I sent it back and paid her for the next month. I also decided to take the opportunity to tell her I would be gone most of the time for the next couple of months at least. I might come back on some weekends, but it would mostly be vacant. She indicated that was just fine and she would stop by occasionally just to make sure all was well with the place. Once that was squared away, I got on the phone and started calling places that were located between the first two sites.

Craigievar castle and Culdees Castle Estate were the first two sites we would be working on. They were about two and a half hours apart, so I decided that Dundee was the most central location for us to be and would provide all the amenities we might need for such a long stay. After calling around and doing some research online for lodgings, I finally settled on a place that was situated on the northernmost edge of the city. It appeared to be a quaint little hotel that had about six units associated with it. The first floor was the lobby, dining area, a sitting room, and a good-sized conference room that seemed to be equipped with everything you might need for business meetings. It had a large conference table, about 10 chairs, printers, a smartboard on the wall for presentations, and a small fridge for beverages. The pictures of the dining area were so gorgeous. The woodwork and furnishings looked like they were set right in the heart of the 1800's. It had a large wood-burning fireplace and just seemed so cozy. For some reason, I couldn't wait to sit at one of the small dining tables and have a relaxing dinner while watching the fire blaze.

There were 2 units per floor. Each unit had its own little sitting room, kitchenette, and a primary bedroom and bathroom. Each bedroom had a king-sized bed and fireplace. They looked like the bedrooms I had dreamed up in my mind when reading my favorite Scottish romance novels. I liked that they each had their own living rooms and kitchens so that if we needed to just be alone and have meals and time to ourselves, we had that option. Or, we could dine in the dining room as they served three meals a day. They also offered room service which is certainly something I might take advantage of. This was the perfect place for Sam and I to be comfortable, close in proximity to each other for work meetings, and centrally located between the two work sites.

I called the place, which was named The Rose Lodge, and the sweetest Scottish voice answered the phone. He introduced himself as Callum and asked how he could be of service. I explained our situation and who I was, and asked if he had two units available for that long of a duration. And, if possible, if those two units could be on the same floor. He said, "Oh aye dear, that's no 'a problem. Would ye rather be on the first level or second?"

"I suppose the second level will do just fine, thank you" I replied.

"Aye, of course dear. We also offer a meal plan package that's included in your stay if you're interested. It will provide three meals a day that can be taken in the dining area or in your private room. If ye don't use all the meals during yer stay, we'll reimburse ye at the end of yer stay to discount that number of meals. Would ye be interested in that service, ma'am?" he asked.

"Yes, I'm certainly interested. I would like to have a price quote with the meal package and without. I have a business budget I'm responsible for, so I need to make sure I don't go over that before I commit." I responded.

"Ok, dear. What will the dates of yer stay be?" he asked. "If it's a long duration, I can offer ye the long-term rate" he stated.

"   We will need to check in on Friday, September 5th. We will definitely be there until November 7th, but there's a chance we may need to extend our stay beyond that date too" I told him.

"Yes, love…we can make that happen. Give me a minute, dear, and I'll have a quote as ye say" he said. "Ah, yes, yer total for a 3 month stay wi'out the meal plan is 6,010 pound. Yer total wi 'the meal plan is 8,162 pound." he said.

After some quick figuring in my head, I decided the meal plan would definitely be worth it. The total with the meal plan was still under my allotted budget for a three month period, so I figured I was making a good deal here.

"That sounds great. I would like to include the meal plan please" I said.

We worked out the rest of the reservation details and I was able to pay over the phone. While on the phone, Callum said his last name is Andrews and his wife's name is Maggie. They run the lodge together and it has been in his family for multiple generations. I told him what a small world it is because my last name was also Andrews. He determined that we must be of some distant relation and we both playfully agreed we were long-lost cousins. I could tell immediately that I liked Callum. He seemed particularly concerned about making our stay comfortable and was already trying to anticipate any needs we might have.

It was Friday afternoon and the office was quiet. Most of the staff had taken the rest of the day off, so there were only a couple of people left. Sam had been out of town for a couple of meetings for the last couple of days. Ms. Graham, Mr. Eden, myself and Allison were the only ones left today, so we skipped our normal tea time. Mr. Eden came around at about 4 and said he thought we should all knock off early today. I didn't waste any time heeding that advice and practically had my stuff packed up before he finished that sentence. It had been a busy week and I was looking forward to a nice, relaxing weekend. I didn't have any plans and I was kinda excited about it.

Since Sam was gone, I called an Uber for a ride home today. I chatted with Allison outside on the sidewalk as we both waited for our rides. My car arrived first so we said our farewells and wished each other a good weekend. My brain zoned out on the way home and I didn't even remember the ride once the Uber driver parked outside my apartment. Once inside, I threw all my stuff on the counter and plopped down on the couch. I ordered take out on my app and decided to spend the night binge-watching the latest Netflix show I had discovered. I had exactly two weeks from today to prepare for our work excursion, so I needed to get some things taken care of before we left. I also knew we were going to be busy, so the main item on my agenda was to enjoy relaxing while I could. The next three months were probably going to be a whirlwind. Sam had bought me a new laptop and phone for work, so I brought those home with me to get them set up and figure them out.

The next morning I woke up at about 7:00. That was sleeping in for me; considering I usually got up around five every morning. I got up lazily, went and made myself some coffee, and came back to bed. I opened my window and listened to the sounds of the world outside while I scrolled through social media, texted back and forth with my parents, and sipped my coffee slowly. It was such a nice, slow start to a good day of nothingness.

About an hour and a half later I decided that I had been lazy enough and it was time to get some exercise in. The sun was shining outside and I could hear the birds chirping. I didn't feel like going to the gym today, so I decided a walk or run outside would be nice. In fact, I thought I would head to the trails around Arthur's seat as Sam had suggested. I looked at Google Maps and saw that it was just over a mile to get there from my apartment. I figured this could be a long walk or run since I didn't have any plans for today. I quickly got ready and put on my long-sleeve running top over my tank top, leggings, and my running shoes. I also took a running waist belt to hold my key and a credit card. Just in case I needed to stop for some emergency shopping or a meal along the way home. I also had my phone, earbuds, and sunnies in tow. I headed out the door and walked along the sidewalks as I let Google guide my direction. I strolled at first so I could enjoy seeing all the different shops and restaurants along the route. I just wanted to take in the sights and people at a slow pace for now. It didn't take me long to reach the outskirts of Holyrood palace and I continued toward the park and trails surrounding it. I decided to get serious about my exercise and I started my jog. It was a beautiful morning and it was starting to heat up. I was probably going to have to stop and take off my long sleeve shirt before long.

I really didn't like running much, but I didn't mind it today. I had music going in my ears and I was enjoying the sights as I ran. People were out in the open spaces playing with their kids and sitting around on the grassy areas. Others were walking, jogging, or heading up the trails toward

Arthur's seat. It was a busy area with ice cream trucks parked along the way for all the kids.

As I continued to run, I saw someone running toward me on the same path that seemed familiar. As I got closer, I realized it was Sam. He was jogging and had his earbuds in too. We approached each other and I began to smile, but I could tell he didn't recognize me. I had my hair in a ponytail, very little makeup on, sunglasses on, and I was wearing something he had never seen me in. I could see why he wouldn't recognize me. So, I took my sunglasses off and moved over on the path right in front of him so that he would have to run straight into me. I could see a look of concern come over him, until he saw my smiling face. Once he realized it was me, he began to slow down and return the smile. We both laughed and slowed to a stop in front of each other.

"Hey, did you think I was gonna run you down?" I asked.

"Yeah, I wasn't sure what was going on. I'm sorry, I didn't recognize you," he replied.

I half-laughed and said, "It's okay. I look quite a bit different than I usually do for work."

"Are you just out for a run this morning?" Sam asked.

"Yes, I figured today was a good day to take your advice and hit these trails. It's a beautiful day, so I decided some fresh air instead of stale gym sweat was a good idea," I replied. I continued, "I've already walked and ran about two and a half miles, so my journey back home might be slow." I laughed at myself and rolled my eyes. "How did your meetings go the last couple of days?" I asked.

"Good, they were very productive meetings," he said.

"That's great," I responded.

After we stood there looking at each other awkwardly for a few seconds, I said, "Well, I guess I better start heading back home."

Sam said, "yeah, I was just running back toward home as well. Do you want to walk together?"

"Sure," I responded....maybe a little too fast.

So, we strolled alongside each other as we found our way back toward our general areas. We talked as we walked, but I tried to stay away from work talk. I didn't want him to think I wasn't capable of having a conversation about anything else. I began asking Sam questions about himself. He told me about his parents and two brothers. I had lots of questions about his family and what they thought about him moving so far away. He said his parents weren't thrilled at first because they knew they wouldn't see him much, and he probably wouldn't get to come home often for holidays. They apparently were a pretty close family and always spent the holidays together, so that was going to be a big change. Both of his brothers still lived in St. Louis where his parents were. They were both married and had children, and Sam talked very fondly about his nieces and nephews. Sam admitted that he didn't know how he was going to feel when Christmas time came around and he wouldn't be with his family. I got the distinct impression that he was a little lonely and already dreading that time of year.

Then it was Sam's turn to ask me questions. I could tell he was working up the nerve to ask me about my family which was probably going to lead to details about my husband's death. It was inevitable. I just had to brace myself to retell the story. I tried to have some pity on him and just give him some answers without making him ask. I told him about where I had lived in Texas. I told him about my parents and that I was an only child. Then I told him about Michael. I told him how Michael and I had met, about our life together, and who Michael was. I told him more about Michael than I really had meant to, but Sam just listened and was so easy to talk to. I think, for some reason, I just needed Sam to know who Michael was. I needed him to know my past so he could understand who I was and how I had gotten to this point in my life. We continued to walk at a slow pace while he asked questions and I answered. Sam finally asked how Michael had died.

I told him that Michael had died in a tragic car accident. It wasn't exactly accurate, but I didn't want to bring down the mood by going into all the details of the accident. I figured the details didn't really matter cause they weren't going to change anything, so I kept it vague. I explained that after Michael died, I decided I needed a change. I couldn't go home everyday to an empty house full of nothing but memories. And I couldn't keep going to work everyday where I used to see Michael daily. He had filled every aspect of my life and I couldn't get away from the pain. So, I decided to make a big change and move. I was fleeing, but I was simultaneously moving toward something huge for myself.

Sam asked me why I decided to move to Edinburgh, Scotland of all places. I told him that Michael and I had visited years ago and really loved the city. I felt like it was somewhere I could live and would be a great adventure. I knew the language and I had a good understanding of the culture so I felt like I could handle it. I knew I had to move and if I was going to move, then I needed to challenge myself and go big. It was an opportunity for me to seize.

Sam nodded in understanding and told me he was yet again impressed with my courage and tenacity. I thanked him for the compliment, but I really didn't feel that impressive. I felt like most days I was just hanging on for dear life and flying by the seat of my pants. Then I returned the compliment and told him that it took him just as much courage as it had taken me to move away from everything and everyone you knew.

"You mentioned once that you had gone through something traumatic that changed your perspective and caused you to make a change too, right?" I asked.

Sam responded, "Yes, I was also involved in an accident that made me reevaluate my life."

I said, "I'm so sorry. Were you injured?"

Sam said, "No, not really. I wasn't really in the accident. I saw the accident happen and it really spooked me. People were hurt badly and it was scary. It changed me. I actually flew home to Illinois the next day to stay with my parents. I quit my job about a week later and decided I needed something different. Something about that accident rattled me. It shook me to my very core. My parents thought I was overreacting and being rash, but really it was just a turning point for me that had been a long-time-coming. I started searching for jobs overseas immediately. Within just a few weeks, I had found the job listing for Eden & Associates. I had a Zoom interview with Erick initially. Then, he flew me to Edinburgh to have a sit-down, in-person interview. That interview lasted about three hours. It was the longest interview ever, but it was really laid back and I knew after that I was meant to be here. He made me feel at home and we agreed on all business perspectives. I flew back home and within another week, Erick called me to offer the position. I accepted right away and told my parents I was moving. That was at the end of March. And, well, you know when I moved over here because we were on the same plane."

"Wow," I said. That was a pretty bold move. "Do your parents still think you're crazy?" I asked.

"No, they've resolved themselves to the idea. I talk to them on the phone pretty often and I think they can hear the difference in my voice and thoughts," he said. "I'm happier. I can feel it. Even though everything's different and I don't have my family and friends here, I'm doing better than I was before. I've also made at least one friend that keeps me entertained," he said as he winked at me.

I felt myself blush slightly, smiled and said,"Well, I'm nothing if not entertaining. And the feeling is mutual." By this time, we had wandered up the royal mile and were strolling among the tourists. It was nearing 11:00 so a few people were out and about, but it wasn't packed like it could be. As we continued to stroll, the smell of the opening restaurants was beginning to waft out into the street and my stomach literally roared. I was starving. Almost as if he could read my mind, or maybe he actually heard my stomach growl, Sam asked if I would be willing to join him for some lunch.

"I thought you'd never ask. I'm starving to death," I responded with a big goofy grin.

"I know a place on Victoria street where we can get great fish 'n chips if you're interested?" he quipped.

"Perfect!" I answered. We were sort of doing some touristy things and I was here for it. I wanted to soak it all in. We walked to Victoria street and I noted that I never got tired of seeing all the quaint multi-colored facades along the street. Sam led me to Bertie's Proper Fish 'N Chips. We went up the narrow stairs and along the wooden planks of another narrow hallway. There we were greeted by the hostess and she led us into the circular dining room. There were tables all around a grand circular, winding staircase that was lit up by a huge multi-globe chandelier. The hostess placed us at a small table on the far side of the room near a window. The ambience was like something out of a movie.

The waiter came at once and greeted us and asked us what we would like to drink. Sam ordered a flat water and a beer. Since he was having a drink, I decided 'why not.' I also ordered water and a cotton candy martini. There was a picture of it on the menu and I was intrigued. Anything called cotton candy couldn't be bad.

Once the drinks arrived, Sam and I both laughed at my drink immediately. It was pretty elaborate. They lit it on fire and then poured something in that looked like cotton candy. People all over the restaurant were watching. Then we ordered our fish 'n chips and an appetizer. Sam looked at me with raised eyebrows like "can you really eat all that food?" and I said, "What, I told you I'm starving," as I smirked. Our appetizer arrived quickly and I proceeded to chow down. I think Sam was either disturbed or truly impressed with the fervor with which I put the food away. We enjoyed our lunch together. We talked and laughed. A lot. We were becoming more and more comfortable together and both started to let our guard down quite a bit. Our sarcasm and senses of humor were starting to bubble to the surface, and we were finding out we were very much alike.

Sam was also a gorgeous man… without a doubt. His hazel-colored eyes, dark hair and eyelashes, and chiseled jaw made him easy to look at. He was slim and fit, but his shoulders were broad. He was wearing a ball cap today which was a different look. I had only ever seen him dressed up at work, so this casualness was a good change. He was also wearing a long-sleeve, black dri-fit shirt and longer basketball type, black shorts. I saw, when he sat down, that he had muscled long legs with dark hair. I realized in an instant that I might be looking at him like he was dessert, so I quickly bit my bottom lip and looked away. He was beautiful, but I needed to keep my mind in the professional zone. Then, as if I hadn't even thought of it, I remembered what I looked like today. I had on black leggings and my running shirt. They were both fitted and tight and probably showed off everything I had. But, I had on very little makeup and my hair was up. I had probably sweated off any hope of looking decent. He looked good in this casual look. I just looked like I needed a shower.

I excused myself to go to the restroom. On the way, I ran into our server and asked if I could go ahead and pay the check. I had my credit card in the pocket of my leggings, so I slipped it to him and he ran it quickly. I quickly added a tip and thanked him for his service. When I came back from the restroom, Sam was scrolling on his phone and scowling at something. I told him he looked like his dog had just died and he laughed.

"No, I was just reading a work email. Apparently, Mr. Harris from the HES foundation wants to meet with us a couple of days before the scheduled start to review the plans. He wants to meet on September the 3rd, but I know we're not supposed to go until the 5th. I need to check the calendar to see if it's possible and then see if we can change our arrival date for the hotel, " Sam said with some mild irritation.

"Ok, well that's no problem. I can help you with that," I responded. I quickly got on my phone and pulled up our shared Google calendar and checked his appointments. "It looks like you don't have any important meetings scheduled. Everything on the calendar can be taken care of remotely, or I can do it," I said. Before Sam could respond, I dialed the number to The Rose Lodge and Callum answered on the first ring. "Hey Mr. Andrews," I said.

He said, "Hello to ye too, Mrs. Andrews," and we both laughed. Sam could hear our conversation and gave me a puzzled and amused look at the same time.

"Callum, we really need to move our check in date to September 3rd. Is that possible?" I asked.

"Oh, aye…you betcha dear. It's available for the same rooms so I'll make the change now. I'll send you a confirmation email, love," Callum said.

"Callum, you are the best. I don't care what anyone else says," I giggled into the phone. Callum responded with a resounding laughter that could be heard through the phone and across the restaurant. Sam just looked at me in amusement and shook his head like he couldn't believe the exchange he just heard. Callum and I ended our conversation and I hung up. Sam continued looking at me with a bewildered look.

"Ok, it's all taken care of," I said. "Would you like me to respond to Mr. Harris 'email and let him know we'll be there on the 3rd?" I asked Sam.

Sam continued to look at me like he couldn't believe what had just happened.

"What?" I asked.

"I can't believe you just made all that happen in like two minutes. And, I'm also amazed that you seem to be new BFFs with Callum…..whoever that is," Sam retorted.

"Ha!" I laughed. "Callum is the owner and operator of the hotel we're staying at in Dundee. He and his wife Maggie run it, and their last name is Andrews. We've decided we're obviously long lost cousins. He's been so sweet and easy to work with," I reported.

Sam just looked at me while smiling for a moment longer. He said, "You really are something else, you know that?"

"Yep, I know," I replied mischievously. We smiled at each other and then I asked, "Are you ready to get out of here?"

Sam said, "Yeah, but we need to pay the check so we don't get arrested today."

"Oh, I already took care of that," I told him.

"What? When?" Sam asked with a confused look.

'You're too slow, Strickland," I said with a grin as I started getting up from the table.

Sam huffed with half amusement and half irritation that I had snaked the check out from under him without him knowing. He slid out of his chair and followed me through the restaurant and out the entrance onto the street. It was about a mile or more to get back to my apartment and the weather was still nice, so we decided we would walk together. We strolled leisurely as we took in the sights. We didn't talk a whole lot, but just enjoyed each other's company.

As we neared the street of my apartment, we had to cross a busy intersection. Apparently, I forgot where I was and went to step into the street to cross, but didn't look to my right. A car was coming and I was looking left as we do in the U.S. The next thing I knew, a horn was blaring and I was being jerked back by a strong hand grasped to mine and an arm wrapped around me. Sam had grabbed me and pulled me out of the way, and I landed nuzzled up to his side. I was scared and breathless and looked up at him.

"Are you okay?" he asked.

"Yes, I'm so sorry. I don't know what I was thinking. I wasn't.. I guess," I said as I looked down at my feet. I was so embarrassed.

Sam squeezed my hand and pulled me in closer to his side as he said, "hey, it's okay. I've done it too; believe me." I looked up at him as he held me closer and our eyes met. I was pressed into his side and I could feel his muscled hard body against mine. He looked down at me and I had never been more aware of our height difference. He was at least 6 '2" if I had to guess, and I had to crane my head back to look up into his eyes. They were serious, blazing, and compassionate all at the same time. We stood there, locked, for what seemed like forever. Neither of us wanted it to end.

"Thank you," I said as I rose up on my tiptoes to give him a kiss on the cheek. It was a sweet, gentle kiss that lingered just for a moment. He looked back at me with even more fire in his eyes.

"Anytime," he replied as held my gaze. I can tell he wants more, but he's afraid. I'm guessing he doesn't want to cross any boundaries without my explicit consent. He's not only worried about our professional relationship, but he's worried how I'm going to feel as a widow. He wants me to make the move and he's trying to be respectful of my feelings, but the look on his face tells me it's getting harder and harder for him to resist.

I pulled back from him and I turned toward the street to cross, but I kept my hand in his and let him know I wasn't willing to let go yet. We successfully crossed the street this time and reached the front steps of my building while still holding hands. I let go of his hand so I could retrieve my key from my running waistband. Sam instinctively followed me up the stairs to the door of my apartment, and I unlocked the door. He stood outside the door of my apartment and I turned to squarely face him. We looked at each other without words for a long moment. Finally, I couldn't wait any longer. I stepped forward and reached my arms up and around Sam's neck. I settled my hands around the back of his head and neck and gently nudged his face down toward me. I leaned up and neared his face with mine while our eyes were fixed on each other. I felt his arms wrap around my waist and his strong hands landed on the sides of my waist.

I could hear our breathing quicken together, and feel Sam's heart rate speed up. I glanced at his lips and then back to his eyes. That was all he needed to know and he hungrily leaned into me and pressed his lips into mine. It was soft, sweet, and sensual. He moved his lips slowly at first and then deepened the kiss for a long while. We finally broke apart and stepped back from each other just a hair. Sam looked at me and said, "Will you have dinner with me tonight? Please?"

I slowly smiled and said, "Tell me what time."

Eight

The following week and a half were weird and exciting. We spent our days at work busy getting ready to basically move our office and personal lives to Dundee for the next 3 months which required a ton of planning and work. The vibe between Sam and me was strange. We had one kiss, and went to dinner together on Saturday night and had the best time. But, since then, things seemed to have resumed back to "friends" status. Sam picked me up Monday morning for work and things went back to how they had been. We chatted easily like we had always done, and I caught him looking at me a couple of times in the way that he does, but other than that, it was like he had forgotten what happened between us over the weekend. It was so weird, but I didn't feel like I could say anything about it, so I just played along and followed his cues. Maybe he felt weird about the whole 'boss vs assistant 'thing and wanted to back up? I don't know....but

I didn't have the emotional capacity to try to figure out what he was thinking or feeling. So, I just moved forward and focused on work.

Everything was fine at work. I had wrapped up all the final details of our work trip and we were set to leave early Wednesday morning. On the way to work on Tuesday morning, I told Sam that I would be leaving work early to go home and finish packing so he didn't need to give me a ride. He seemed somewhat shocked and caught off guard by that, but I'm not sure why. I let him know that I had cleared it with Mr. Eden and he was totally fine with that, so I would be headed out of the office by 3:00pm. Sam nodded in agreement, but was relatively quiet after that. Almost as if he was hurt by it somehow. I don't know what he was thinking. And, I've given up trying to interpret his feelings by his level of quietness.

By 2:30 I had gotten everything done on my to-do list, so I popped my head in Sam's office to check in with him. "Sam, is there anything else you need me to do before I head out today?" I asked.

He turned in his chair toward me, looked at me and said, "No, I guess not. I think everything is ready to go."

"Great! So, I'll see you in the morning, then? What time should I expect you?" I asked.

"I'll be outside your apartment around 6:00 am. Is that ok?" he asked.

"Sure," I responded. "I'll see you then," I said as I smiled sweetly at him. He did not respond with a smile, but remained stoic. I definitely got the sense that something is wrong, but I can't figure it out and I don't feel like here and now are the right time and place to inquire, so I let it go.

I collected my things and went downstairs. I said goodbye to Allison and went out the front door of the office to wait on the sidewalk for my Uber ride. The app said my driver was about eight blocks away, so I was probably going to be waiting for a few minutes. Traffic at this time of day can be horrendous. I decided to sit down on the steps to wait and just as I was sitting down, I heard the door open. Sam came out of the office and closed the door behind him. He looked….troubled or worried. I stared up at him and he just looked at me with a facial expression that I could not decipher.

"Is something wrong?" I asked.

"I don't know…..you tell me," he said.

"What? What do you mean?" I quizzed him.

Sam said, "Well, you seem quiet or mad at me or something."

I truly was so surprised. I didn't even know how to respond and just looked at him for a few seconds. I mean, if anything, he's the one that has seemed quiet or mad for the last week and a half. Like, what the heck? "I'm not mad," I responded. "Not at all. I'm not sure why you would think that," I continued.

Sam continued to just look at me. He shoved his hands in his pockets and looked down at his shoes. He wasn't going to say anything, so I had to be the one to talk about the proverbial elephant in the room. "Sam, things have been weird between us for the last 10 days. You've been quiet and things between us seemed to have gone back to the way they were before our day and evening together. Before our kiss," I whispered. "I know we need to keep things professional at work, but even when we have time alone you don't seem interested any more," I added.

Sam looked up at me with a shocked, desperate look on his face. He stepped toward me to close the distance between us. He brought one hand out of his pocket and reached toward my arm to touch me. "That's not true at all," he said as he kept his voice low. "I'm very interested. You're all I can think about," he said. I think he could see the look of confusion on my face, so he tried to explain. "I think I'm just struggling with how to keep things professional at work and not let everyone know our business, and then turn that off when we're alone," he continued.

"Well, I get it. It's kind of difficult…. and weird," I conceded. "But, I would like to try to figure it out. Together," I said as I searched his eyes. He looked at me and gave me a slow half grin.

"Yes," he said. "I know we need to maintain some decorum of professionalism at work. And this trip is going to be especially difficult because almost all the time will be work time, so I just don't want us to struggle and mess things up. I need your help at work. I can't do this without you. But, I also…..want you," he said as he slid his hand down my arm and squeezed my hand. His eyes had a fire in them that seared into me.

The level of excitement that his touch and words caused in my gut was almost alarming. I really liked this man and he made me feel something I hadn't felt in many months. Alive. I looked back into his eyes and returned the squeeze. "I feel the same," I said. " I just ask one thing though," I continued.

"What's that?" he asked.

"That you talk to me instead of going quiet. I can't read your mind, and you can't read mine. I don't want to play the guessing game. I'd like you to just talk to me and let me know when you have concerns. Both professionally, and personally," I said.

"Done," Sam replied. We smiled at each other and then let go of our hands. "I'll see you in the morning bright and early," Sam added.

"Bright and shiny," I clarified with a big smile. I could see Sam's whole body relax as he stepped back from me. My Uber driver had arrived, so I said goodbye and headed toward the car. Sam stood on the steps for just a moment to see me off and I saw him go back inside once the car had pulled onto the street. There was a part of me that relaxed too as I took a deep breath and settled into the seat of the car. I was suddenly kind of exhausted. Like I had been tense and holding my breath for a week.

I spent the next few hours at home doing laundry and packing. It was proving to be tricky because I was going to potentially be away from home for so long, but Sam only has a certain amount of room in his car for luggage. So, I was having to be really selective and creative with my packing skills. I ordered take out for dinner around 5:30, so I thought I would keep working until my food arrived. About 15 minutes later, my door buzzed and I was impressed at how fast they had delivered my food. I looked through the peephole to make sure it was my food delivery, but I was surprised. It was Sam.

I opened the door and said, "hey, what are you doing here?"

He stepped in the door without saying a word. I closed the door and turned to face him. He grabbed me and wrapped his arms around me tightly. I reciprocated by wrapping my arms up around his neck. He buried his head into my neck and hugged me close. His body was warm and it felt good to be hugged. We stood like that for a long moment before Sam lifted his head and pulled back slightly to look at me. His eyes searched mine and I smiled slightly. I was still taken aback and surprised at his gesture of intimacy. I looked into his eyes and tried to let him know how much I loved this moment without saying the words. Sam leaned down and slowly put his lips on mine. His lips were soft and gentle. It felt as if his kiss was telling me that he wanted me, but he was leading into this relationship slowly. It was exactly what I needed to hear.

Our moment was jarringly interrupted by the sound of the door buzzing. My food! I had forgotten all about it. In fact, I think I had forgotten that I even needed to eat.....ever. I was convinced I could live on Sam's hugs and kisses alone by this point. I answered the door and handed the young teenage boy a tip while taking my bags of food from him. I closed the door and turned to Sam. "Dinner," I said. "Would you like to stay and share with me? I have plenty," I asked Sam.

"It smells delicious and thank you, but I better get going. I need to get home and pack too. I haven't even started," he said sheepishly.

"What? Oh my gosh…you're going to be packing all night long," I laughed.

"I know. Don't remind me," Sam said and he leaned down and gave me another quick, but slightly lingering kiss. "I'll see you in the morning. Bright and shiny as you say." he said teasingly. I smiled and swatted at him playfully as he opened the door.

I closed the door and turned toward the kitchen when I heard a knock and "lock the door."

I locked the door and shouted, "yes, Mr. Strickland." I heard him harrumph and then trod down the stairs. I smiled to myself and I was suddenly way more excited about the next three months.

I finally finished all my laundry and packing. I laid out my outfit for tomorrow and then jumped into the shower. I was going to get up extra early in the morning to get in a jog and some squats. I wouldn't be able to go to the gym because they don't open until six each morning and Sam would be picking me up at that time. So, I set my alarm for four and climbed into my bed by eight. I did a little reading, but it didn't take long for my eyelids to grow heavy. I put my book on the nightstand, turned off my lamp, and rolled over to go to sleep. My heart was content. For the first time in a long time, I didn't feel alone or sad. I was genuinely looking forward to the coming days and weeks.

My alarm rudely woke me up at four and I couldn't believe it was already time to get up. I felt like I had slept for about an hour. Even though I was sleepy and groggy, my mind immediately went into overdrive thinking about all the things I needed to get done this morning before Sam arrived. Those thoughts got me going, so I crawled out of bed and headed straight for the bathroom. I brushed my teeth, put on my workout clothes and shoes, pulled my hair into a ponytail, and headed out the door. It was still slightly dark, but the sun was beginning to rise so the streets were easy to see. I set out with a fast-paced walk to get myself warmed up and then started jogging after about 2-3 minutes. My tracking app let me know when I had reached two miles and I was feeling lucky that I had calculated my course well enough to be back near my apartment at the end of my two miles. I decided to run up and down the stairs a few times, and then I went inside my apartment and got about 100 squats in. By this time, I only had about an hour to get ready, so I put myself into high gear. Somehow, by sheer luck I think, I was downstairs with my two suitcases, backpack, my purse, and my work tote by 5:58am. I looked like a pack mule standing on the sidewalk waiting. Sam drove up at exactly 6 am and looked shocked. He opened the door to the car and I said, "what's wrong?"

He replied, "nothing, I'm just astonished that you got all that gear down those stairs by yourself."

"Ha! I'm stronger than I look," I retorted. "I even got up and worked out this morning, thank you very much."

" Very impressive, Mrs. Andrews," Sam quipped. He smiled at me while simultaneously lifting my suitcases into the trunk of his car. I slid into the passenger seat and settled in for the drive. Sam got in and buckled his seatbelt. Then, he handed me a large cup of coffee. He had stopped for coffee on his way and it was the largest, hottest, most divine cup of caramel latte I had ever had. I thanked him profusely, took a long sip, and let my eyes roll back in my head at my delight. He grinned and we were off on our adventure.

The drive was just about an hour and a half to our hotel. I had seen this scenery before when Rachel and I took this trip, but it was still breathtaking. We drove for a while just chatting and talking about the business ahead of us. I had the itinerary for the next couple of days and reviewed it with Sam. He seemed genuinely impressed at my organization and all that I had accomplished. I had spent several weeks making phone calls and getting all the puzzle pieces to fall into place at the right time. Sam also seemed relieved to know that I had it all in hand. I think the scale of this job was stressing him out, but he would never say that.

After about 45 minutes, I had to request a pit stop for the restroom. I really didn't want to be the one delaying us, but my bladder wouldn't survive this whole drive. "Sam, I'm so sorry, but I really need to stop for the restroom if you don't mind," I said.

Sam looked at me and said, 'Of course, no problem. I'll pull into the next stop we see."

Luckily, there was a stop within the next five minutes down the highway, so Sam pulled into the area. There was a rest area and a Starbucks so I decided that I would use the restroom there. I tried to hurry as fast as I could and got back to the car quickly. Sam was out of the car and waiting beside it. I assumed he just needed to get out and stretch his legs too. He watched me walk out and across the parking lot all the way back to the car. I smiled and said, "Ok, think I'm good to go now," as I smiled broadly. We hopped in the car and jumped back onto the highway in no time.

As we settled back into the drive, Sam reached over and grabbed my hand to hold it. I looked at him and he said, "Is this okay?"

"Yes, absolutely," I responded with a smile. We spent the rest of the drive talking about the scenery and our parents. I mentioned that my mom and dad would love to see all the highland cows and sheep in the green pastures. They both grew up on farms, so they would appreciate the rolling hills of farmland. Sam talked about his hometown of St. Louis and his parents. His mom was retired now, but she had been a teacher for many years. His dad is a pharmacist and owns his own pharmacy. Sam said he's been talking about retiring for several years, but Sam doubted that he would actually retire anytime soon. It sounds like his dad is really attached to his business and is having a hard time letting go.

"Oh, I bet your dad and I could have some great conversations about drugs," I laughed.

Sam said, "oh yeah…I forgot you were in pharmaceutical sales. I bet you two would get along great. You'd be talking shop and boring the rest of us," he said with a wink.

"I'll have you know that pharmaceuticals are a riveting conversation piece," I retorted with a smirk.

I proceeded to tell Sam that my mom was also a teacher and she would be retiring after the next school year. She had taught elementary age the whole time.

"And what about your dad?" Sam asked. "What does he do?"

"Well, he's actually a hospital administrator. He's currently the Chief Financial Officer for a hospital near where I grew up. That's kind of how I got into the pharmaceutical sales area. He knew several of the companies and reps, so he encouraged me to go that route," I explained. "I think he'll probably retire in a few years too. I think my parents want to travel before they get too old, so he'll be working on getting out."

"Sounds like our parents might get along really well if they were to meet," Sam said. "They seem to have a lot in common," he continued. Sam looked at me to see how I was going to respond to that. It was a little early to be thinking about our parents meeting, so he looked like he regretted saying that almost immediately.

I did think it was a little soon to be going there, but I tried to nonchalantly respond with, "Yes, I'm sure they would," I replied. However, I didn't look at Sam and just kept looking out the window as if I were preoccupied with the scenery. But inside, I was panicking at that thought.

I was nowhere near ready to even tell my parents I might be involved with someone. In fact, when I talk to them about my new job, I only refer to Sam as "Mr. Strickland" and I keep it short. I haven't told them anything about him because I don't want them to even think that I might be interested in someone. The truth is, I'm afraid of their judgment. I'm afraid they're going to disapprove of me being involved with someone only 7 months after Michael died. They'll think that's too soon, and that I've lost my mind.

Maybe I have lost my mind. Maybe it is too soon. Maybe I've jumped into this because I'm lonely. If I were still living back home, I probably wouldn't dare become involved with someone this quickly after Michael's death. I can do it here because no one knows me and they can't really judge what they don't know. There's suddenly a pit in my stomach and I feel guilty. I became quiet and kept looking out the window.

After a few minutes of silence, Sam squeezed my hand and said, "Hey, are you okay? You got really quiet all of a sudden."

I looked over at him and decided that I needed to tell him what I was thinking. That's what we had agreed on. To not make the other guess at our thoughts. "Yes, I'm fine. I'm just feeling a little guilty."

"About what?" Sam asked.

"To be honest, I feel guilty that I've started this relationship with you so quickly after Michael's death," I answered. He squeezed my hand again and looked at me with compassion. I was afraid that declaration would scare him or make him uneasy, but it didn't. He just let me talk it out.

"I haven't told anyone about us. I'm afraid to. Even my parents. I think everyone will judge me and think I've lost my mind for beginning this so soon. It's only been seven months," I said. "They already thought I was nutty for moving across the world, by myself, and starting a whole new life," I added as I tilted my head down.

Sam looked straight ahead and held that stoic look he can have, but he didn't let go of my hand. He just let it sit in the air for a bit. Finally, he said, "I can understand why you wouldn't want people to know yet. Krista, I don't want you to worry about me. We'll take this as slowly as you want. You tell people when you're ready. I'm a pretty private person in general, so it's not like I'm gonna go blabbing to people about us. I'm happy to follow your lead. I just don't want that to be a worry for you." He went on to say, "I didn't mean for my comment about our parents getting along to alarm you."

"I know you didn't," I said. "I really appreciate you being so patient and understanding of my feelings about this."

By this point, the Google Maps girl let us know we were nearing our destination. Thankfully, just in time, because the mood was a little thick right now and we needed something to break the tension. After several turns and lots of navigation, we finally arrived at The Rose Lodge. It was just as charming in real life as the pictures had shown. Sam parked the car and we got out to collect all of our things. It was nice to stand upright and stretch my legs. I rounded up my backpack, purse, and work tote; and Sam had gotten all the suitcases out of the trunk. He insisted on carrying all of them into the lodge. Once inside the grand front entrance, there was a quaint foyer area with a large front desk. The woodwork of the desk, staircase ascending up and behind the desk, and the wood flooring were astonishing. It looked like something out of the 18th or 19th centuries. The charm of the furnishings and the smell of wood polish caused me to feel oddly nostalgic for something I had never even had.

We approached the desk and Sam set the suitcases on the floor. There was no one around, but I heard a voice from behind us say, "Hiya, can I help ye?" and I knew immediately, without even looking, that it was Callum. I turned to see him entering the foyer from a large arched doorway on our left that appeared to lead to a grand sitting room with a giant fireplace. There was a similar arched doorway on our right, just at the foot of the stairs, that led to the dining room area.

I smiled brightly and said, "You must be Callum. I'm Krista Andrews. We spoke on the phone. You know.....your long lost cousin."

His eyes lit up and twinkled as his face transformed into the broadest, most jolly smile I had ever seen. He responded instantly with a hearty laugh and outstretched arms while saying, "Cousin. It's so good to see you!" We both laughed and Sam was looking between us like we had both grown two heads. He couldn't figure out what was going on. Callum approached us and reached out his hand to shake Sam's and introduced himself. "Callum Andrews. You must be Mr. Strickland," he said.

Sam responded by shaking his hand and saying, "Yes, sir....that's me. Nice to meet you."

Callum rounded behind the large front desk and quickly started looking up our reservation on the computer. While he was busy clicking away on his keyboard, he chatted with us about how our drive was and whether we had run into any weather on the way. Once he had our information pulled up, he began giving us the details of our stay.

"Mrs. Andrews, you will be in number 4, and Mr. Strickland will be in number 3. They are right across the hall from each other on the second level. There's no lift, but I'm happy to help ye up the stairs with your bags. Lunch will be served at 12 noon sharp each day and you have a window from 12:00 to 1:30 to be served either in the dining area or in your rooms if you prefer. Dinner is the same and is served between 6:00-8:30 each evening. Breakfast is a buffet that is served every morning from 6:00 am to 9:00 am. If you miss meals, we always have a variety of snacks available in the pantry and cold storage in the grand sitting room there to ye left." Callum went on, "Will ye be needing lunch today?"

I chimed in, "Mr. Strickland will not be needing lunch today as he has a business luncheon, but I will want to eat here. I'll take it in the dining area if that's okay?"

Sam quickly snapped his head in my direction with a slight look of concern. He said, "Mrs. Andrews, are you not planning to join me for the lunch meeting today?"

I said, "Oh, I'm so sorry. I didn't realize you would want me there. I'm happy to attend the lunch meeting if that's what you prefer."

"Yes, I think that would be best if you don't mind," Sam replied.

"Very well then. Business lunch it is. Scratch that, Callum. I'll be joining Mr. Strickland. However, I do think we'll want to dine here this evening, is that right Mr. Strickland?" I turned to Sam. He agreed and Callum wrote us down for the dining area.

We then followed Callum up the stairs with all our bags. I briefly poked my head into the dining room and it looked exactly as it had in the pictures. A large fireplace on the far side of the room was the centerpiece of the space. There were small tables for two to four people scattered around the room. Two of the small tables were situated in front of a large bay window that gave a great view outside. I had already determined in my head that it would be a great place to sit and have coffee in the mornings. All of the tables, trim, and flooring were a dark mahogany type wood that gave the space a rich, warm feeling. The windows were draped with thick velvet curtains that were a deep blue color. They matched the blue and green plaid wallpaper on the walls. I would never have thought to put those colors up in a space, but they looked so good and it was very traditionally Scottish. I was in love.

We followed Callum up the stairs, and in true gentlemanly fashion, neither he nor Sam would allow me to carry my own suitcases. Once we were on our level, Callum opened our doors for each of us and handed us our keys. He made sure we were settled in nicely and bid us farewell.

"If ye have need of anything at all, just call down or come find me," he said as he headed back toward the stairs. After putting my stuff down, I went across the hall to Sam's room. His door was open so I went in to make sure everything was to his satisfaction. His room was very nice with a large bed, sitting room, small kitchenette and all the amenities you could possibly need.

"I hope you have everything you need here," I said.

Sam turned to me and said, "It's really perfect. You've done an excellent job of finding the perfect accommodations for us. And I can see why you are so fond of Callum. He's a hoot." Sam continued.

"Isn't he?" I replied. "I think we'll be very comfortable here. They even have a conference room with high tech amenities that you wouldn't expect based on how everything else looks. I'll have to go down and scope it out. I figured if you needed to have any meetings, that would be a good place to do it. Callum said they would be happy to provide beverages, snacks, or even a meal in there for meetings if you need. And, it will be included in the overall meal package that the company has purchased."

Sam just looked at me with a slight smile and said, "You really have thought of everything, haven't you?"

"Well, that's what you're paying me for so let's hope so," I replied with a shrug of my shoulders. We both chuckled, and then I told Sam I was going to go get unpacked before it was time for our luncheon.

He said, "I hope it's okay that I put you on the spot to go to lunch with me. I just want you there at any and all business meetings if possible. I'll feel better knowing you're in the loop and can help me remember things and stay organized."

"Oh sure, I don't mind at all. I'm looking forward to it. But....I do have a question. How should I dress for this meeting? Is it business attire, or more casual?" I was currently wearing wide leg jeans, black slide mules with a pointed toe, a white bodysuit, and a fitted black blazer.

Sam said, "You look perfect and should go as you are. I'm going to wear jeans and a blazer too."

"Ok, good. Then I'll go get unpacked and situated. I assume we'll need to leave at about 11:30? Google says it'll take about 15 minutes, but I figure we'll want some wiggle room so we're on time," I said. "Also, Sam, do you need anything ironed? Like, do you need a shirt ironed or anything?" I asked.

"You would iron for me?" Sam asked with a puzzled look.

"Well, yeah. The job description was office AND personal assistant. So, if you need those kinds of things done, you need to tell me. I'm happy and eager to help you however you need. Don't be hesitant to ask," I said.

He looked at me with such admiration and love in his eyes. Like he was so relieved and appreciative to have someone that genuinely wanted to help him no matter the task. It gave me such satisfaction to be able to be that person for him. For some reason, I got the impression he had never had someone that was available and willing to be that for him. This was new to him, and that was both exciting, and a little bit sad.

Our business lunch went off without a hitch. Mr. Harris was very pleased with the plans we laid out to him for the beginning of the project. It seemed like our detailed plans helped to alleviate some anxieties for him. I could tell that I would need to communicate with him frequently to let him know what was going on. He was the type of person that would need to know what to expect during each phase of the projects. Tomorrow, we would arrive on site to meet the crew and get started. I had some phone calls to make this afternoon to make sure everything started smoothly. This was all so new to me, but I was so excited to be a part of it.

Nine

The next couple of weeks were insane! Our plan involved starting reconstruction work on the Craigievar Castle and once that project was up and running smoothly, then we would initiate the Culdees Castle Estate. Craigievar was about an hour and a half drive away, so we were getting up early each morning to make it there by 8:00 and getting back late in the evenings each day. Sam and I were putting in long, 12-14 hour days, 6 days a week. It was brutal. I was getting up around 4:30 each morning to work out before getting ready for work. Luckily, we dressed very casually for the job site, so planning my work attire was easy and saved me time. Most days, I just wore leggings, a sweater, and rain boots with a rain jacket.

After about two weeks of getting that project off the ground, we went to the Culdees estate and did the same there. We had established a good foreman from the crew working on Craigievar, so we trusted him to keep the plan on track and report to us frequently. I was basically the one he would report to and then I would relay any specific questions to Sam that I couldn't answer. Which was a lot, because I was by no means a structural engineer and sometimes it felt like they were speaking a different language. I tried to listen, observe, and soak in as much as possible, but these people had experience and training that I didn't have. However, I will say, I felt like I was doing a pretty good job of organizing and taking care of peoples 'needs on site. The foreman, his name is Jameson, was really good at letting me know what they needed. I tried to anticipate their needs as much as possible and I think he appreciated that. He had told me several times that he felt I was keeping things moving well and taking care of problems faster than he usually experiences on job sites. That made me feel like I was hanging in there at least.

I barely saw Sam throughout the day. We texted a ton and talked on the phone when there were issues that required more conversation than text. We would see each other in passing, but there wasn't time to hang out and chat. Lunch time on site was really the only time I saw him during the day, but I was usually busy during that time checking in with workers trying to help solve problems. Basically, I would only see Sam on the ride to and from each day. And honestly, we were so tired that we hardly even talked on the drive.

Six weeks into the projects, both sites were up and running full speed. Things were essentially going well with only a few hiccups here and there. At this point, Sam and I were going in different directions. The foreman of the crew at Culdees was not as great and reliable as Jameson was at Craigievar, so Sam had to spend more time there. Sam often wanted me to be at the opposite site from him to make sure things were going smoothly and to keep a finger on the pulse of what was going on. Then, he would want to go check in at the other site, so we would switch. That system worked pretty well, but it did nothing for our personal relationship. We hardly saw each other at all.

By the end of the sixth week, Sam had decided that we needed to take a break and not work the whole weekend. The crews would still work on Saturday, but he and I would not be there. However, we would be "on call" so to speak and available by phone to answer questions and help make decisions if needed. I was so grateful he made that decision. I was absolutely exhausted and needed a couple of days to catch up on rest. We were quiet on the drive back to Dundee Friday evening. We got back to the lodge around 7 pm and I had called ahead and had spoken to Callum about our dinner order. When we walked in, Callum immediately ushered us into the dining area and seated us at a table by the fireplace. No one else was in the dining area. Friday nights tended to be a lighter crowd because most people went out on the town for dinner. Sam and I were grateful that it was quiet and we had it to ourselves. The fireplace had a nice fire going and sitting there listening to the crackling of the logs was peaceful. Callum and Maggie had memorized what we wanted to drink and had a couple of drinks and flat water already on the table. They treated us like royalty. Callum brought out our dinner plates within seconds of us sitting down. I had steak and pasta with a nice side salad, and I had ordered Sam a steak and chips. He also got a side salad, but Sam rarely touched anything green.

Sam and I were able to settle in and enjoy our dinner together. We talked a little about work, but then our conversation drifted off to more personal exchanges and it was nice to not talk about work for a while. We talked quite a bit about what we were missing from home, about how we grew up, and some of our childhood memories. Then, somehow, we got on the topic of Michael. Sam asked me questions about our marriage and why we hadn't had children. I could tell he was a little nervous to ask that question, but I didn't blame him for asking.

"We tried to have children. We both wanted them, but we couldn't ever conceive," I said. I'm sure my face was sad because Sam reached across the table to hold my hand as if to say he was sorry for that pain. "After years of trying, and even going through IVF, and spending a fortune, we finally decided it just wasn't in the cards for us. So we stopped putting pressure on ourselves to have kids and we just decided to enjoy each other. So we did." I explained.

Sam held onto my hand across the table, but we both remained quiet. Sam took a drink of his whiskey on the rocks while I stared out the bay window. It had begun misting outside again and the overcast skies reflected the mood in my heart at the moment. I was remembering the sadness both Michael and I felt every time I took a pregnancy test and it was negative. It happened over and over. Each time though, Michael was the one who stayed positive. He was such a reserved, quiet type of guy. He was always positive even in the face of devastation and hard times. He was my constant. I could always rely on him to be strong and keep me going; no matter the situation. It was such a good feeling to have someone looking out for me, and I always felt like he could make any bad situation better. Sadness filled me and I wondered whether I had been that for him. Did he feel that way about me? Did I lift him up enough over the course of our marriage?

Before I knew it, I was crying. Silent tears streamed down my face as I sat there looking out the window at the dreary landscape. My heart felt broken all over again. I missed Michael so much sometimes I could hardly take in a full breath. My chest felt tight and my heart literally felt like it would break. The weight of the last few weeks was heavy. I was exhausted and the loss of Michael was bearing down on me all over again. Sometimes, I felt like this grief would go on forever. I'd had breaks from it over the past few months, but it rolled through in waves and I never knew when they were going to hit. I looked over at Sam.

His face fell when he saw mine.

"Krista, are you okay? What's wrong?" Sam asked. He looked more concerned than I'd ever seen him. He scooted his chair closer to mine, never letting go of my hand. He leaned in close to me and looked into my eyes.

"Yes, I'm so sorry. This is embarrassing," I said as I frantically wiped tears from my cheeks. I attempted to get my act together and dry up my tears. I was so humiliated for allowing myself to get emotional in front of Sam and in the dining area. Thank goodness there was no one else in the room. Sam was basically sitting right beside me now and he wrapped his other arm around me. He pulled me close to him and somehow that made the tears flow even more.

"Krista, what can I do?" Sam pleaded.

"Oh, nothing. I'll be fine. I'm so sorry for being an emotional mess," I replied.

"Please don't apologize," Sam said. "Talk to me. What's going on?" he urged again. "Was it me asking about you and your husband having kids? I'm sorry I brought it up," he said.

"No, please don't apologize. I'm glad you asked and I really don't mind telling you about Michael and our marriage. In fact, I want to . It was a great marriage and I want you to know about us. But, you just have to know that my grief takes over sometimes. It's only been eight months and most of the time I handle it well. Other times, not so much. The grief sneaks up on me and usually strikes me at the most inopportune times," I told him. "I think I'm tired too, so I'm probably on the emotional cliff...so to speak."

"Please don't be sorry, Krista. I want you to talk about Michael, your marriage, and the sadness. I want to be the person that you lay that on. You can trust me and you should never, ever feel embarrassed for feeling whatever you feel. Whenever you feel it," Sam encouraged. He leaned in and brushed a kiss against my temple. It was sweet, tender, and reassuring. I squeezed his hand as I looked at him and we held eyes for several seconds.

"Thank you, Sam. You have no idea how much I needed to hear that. Thank you for not running the other way," I said as I slightly smiled. I was trying to lighten the mood a bit. Sam gave me a half grin in response and pulled me in for a closer hug. Then, we sat and held hands, sipped our drinks, and stared out the window together for a long while. He let me just sit there and think. And be sad for just a little while longer.

I finally decided that I was done being sad for the day. I had grieved all I could for today and needed to snap back to reality. That was the thing about grief for me. I could only handle it for so long and then I needed to pull myself out of it. If I didn't, I feared it would pull me completely under and I wouldn't make it out. And somewhere in my brain, I could always hear Michael saying, "You can't dwell. You gotta move forward."

Sam and I decided it was time to call it a day. It was nearing bedtime and we were both so tired. We headed up the stairs to our rooms. It was mid October now and the Scottish weather had turned cold. The stairwell felt drafty and I shivered a little as we trudged up the stairs. When we got to our doors, I asked Sam if he would mind helping me get my fireplace in my room going. He of course agreed and followed me into my room. Each day, the staff cleaned our rooms, made our beds, and restocked the wood for our fireplaces. Sam never used his fireplace because he's hot natured and loves the chill of the room. I, on the other hand, did not like being cold at night so a warm, cozy fire was exactly what I needed right now.

Sam headed straight for the fireplace and began loading the logs onto the grate. Then he used the kindling strips and the striker to get it lit. In no time at all, the fire was absolutely roaring. While he was working on that, I went to the bathroom and took a quick shower. I came out in my pj's and had washed all my makeup off. Sam rose from the fire and turned to face me. For the first time ever, he saw the casual version of me. I was ready for bed with my hair up in a bun and no makeup. It was a different look for sure. Part of me was a little embarrassed for him to see me like this, but the other part of me was so incredibly exhausted that I didn't even care. Sam walked toward me and looked me over. Then he smiled.

"You look cozy," he said as he was smiling.

"Yes, I know it's a much different look than you usually see," I said shyly as I twirled a strand of hair that had fallen down my neck and looked to the floor.

Sam lifted my chin with his hand so that I met his gaze. "You look beautiful," he said. He held my eyes for a few seconds and then he slowly leaned in and kissed me. It wasn't a passionate kiss. It was a sweet, soft kiss. It was to let me know what he felt for me without saying a word. Without any pressure.....just tenderness.

"I know you're tired. We both are. But, do you have any specific plans for tomorrow?" Sam asked.

"Well, nothing major. I'm hoping to sleep in a little, have some coffee in bed, and just have a slow start to the day. I need to take our laundry into town and drop it off. I had also hoped to do a little shopping to restock on a few things. Other than that, I don't really have any plans. Do you need something?" I asked.

"I would just like to spend the day with you," Sam answered. "We can do whatever you want or need to do. I just would like to hang out with you and NOT talk about work," he said emphatically as he smirked. "Would that be okay with you? If you'd rather not, that's completely fine. You might rather just have a day to yourself," he said.

"No, no, that sounds wonderful," I replied.

"Good," Sam said. "I'll bring you coffee in the morning." Then Sam leaned down and kissed me again. After a long, more passionate kiss, he wrapped me in a tight hug. I desperately needed that hug and I felt my whole body melt into his. He held me there for what felt like five minutes before backing away and saying goodnight. I closed the door and locked it behind him. Without wasting a single second longer, I climbed into bed and slid down under the comfy comforter. My head hit the pillow and that's the last thing I remember.

The next thing I knew, I heard knocking at the door. It took me several seconds to figure out where I was. My eyes were heavy and I couldn't quite focus on my surroundings. The knocking came again after a few moments and I finally remembered where I was. It must be Sam. I quickly looked at my phone and it said 8:36. I couldn't believe I had slept this late. I never sleep this late. Usually, sleeping in for me is 7:00 at the latest. I stumbled out of bed and opened the door. Sam was standing there with two coffees in hand.

"Good morning sleepy head," he said with a smile. He walked in while I shut the door behind him. I bet I looked a mess, but I didn't even care. I crawled back into bed and Sam handed me my coffee. I thanked him as I propped my pillows up to lean against. Sam went over to the fireplace and quickly threw a couple of logs on and relit it. I didn't know how he managed to get a fire going so quickly, but it warmed up the room almost instantly. The crackling sound, coupled with the pitter patter of the rain outside my window, made my warm coffee taste all the sweeter. Once Sam was finished with the fire, he stood and walked over to the chair and pulled it across the floor so that it was next to the bed. He sat and sipped his coffee while we talked. We talked about all the things we would do today and about the weather. It was going to be a nasty day out, but that wasn't going to stop us.

After I finished my coffee, I told Sam I would get dressed and be ready to go in about 45 minutes. He said he would meet me downstairs and left my room. I showered and got dressed as quickly as possible. I dried my hair, but I just left it straight. There was no point in curling it in this wet weather. I looked in the mirror after my hair and makeup were finished. My long, dark hair reached down my back to near my bra strap. I tried to emphasize my blue eyes with a dark eyeliner and shades of brown eye shadow. My black lashes were long and nearly obscured my eyes completely. My dark eyebrows matched my hair, and I topped off my look with a bright red lipstick to contrast. My eyes were a little tired looking with dark circles that I had managed to camouflage with concealer. I put blush and highlighter on my cheeks to give them a little life. Once I was satisfied with my look, I grabbed my purse and rain jacket and headed downstairs. As promised, Sam was waiting in the foyer at the foot of the stairs. He looked up at me as I was coming down and had a look of adoration on his face. It thrilled me to my very bones for him to look at me like that.

We jumped in Sam's car and I side-seat navigated us to our first stop, which was dropping off our laundry. I had found this quaint little shop that does laundry...it was actually Maggie's suggestion. Two young women owned it and they would do all our laundry in one day and then have it delivered back to the lodge. It was fantastic and was really very affordable considering what they do. They even dry clean and press some of Sam's business clothing when I ask them to specifically. After dropping that off, we decided to head into Dundee city center to do some shopping. I really needed to bulk up my winter wardrobe. The autumn temperatures were getting frigid and winter was right around the corner.

We found a shopping area downtown and hopped from one store to another until I had found most everything I needed. Sam even bought a couple of new shirts and a coat as well. Next, we ducked into the cutest little bookstore I had ever seen. I loved the smell of bookstores. We both browsed in our own sections until we each had found a couple of books we couldn't live without. Sam insisted on paying for both our books despite my protests.

By this point, it was well past 1:00 and we were both starving. The owner of the bookshop gave us a couple of restaurant recommendations, so we decided to check out the closest option. It was a sweet little cafe with a bar and several small tables. It was pretty full, so we decided to sit at the bar. We chose to sit at the end corner where there weren't any other people sitting so we could eat and talk in peace together. I ordered a pasta dish and Sam ordered a steak pie. The food was delicious and the ambiance was perfect. We ate and talked and just generally enjoyed each other's company for over an hour before deciding to move on with our day.

We basically spent the rest of our day just exploring the city. We drove around, walked the harbor side where Rachel and I had biked, and visited the HM Frigate Unicorn. That was a unique experience.

Around about 6 pm we decided that we had probably had enough exploration for one day and made our way back toward The Rose Lodge. Just before arriving back though, Sam said there was a little pub he had been wanting to check out, so we decided to stop in for a couple of drinks and possibly dinner if it looked good. It was the neatest little spot and had a great atmosphere. There weren't very many people there, but it was still kind of early in the evening. Especially for Scots. They seemed to be a late-night type of culture. The bar stretched all along one side of the pub with high- top tables scattered all around. In the back, there was a small stage and a dance floor. The pub had that old-world charm with exposed duct ceilings and old exposed bricks for the walls. The bartender greeted us as we came in and told us to pick a table. Sam led me back toward the back where the stage was and we picked a table that was wedged between the corner of the bar and the wall. A sweet waitress came over immediately and introduced herself and took our drink order. I decided on a gin and Sam went for his trusty whiskey. She returned with our drinks and some flat water as well. She also gave us a couple of menus and Sam and I looked over them. He asked if I would like to eat dinner here or at the lodge, and I figured the food here would be as good as any.

By the time we had finished our meal, which was absolutely fantastic, the band had come in and started setting up. The waitress told us they were a local group that played here once a month, and she was obviously a big fan. She said they had some of their own songs, but they mostly played cover songs. She indicated we would probably love them because they cover a ton of American songs. We were intrigued so Sam and I decided to stay for a while longer to hear them play. We ordered another couple of drinks after our waitress cleared our dinner plates. By this time, the rest of the restaurant was starting to fill up and the noise level with the clinking of glasses and the chatter of voices was at a low roar.

Sam and I were thoroughly enjoying each other's company today. Being with him was easy. He was so laid back and never seems to get too bothered by anything. He was really genuine and down to earth. He talked about his family with the highest regard, so that makes me feel like he's just really a good person. I asked him more about his decision to move here and the accident he was involved in before coming here. I could tell that he was still pretty hesitant to talk about it or relive it. It must have been really horrible for him to not want to talk about it because he seems to be an open book about everything else in his life.

"The accident changed my life," Sam said. "It was something that I'll never forget and made a big impact on how I view life. It can be so fleeting and precious. Experiencing that just made me realize that I didn't want to take anything for granted," Sam added. I began my sentence to probe a little further into the details of what had happened, but just then the band began to play and it got loud quickly. I decided to drop the subject for now and enjoy our evening together.

After a few songs, Sam and I were hooked. Our waitress had been right…this band was awesome and they were playing a lot of old 60's, 70's and 80's rock songs from the U.S. It was so nice to have a bit of home and reminisce a little. Sam and I sang along and talked about our memories associated with each song. About seven or eight songs in, the band decided to slow things down a bit and started playing a slow song. Nearly every single table stopped what they were doing and went to the dance floor. Sam and I giggled at the mass exodus to the dance floor. Then, as I was taking in the sight of all the people pairing up, Sam stood up from the table and held out his hand.

"Would you mind dancing with me, Krista?" Sam asked. I hesitated for just a split second, and then smiled in response. I took Sam's hand and let him lead me to the dance floor. It was already jam packed with people, but Sam and I inched our way in between the others. Sam wrapped his arm around my waist and pulled me in close. I put my right hand in his and wrapped my other arm up and around his shoulder. The band was playing "Faithfully" by Journey. It was the best slow dance song I could possibly think of at that moment. Sam pulled me in even closer and my breath hitched. Suddenly my heart rate went up and the spark between us was undeniable. Sam's body was hot. I could feel the heat emanating through his shirt, and I could feel his strong, muscular back tighten at the touch of my hand. We stared into each other's eyes for a long moment before I relented and nestled my face into his neck. He smelled divine and it made my stomach clench with excitement. I was completely attracted to him and had a hard time staying composed. I think he was feeling the same way by the way he looked at me. I let go of his hand and reached my right arm up around his neck. He reciprocated and wrapped his now free arm around my back so that I was fully engulfed. We continued to sway to the music and I could feel his heart pounding against me.

All too soon, the song ended and the band launched into the next rock song returning the crowd to their seats. Sam and I stood there frozen to each other until we finally felt like we needed to break it up and go back to our table. We both sat down and took a drink of our drinks. The waitress returned and asked if we needed anything, and Sam looked at me and said, "I think I'm ready to get out of here." His gaze was burning into me and I understood what he was feeling. There were suddenly too many people around us.

He paid the tab and stood. Sam took my hand and led me out of the restaurant. Once we stepped out onto the sidewalk and walked out of the way of the door, Sam turned and grabbed me by the back of the neck and pulled me into the most passionate kiss I could ever imagine. His lips were soft and gentle, yet possessive and hungry at the same time. It was like he couldn't wait another millisecond to have me. He became bolder with his kiss and touches than he had ever been with me. I had the feeling he was on the verge of losing control and that wasn't typical for him. His hands roamed over my body as he kissed me. They wandered down my back, along my waist, and teased by sliding down my bottom and leg. I felt his other hand slide to my waist. His thumb slid under my shirt and brushed my side causing a sensation of electricity to shoot through me. I, on the other hand, was doing some exploration of my own. I couldn't help but slide my hands along his waist and felt the ripple of his hard ab muscles. His body was hard. He was tall, strong, and completely sexy. Both of our breathing and heart rates were at full speed by this point.

Sam slowed the rhythm of the kiss and ended it sweetly. He pulled away slightly and looked into my eyes. He didn't say a word, but it was like we were passing secret messages to each other. He took a deep breath and slid his hand down to mine to hold it. "We better stop making out on the sidewalk, don't ya think?" Sam joked. I laughed and nodded in agreement. We turned and walked hand in hand back to the car. Sam opened the car door for me and I settled into the passenger seat. I took a long deep breath as he rounded the other side of the car and tried to slow my racing mind and heart rate.

The drive back to the lodge was quick and we were walking up the steps of the lodge within just a few minutes. It was about 10:00 by that point so we were trying to be quiet as we entered the lodge and headed upstairs. When we got to our doors, we paused and looked at each other while holding hands. There was a part of me that was afraid of this moment. We were clearly extremely attracted to each other, but I was not the type to sleep with a man outside of marriage and that was pretty unusual in this day and age. Not only was I not ready for that level of intimacy, but I was desperately afraid Sam wouldn't understand that. Most men these days wouldn't. I had only ever been with Michael, and I wasn't well-versed in having this kind of conversation. I didn't know what to say and I think Sam interpreted that on my face.

"Krista," Sam said. "This relationship is going to go exactly how you want it to go. I'm never going to pressure you to do more than you feel comfortable with. I'm sure you've noticed that I'm enamored with you and I'm having a hard time keeping my hands off of you. But, I'm not going to push you," he added.

I smiled slightly and dipped my head down to look at the floor. I was so relieved. I decided to be honest and say exactly what I was thinking. We had promised each other that. I looked back up and into his eyes. "Sam, I feel the same way about you. But, I've never been with anyone but Michael. We waited to be....you know.... Intimate...until we were married. And that's how I still feel about that. Call me old fashioned, but I think that's sacred and should be saved for marriage. I'm falling for you, Sam. There's no question about that. I'm hoping this relationship between us will continue to grow, but I need you to be patient with me. My husband tragically died only eight months ago and it's going to take some time for me to close that door completely. I'm still in the grieving process. As you unfortunately witnessed last night," I quipped.

Sam squeezed my hand and pulled me into a tight, warm hug. "I completely understand. As I said, it's your show.... you call the shots. I'm happy to go at whatever pace you set," Sam said. "I do appreciate you being honest and upfront. It's nice to be with someone that I don't have to guess at the rules of the game." Then Sam gave me a final goodnight kiss that was soft and caring. I stepped back and wished him a good night and then unlocked my door. He waited for me to go inside and lock the door. Then I heard him unlock his door and close it behind him. I leaned against my door with my head resting back and closed my eyes. I took the deepest, most cleansing breath I had taken in a long time. It had been a good day and I was happy. Happiness had eluded me for so many months that I was thankful for days and moments like today. My heart was full.

Ten

I awoke to knocking at my door. My brain was aware, but my eyelids betrayed me and I couldn't force them open. I lay there for a few seconds more until I heard the knocking again. It wasn't urgent knocking, but was light and gentle with only about three raps at a time. I finally forced my eyes to open and reached over to grab my phone from the nightstand. It read 8:49. I couldn't believe I'd slept in this late again. I never sleep this late. I slowly sat up onto my elbows in the bed and looked around the room. When my eyes were adjusted, I pushed back the covers and got up out of bed. I slipped on my robe that was lying at the foot of the bed. I wrapped my robe closed and tied the belt to it as I walked to the door. Once again I heard the light knocking on the door. I unlocked the door and opened it just a crack to see who it was. Sam was standing there with coffee and a bag of what I assumed was breakfast in his hands.

"Good morning, sleeping beauty," he joked. I smiled as I pulled the door open wider and motioned for him to come in.

"Good morning. I can't believe I slept in this late again. Two days in a row," I responded.

"You must be tired," he replied. "I brought you some coffee and bagels, but I completely understand if you want to go back to bed," Sam added.

"No, no….it's time for me to get up," I said. "Thanks for bringing breakfast. Especially the coffee," I added as I took the first sip. It was warm and delicious. Sam had ordered exactly what I liked.

"What are your plans for the day?" Sam asked.

"Well, I'd like to take a walk, depending on the weather," I said as I peeked out the window. The sky was a mix of overcast clouds and sunny patches. It didn't seem to be too windy, so it might be a decent day for a walk.

"What are you doing today?" I asked.

"Actually, Mr. Hess called early this morning and asked if I would be willing to go to the work sites with him to look things over. He's going out of town for a couple of weeks, so he wants to catch up on the progress of the projects before he leaves. He's picking me up in just a few minutes," Sam said.

"Oh…well, do I need to go with you?" I asked. I'd be happy to go along and I can be ready in about thirty minutes." I added as I hopped up and started going into action to pull myself together.

"No, no… you don't need to go, Krista. You stay here today and enjoy your day. You need and deserve some rest and time to yourself. I can take care of this," Sam said as he stood up and walked over to me. He stopped me and lightly grabbed my shoulders to face him. He looked at me gently and with compassion in his eyes. "Enjoy your day and I'll see you in the morning bright and early. I'll probably be back late tonight, so I'll see you in the morning when we leave for work," Sam added.

Part of me was relieved to have the day to myself to relax, and the other part of me was a little sad that I wouldn't see Sam until tomorrow. I'd gotten used to spending every day with him. Sam gave me a quick hug and kiss and said he needed to get going. Mr. Hess would be arriving in just a few minutes and he wanted to be downstairs and ready to go. After seeing him out, I crawled back in bed and continued drinking my coffee and enjoying the breakfast he had brought for me. I had opened the shades to my window and was now looking outside just sort of daydreaming. The view was breathtaking and I decided that getting out for a walk was exactly what I needed to do. I got dressed, put on makeup, and did my hair into a half up, half down style so I could keep it mostly out of my face. I layered up so that I could stay warm, but be able to shed layers if I got hot on my walk.

I spent a big part of the morning walking around Dundee. It turned out to be a pretty nice day and didn't rain on me at all. The wind was light so I stayed nice and cozy in my layers, but wound up taking my rain jacket off and tying it around my waist. Along the way I found some quaint little shops with clothing and accessories so I decided to check them out. I actually took my time and properly shopped. I wound up buying several items. I found a new pair of shoes, a new bag that I thought would be perfect for work, a couple of sweaters, and a nice dress that would work for a night out or a business dinner. I also stumbled into a cozy little bookstore and browsed around for a little while. The shopkeeper was a lovely woman that I would place in her fifties or so. She greeted me and asked if there was anything specific I was looking for. I told her I was really just looking, but interested in a fictional romance novel if she had any suggestions. She guided me to a section with several choices and showed me three books she had read and said they were all worth the reading. I chose one of them and got in line to pay. The nice lady assured me I wouldn't be sorry for reading this selection and bid me a nice day as I was leaving. The people here were so nice and friendly. It made me a little homesick for Texas because it had a similar vibe. Everyone was so down to earth and good-hearted. I thought of my parents and wondered what they were up to. I hadn't talked to them in a couple of weeks. We had texted a few times, but we hadn't actually spoken on the phone. I was missing them. I looked at my phone to check the time. It was 12:10 pm here, so that meant it was 6:10 am there. Too early to call, but I set an alarm for 3:00 so I could call them then.

My parents have been so good to me over the past nearly nine months. They had been there for me through every single step of the grief. They were my first call when I received the news that Michael had been in an accident and taken to the hospital. My dad met me there and was by my side when the doctors gave me the news that Michael didn't survive. I remember that moment like it was yesterday. Most of the days and weeks to follow were a blur, but I remember that moment vividly. I had been placed in a consultation room that consisted of a small armchair and a small loveseat with an end table. The table had a lamp on it with a phone and a box of tissues and a few magazines. It was quiet and lonely in that room. After waiting there for what felt like eternity, the door suddenly opened and a security guard had led my dad to the room. He entered and immediately sat beside me. He grabbed my hand and asked me what I knew. I told him that I had received a call from the sheriff telling me to meet Michael at the hospital. That he had been involved in an accident and the ambulance had taken him here. I remember starting to shake and tears welling up in my eyes.

"Dad...I really don't think Michael survived," I said as I started crying. He asked why I thought that and I told him, "the way the triage nurses looked at me when I arrived. They looked at me like they pitied me, dad, and they've all been overly kind. It's like they know he's dead, or that he won't survive, and they feel sorry for me." I started crying harder and was losing control. My dad grabbed me and pulled me in to hug and hold me. We sat like that until I finally calmed down. He continually tried to reassure me and let me know that everything would be okay, but I knew it wouldn't. Somewhere deep down, in the pit of my stomach, I knew it wasn't going to be alright. I could feel it. Michael was gone.

After about forty-five minutes of sitting in that room, a doctor finally came in. He knocked a couple of times before entering. He was an older gentleman and he looked haggard and tired. He looked like he had been sweating and his face was sad. This was it. I braced myself to hear what my body already knew.

"Mrs. Andrews, I'm Dr. Tanner. I'm one of the Trauma Response Physicians here," he introduced himself. I told him my name and introduced my dad and then we waited. Holding our breaths for his next words. "Mrs. Andrews, I don't have good news for you," he said as he lowered his head and briefly looked at the floor. He went on, "your husband was brought in about an hour and a half ago. He had been submerged into cold, frigid water and was under for a long time according to the first responders on scene. His core body temperature was too low and his lungs were full of water. His heart stopped and he stopped breathing. We attempted CPR for about 40 minutes once he arrived here. I know the first responders were also doing CPR as they were en route to the hospital. We gave him several rounds of medication, but we couldn't get his heart rhythm back and we were unsuccessful at resuscitation. I'm sorry, Mrs. Andrews, but your husband did not survive."

And there it was. What my body already knew, but my brain was still trying to process. The love of my life was gone just like that. Fifteen years of love was lost. So many thoughts ran through my head all at once. I will be going home to an empty house tonight. I would wake up tomorrow and Michael wouldn't be there. My mind flashed to the day we met, then to our wedding day, and then to that morning when we had said goodbye to each other like it would be a normal day. It wasn't a normal day at all. It was the end.

My mind snapped back to reality with the sound of a cab honking on the street. I looked up to get my bearings. I had been walking the streets, deep in thought, and hadn't been paying attention to where I was going. I looked around several times and didn't recognize my surroundings. I pulled out my phone and checked my location on Google maps. I was about five miles away from the lodge. I was also suddenly exhausted. I decided that I would grab a cab back to the lodge and eat lunch there. I found a cab and slid into the back seat and gave the driver the name of the lodge. He nodded and said he knew it as he pulled away from the curb. Within minutes the cab pulled up to the entrance of the lodge. I paid the driver, or swiped my card rather, and got out with all my bags. I trudged up the steps of the lodge and into the front door. The large clock that hung on the wall behind the front desk read 1:45. I only had about 15 minutes to try to get some food for lunch in the dining area. I walked into the dining area which was completely empty. I sat down at the same table that was located between the fireplace and the large bay window. Mrs. Andrews appeared shortly out of the kitchen swinging door and greeted me.

"Oh, good afternoon dear," she greeted. "Ye look a bit weary, love. Are ye okay?" she asked.

"Yes, Mrs. Andrews. I'm fine, thank you. I've been walking most of the day and I'm just tired and hungry. Is it too late to get some lunch?" I asked.

"Oh absolutely dear. What would ye like? We have soup, beef and mash, or I can make ye a sandwich if ye like," she said. I decided on a half sandwich and a bowl of soup. Mrs. Andrews patted me on the shoulder and said she would have it right out. She disappeared back into the kitchen and I took off my jacket and settled into my chair. I didn't realize it, but I was kind of chilly and the warmth of the crackling fire was comforting. Mrs. Andrews reappeared within a minute with a glass of water and a hot cup of tea with milk. She set them down on the table and said, "ye look like you could use a good cup of tea, dear."

She was right. I needed that tea. I sipped on the hot tea as I enjoyed the fire. The weather outside was starting to take a turn and I was thinking that I got lucky with having good weather for most of the day during my walk. I felt sad though. Allowing my mind to rehash the events of Michael's death had stolen a little of my happiness today. I was suddenly feeling very alone.

Mrs. Andrews returned just at that moment and brought my food. It was exactly what the doctor ordered. A heaping bowl of minestrone soup and a half of a chicken salad sandwich on rye. My mouth was watering and I hadn't realized how hungry I was until just now. I made short work of my lunch and it was fabulous. After finishing, I thanked Mrs. Andrews and headed upstairs with all my bags. Once in my room, I dropped the bags on the floor and crawled into bed. It was now almost 3:00 so I decided to call my parents. My mom answered and sounded so excited to hear from me. It was wonderful to hear her voice. We talked for nearly an hour. As we were winding up our conversation, my mom asked, "Krista, do you have plans for Thanksgiving? I know they don't really celebrate that there, so I was just wondering if you might be able to come home? Or we could even come for a visit there if you like?"

"I hadn't really thought about it yet, but I would really love it if you guys could come visit. I will still have work, so I don't think I can come home, but we could celebrate here," I said.

"Honey, we would love to come there. We'll plan on that. We'll probably stay for the whole week of

Thanksgiving, but you shouldn't feel obligated to entertain us the whole time. We'll do some sightseeing. I know you will have to work most of the time," mom said.

"That's great, mom. I'll work on finding you a place to stay. I might even be able to find somewhere close to me. I'm not sure if we'll be on the worksites near Dundee or back in Edinburgh. I'll find out and let you know. When you book flights, let me know," I said excitedly. This brightened my mood. My sadness had lifted and hope was returning. We ended our call and I was giddy. I suddenly realized how much I missed my parents and now I couldn't wait for the next few weeks to go by. And then my thoughts turned to Sam. What was I going to do about Sam? I would have to introduce my parents to him because he was likely going to be around. Even if just in a professional capacity. I wasn't sure I was ready to let them in on my personal relationship with Sam. I wasn't sure they would approve or understand. The thought of dealing with that caused me some anxiety, but overall I was really excited to know my parents were coming to visit.

The rest of the evening and night were very relaxing. I binge-watched some tv, cleaned up around my room, got reorganized, put away all my laundry, and got my clothes and things ready for work tomorrow. I had dinner brought to my room and continued my binge-watching. I fell asleep early at probably around 8:30, but I woke up at about 10:30 to the sound of noise in the hallway. I got up, unlocked the door, and poked my head out into the hallway to see what the noise was. It was Sam. He looked surprised to see me and said, "hey, what are you doing up?"

"I heard you coming up the stairs, I guess," I said. "How was your day?" I asked him.

"It was good. Mr. Hess was very pleased with the progress," Sam replied. "I'm exhausted. It was a long day," he continued. "How was your day?" he asked.

"It was good. Lots of relaxing, and a little shopping," I said as I grinned.

"That's great," he said. He reached up and put his hand on the side of my face. He looked at me lovingly for just a moment and then that look turned to desire. He leaned down and kissed me. It was a passionate kind of kiss that let me know that he had missed me today. His other arm found its way between my robe and my nightgown and wrapped around my waist and rested just at the top of my bottom. Teasingly placed, it sent a spark through me that I felt low in my stomach. Sam kissed me like he hadn't seen me in years. I reciprocated the passion and leaned into his body with mine. The heat between us was palpable. Finally, Sam reluctantly pulled away and we both attempted to catch our breath. "I better get in my room and go to bed before things get too heated," he said as he smiled. "I'll see you in the morning, Krista." And then he gave me one more sweet kiss.

I closed and locked my door, and returned to bed. My mind replayed the events of the day as I pulled the covers back up and turned my lamp off. My emotions had been all over the place today, but it was a good day. It ended on a happy note, and I was once again looking forward to the next several weeks. Grief struck again today, but I had conquered it once more. I could only hope that one day the grief would subside completely and I could remember Michael without the weight of despair.

Eleven

I could see mom and dad walking down the long corridor toward baggage claim. They were a sight for sore eyes and I was holding myself back from running and tackling them with hugs. I spotted them before they saw me so I was just waiting for them to look up, and when they did they both broke into the biggest smiles I had ever seen. I was giddy with excitement and I walked quickly to meet them. As we approached each other, my smile turned into tears. I was so happy to see them and my emotions got the best of me. All the things I had felt over the last several months seemed to compile into this moment and I couldn't hold back feelings.

I embraced my mom in the longest hug and my dad wrapped himself around the both of us. No one spoke. We couldn't. We were all so overwhelmed with emotion that we just needed to stand there and soak each other in. After what felt like several minutes, I finally broke from our hug and stepped back just a bit to look at their faces. My mom had tears welling in her eyes. She was beautiful. The tears in her eyes caused her blue eyes to turn a shade of turquoise. Dad had a look of compassion and relief on his face, and he let out a deep sigh like he'd been holding his breath for the last few months.

Once we had regained our composure, we started heading toward the baggage carousel. They had just begun sending out the luggage, so we worked our way into the crowd. Mom and Dad had a total of four, large checked bags. Not to mention they had a small carry on each and they were both carrying backpacks.

"Good grief," I exclaimed. "I thought you guys were only here for about 10 days. Did you decide to move here?" I teased.

"I told your mom we were bringing too much," dad said as he rolled his eyes.

"You never know what you might need and what the weather is going to be like," mom replied. "Besides….you never know. We might stay longer," she said with a half offended and half joking tone.

"Well, the good news is that my boss has given me the whole week off. He's American too so he knows how important this week is to us. So, we'll be able to stay in Edinburgh and I was able to get you an Airbnb apartment in the same building where I live. I reached out to my landlord and it just so happens she had an extra place available," I explained. That seemed to please my parents to no end and they were excited that we would get to spend a week together.

"That's so wonderful!" my mom said. "Is your boss going back to the U.S. for Thanksgiving?" she asked.

"No, he's staying here. He said he was going to work some, but he'll take off for Thanksgiving Day and the following Friday," I told them. "You know we've been staying in Dundee since the beginning of September. He's still there, but said he's going to come back to Edinburgh late Wednesday night," I said.

"Oh, well…do you think we should invite him to Thanksgiving dinner with us?" my mom asked. "I mean, I'd hate for him to spend the holiday alone." she added. Mom was always the one thinking about the feelings of others. She never wanted anyone to feel left out or lonely.

"Ummm, I don't know… maybe," I replied reluctantly. I wanted to invite Sam, but that would probably be really awkward and difficult for us to act like we aren't in a personal relationship in front of my parents. I don't know if my acting skills are that good. And, I certainly didn't want to give them any reason to question it. "I'll see what he says, but I doubt he'll want to horn in on our time together," I added.

"Oh honey…you have to invite him," mom said. "I can't stand the thought of him being alone for the holiday."

"Ok, ok, I'll invite him," I responded with a slight scoff.

We made our way outside the airport and I had an Uber waiting for us. We loaded all the luggage into the trunk and piled into the car. My mom and dad were absolutely thrilled to hear the driver speak in his Scottish accent, so they talked to him the whole way to my apartment building. It was fun to watch them see all the streets and architecture for the first time. I could tell they were in love already.

Once they were settled into their apartment, which was one floor above mine, they came down to my place to catch up. It was about nine in the morning at this point because they had flown the overnight flight. I made them some breakfast and a huge pot of coffee. I had made sure that I had the type of creamer mom liked. I had to make it myself basically because they don't have the same types of creamers here in the UK that they have back home.

We ate, sipped our coffee, and talked for a long time. It was nearly noon and I could tell that they were exhausted. I encouraged them to go take a long nap and try to get caught up on sleep. I assured them we would have plenty of time together. I promised I would come wake them up and we would go to dinner at around 7 so they could stay on track with a good schedule.

They didn't hesitate to follow my advice and headed upstairs. Just as I closed my door, my phone dinged. It was a text from Sam.

"Hey there. How are you? Did your parents make it okay?" he asked.

"Hi! Yes they're here. They just went to take a nap. They're exhausted from the trip. lol How are you?" I replied.

"Missing you already," Sam wrote..

"I miss you too, Sam. Would you be interested in having Thanksgiving dinner with us? We'll probably just go to a restaurant here in town. My mom is upset to think you'll be alone for the holiday and she's not likely to accept you saying no," I said.

"Sure, I'd love to actually. But do you think that's a good idea? I know you're worried about them finding out about us right now," Sam asked.

"Well, yeah I think we're gonna have to be careful about that, but I'd really like it if you'd join us," I said.

"You got it. I'll be there. Just let me know a time and place," Sam replied "I'm going to miss you this week, Krista. I've gotten used to seeing you everyday."

My heart squeezed. I was going to miss him too. I already did miss him and it's only been a couple of days. I was so excited that he would be joining us for Thanksgiving dinner. "I'll miss you too, Sam. It's going to be so hard for me to keep things professional on Thursday after not seeing you for several days," I said. "Have a great week, and I'll see you soon," I ended. He replied with a heart emoji.

The next few days were so much fun. Mom, dad, and I spent every single minute as tourists and packing in as much sight-seeing as we possibly could. We laughed, talked, and just genuinely enjoyed each other's company. It had been a long time since we had spent this kind of time together. And, the last few months had been overshadowed with nothing but grief and survival for all of us. We hadn't been able to even sit and have a normal conversation until now. It was refreshing and I think we all needed it to heal.

By Wednesday, we had worn ourselves out with all the activities, but it had been so much fun. We were sitting at an outdoor cafe at the Hay Market and just having a late lunch and enjoying the rare bit of sunshine. Lots of tourists were walking by which made for great people-watching. After being fairly quiet for quite a while, dad spoke up and said,"You seem to be healing well, Krista. I think this place and these people have been good for you." I looked at him and there was a brief moment of understanding that passed between us without uttering a single word. He continued, "I'll be honest, I thought you were nuts for coming here by yourself. And I was truly a little bit hurt that you wanted to get away from home.I thought that your mom and I would be what you needed. But now I can see that this was the right move for you. You seem so much happier, and I'm incredibly proud of you."

My eyes were leaking again. I needed to hear those words. I needed them to understand why I did this. Why I moved here and desperately needed the change.

"I am happy here, Dad. I still struggle with my grief and it sneaks up on me when I least expect it. I suspect it will be that way for a while, but this place has helped me a lot. I don't think I could've stayed in Texas and healed the way I needed to," I told him. "I'm also so glad I got the job I have. It has been a much-needed distraction and something to keep me busy. And the people that I work with are life-savers," I added.

I went on to tell them about everyone in the office and how Mrs. Graham had taken me under her wing. I told them about my interview, our initial meeting with Mr. Hess, my role on the job sites, and the projects in general. They were very interested to know all the details of such a unique operation. They also asked a ton of questions about Sam. I think they were just interested in him because he's American and they wanted to hear his story, but it made me squirm to talk about him and try to keep a poker face about our relationship. I was so scared they could see right through me and I was really worried they would be able to tell when Sam and I were around each other. I didn't know how I was going to handle that at dinner tomorrow. Part of me was so excited to see him, but the other part of me was so anxious about spending that time with him and keeping my feelings for him secret.

The next morning we all slept in and then Mom and Dad came down to my place midmorning for a late breakfast. We had really been enjoying our coffee time together in the mornings. That's when we got most of our chatting and catching up done. We had talked a lot about Michael and his death too. It was painful to talk about, but there was a part of me that needed to discuss it with my parents to help me move on. They shared their feelings about the whole thing and it made me realize that they had grieved so much too. I guess I had never stopped to think about how his death affected them. I was too busy focusing on my own grief, but now I could see how much they had hurt over this.

We spent the afternoon hiking and I took them up Arthur's seat. I was pretty impressed they hiked it so well. It's not for the weak of heart and my mom is deathly afraid of heights, so her agreeing to do it was impressive. It was good for us. We needed the fresh air and exercise after the heavy topic of discussion this morning.

Once we were back at the apartments, we all showered and dressed up for our dinner. We had agreed on dinner at Gaucho Edinburgh at 7:00 pm and we were all dressing up in our finest. I had decided on the black dress I bought in Dundee for the occasion. I slid my black strappy heels on my feet and stood in front of the mirror on the back of my bedroom door to check my final look. My hair was loosely curled and I had achieved the blowout look; although I was sure the Scottish rain would put an end to that by the time I got to the restaurant. My makeup was on point. I had chosen a smokey eye and a dark red lip for some color. I was sure that Sam was going to appreciate my choices tonight and that excited me, but at the same time I admonished myself for thinking that way. I needed to keep it professional tonight. I couldn't risk letting my guard down. It was going to be so hard to be professional, but not make Sam question how I felt about him.

Sam was meeting us at the restaurant, so we took an Uber. When we arrived, we were about fifteen minutes early. I gave the host my name and told him we had a reservation for four. He let me know that we were the first to arrive and he led us to our table. The restaurant was gorgeous and the ambiance was perfect for this evening. Mom, Dad and I settled into our seats and dad went ahead and ordered water and a bottle of red wine for the table. After about ten minutes, I looked up and saw Sam walking in. I nearly lost my breath. I hadn't seen him in about a week and the sight of him made me shiver. He was dressed in a dark navy suit with a white button down shirt, but no tie. It was the perfect outfit for the occasion and he looked better than I wanted him to at this moment. I didn't know how I was going to maintain my composure. All I wanted to do was go give him a hug and kiss. I could see the host showing him where our table was and Sam looked over to see. We made eye contact and we both froze for a split second. Luckily, mom and dad were in a full blown conversation while perusing the menu together, so they were distracted. It was a good thing because if they had seen how we looked at each other, the jig would have been up immediately.

I blinked and smiled at Sam to break the moment. He smiled back and began to make his way toward the table. I stood from my seat and greeted him as he approached. "Hey Sam, it's nice to see you," I said. My mom and dad looked up and quickly put their menus down so they could stand to greet Sam as well. My mom said, "Oh Mr. Strickland, it's so nice to meet you," as she hugged him. Only my mom would hug my boss when meeting him for the first time. I could tell Sam was a little surprised by this, but then his face turned to a look of humor and happiness. I think he secretly enjoyed getting some motherly attention. My dad shook Sam's hand and introduced himself and then motioned for Sam to sit and make himself comfortable.

Sam sat between me and my mom, and my mom immediately began quizzing him about who he was and where he came from. My dad interjected and said,'You'll have to forgive the inquisition. She does this with everyone." We all laughed and my mom slapped my dad's arm playfully and rolled her eyes. The waiter returned with the bottle of wine and began to pour everyone a glass.

"I hope you don't mind, Mr. Strickland, but I took the liberty of ordering wine for the table. Feel free to order something else if wine isn't your thing," my dad said.

Sam said, "Wine is perfect. And please call me Sam. Mr. Strickland is my dad." My Mom and Dad chuckled and they all agreed to a first name rule. We proceeded to enjoy our time together and talk about everything from family to work. Sam tolerated my mom's endless questions and answered everything she fired at him. We all ordered our food and then mom and dad both excused themselves to the restroom.

When they were out of sight, Sam reached over and placed his hand on my back. He leaned close and whispered in my ear, "You look extraordinary." I looked at Sam and our eyes locked for a long moment. The look between us was saying how much we had missed each other, and how much we needed each other without saying any words.

"I've missed you this week," I whispered back. "I'm so glad to see you, but tonight's proving to be harder than I expected. I don't know if I can hide my feelings for you. All I want to do is kiss you right now," I told him. He smiled a steamy half grin at me and then we both pulled away from each other as my parents rounded the corner on their way back from the restrooms.

The rest of the night was the most wonderful Thanksgiving dinner we could have possibly had. We laughed, shared stories, talked about our families, and just enjoyed each other's company. It felt very comfortable and there wasn't even a hint of tension among us. It was everything I needed it to be.

Sam insisted on driving us back to our apartment building rather than taking an Uber, so we climbed into his car and hit the road. He parked on the curb just outside our building and got out to help us out of the car. He opened the door for me and my dad opened the car door for my mom. My mom of course made a comment about what a gentleman Sam was. We all said our goodnights and agreed that it had been a wonderful holiday away from home. Mom, dad, and I walked up to our apartments and they wished me a good night as they continued up the stairs to their flat. I unlocked my door and went inside. I had no more than set my purse on the chair when I received a text from Sam.

"Can I please sneak up to your apartment for a proper farewell?" he asked.

"Of course," I replied. "Hurry!"

Within seconds I heard Sam coming up the stairs so I unlocked the door and opened it. Without saying a word, he came right into my apartment and I closed the door behind him. I turned to face him and before I could say a word he swept me up into his arms and started to kiss me with the fiercest amount of passion possible. It was like he had been starving all week and was set to devour me now that he had the chance. I felt the same. I lost my breath and grabbed the back of his neck with one hand and instinctively shoved my other hand up his side and around his back. I touched every inch of his toned back that I could.

Sam's hands roamed over me and he was more bold than he had ever been. It was a side of him that he rarely displayed; if ever. It was clear how he felt about me. He wanted all of me. I ran my hand up through the back of his hair and grabbed it with a slight pull. Sam groaned low in his throat and that move caused him to become even more aggressive. He gently pushed me back against the door and leaned against my body while still kissing me. He pulled away from my lips and moved his kisses down the side of my neck while continuing to explore with his hands. After several minutes, the make-out session was growing more and more intense. Sam finally pulled away from the kisses and stopped. We were both breathing heavily as he looked down at the floor like he was trying to compose himself.

"What's wrong?" I asked.

"Nothing," he said. "I just need to stop before this goes any further. Or before I can't stop myself," he said as he brought his eyes to mine.

" Yeah, I know," I responded. "I'm glad you have some self control because mine is apparently gone," I laughed. Sam smiled and stood back from me just a step.

"I better get going. Thank you for tonight. It was really nice and I like your parents. It's been a great Thanksgiving and I'm thankful for you, Krista," Sam said.

"Happy Thanksgiving, Sam," I said as he gave me another quick hug and kiss. It had been the most wonderful holiday away from home that I could imagine.

Twelve

With Thanksgiving over and done with, we had about four weeks until Christmas. Eden & Associates were planning to be closed for about ten days from Christmas Eve until after the new year, so both projects would go full steam until then and the work would be halted during the holidays. Mr. Hess had agreed that giving the workers a good amount of time for the holiday break would be best for everyone. At that point, we would be about four months into the project for the first phase. We were actually ahead of schedule for this first phase, so a holiday break wasn't likely to hurt our progress.

On Monday morning, Sam and I left around 5 am to head back toward the worksites. My mom and dad had left on Sunday to head to London to spend a few days before flying back to the states. Sam and I were rested up and ready to tackle the next few weeks. We were going to be putting in long days, six days a week for the next four weeks. I was truly looking forward to it. Both projects had made so much progress and it was really amazing to be a part of something that gave me so much satisfaction to watch the work get accomplished. The sheer amount of teamwork and planning that it took for such a large undertaking was astonishing. On paper and in theory it seemed impossible, but everyone just made it happen.

Once Sam and I arrived in Dundee and back at The Rose Lodge, we literally threw our bags in our rooms and immediately went to work. Sam jumped back in his car and headed toward the Craigievar Castle to spend the day there and see what Jameson had been up to. He was generally very good at keeping us in the loop, but Sam felt like he needed to check in. Meanwhile, I was headed to the Culdees Castle Estate to see the progress going on there and see if they needed anything. I generally hired a driver, paid for by Eden & Associates, to get me around when Sam was going in the opposite direction. It was nice because I could spend the whole ride there getting caught up on work.

I arrived at the Culdees site at about 10:00 am and immediately noticed that something seemed off. The scaffolding was up and large pieces of equipment were sitting on site, but nothing was happening. There were no workers and there didn't seem to be any movement. I thought this was kind of odd, but I just figured maybe they were working inside or somewhere I couldn't see from my viewpoint. I got out of the car and slung my backpack over my shoulder. I zipped up my rain jacket over my coat. It was freezing, overcast, and lightly misting rain...sideways. It was miserable, but I was prepared in my fleece leggings, sweatshirt, down coat, and rain jacket over the top of all that. I had on my rain boots, a beanie hat, and gloves. I trudged through the slightly muddy muck of the grounds toward the main entrance of the castle. I spent several minutes roaming around the grounds and couldn't find anyone. There were no workers or people anywhere. It looked like all work had halted. I finally pulled out my phone and texted Sam.

"Hey there. Question- have you heard from the foreman of the Culdees project recently? 'I asked.

Sam responded quickly with, "No. Why? Is there a problem? '

"Well, there's no one here. There are no workers and it looks like work has halted. I can't tell that any work has been done since we were last here" I texted back. Sam quickly called me.

"Hey, I'm sorry to bother you with this, but I'm not sure what's going on," I said to him on the other end of the line.

"The last time I was there was the Saturday before Thanksgiving," Sam said. "Mr. Murray was there and oversaw the work that day. Well, overseeing is probably an overestimation of what he was doing. It was more like sitting around and being lazy. In fact, he and I had a small exchange about some of the work that was happening. I noticed that some of the workers were working on that north wall, but they had failed to shore it up properly before starting on it. I pointed it out to Mr. Murray and he acted like it wasn't a big deal. I let him know that it was a big deal. Not only for the integrity of the work, but also for the safety of his crew. I could tell he didn't like what I had to say, but he begrudgingly corrected the situation while I was there" Sam told me.

"Well, I'm going to give him a call and see what's going on," I said. "I'll call you back when I find out what the deal is," I added. Sam and I both hung up and I began searching for Mr. Murray's contact information on my phone. I was sitting on one of the scaffolding boards as I was looking at my phone for his number. I dreaded making this call and talking to Mr. Murray. He was a grumpy codger that seemed pretty uninterested in working. On top of that, he gave me the creeps. He always seemed irritated that he had to even communicate with a woman about his work, much less report to me or take direction from me in any way. He was nothing like Jameson. Jameson was friendly, respectful, kind, and hard-working. He genuinely took pride in his work and the organization of the project. Mr. Murray on the other hand, couldn't care less. He just showed up for the paycheck, and was completely put out when you asked him questions or gave directions. The way he looked at me gave me chills....and not in a good way.

I clicked on Mr. Murray's number and brought the phone to my ear and I instantly heard ringing both in my ear and also from somewhere close to me. I looked up and saw Mr. Murray walking toward me. I hung up the phone and greeted him with a smile. He did not return the smile.

"Good morning Mr. Murray, I was just trying to call you," I said. He did not respond. As he walked closer, I could tell something was off. He looked angrier than usual and his eyes were bloodshot. He looked terrible. He almost looked sick and unsteady on his feet. "Are you okay, Mr. Murray?" I asked. He continued to stare at me without saying a word as he approached. As he got within about three feet of me, I figured out why he looked so bad. He was drunk. He smelled like he had been on a five-day bender. That explained the unsteadiness and bloodshot eyes. My eyes narrowed on him and my expression changed from inquisitive to disgusted instantly.

"I'm none of yer business," Mr. Murray responded. His eyes narrowed back on me and his face remained stoic.

I hopped down from the scaffold board to stand before him. It was my non-verbal way of letting him know that he couldn't talk to me that way. "What's going on, Mr. Murray? Where is everyone and why isn't anyone working today?" I asked pointedly with my shoulders squared up.

"I don't need to explain myself or this operation to you," he responded.

That pissed me completely off. The nerve of this guy. Who does he think he is? I may not be the top boss, but I'm very closely connected to the ones who are. "I beg to differ, Mr. Murray," I retorted. "I'm the project manager of this site today and it's your job to report the progress to me," I said.

He gave me the most murderous look and said, "I decided that if you all got to have time off, then so did our crew. I told them we would resume work when you lot returned to work. Do ye have a problem with that?"

"Yes, I absolutely have a problem with that. It's not within your job description or discretion to take time off without our approval. I know for a fact you did not discuss that with Mr. Strickland," I replied. "In fact, if you would like to keep your job, I strongly suggest you get on the phone and get the crew back on site and working as quickly as possible," I said fuming.

Before the end of my last word in that sentence, my eye and face exploded in pain. I felt a hit with an instant searing pain on my cheekbone that was quickly followed by a sensation of burning. My sight in my right eye went black and as I grabbed my eye and face I stumbled back into the scaffold board I had been sitting on moments before. I caught myself with my left hand to stay upright. I was stunned and not altogether certain what had just happened. I looked up to see Mr. Murray standing in front of me with a face of anger, breathing hard, and his fists clenched at his sides. Before I could even think of what to do next, he hit me again and I fell to the ground. Everything went black at that point.

I awoke slowly and realized I was lying on the ground in the courtyard by the scaffolding. My right eye wouldn't open and my sight was dim. I tried to look around but was struggling to see anything clearly. After a few moments, I was able to raise up to my elbows and look around the courtyard. I reached up with my right hand to feel my face. It was very swollen and sensitive to the touch. I was also bleeding as there was fresh red blood on my hand as I pulled it away. My vision was blurry, but I could see that no one was around. I sat there in shock for several minutes before attempting to get up off the ground. Once I was up, I had to lean against the scaffolding board because I was dizzy and just a little bit queasy. Then I heard my phone ringing, so I began looking around to find it. I followed the sound of the ringing and finally located it half-buried in the muddy area about ten feet away from me. I had been holding it when Mr. Murray struck me and it must have flown out of my hand when I went down.

I wiped away as much of the mud and dirt as I could. Then I saw that I had missed twelve calls from Sam. Geez…how long had I been down? Then I looked at the time on my phone and it read 11:52. Oh my gosh. I had been out for a while. I dialed Sam as quickly as I could, although it was a struggle because I couldn't see very well.

Sam answered with a panicked sound in his voice. "Krista, are you okay? I've been trying to call forever, 'he said.

"Hey….I'm sorry," I said. "Ummm, I found Mr. Murray," I responded.

"Ok, well what's going on?" Sam asked. "You don't quite sound yourself," he added.

"Sam, don't freak out, ok?" I implored.

"Well, now you're worrying me," he replied.

"He was drunk, Sam. I confronted him about not working and how no work was being done. He got very angry and hit me. Twice," I told him.

"What???" Sam asked. I could hear the panic and immediate rage in his voice.

"I'm pretty certain I was unconscious for a while, Sam. I just woke up and found my phone," I explained.

"Krista, are you okay?" Sam asked.

"Yes, I'll be okay, but I may need stitches. I'm bleeding quite a bit and it's not stopping," I said.

"Krista, I've already called the driver that dropped you off this morning. He's on his way back to you. I called him when I couldn't get a hold of you. He should be there soon if he isn't already. I'm going to have him take you to the nearest hospital and I'll be there as soon as I can. I'm already on my way," Sam told me.

'Ok, thank you, Sam. I'm so sorry about this," I said.

"What? What in the world are you sorry about? You have nothing to apologize for," he said. "I'm sorry this happened. I feel horrible. I should have been there with you."

"Oh no, don't feel bad. This isn't your fault either, Sam," I said. Just at that moment, I saw the driver walk into the courtyard of the castle and spot me. The look on his face was one of total alarm. I must have looked so bad because he looked totally panicked and ran over to me.

"Sam, the driver just got here. I'm going to go and I'll see you at the hospital, ok?" I said.

"I'll be there as fast as possible, Krista," Sam said. I could hear the emotion in his voice. He was panicked and feeling powerless.

I don't remember a whole lot about the ride to the hospital. The driver helped me to the car and put me inside. He had some towels in the car and had me hold one to my face. I'm pretty sure I fell asleep on the way there because the next thing I knew, he was waking me up by tapping me on the shoulder. I jumped awake and he apologized for startling me. He walked me into the hospital and explained what had happened to me. I was able to answer most of their questions but was still pretty groggy and struggling to stay awake.

The next thing I knew, I was waking up to the sound of two male voices talking. My eyes adjusted and I could see that Sam and a doctor were discussing something, but I couldn't quite make out what was being said. I began to prop myself up to sit upright in the bed and I saw Sam look over at me. He left his conversation with the doctor and came over to me.

"Hey, how are you?" he asked.

"I've been better, I think," I said with a slight smile.

I reached up to touch my face and Sam stopped me.

"Don't touch it, Krista. You have fresh glue stitches so you need to leave it alone for a while," Sam said.

Without even seeing it, I could tell how swollen it was. My eye was almost completely swollen shut. The doctor proceeded to let me know that they had done a CT scan and did not see any serious damage. It was mostly superficial, but a lot of swelling. He said it would probably take three or four weeks to start to get back to normal, but that he had the plastic surgeon consult and he said it shouldn't scar too badly. The doctor told us the police would be here soon to take my statement. I looked at Sam with a puzzled look. Sam explained that he had called the police to file a report and charges on Mr. Murray.

After the doctor left the room and Sam and I were alone, Sam came back over to the bedside and sat in the chair beside me. He looked at me and sighed deeply as if he had been holding his breath for the last several hours. He grabbed my hand with one hand and reached up with his other hand to caress my hair. He gently tucked my hair behind my ear lovingly and stared into my eyes. Or one eye at least.

"Krista, I'm so sorry," Sam said. I'm pretty sure I could see what might have been traces of tears in his eyes.

I squeezed his hand and leaned over and wrapped my arms around him. I hugged him for a long while and he hugged me back tightly. I could feel the tension and worry in his body. "You don't need to be sorry, Sam. None of this was your fault. That guy is just a crazy drunk. How could we have known he would be unhinged?" I replied.

"I know," he said, "But I just feel awful that this happened to you. It should have been me," he said as he looked painfully guilty. I grabbed his face with my hand and tilted his chin up to me. I leaned over and kissed his lips softly and then leaned my forehead to his and closed my eyes. I just wanted to rest there for a moment.

Then there was a knock on the door and it opened. Two police officers entered the room and asked if they could take my statement. One was a male and the other a female. The male officer asked most of the questions and was taking notes. It seemed like the female officer was there just as support. Over the next several minutes, I gave my account of what had happened with all the details I could recall. I could tell this made Sam very uncomfortable to hear everything.

I'm sure he was imagining it in his head and becoming angrier by the second. I squeezed his hand to let him know I was okay. The police officer finally had my total statement and told me the Crown office would make a decision on whether to press charges based upon the evidence.

Then the female officer asked if she could take pictures, so I sat up and allowed her to get images from several different angles. I had not seen my face in a mirror and she showed me some of the pictures. It was shocking. It looked pretty bad. I looked at myself in the bedside table mirror and then I looked at Sam. I could feel hot tears welling up in my eyes and my lip began to quiver. I was trying so hard to keep it together, but I was suddenly overcome with emotion. I think seeing my face in the mirror and thinking about the events of the day had finally caught up to me and I could no longer control my emotions. The tears started falling.

Sam rushed back to my side to comfort me. I kept apologizing for being emotional and he was shushing me and telling me not to worry. He lovingly stroked my hair and kissed me on the forehead and temple as I cried. I could tell this made the officers feel very uncomfortable so they excused themselves quickly leaving Sam and me to ourselves. I finally calmed down and stopped crying, and then I felt exhaustion come over me. Sam told me to sleep and he was going to go get me some food.

I awoke about an hour later and Sam was at my side. He had brought food and I was absolutely starved. I looked at my phone and saw that the time was about 6 pm. Then the nurse came in and gave me some more pain meds. She let us know that I was discharging, and that Sam could take me home. I sat up and ate my food and within about another hour, we were packed into Sam's car and headed back to Dundee.

I slept the whole way there and woke to Sam calling my name softly. He got out of the car and came around to help me out. He walked me into the lodge where Maggie and Callum met us in the foyer. They seemed to know what was going on and jumped into action helping us up the stairs. Sam walked me into my room and helped me sit on the edge of my bed. Maggie was rushing around and doing who knows what, but she eventually came over to me with my pjs and a hairbrush in her hands. Sam left the room and closed my door. Maggie told me that she was going to help me change out of my clothes and into my pajamas, and then she would brush my hair for me. I was too tired to be embarrassed, or to refuse the help. We made quick work of our efforts and before I knew it, I was tucked into my bed.

Maggie left me with a glass of water by the bedside and the TV remote close to me in case I wanted to watch tv.

Sam came back into the room followed by Maggie and Callum. Callum and Maggie rolled a rollaway bed into the room and Maggie quickly put a fresh set of sheets on the bed. She worked so fast I barely had time to question why they were doing this. I guess Sam saw the look on my face, so he began to explain.

"Krista, you took a hard blow today and you were knocked unconscious. The doctor gave specific instructions that we needed to be on the lookout for concussion. He said you shouldn't be left alone and someone needed to monitor you for at least the next 24 hours, so I'm going to stay here with you. I promise my intentions are good....mostly," he said with a smirk.

I laughed and my eyes darted to Callum and Maggie. They were both giggling under their breaths and looking at each other like they knew better than that. I guess the cat's out of the bag with our relationship. Maggie and Callum both seemed to understand where Sam and I stood with each other, and it was way beyond just a professional relationship. I didn't argue with the plan and Sam sat down in the chair across the room as Maggie and Callum said goodnight and left the room.

I watched as Sam settled himself into the room. He was dressed in his pajamas which consisted of pajama pants and a t-shirt. I don't know how he could possibly make that outfit look sexy, but he nailed it. Then I watched as he added logs to the fireplace and lit it. It roared into large flames in no time and quickly warmed up the room. It was so cozy and had an immediate effect on my eyelids. I could no longer keep them open. Sam walked over and kissed me on the head and said, "sleep. I'll be right here if you need me." I allowed my eyes to close and quickly drifted off. I felt safe and well taken care of.

Thirteen

I woke the next morning with the biggest headache I could ever remember having. When my eyes slowly peeled open, I immediately felt the throbbing, and initially couldn't quite figure out why my head hurt so badly. Then I remembered the events of the previous day. Sam. Oh yeah, where is he? I looked over to my left and there he was. He was sleeping so peacefully on his rollaway bed. Then I looked over to my right at the fireplace which had long died out. No wonder it felt chilly in the room. I slowly moved to sit myself up on my elbows and reached over for my phone on my nightstand. It was 3:47 in the morning. I figured my headache probably woke me early and I needed to take some medicine.

I decided to slip out of bed as quietly as possible and go find my pain meds. I quietly walked over to the dining table where I had seen Sam put the medication bottles. I did my best to use my phone light to check the bottles to make sure I was getting the right medicine and dosage. Then I went back to my nightstand to get my water bottle. I gulped the pill down and then decided to slip on my robe that was lying at the foot of my bed. It was so cold in my room. The weather outside had obviously turned even colder overnight. I looked down at Sam again and realized that he was curled up on his side with only a thin blanket covering him. I surmised that he was probably cold too, so I decided that getting some logs on the fire and restarting it was necessary. I just wasn't sure how I was going to be quiet about doing it.

I tiptoed to the fireplace and carefully picked up one log at a time from the log rack and placed them gently into the log stack. Then I found the little starter sticks that Sam had been using to help to get it lit. They were kind of like a kindling substitute and very handy. I grabbed the striker and pressed the button. The clicking was a little loud for such a small device. I began to light the kindling sticks and the flames licked up quickly. The next thing I knew, I heard Sam say, "What do you think you're doing?"

I looked back over my shoulder and said, "Oh, I'm sorry to wake you. I was trying to be quiet. It's just chilly in the room so I thought I would get the fire going again."

As Sam slipped out from under his blanket and got out of bed, he said, "Krista, that's what I'm here for. You shouldn't be doing that. You should have woken me up." I could tell that he was slightly annoyed at me as he walked over to the fireplace and squatted down beside me.

"Yeah, but look. I did it," I said as I beamed a proud smile at him. He smirked in a half annoyed, half humored fashion and then began stoking the fire with the poker.

"How are you feeling?" Sam asked.

"I woke up with a fierce headache, so I got up and took one of the pain meds," I replied. His face again showed some slight irritation with me that I had not awakened him and let him do these things for me. "What?" I asked. "I'm not going to wake you up to wait on me hand and foot when I can do something for myself. That's ridiculous," I continued.

Sam rolled his eyes at me and said, "That's why I'm here. I want to do those things for you. You just need to let me." I smiled sweetly and patted him on the shoulder as I stood to return to the bed. The pain medication was starting to kick in and making me a little sleepy. As I turned to walk back to the bed, I got a little dizzy and stumbled sideways just a bit. Sam instantly jumped up to catch me. Once he had me steadied, he gave me a "I told you so" look and walked me back to the bed. I took off my robe and slid back under the covers. Sam tucked me in and said, "I'll have breakfast and coffee ready for you when you wake next." I couldn't even respond. My eyelids were so heavy all I could do was drift away.

Sure enough, I woke up at around 6:30 to Sam closing the door. I looked over and saw that he had coffee and a sack of food in his hands. He walked over to the bed and set the coffee and food down on my nightstand. I rolled onto my back and slid myself up to a sitting position while readjusting my pillow behind me. I felt much better now and my headache was almost completely gone.

"I grabbed you some food and coffee. I have to get going and go to the job site," Sam said. He had clearly showered, shaved, and put on fresh, clean clothes. He smelled and looked yummy.

"If you'll give me about 45 minutes, I can be showered and ready to go too," I said. Sam whipped his head around and looked at me like I was crazy.

"You're not going to work, Krista. You need to rest. Doctor's orders," he insisted. "The doctor specifically said you would need at least a week to recover before you could resume a full work schedule. Even when you go back, you probably shouldn't start out with a full day."

"But I don't feel that bad, Sam. I'm pretty sure I can do it," I said pleadingly.

"Krista, I have no doubt in my mind that you COULD do it….., but you shouldn't do it," Sam said sternly. "I'm going to go to Culdees this week and manage things there and find a new foreman. Mr. Hess already knows what has happened and is totally understanding of the possibility of a small setback on the timeline," he said. "You need to stay here and get some rest."

To that I frowned and said, "But what am I going to do all week? I can't sleep the whole time. I'm going to get so bored." I couldn't stand the thought of staying in my room for a whole week and sleeping or resting. That sounded like absolute torture. Surely, I would be able to return to work in a couple of days. I agreed to stay in bed today, but in my head I was already scheming on how to convince Sam that I would return to work sooner.

Sam responded with, "You need to rest for at least a couple of days and then you could consider returning to work by doing remote work and computer stuff. But you're absolutely not returning to the work sites until next week at the earliest." He said it with such authority. I'd never seen him be so bossy and commanding. It was almost sexy to see him be firm and put his foot down. I really didn't know he was capable of that.

I relented my arguments and proceeded to dive into my caramel latte, and scone with jam and clotted cream. My favorites. And Sam knew it. That thought made my heart squeeze a little. Sam walked over and sat next to me on the edge of the bed. He looked at me intently as I stuffed a bite of scone into my mouth and smiled at him with a mouth full of food. He chuckled and then leaned forward and kissed me on the lips. It wasn't a deep kiss, or long, but it was sweet and packed with meaning. He really cared about me and it showed. Sam said his goodbyes and then left for the day. I clicked the tv on as I heard him trodding down the stairs. The rest of my day consisted of tv watching, eating, sleeping, and repeating.

By Friday morning, I was convinced I was going to have to be committed to an insane asylum. I couldn't take it any longer. I had caught up on all the remote, computer work that I could possibly find to do. I had even emailed Mrs. Graham and asked her to give me some tasks that I could do because I was so bored. I had binge watched tv, read two books, and had milled around downstairs with Maggie and Callum just to have some company. I couldn't take it any longer. I had to get outside.

I went downstairs and walked out onto the front steps to see what the weather was like. The sun was shining, but it was completely frigid out. I couldn't help myself though. I was bound and determined to take a walk. I went back upstairs and bundled myself up as much as physically possible, and then I came down and told Maggie and Callum where I would be. Maggie said, "Are ye sure ye should be going off by yerself, dear?" I assured them I would only be gone for about 45 minutes to an hour and I told them the exact route I was going to take. They promised to come look for me if I wasn't back in an hour.

Before they could argue, I spun on my heels and basically ran out the front door of the lodge. The sun hit my face and the brisk, chilly morning air filled my lungs. It was wonderful. Normally, I would hate going out for a walk in such cold weather, but I was so desperate to get out that I almost appreciated the cold. I walked along the natural path that had been created by other pedestrians over time. It was wedged between the sheep pasture that sprawled across the landscape and the road leading to town. Other walkers, joggers, and bikers used the path as well, so I felt totally comfortable and didn't feel alone. My walk was glorious and just as promised, I arrived back at the lodge well-before my hour was up. I felt refreshed and like my battery had been somewhat recharged.

I headed up to my room and took off all my layered coats and clothing. I was quickly freshening up with the intention of going back downstairs to have an early lunch when I heard a notification ding on my computer. I walked over to my table and sat down at my computer. It was an email with the heading "Autopsy M. Andrews Report" sent to my personal email address.

It had been nearly 10 months since Michael died in that accident and the M.E. was just now finalizing the autopsy report. That subject line immediately put a damper on my previously recharged mood. I wasn't sure I was ready to read these findings. I wasn't convinced they were going to tell me anything new, but I just wasn't ready to take my heart to that sad place again. I decided, in light of the last few days, I didn't need to read it quite yet. My mental health couldn't handle it right now, so I left it alone. That would be for another day.

The next few days were not quite so bad because it was the weekend and Sam was off to stay with me and keep me entertained. I begged him to take me somewhere on Saturday so I could get out and about. He didn't fight me when I jokingly told him I was going to run away if he didn't let me out of prison.

On Saturday we decided to drive to St. Andrews and check things out. I hadn't been there yet and was dying to see the sights. I was feeling good and hadn't had any headaches or dizziness in several days. I was no longer needing any type of pain medication, so he was convinced I could probably handle the journey. The drive was only about half an hour, so it was a great little trip. The scenery was gorgeous as usual and crossing the Tay Road Bridge was fun.

We arrived around 9:00 in the morning and Sam drove us directly to an apartment he had secured online. He had taken care of all the arrangements in a matter of a few minutes. It was so nice to not be the one taking care of things like that for once. The apartment was located very near the golf course and within walking distance of basically everything. It had two bedrooms and one bath with a small kitchen. It was cozy and quaint.

Sam and I spent the day walking around, exploring, shopping, and eating at some of the local cafés.

It was a wonderful day and evening. It did my soul good. Getting out and spending time with Sam was exactly what I had needed for complete healing. The next morning we slept in, had a late brunch, and then got in the car and headed back to Dundee that afternoon. By Sunday evening

I had convinced Sam that I was ready to return to work the next morning. He had seen that I was able to handle all the activity and my wounds were healing nicely. I had also sarcastically threatened to quit my job and find another one if he didn't let me work. Sam scoffed at that and said, "Fine, you can come back tomorrow. Besides....I'm not doing a very good job without you, so I kind of need you to fix all the stuff I screwed up this week." I smiled and jumped up and down with excitement. I had finally gotten out of head trauma jail.

Fourteen

The next couple of weeks at work were jam-packed busy. Sam and I were once again splitting our time between the two sites. I had managed to find a new site manager for the work crew at Culdees and he was a God-send. He stepped in and took charge immediately and showed great initiative and organization. I was so relieved because I didn't know enough about what needed to happen with construction to do it myself, and Sam couldn't be in two places at once.

I spent a lot of my time planning out the projects and getting organized for when we returned after the holiday break. I also had a ton of personal planning to do as well. I had decided that it was time to return home to the states for a visit. I had avoided going home and facing some of the business I left there regarding our house and some of Michael's affairs. I had basically left everything after renting out our house and headed to the UK. Now it was time to go check in and button some things up. I needed to see family and spend some time getting some of those things taken care of. My biggest problem at the moment was figuring out how to tell Sam that I was going back to the U.S. for Christmas. He didn't have any plans for Christmas and I hated the idea of Sam being alone for the holidays.

That evening, during dinner back at the lodge, I broke the news to Sam that I had decided to return to the states for Christmas. When I told him, he was mid-bite and briefly halted his bite and looked up at me for a moment to search my face. He quickly put his poker face back on and returned to what he was doing, but I could tell that he was somewhat disappointed at that news. He quickly said,"That's great. You probably need some more time with your family. I'll miss you, but I hope you have a wonderful visit with them."

"Well, what are your plans for our holiday break? Are you going back home?" I asked.

"No, no, I'm just going to stick around Edinburgh and catch up on sleep and work," Sam replied. The mental image of him being alone on Christmas morning was killing me. But, there wasn't much I could do to change that. Inviting him to spend Christmas with me in Texas wasn't an option. My parents and family wouldn't have a problem with it, but they would quickly catch on that there is something going on between Sam and me. I couldn't risk them finding out and then have to face the judgment that would be certain. So, I just had to be ok with Sam being alone for Christmas.

The next morning I booked my flight to Dallas. I would leave in two days, so I had a ton of stuff to get done. I needed to wrap some things up for work, do laundry, pack, and also get some things done for Sam as well. Instead of going to work for the next couple of days, I spent my time doing personal errands for Sam and then I took a train back to Edinburgh to get myself packed and ready for my flight. Sam agreed to drive back to Edinburgh Thursday night so we could have dinner together and then he would take me to the airport on Friday.

Thursday night came quickly and I had just finished up my packing when Sam arrived. He texted me when he was close, so I met him down on the street so we could go straight to dinner. As soon as I stepped out the door at the ground level, I saw Sam pulling into an empty parking spot on the street. I jumped in the car and turned to see Sam smiling at me. It was good to see him. It had been a couple of days and felt like it had been weeks. I don't know how I'm going to be away from him for ten days while I'm gone.

Dinner was wonderful. We ate at a lovely, quaint little pub Sam had learned about from some clients. It had a great atmosphere and the food was really good. We were able to relax and enjoy each other for a couple of hours, and we didn't talk about work even once.

After we finished, Sam drove us back to my apartment and he walked me upstairs. My flight was at 9:00am the next morning, so we both decided we probably needed to get some sleep. Once I unlocked my door and stepped inside, Sam quickly followed me in and closed the door behind him. The next thing I knew, he grabbed me by the waist and pulled me into him with his right arm and his left hand came up to cradle my face and neck. Sam pulled me so close that we were nose to nose and just took a moment to look into each other's eyes. I could sense something electric between us. Not just physical attraction, which was definitely there, but something more. A kind of unspoken connection that had formed between us that was quickly becoming stronger than either of us had expected. So much passed between us without even saying a word. Then, Sam leaned down and kissed me with more passion than I thought was possible. There was something between us that was incredibly unusual. I had thought that what Michael and I had was special....and it was. But this. This was different. This was unlike anything I had ever felt before. I think Sam felt the same way and we were both trying to figure out how we could feel so attached to each other in such a short time of knowing one another. And as more time elapsed in our relationship, the stronger the pull was. For most couples, the initial attraction starts to wane and fade into something else. But, for Sam and I….it was growing stronger and we were both struggling to make sense of it. Yep, the next couple of weeks were going to be hard.

Sam finally released me and stepped back; although I could see the reluctance on his face. I could see the restraint he was employing. After a few long seconds of watching each other, he said, "I'm really going to miss you. It's going to feel weird here without you."

"I hate the thought of you being alone for Christmas, Sam," I said.

"Don't worry about me. I'll be fine. But I will miss you," Sam replied. He reached up again and caressed my face with his hand.

"I should go," Sam said. "I'll pick you up in the morning at about 6:00," he added.

"Ok, I'll see you then," I said. Sam walked out and turned to go down the stairs as I closed the door behind him and locked it. For some reason, I suddenly felt very lonely and a void that I was surprised by. I did my best to shove those thoughts and feelings aside and went to shower before bed. Tomorrow was going to be a long travel day and I needed some rest.

As always, Sam was five minutes early to pick me up the next morning. He knocked on my door and I answered with all of my bags and belongings strapped on me like a luggage cart. He giggled when he saw me and immediately started off-loading luggage and helping me to carry it all down stairs. Once it was all loaded into the car, we both slid into our seats and Sam headed toward the airport.

As expected the airport was a madhouse. There were people everywhere and finding a place to drop me off proved to be stressful. Finally, Sam managed to pull into an open spot on the curb just outside of my departure terminal. He helped me unload my luggage from the car and I once again strapped everything to myself. I didn't have a free arm or hand to hug him with, but he stepped in and hugged me tightly. Then he gave me the best 'goodbye 'kiss ever and he said, "I hope you have a good flight and enjoy your time with family."

I smiled in return and said, "I will call you when I get there. And probably again the day after that. And maybe each day. And definitely on Christmas day." He chuckled at me and told me he was looking forward to it. I then turned with my luggage to head inside. Sam watched me walk in and gave me one last wave and smile as I turned to see him.

The flight took off on time and I was grateful there weren't any delays. I had managed to book a direct flight into DFW so I didn't have to worry about layovers or delayed connections. I did not book first class this time because the flights were already astronomical, having booked last minute right before the holidays. I didn't think upgrading to first class would be worth spending everything in my bank account. But after about five hours in economy seating, I was starting to regret that decision. Sleep eluded me and I couldn't get my legs stretched out enough to be comfortable. I seriously considered taking one of those sleeping pills the doctor had given me after Michael died to just knock me out for the rest of the flight. I didn't. But only because I was afraid it would knock me out and I wouldn't get off the plane. Or worse, someone would have to drag me off the plane.

In an effort to get my mind off of how uncomfortable I was, I got out my laptop and decided that I would check emails. Most of them were junk, but there were a few that required some attention. I spent the next several minutes responding to those, and then remembered the email I had received regarding Michael's autopsy report. My heart wanted to keep avoiding that email, but my head told me I needed to just rip the band aid off and read through it. Now was as good a time as any.

I clicked on the email and downloaded the PDF version of the report. Once in the report, I could see that the report was organized in sections with Michael's demographic information at the top. They had included typical information such as his age, weight, height, and sex. The report went on to describe the condition of his body upon examination. Reading some of this information was really difficult. They described him and his body features so matter of factly and made him sound like an object rather than the man I had loved. I tried not to take it personally, but it was really hard to hear some of the descriptions as if they were everyday, mundane things to say about someone's body.

The examiner described the exterior of the body with comments related to the head, neck, torso, and extremities. He, or she, also described Michael's personal effects like his clothing and his ring and watch. The description indicated that bruising was found on Michael's sides just under his arms. According to the report, this was indicative of suspected markings from rescue attempts. In addition, Michael's hands, forearms, and upper chest areas had many small lacerations that may have been caused by glass or during rescue efforts. I remembered seeing those on his body at the hospital. I had insisted on seeing him even though everyone, including the trauma physician, tried to discourage me from viewing him. Once the funeral home had him, they did their best to cover those cuts.

The internal examination revealed fluid in the pleural cavities, overexpansion of the lungs, and middle ear rupture indicative of drowning. The flashes and mental images in my mind were devastating. The words on the screen depicted my husband's tragic death and all I could think about was how scared and alone he must have felt. Tears welled up in my eyes and I had to look away from the screen for several minutes to keep my composure. The thought of him struggling for his life was ripping my heart wide open. The fact that he went in to help save lives and wound up losing his own was just unbelievable to me. He was dealt a very raw deal and I was crushed by his loss all over again.

I sat there in my plane seat thinking about his death and struggling to come to peace with these facts. I still could not wrap my head around the fact that someone could be lost trying to just be a good human. It was like he had been punished for trying to do something good for someone else. It was so unfair. I took a deep breath and tried to slow my breathing. I felt like an elephant was sitting on my chest and my heart was breaking all over again.

Then my mind went back to a detail in the report. Michael had bruises on his sides, under his arms. This must have been where someone had tried to pull him free. The sheriff had told me that another bystander had jumped in to help Michael get the girls free from the car. They told me it was a man, but no other details about the rescuer were given due to privacy regulations. The sheriff also told me that the man attempted to rescue Michael when he became trapped after getting the girls out of the car.

Apparently, the man helped the girls up to the surface of the water and other bystanders helped to pull them out of the water. The man noticed that Michael had not come up so he went back down to find him. The police report indicated that Michael had gotten caught on something and could not free himself. The unknown man had obviously attempted to pull Michael free by linking his arms under Michael's and around his sides. He was obviously unsuccessful and had to come back up before he ran out of air. The sheriff told me later that the man was devastated and visibly upset that he had not been able to save Michael. Again, I imagined this mystery person in that moment and my heart hurt for him too. What a horrible experience that must have been. It was an overall crappy situation for everyone involved. And there was absolutely nothing that would ever change it. So concrete and absolute.

I closed my laptop and promised myself I would never have to read another autopsy of a loved one for the rest of my life. My mind was numb and my body was exhausted. Being home with family and celebrating Christmas for the first time without Michael was going to be excruciating. I suddenly wished I had not left Scotland. I took a long swig of my whiskey on the rocks and savored the burn in my throat because it momentarily took away the hurt in my heart. I closed my eyes, leaned my head back, and prayed that sleep would take me so I could avoid the ache in my soul.

Fifteen

Mom and dad were waiting for me on the curb just outside the arrivals terminal at the airport. I had collected my luggage and met them outside. Dad quickly threw my luggage in the back of his truck and mom and I climbed up into the cab. It was good to see them even though I had just seen them a few weeks earlier. Somehow, it was different seeing them on home turf. We chatted and caught up about the last couple of weeks on the drive home. We were headed to their house and that's where I would be staying since my house was rented at the moment to a sweet family with two beautiful young children.

The drive was about an hour from their house so we had plenty of time to talk about all the things that had changed in our hometown over the last several months. Mom gave me the rundown on all the Christmas activities and get-togethers that were planned with family and friends during my visit.

Part of me was eager to see family and friends, but there was a part of me that knew it was going to be hard without Michael. And there was sure to be some awkwardness with people because they didn't know what to say or how to act around me. I had felt that before I left for the UK and it's honestly one of the reasons I wanted to get away. I couldn't stand the struggle everyone appeared to have coping with Michael's loss. They treated me differently. It was as if they no longer knew how to talk to me or be around me without him. Like we were so connected that we were one person, and no one could figure out how to move forward with me being one individual without him. It was just all so weird and hurtful that I couldn't stand it. I had to go.

Now, I would have to face that again. But, I felt better prepared to face it now than I did a few months ago. I had a plan in my head that I was going to have to let people off the hook and address the elephant in the room so they would feel better. I probably shouldn't have to do that, but in the end I think that's the only way to help people move forward and be able to talk and interact with me without being weird and uncomfortable.

As mom and I were chatting in the truck, dad turned into their driveway. I stopped talking mid-sentence and audibly gasped. It had been a long time since I'd seen home and it took my breath away. The memories and nostalgia got the best of me in that moment.

Dad slowed the truck on the gravel driveway and everyone got really quiet. I could hear the crunch of the gravel beneath the tires as we approached my childhood home. It was just after dark at this time and my parents had their house decorated for Christmas. They had always been so good about decorating and celebrating holidays to their fullest. The house had been trimmed in white lights that edged the rim of the roof and windows. White lights were also wrapped in the trees in the front of the house. It was beautiful and instantly brought me back to my childhood. Somehow, my heart needed that at the moment.

"Oh my gosh, guys….the house and lights are beautiful," I said in astonishment.

"I'm so glad you like it," my dad said. "Your mother made me hire it out this year and I basically had to rip off my left leg to pay for it," he grumbled. My mom rolled her eyes and playfully swatted him on the arm to show how ridiculous he was being. I couldn't help but giggle a little at their typical married couple exchange. I secretly knew that my dad would do anything for my mom. He would move heaven and earth if she wanted it done. But, he was also probably going to fuss about it too.

Dad parked the truck just outside the garage so we could get out and get my luggage out. Mom and I rolled my stuff into the house while Dad pulled into the garage. I went straight to my old bedroom. To my surprise, mom had completely redone the room with all new furniture, paint, and bedding. It didn't look the same at all. It was beautiful and as usual I was impressed with her taste. When I looked at mom with surprise on my face, she said, "Well, I just thought maybe you might like a change. New memories to be made instead of dwelling on old ones." It was like she knew me better than I knew myself. Most people would probably want to keep everything the same if they lost a loved one, but to me that was more painful. It was just a constant reminder of the one you lost. It's the primary reason I moved to the UK after Michael died. I needed change. I couldn't stand the thought of dwelling in the memories and pain. I needed to move forward.

Mom let me get settled in my room and unpack my suitcases while she prepared dinner. Just about the time I had all my clothes stashed away in the closet and drawers, I was beginning to smell a heavenly aroma coming from the kitchen. Mom was one of the best cooks I knew, and always managed to concoct something wonderful. I did not get that trait from her. I detested cooking. The smell drew me to the kitchen where I found her bustling about trying to pull all the parts together. My dad was sitting in his recliner watching a boring documentary on the myths of ancient Rome. What a snooze fest.

"Mom, is there anything I can help with?" I asked.

"No, honey. I've just about got it all together," she replied. I knew better though so I went to the cabinet and began to get the plates, silverware, and napkins out and put them on the island countertop. Mom had everything ready in no time and she called dad over to come fill his plate. She had made fried salmon patties, macaroni and cheese, broccoli, salad, and dinner rolls. It was one of my favorite meals when I was growing up. I was going to have to be careful over the next couple of weeks or I would gain twenty pounds and not be able to fit into any of my clothes.

We sat at the island barstools and enjoyed our dinner together. It had been a very long time since we had enjoyed a meal at home with just the three of us. Mom had retired and dad was planning full retirement at the end of the year, so he only had a couple of weeks left. I was truly surprised that he was really going to do it. I never thought I would see the day come, but he seemed really excited about it. He and mom had plans to travel quite a bit so they spent most of our dinner talking about the places they were planning to hit first. The dinner was delicious and the relaxed conversation that didn't revolve around Michael's death was much needed. I just wanted normal and they were giving it to me.

Soon after dinner, I headed to bed. I was exhausted from the flight and travel day, so early to bed was in order. I said goodnight to my parents and went to shower. It was two in the morning in Scotland and Sam was probably asleep, but I texted anyway just to let him know I had made it safely.

"Hi! I made it safely to Texas. At mom n dad's and about to shower and go to bed. Hope your day was good. Miss you already."

I figured Sam would see it the next morning when he woke up, but to my surprise my phone dinged immediately with a response.

"Glad you made it safely. Things are not the same without you here. Already. Miss you too. More than you know. Call me if you get a chance."

I smiled as I read the text. I had butterflies in my stomach from just reading his text. "More than you know," he said. Wow. I was really falling hard for this guy. I truly missed him and there was a moment of sadness in my gut that I didn't feel like I could share him with my family yet. I was torn between being happy with Sam, and being respectful toward Michael.

I responded with, "Will do" and a heart emoji. I laid my phone on the nightstand after plugging it into the charger. I turned off the lamp and the room was immediately dark with the exception of the dulled hue of the Christmas lights shining in through the window. My mind wandered over the events of the day and what was to come over the next couple of weeks. Ultimately, Christmas was going to be good and I was really looking forward to seeing several people. On the other hand, I knew I was going to have to face dealing with some things that would force me to think of Michael and his death, so that was going to be hard. Lastly, my mind flashed to Sam and I could see his face, his slight smile when he was amused with me, and how warm his body felt when he pulled me in for an embrace. My eyes slowly closed and I drifted off to sleep with that thought.

I woke the next morning feeling well-rested and so cozy in my bed. I rolled over to check the time on my phone and it read 11:23. What? I couldn't believe I had slept that late. I never sleep late. I really didn't even know I was capable of that anymore. I hadn't slept past 9:00 in the morning in years, and that was usually when I was sick. I quickly got up and threw on my robe. The hardwood floor was cold in December and I wished I had brought my slippers. As soon as I opened my bedroom door, I could hear noise and movement coming from the kitchen. I found mom milling about in the kitchen with the tv on HGTV in the living room. Mom smiled as soon as she saw me and said, "good afternoon, sleepyhead," sarcastically. I laughed and walked over to give her a hug.

"I guess I was really tired," I said. She smiled again, patted me and then ran her hand through my hair like she did when I was little.

"Yes, I should say so. I didn't want to wake you. I figured you needed the rest," she added.

Today was Saturday and mom had hinted that she would like to spend the day shopping. I had wasted half our day by sleeping, so I quickly got dressed and ready so we could head to the shops. It was a lovely day spent at local shops and then larger chain stores closer to the city. The crowds were crazy with it being this close to Christmas, but it didn't matter. Mom and I were just happy to be together. We both only had a few gifts that we wanted to get so we weren't stressed or in a hurry. We enjoyed a late lunch, or early dinner, in one of the cafés downtown. Mom called it "lupper." Then we hit the pavement for a little more shopping. By the time we were done and got back home, it was nearly 8:00 that night. Dad was back to watching boring tv and reported he had leftovers for dinner.

After settling down for a bit, we all found ourselves sitting around the dining table and Dad brought out a deck of cards for some games. We sat and played cards, talked, and laughed for the next couple of hours. Mom made some hot apple cider spiced with rum which had been a tradition around the holidays for several years running.

At some point, we got around to the topic of my job and the details of our current projects. For some reason, both mom and dad seemed really interested in those projects and how the operations of the company worked, so I indulged them with as many details as I could. They were pretty impressed with the amount of knowledge I had gained in just a few months with something so outside of my field and educational level. Of course, I told them quite a bit about Sam and what I do for him. I explained his job and role in the projects and how I'm essentially his right-hand man, so to speak, both professionally and personally. I talked about the details of our daily routines, staying at the lodge, told them about Maggie and Callum Andrews, Mrs. Graham, and all the other components of my life there in Scotland.

When I finally stopped talking, I looked up and realized that my parents were looking at each other with smirks on their faces like they were sharing knowing looks between them. I looked back and forth between them and said, 'what? Am I talking too much? I'm sorry….

Dad said, "No, no, don't be sorry. It's just nice to see that you're happy and have so much to talk about.'

Mom interjected, "Yeah, especially about Sam." My eyes darted to her face and she was smiling like the Cheshire cat. I was shocked and didn't really know what to say. Had I been that obvious when talking about Sam? I thought I had managed to keep it professional so they wouldn't pick up on my feelings for him, but I guess I wasn't as sly as I thought.

When mom saw my face and probably interpreted my thoughts, she said,"Krista, it's ok to like him. It's ok to be happy. You don't have to hide that from us. We want that for you. We want you to love again.'

I couldn't believe what I was hearing. I could feel my face turning flushed and tears stinging at the back of my eyes. I stayed silent for a long moment not knowing what to say. Dad placed his hand over mine and patted it. "Honey, we think Sam is a great guy. He seems like a real gentleman. He's smart, funny, has a great job, and appears to be the calm among your storm. It's ok for you to fall in love again. In

272

fact, I'm pretty sure that's what Michael would have wanted."

I looked up at my dad's face and the tension that I had been holding in broke loose. The tears started to fall and I couldn't stop them. Both of my parents were surprised and immediately tried to console me. "You don't think I'm awful for falling in love so soon after Michael's death? Doesn't that make me a horrible person? What's everyone going to think?" I cried as I lost complete control of my emotions.

My mom jumped up and came over to hug me. She held me tight and kissed me on the head until I began to calm. My dad never let go of my hand. "Krista, it doesn't really matter what anyone else thinks. You have to do what feels right to you in order to heal. We certainly don't think less of you for finding a new love," my mom said. "If Sam loves you, and is helping you to move forward in life, and you love him.....well, I think that's absolutely incredible. You hang on tight and don't let him go," she added.

I felt so much better about the situation once I had calmed down. There was still a part of me that was guilty and worried about what others would think, but a larger part of me was completely relieved that my parents knew and were supportive of my new developing relationship with Sam. I was starting to feel that weight of grief being lifted off my life. Like I could finally take a deep breath for the first time in nearly a year. My parents were right.... Michael would want me to be happy. That's all he ever wanted for me. And Sam makes me happy.

Sixteen

Christmas morning came and I could tell my parents were doing their best to make it special and to keep me busy. As soon as I awoke and came out of my room, my mom shoved a cup of coffee into my hands and greeted me with an excited smile. The coffee smelled yummy and that first sip hit me right in my soul. Mom had used her Gingerbread cookie Christmas creamer and it was absolutely lovely.

Mom led me to the living room where Dad was sitting in his recliner with Christmas music playing on the tv with one of those crackling fire screensavers going. He had the actual fireplace roaring too so the Christmas ambience was perfect. Dad hopped up out of his recliner and put his Santa hat on and began grabbing presents from under the tree. He placed no fewer than ten presents at my feet where I was sitting on the couch. I could tell they had bought me more presents than ever because they were compensating for this being my first Christmas without Michael.

We opened gifts together, laughed, and reminisced about our memories of my childhood and of Michael. It was nice. I was finally able to share memories about Michael without crying or slipping into the deepest depression. I was starting to feel like his death wasn't going to crush me forever. That I was going to be able to move on, but still love and remember him without the utter heartbreak.

The day after Christmas I decided that I needed to take care of some things that I had been avoiding. The first thing I needed to do was go get a copy of the police report from Michael's death. I hadn't ever gone to get it just because at that time I didn't really want to know. I preferred to stick my head in the sand and avoid all the details surrounding his death. The sheriff had told me quite a bit and that was all I really wanted to know, or could handle knowing, at that time. But now, I felt like I was ready to read it so I could process it and file it away in my brain forever. Reading the autopsy report had been difficult, but I had survived it and I figured that had to have been way harder to digest than the police report.

The other thing I needed to take care of was putting our home up for sale. I decided that I was probably never going to live there again. Even if I moved back to the states and to Texas, I really didn't want to move back into that house. It was a wonderful home for Michael and me, but I didn't think I would be able to live a new life while dwelling in the memories of my old life. I had spoken to the current renters right before Christmas to let them know that I would be placing on the market soon. Mainly to give them a chance to make an offer if they wanted. So, I needed to find a realtor to list it. I had asked Mom if she would go with me to help take care of those things and she agreed.

We got ready pretty early and headed toward Denton, which is the town where Michael's accident happened, so we had to go to their police station to get the report. It's about a 30 minute drive, so I drove Mom's car. She enjoyed playing passenger princess and getting to relax. She wasn't a huge fan of driving in traffic on a busy expressway, so she was eager for me to sit behind the wheel. Once we got close, I plugged in the address to help get us to the right location. We pulled in and I parked the car right in front of the door. I put the car in park and subconsciously took a deep breath. Mom asked, "are you ok? Do you want me to go in with you?"

"No, you don't need to do that. It should be pretty straight forward. They told me over the phone I just have to sign for it," I told her. "I'll be right back," I added. I walked through the front door and realized I had more trepidation about doing this than I'd realized. I could feel myself tensing up and holding my breath. I walked to the front desk and an officer greeted me and asked how he could help me. I told him who I was and that I needed to pick up a copy of the police report for an accident involving Michael Andrews. They had given me a case number over the phone previously, so I gave that to the officer and he quickly looked it up on his computer. He printed it out and then had me sign and date indicating that I had received it. Then he handed me the report and wished me a good day.

I slid back into the car and once again took a deep breath of relief. Mom said, "Well, what does it say?"

"I haven't read through it yet, mom. I'm probably going to wait until we get home," I said. She looked somewhat disappointed because she was curious to know the details too. I knew I was going to need some quiet, alone time to read through it and process it. I put the car in reverse and said, "You said you have a realtor that can help me?" This was my cue to Mom that I was done talking about the police report for now. She relented and began giving me directions to the real estate agent's office.

After talking with a very nice agent about listing my house, we headed back home. I was happy and satisfied with the agent's plan for listing the property. She was going to reach out to the renters, go take pictures, and get it listed by the end of the week. I told her that I would be returning to the UK in the next few days, so she agreed that the transaction could take place with electronic signatures. Or if worse came to worst, I could assign one of my parents as a proxy to the sale. She felt like the house would probably sell pretty quickly given its location, size, and amenities.

I was ready to sell it, but at the same time it was going to be hard to give up the memories. I would also have to face going through the storage at some point and getting rid of Michael's stuff. I did not look forward to that, but I would put that out of my mind for another time. My mom and dad had agreed to help take care of whatever I couldn't do since I wouldn't be here.

Once we got back home, I was suddenly exhausted. It was only about three o'clock in the afternoon, but I think the contents of the day had worn me out emotionally. I decided to go lie down and rest in my room and possibly take a nap. Mom gave me a hug that lasted a little longer than the average hug and I knew she was feeling bad for me. I felt bad for her too. It must be so hard on a parent to have to watch your child endure so much painful loss and not be able to do anything about it.

I closed my door, turned on the ceiling fan, and crawled into my bed. I looked at my phone and decided that a call to Sam might be what I needed. It was about 9:00pm there so hopefully he would be up and able to talk. Sam picked up after only one ring and greeted me with, "Hey there, darlin." It made me smile.

"Hi, how are you?" I asked. But before he could even respond, I followed with, "I miss you. Like….a lot."

I could almost hear Sam smile over the phone and he said, "I'd be better if you were here. I miss you too." And with that, my exhaustion lifted. Sam and I talked for nearly an hour about how our Christmas was, his plans for the next few days, and I filled him in on my day. He is a good listener and just let me vent all my sorrows and frustrations with dealing with continued issues around Michael's death. I told him about the autopsy report and police report, but I didn't give any details. I didn't want to be a Debbie downer by getting into the specifics.

Sam said that he spent Christmas day at Erick Eden's house and it had been pretty good. Erick had invited Sam because he knew he was alone, so Sam took him up on it. Erick apparently had a huge party that included his own family, but also a lot of friends and colleagues. Sam said Erick's wife had a gift for every single person there. I could tell Sam was impressed with that level of kindness and forethought. They had a big Scottish spread of food, drinks, played games, and just hung out and mingled for several hours. Sam said it wound up being a lot of fun and he didn't feel lonely at all. I was so relieved to hear that and was appreciative to Erick for being that kind of person to take care of and think of others. Sam said Mrs. Graham was there too and she had given her best effort at making an "American" apple pie just for Sam. He said he had some of it last night and again this morning for breakfast so it must have been pretty good. My heart was happy to know that Sam had been taken care of for Christmas, but I couldn't wait to get back to see him.

After talking for quite a while, I decided Sam probably needed to go to bed so I said goodbye. "I'll see you in about 4 days," I told him.

"Oh, are you coming back a little early?" he asked.

"Yes, I've had a great time here, but I'm ready to get back." I replied.

"That's the best news I've heard in a week," he said. "Can I pick you up from the airport?" he asked.

"I thought you'd never ask," I countered.

We made plans for him to pick me up and I let him know which airlines, terminal and the time. We reluctantly said our goodbyes and just before I hung up the phone Sam said, "Krista..."

"Yes?" I answered.

"Thank you for calling. I've missed you and I can't wait to see you," he added.

"Same here, Sam," I said. "I'll see you in four days. I hope you're ready for a big hug," I joked. We hung up and I felt giddy and sad all at the same time. I truly missed Sam and was a little heartsick not being with him.

The next few days went by quickly. Mom, Dad, and I spent every minute together just hanging out and enjoying our time. We visited with some of my aunts and uncles, had dinner with family friends, went to the movies, and just generally hung out and soaked up every minute we could together. Mom and Dad even started planning their next trip to visit me in Scotland. It sounds like they're planning to come in February around the time of Michael's death anniversary. They didn't say that's why they chose that time, but I know it is. They think I'll struggle with that time and they want to be available to take the sting away. I appreciated that about them. They're always trying to help and dull the pain for me. Even as a grown up adult, they're still parenting. I guess that never goes away. I love them for it, too.

By Saturday, it was time to fly back to Scotland. Luckily, I had another direct flight from Dallas to Edinburgh and my dad had insisted on paying for me to upgrade to first class. I argued with him for at least ten minutes trying to get him to give in, but he absolutely insisted. I hated for them to spend that kind of money on my comfort, but dad just wasn't having it. They dropped me off at the airport around 2:00 in the afternoon. My flight was scheduled to depart at 5:20 and so far everything was on time according to my airline app. I got my luggage checked in, got through security really quickly, and then had more than two hours of time to kill before my flight. I got a Starbucks iced coffee and found a comfy spot near my gate to waste a little time. I bought a book at one of the little airport stores and started reading while I enjoyed my coffee. My mind flashed back to the last time I was in this airport headed to Scotland and I remembered how much different I felt then. I was in about as much grief pain as a person could be in at that time. I just wanted to sleep and numb myself from the pain. Things are different now, thank goodness. I'm so glad that I have moved beyond that time. A person can only take so much grief and heartache without some relief from it. I was proud of the progress I had made and where I currently was in my life. I had survived something horrible and tragic and was moving forward.

Nine million hours later (or what felt like that long), we had landed in Edinburgh. The local time was about 8:00am. Once I took my phone off airplane mode, I was able to text Sam and let him know I was on the ground. My stomach did actual flip flops at the thought of seeing him. I was more excited than I had been in a long time. And nervous for some reason. I had missed Sam so much and realized that I was truly falling in love with him, so I was suddenly nervous and worried about whether he felt the same way.

I followed the crowd of people that got off the plane to baggage claim and waited impatiently for them to unload our bags to the carousel. I secured a spot to stand and wait. I had my backpack on, and my carry on beside me. Luckily, my big bag was one of the first ones out so I grabbed it and hoisted it over the edge. Once all my things were collected, I headed toward the doors to meet Sam by the curb for arrivals. I strolled out onto the sidewalk and looked around with my phone in my hand. Sam and I had been texting back and forth so we could find each other. I looked at my phone, and then looked back up to try to find him on the street. I looked to my left and didn't see him and then I turned to my right and immediately locked eyes with Sam. He was walking toward me and was smiling. He took my breath away. He was so good-looking and was a sight for sore eyes. I started rolling my luggage and walking toward him. As we got closer to each other, Sam's look turned from smiling to intense. His steps sped up and when he reached me he wrapped his arms around me and picked me up in a full embrace. I equally launched myself into his arms and wrapped my arms around his neck. I buried my face into his neck and breathed in his scent. Oh my heavens....I have missed this man. Sam pulled back slightly from our embrace and kissed me like he was dying of thirst in the desert and I was the only water within a thousand mile radius. He kissed with hunger and heat. He was possessive and demanding....but in a good way. He was taking control. Showing me what he wanted and felt. I reciprocated every movement. We finally broke our kiss and stepped back from each other. We stared into each others 'eyes for several moments before breaking into smiles and returning to our hug.

"God, I missed you, Krista. Have I said that already?" Sam laughed.

"Yes, you mentioned that once or twice," I replied with a smile. "I feel the same. It's so good to see you," I added.

Sam helped me get my luggage into his car and then opened my door for me to settle in. Once inside the car, Sam pulled out onto the street and started our journey to my apartment. Sam reached for my hand and held it the whole way home. I was so completely happy. I felt warm and fuzzy inside and I'm pretty sure I had a goofy smile plastered to my face for the whole ride home. Once we pulled up to my apartment, Sam helped get my luggage out and up the stairs. We rolled everything into my apartment and then Sam stood by the door like he was going to leave.

He looked at me and then said, "I know you just got home and you're probably exhausted, but would you be interested in hanging out with me today and having dinner tonight?" He went on, "You probably want to unpack and maybe take a nap, huh?"

"I would like to take a nap, but I absolutely want to spend time with you today," I replied. "Just give me about three to four hours to unpack and grab a short nap, and then I'll be ready to go," I said.

Sam winked at me with a smile and said, "Sure thing. I'll be back at say 1:00 to pick you up?"

"Sounds perfect. I'll see you in a few hours," I responded. We smiled at each other and Sam gave me one more long, heated kiss before he slipped out the door leaving me breathless. My brain was foggy, but my heart was full to the brim. Happiness felt good.

Seventeen

S o, tell me about your trip. How was Christmas?"
Sam asked as we walked. It was New Year's Eve
day and we had decided to go on a hike together.
The weather was very cold and somewhat windy, but it
wasn't raining; which is a small miracle in Scotland. We
bundled up and set out for our hike. I really didn't know
where we were going so I left it up to Sam.

We jumped in his car after walking a few blocks from
my apartment, and headed toward one of the points of the
Water of Leith Walkway. It follows the river and Sam said
he hoped it would be a peaceful area where we might even
see some wildlife. It sounded heavenly to me. Getting out
of the city occasionally was good for my soul. Especially
since I was raised in the country. Edinburgh is by far the
best city I've ever been in, but a city is a city and sometimes
I just need to get away from the hustle and bustle.

"It was good. Really good actually. I was kind of dreading it, being that it was the first Christmas without Michael, but it wasn't as bad as I thought it might be. My parents went out of their way to make it really special and easy on me," I told him. He smiled, grabbed my hand and squeezed it. "They also know about you," I said as I looked at him shyly.

"What do you mean they know about me?" Sam asked. "You mean like….they know about our relationship?" he questioned in surprise.

"Yes, they know. I didn't really have to tell them. They already knew. They basically brought it up to me one evening while we were playing cards at the kitchen table. I was shocked, but I guess they could already tell there was something between us when they visited. And, in the way I talk about you in conversation," I told him. "I was kind of embarrassed about it, but they told me I was being ridiculous.'

"So, they were okay with us being in a relationship? They didn't give you a hard time about it or make you feel guilty? Sam asked.

"No. In fact, they encouraged it. They said they could tell that I was happy and that's all they really wanted for me. And they said that's what Michael would have wanted too," I explained.

Sam squeezed my hand again and looked at me with happiness and relief in his eyes. I didn't know if he was relieved for me, or for himself. Maybe it was both. Maybe he felt more free to be ourselves and share in a life together now that my parents knew. I know I certainly felt a huge burden off my shoulders.

We pulled up to the parking area and got out of the car. The wind was brisk and there was a severe bite to the chill in the air. We were going to have to walk fast to keep me warm during this hike. We quickly found the trail and Sam guided us on which direction to go using his trail app on his phone. This trail is about twelve miles long, so we should be able to go for as long as we want today.

We set out at a quick pace and Sam made a comment about how fast I was walking. I laughed and told him I would freeze to death if I didn't keep my speed up. After about a mile, I started to heat up and slowed my pace quite a bit. Sam and I were really enjoying the scenery and just talking about life as we walked. And as the day drew on, the sun came out and started to heat things up a little.

After we had settled into a nice pace together and talked about random things for a while, I told Sam about the details of the autopsy report. He listened while I explained what I knew about the findings and the police report I had received. Sam was quiet and didn't ask a lot of questions. He just let me tell it all and listened to my thoughts on the how's and why's of the whole situation. There was something really therapeutic about explaining it to someone who had no knowledge of the whole ordeal. Someone who didn't know Michael and was a completely objective listener.

Sam's face was intense while I was telling him the details. For the first time, I began describing that whole experience from that terrible day from my perspective. I had never shared those thoughts with anyone. Not even my parents or close friends. To have Sam listen and just be in the same space with me while I recounted that day, the day of the funeral, and the days in between, was helpful. I needed to get it out. To share the information with someone else. It had been nearly a year at this point, and this was the first time I was freeing myself of the burden of that storyline.

When I was done purging my story, I stopped talking and we kept walking. Sam grabbed my hand and pulled me to a stop. I turned to look at him and he drew me into a hug. He wrapped his arms around me without saying a word and just held me there for a long time. Within seconds of that embrace, I let out a breath and tears began to flow. My body was suddenly desperate to rid itself of pent up emotion. I cried quietly while the rest of my body shuddered from the grief. Sam held me tightly. He didn't say a word. He just stood there and held me. I got the feeling that he was prepared to stand there and hold me for as long as I needed. Thank goodness there were no other hikers on the trail at that time or I would have been so embarrassed.

When I finally felt like I had gotten all the feelings out, I pulled back from Sam and looked up at him. I wiped my tears from my face and tried to pull myself together. "Thank you," I whispered.

"You don't need to thank me," he replied as he caressed my cheek with his thumb. "I'm here for you, Krista. Anytime you need," he added.

We decided to turn back at this point and head to the car. By the time we got back to the car, we had gone about six miles. Between the therapy session and the physical exertion, I was exhausted. We headed back toward the city center and spent most of the drive in silence. I was quiet because I had pretty much used up my word quota for the day, but I wasn't quite sure why Sam was so quiet. I wasn't sure if he was just trying to give me some time to recover, or if something was bothering him. He was staring off into the distance at the road ahead of him while driving. He seemed lost in thought and almost bothered about something. Maybe I had just worn him out with all my emotions today. I shrugged it off and decided that we were probably just both really tired.

We arrived back at my apartment around noon. When we got there, Sam made no attempt to get out and walk me up which was kind of unusual. He generally always gets out and walks me to my door. Nevertheless, he gave me a hug and kiss before I got out of the car. He said he had some things he needed to do this afternoon, but we made plans to have dinner and celebrate the new year together tonight.

Sam had made reservations at one of the rooftop restaurants, so we were going to dress up and party like we were in our twenties. I'd be lucky to make it to midnight, so I decided a nap was in order for this afternoon. We said goodbye and I got out of the car and watched as Sam pulled out onto the street. Something felt off, but I couldn't put my finger on it. I chalked it up to being tired and emotional. Once inside, I made myself a quick lunch, checked some emails, and then took the most glorious nap of my life. I woke up about three hours later and was stunned I had slept that long. I never sleep that long for a nap.

I did my nails, took an 'everything 'shower, and got dressed in a new black jumpsuit that I got just for tonight. It was all black, strapless, with a low cutout back. It had a few sparkly beads added to the trim around the top near my neckline. It was sexy and exactly the kind of party suit I needed for tonight. I slipped on my strappy black heels, and accessorized with some dainty jewelry. My hair and makeup were on point and I was feeling like a million bucks. I was ready to go by 7:30.

At about 8:00 I heard a knock on my door. I opened the door to Sam standing there looking absolutely delicious. He cleans up so well. He was freshly showered, shaved and smelled divine. My knees nearly buckled just looking at him. He wore a devilish grin that was so faint you couldn't quite call it a smile. He held a beautiful vase of red roses and handed them to me as he walked in the door. He leaned down as he walked by me and gave me a kiss that stole all the air in my body. Oh lordy ... .I may not survive this night. Sam was dressed in black slacks, a white button-down dress shirt, and a black suit coat. He didn't wear a tie and the top button of his shirt was not buttoned so I could see where his neck met his collarbones. There was something so incredibly sexy about that. Good heavens....what was wrong with me? It was like I had never seen a good-looking man before. I needed to pull it together.

We left for dinner right away because our reservation was for 8:30. We were dining by ourselves, but then we were meeting some people from work and other friends at the rooftop bar after our dinner. Our table at the restaurant was perfect. It was a small table for two, but there was plenty of space and the chairs were made of plush velvet and so comfortable. The lighting was low, but we had candlelight on the table and our table was by the window that overlooked the city. It was the middle of winter, so the sun had gone down hours ago and the twinkling of the city lights was in full force. It was breathtaking. Sam and I ordered drinks and he ordered an appetizer for us. I am not a big drinker, but tonight I was gonna have one of my favorite Scottish drinks. Orange gin and lemonade. Sam ordered whiskey as usual.

The meal was absolutely incredible and we spent the next nearly two hours enjoying our food, drinks, and each other. The conversation was good and easy-going as always. Whatever weirdness I had sensed from Sam earlier today had completely dissipated. We talked about work, hobbies, childhood memories, plans for the future, Michael, and everything in between. There was something about Sam that just made me feel comfortable, loved, and not judged. I could let my guard down with him.

After dinner, Sam paid and we moved out to the rooftop bar where we found several of our co-workers and acquaintances already gathered and having a great time. We spent the evening mingling. Sometimes together and sometimes separately. We also spent some time on the dance floor where things really heated up between Sam and me. We struggled to keep our hands off each other and stay public-worthy. At midnight, the whole crowd joined in the countdown initiated by the DJ and we all rang in the new year together.

Sam pulled me into him as the clock struck 12:00 and gave me a burning look and then kissed me like he was going to lose me any minute. It was one of the most romantic moments of my life and suddenly the rest of the world just faded away. We released our kiss reluctantly and looked each other in the eyes.

"I love you, Krista. I just need you to know that," Sam said.

He had the most intense, almost sad expression on his face and it instantly worried me. I searched his face to try to figure out if I was imagining these emotions, or if I was spot on.

"I love you too, Sam. I really love you. Like a lot," I responded.

He smiled at me with relief and pulled me in for another hug. He held me tightly and we stayed like that for a long time while everyone else partied and yelled around us. I'm pretty sure the cat's out of the bag about our relationship now. Our coworkers didn't seem surprised at all about our 'togetherness" tonight. I'm guessing they had us figured out too. Not just my parents. I guess we didn't do as good of a job hiding it as I had thought. I inwardly chuckled at my own naivety.

The rest of the night was full of fun and we stayed up way later than I thought I was capable of. Sam and I finally left the party around 2 am to head home. We decided to leave Sam's car at the restaurant since he had been drinking and we took the train. It stopped near Sam's flat, but we would have to walk several blocks to get back to my apartment and I didn't feel like I could walk that in my heels. So, Sam suggested that we stay the night at his place.

I must have had a worried look on my face because Sam said, "I'll sleep on the couch. Don't worry, I have only pure intentions," as he grinned at me.

"I don't have anything to sleep in or a toothbrush or anything," I said.

"You can sleep in one of my shirts, and I have an extra brand new toothbrush you can use. Stop worrying....I got this," Sam said as he pulled me off the train at our stop. I smiled in return and relented. To be honest, I was more worried about self control sleeping in the same flat as him tonight.

We walked the block and a half to his flat and took the lift up. He unlocked the door and I followed him inside. His apartment was clean and tidy. I don't know why that surprised me. It shouldn't because Sam is the most put-together and organized man I had ever known. He gave me a quick tour and showed me the bedroom, bath, etc. Then he went to his closet and got a t-shirt out for me to wear. He also brought out a brand new toothbrush from the bathroom cabinet and smiled at me sarcastically as he handed it to me.

"I'll just grab a pillow from the bed and a blanket from the hall closet before you get settled in the bedroom," Sam said. "Do you need a glass of water or anything else?" he asked.

"Yeah, a glass of water would be great," I replied. I went to the bathroom and changed, brushed my teeth, and washed my face. I wasn't excited about Sam seeing me with no makeup, but it couldn't be avoided. I came out of the bathroom wearing Sam's shirt and no makeup. Sexy was not how I would describe the look, but Sam looked at me with fire in his eyes. Oh boy...this was going to be hard to control. He had changed into a pair of shorts and no shirt. Oh geez. My mouth absolutely went dry looking at him. I knew he was in good shape, but I had never seen him with his shirt off. My heart rate instantly went up and I was struggling to regulate my breathing. I needed to get it together and put my poker face on.

Sam and I said goodnight and I tucked myself into his bed as he settled on the couch. He left the bedroom door cracked a little so I could hear him lying down on the couch and trying to get comfortable. I felt bad that he was having to sleep on the couch and give up his comfortable bed for me. I lay there looking up at the ceiling and around the room. The moonlight was pouring in through the window and once my eyes adjusted, I could see most of his bedroom. I looked around at all his personal items and the way he had organized his room. I could hear that Sam had fallen asleep because his breathing settled and deepened into a longer, more soothing rhythm. I was restless though. I had too many thoughts racing and being in a new place was not helping. Even though Sam was in the next room, I felt very out of place and lonely. I tried over and over to close my eyes and will myself to sleep, but I just couldn't. I looked at the clock on my phone and it read 4:26. Good grief! This totally sucked.

I couldn't take it any longer. I had started to think of ways that I could maybe leave and go home to my own apartment so I could sleep, but I didn't know how I was going to do that safely. And, I still only had heels to walk in, so there was that. I finally got out of bed and crept quietly into the living room where Sam was sleeping. I walked over to the couch and knelt down on the floor beside him. I gently placed my hand on his chest and whispered, "Sam." He woke instantly with a startle.

"Krista. What's wrong?" he asked as he began to raise up onto his elbows.

"I'm so sorry to wake you. I can't sleep and I'm struggling. I'm so sorry," I said as I instantly regretted waking him up. It sounded so stupid once I said it aloud and I felt bad.

"Oh, don't be sorry. I'm sorry you can't sleep. Is there anything I can do?" Sam asked.

"I don't know. I guess I'm just struggling being in an unfamiliar place. I kind of feel lonely but I don't know why," I told him.

"Would it be okay if I come lay in bed with you? I promise nothing will happen," he said.

Reluctantly, I said "yeah, we could try that."

Sam followed me to the bedroom and we got in bed. I got under the covers, but Sam lay on top of the covers and used the blanket he brought from the couch to cover up with. We settled in and I was facing away from Sam with my back to him. He reached over and put his arm over me. "Is this okay?" Sam asked.

"Yes, it's good," I said. "Thank you for trying to comfort me."

"No problem. I'd rather be beside you anyway," Sam added.

After a few minutes, I turned over to face Sam. I could see his face in the moonlight and he was looking at me. He reached up with his hand and started playing with my hair without saying a word. It felt good and immediately made me relax. My eyelids were finally starting to get heavy and I could feel myself slipping into the beginning stages of sleep. I took a long, deep breath and closed my eyes, allowing sleep to take me under.

I woke the next morning and Sam was no longer beside me. I looked at my phone and it said 11:30. Holy smokes! I have been sleeping like a teenager these days. I sat up on my elbows and cleared the sleep from my eyes. I looked over to where Sam had been and saw a note on the pillow.

"I didn't want to wake you. I went to get the car and coffee. Be back soon. Sam"

I got up and went to the bathroom. I did my best to brush my teeth and hair and then I changed back into my jumpsuit and heels so I could get home. Sam arrived back at his flat about 15 minutes later with coffee and a chocolate croissant. It was just what I needed. Later, Sam drove me home and walked me up to my apartment.

At my door, Sam gave me a kiss and said, "Thanks for spending the night with me. It was the best New Year's Eve of my life."

I smiled brightly and told him how much I enjoyed it. Sam left my apartment after giving me one last hug. He wasn't even downstairs yet and I watched out the window to see him reach the sidewalk. I missed him already and he was only a few feet away from me. "Oh brother.....I've got it bad," I muttered to myself.

Eighteen

arly Monday morning, Sam and I drove from Edinburgh back to Dundee to resume our work for the two properties that Eden & Associates were restoring. We had about two months to get these first two sites completed so we could move on to the next two sites. I had spent the last couple of days getting us both reorganized and packed for a two-month stay. We had no plans to come back to Edinburgh until these projects were completed, so I had a ton of errands to get done.

Rachel and I had spent a day together as well trying to catch up. We had not seen each other in a couple of months because of our crazy work schedules and the holidays. We went shopping, had lunch, shopped some more, and ended with dinner at her uncle's pub. We joked that all we liked to do was shop and eat. It was good to catch up with her, and she wanted to know all about Sam and what had happened between the two of us over the last few months. I told her about Christmas with my parents in the states, and New Year's Eve.

Rachel asked me how I had handled Christmas without Michael. She was a true friend and genuinely wanted to know how I was handling it all. I told her all about the autopsy report and police report as well. She had a ton of questions and I took the opportunity to tell her the whole experience. Now, she was the second person I had told everything to. It occurred to me that this was part of healing. I was finally ready to talk about it all with people that I loved and trusted. She listened intently and I could tell that hearing the details pained her. Somehow, that comforted me. To know that someone else was feeling pain for me. Besides just my parents.

I told Rachel that I had talked to Sam about it during our hike a couple of days ago. I still had this weird feeling about how he responded that day. It was so out of character for him to be so quiet and distant. I couldn't figure out what it was that made him react that way, but the more I thought about it, the more certain I was that I didn't make it up in my head. There was something about what I told him that bothered him. He had been involved in an accident too that had really changed his perspective, so I chalked it up to him reflecting on that. He hadn't really told me much about that time, but I figured he would tell me eventually....when he was ready. Some people just don't ever want to talk about things that cause them trauma. Like veterans that come back from war. Most of the ones I knew didn't really want to rehash it. Sam might be the same way, and I needed to respect that perspective.

Rachel agreed that it seemed kind of off, but she didn't know Sam, so she couldn't really infer much else. "You know, I'd really like to meet Sam sometime," Rachel said.

"Oh yes, I would love for you two to meet. Unfortunately, we'll probably have to wait until we get back to Edinburgh in a couple of months. Unless you happen to come up to Dundee? Then we could meet," I said.

"Yes, I may just do that. I'll let you know if I plan it," she replied.

My thoughts returned to the next days ahead as Sam and I drove to Dundee. The scenery was amazing as always, but pretty dreary weather this time of year. The sky was classic Scotland grey and the mist was heavy. It was brutally cold outside, and every time we stepped out of the car, the wind was enough to blow you away. It was gusty and miserable. I had my coat on and a blanket on my legs and lap in the car. I also had my seat warmer on and still couldn't get warm enough for my taste. Sam said I was going to light on fire, but I was freezing.

We arrived at the Rose Lodge around 7am. Callum and Maggie greeted us outside on the front steps like we were their long lost children. They helped us carry our bags and luggage up the stairs to our rooms, and Maggie immediately insisted on getting us some coffee or tea to warm us. I accepted her invitation for coffee because I never turn down coffee.

We basically threw our stuff in our rooms and then Sam and I said goodbye. We were headed in opposite directions. I called a car service to get to Culdees and Sam went to Craigievar. Once I arrived at Culdees, I met with the new site manager for the crew. He greeted me with a smile, shook my hand vigorously, and introduced himself. "The name is Fin. Ye must be Mrs. Andrews?" he questioned.

"Yes, it's so nice to meet you, but please call me Krista," I replied. "Thank you so much for coming on. Mr. Strickland said you've been doing an exceptional job." Fin blushed slightly and kicked at the rocks under his feet to avoid the compliment.

"Just doin 'my job, but I'm glad to help," he responded shyly.

"Fin, do you have time to get me caught up on the progress and let me know what your crew needs?" I asked.

"O 'course ma'm," Fin replied as he turned to walk with me through the grounds. Fin and I spent the next 45 minutes talking about what had been done and what still needed to be done. He explained the problems and challenges that he anticipated over the next several weeks. Thankfully, Fin came with proposed solutions to those problems. A rare quality for most people these days. I took notes, and Fin and I created a to-do list of things I needed to take care of. After our meeting, I immediately got busy working on my list. I spent the rest of the day making phone calls, getting lunch for the crew, making sure accommodations were still set, scheduling equipment to be onsite, and a thousand other things that had to be done. I was still learning so much about this work and what it entails, but it was so rewarding. I loved to learn and be challenged. It kept me engaged and never bored.

Before I knew it, it was 6:00 in the evening. My driver had arrived to take me back to the lodge, so I packed up my backpack and jumped into the car. It had been a great day, but I was exhausted. I fell asleep on the way back and woke to the sound of crunching gravel under the tires at the lodge. Sam's car was parked outside and I was eager to hear how his day had gone. We had not spoken on the phone or through text today at all, which was pretty unusual, so I assumed he probably had a busy day as well.

As I entered the lodge, Callum greeted me as he always does. After chatting with him for a moment, I peeked into the dining area to find Sam. Callum said, "He's not in there. He went straight up to his room when he arrived about an hour ago." That was weird and very unlike Sam. Perhaps he was just really tired or had a long day. I thanked Callum and headed up the stairs to my room. I unlocked my door and went inside to put my stuff down. I took my coat off and then went across the hall and lightly knocked on Sam's door. I waited for what seemed like too long and then knocked again. Finally, Sam answered the door. He had just gotten out of the shower and was in a t-shirt and jeans. His hair was wet, and he combed it back with his fingers as he opened the door wider.

"Hey there," he said.

"Hi," I returned. "Are you okay?" I asked.

"Yeah, I'm fine," he said. "It was a busy, long day and I wound up doing more manual labor than I had expected, so I needed to shower before dinner," Sam explained.

"I'm glad you're okay," I returned with a smile. "Do you have plans for dinner?" I asked.

"Maggie is currently hard at work making something 'special 'for us," he said as he airquoted and grinned.

"Ok, well we better not keep Maggie waiting or she'll have our hides," I quipped as I smiled in return. Sam asked me to give him a minute to get shoes on and he would meet me downstairs.

I sat at our usual table by the window and fireplace that Maggie had reserved for us. Bless her heart. She treated us like we were her own kids, and I loved her for it. The weather outside the window continued to be blustery and gross, but the crackling fire toasted the room to a lovely temperature. Maggie had a white and gold teapot already on the table, so I poured myself a cup and added a little milk. The warmth of the liquid hit the spot as I settled back into my chair and let my shoulders relax. It has been a long, but productive day.

Sam joined me at the table within just a few minutes and before we could get into our day, Maggie came barreling out of the kitchen with two plates of the most delicious-looking food ever. She had done her best to cook us a traditional, American meal. She made roast beef, mashed potatoes, grilled squash, and macaroni and cheese. It looked fabulous, and the look on her face was priceless. She was beaming with excitement and eager for us to dive in and taste it. Sam and I smiled at each other and wasted no time to give her the reward she was seeking. The food was heavenly and our reactions were clearly all she had hoped they would be. She clasped her hands together in sheer joy and patted us on the shoulders. She left us to enjoy our food as she be-bopped back into the kitchen through the swinging door.

Sam and I giggled after she was out of ear shot and continued our dinner while we shared about our day. After our meal was complete and the dishes had been cleared, Sam made a suggestion. "How would you feel about walking a couple of blocks to the pub and having a drink with me?" he asked.

"That sounds like a good idea," I replied. "Let me go get bundled up and I'll meet you in the foyer," I added. Sam and I walked hand in hand to the pub and found a table in back along the brick wall. Sam went to the bar and ordered drinks and returned to our table. We sat and chatted as we sipped our drinks. As always, the conversation between Sam and I was easy. We talked about anything and everything.

Sam asked how my day of fun with Rachel had been before we left. I told him we had a lot of fun doing the typical girl-day activity.....shopping. He smiled. "Rachel is a good friend. She's so easy to be around, she's fun, and she's a good listener," I said. I went on to tell Sam how I had told Rachel about going home for Christmas, and about the autopsy and police reports. I told Sam how Rachel listened and asked questions and I could tell she truly felt some of the pain that I had experienced. Most of my friends had avoided me or avoided hearing the details because it was painful and made them uncomfortable. I told Sam that I was convinced that I was healing from the experience since I had told him and Rachel.

At this, Sam went quiet. Again. He didn't seem bored with the conversation, just quiet and lost in thought. Distant. There it was again. Something about this topic bothered him. I hadn't imagined it. He was struggling with me talking about Michael's death and the specifics.

"Sam. I can't help but notice that each time I talk about how Michael died, the autopsy report, and the police report, you get really quiet and distant," I said. "Does it just make you sad, or is it more than that?" I questioned. Sam looked at me with an undiscernable look. I still couldn't tell what he was thinking.

After a few seconds of nothingness, I persisted, "Does this bother you because of the accident you were in before leaving the U.S.?" Sam remained quiet, looking at me with sadness.. I could see his mouth twitch as if he was trying to start a sentence to explain, but couldn't find the words. Or didn't want to say.   Despite his reluctance, I continued to press him on the subject. The more I questioned, the more frustrated and uncomfortable he seemed to become.   He fidgeted in his chair, ran his hand through his hair, and looked pained that I was pressing him. "Sam, please talk to me. What is it that bothers you about this?" I pleaded again.

"Krista, if I tell you why this bothers me, you may not look at me the same way again," Sam said.

"What do you mean?" I asked, placing my hand on top of his to reassure him.   "I'm not going to think or feel differently about you for sharing whatever this is," I told him. I was sure Sam was just feeling insecure about his own trauma and was reluctant to talk about it. I felt like he would feel better if he just got it out. Sam looked at our hands and then looked up at me again. Sadness and fear were in his eyes.

"Krista, I don't know how to say this in an easy way, so I'm just going to come out with it," Sam said. I nodded and held my breath to hear what he had to say. I was searching his eyes and face. I waited for what felt like minutes upon minutes for Sam to form the sentence. After a long pause, Sam said, "I was the bystander, Krista." He waited for me to register what he was saying, but I couldn't figure it out. What was he talking about? When he saw that

I wasn't clueing in, he took a deep breath and said, "I was the one that tried to rescue Michael."

Nineteen

I sat there stunned. I searched Sam's eyes and face for an explanation, but I couldn't speak. My breath hitched and my mouth was agape. I could feel tears welling in my eyes as I looked at him. There were tears in his eyes and he looked so sorrowful and sad. He also looked scared and he held onto my hand like he was pleading with me not to let go. I did. I pulled my hand back from his and grabbed the edge of my seat on both sides with both hands. I was gripping hard and looking down, trying to control my breathing. All I could hear was my heartbeat thumping in my ears. My world was spinning and I couldn't make it stop. I had so many questions, but I couldn't even speak.

Sam knew what I was thinking, so he began filling in the gaps. "I figured it out that day we went hiking and you told me the details. I had never told you about my accident, but I knew as soon as you told me that it was me. I was the other bystander that had gone in the water after those girls with Michael. He went in first and I followed him. He went to the driver's side and I went to the passenger's side. The water was so cold and the doors were hard to open." Sam said. I looked up at him in disbelief. He stopped talking as if he could tell I was overwhelmed. "Krista, please let me explain," he pleaded. Tears were falling down my cheeks by this point and I couldn't take another second of this. I wiped my face quickly with my hands and grabbed my purse from the back of the chair. I slung it over my head and shoulder and got up from the table and walked out of the pub as fast as I could. I had to get away.

I ran out the door and into the frigid wind. I wrapped my coat around me and took a deep breath. I exhaled with a shudder and cried out in pain. The tears continued to stream down my face and I turned down the street to head back to the lodge. I walked quickly and kept picking up my pace until I was basically running. I couldn't process it. I didn't want to process it. I ran into the lodge, ran past Callum without saying a word, and ran right up the stairs to my room. I unlocked the door with shaky hands and went inside. I locked the door, leaned my back against the door, began to cry harder as I covered my mouth with my hand, and slid to the floor. It was devastation and pain all over again.

Within minutes I could hear Sam outside my door. His footsteps were quick up the stairs and slowed to a stop outside. He paused and I heard him take a deep, shuddering breath. "Krista," he said softly at almost a whisper. "Krista, please open the door. Talk to me. Please," he begged. I couldn't do it. I couldn't talk to him right now. I needed time. I felt so confused. Part of me felt bad for Sam because he didn't ask to be in this situation. The other part of me was angry and hurt. He hadn't told me. He knew the other day when I told him the story on our hike. He knew then. That's why he was so distant and quiet, but he didn't say anything. And he wasn't going to tell me. I had to basically force the issue and make him tell me. Why?

I got up off the floor and walked over to my bed. I took off my coat and purse, and then lay down on the bed. I cried and cried. I eventually heard Sam leave my door and go to his room. I cried until I fell asleep. I awoke at about midnight because I was freezing. I got up and went to the bathroom. I could see in the mirror that my eyes were red, swollen and puffy. I began crying again. My heart was broken all over again and I was mad that I was still having to grieve. I put my pajamas on, brushed my teeth, washed my face, and then went back to the living room. I placed logs into the fireplace and used the kindling sticks to get a fire going. Within minutes the fire was roaring and the room was heating up. I walked back to bed and crawled in. I decided I would sleep forever and closed my eyes. I couldn't hurt if I were asleep.

Unfortunately, I awoke at 4am again. I sat up and looked around the room. I couldn't do it anymore. I needed to go. I needed to get away from this pain. I spent the next thirty minutes packing my bags. I hauled them downstairs and left them in the foyer. No one was at the desk, but I could hear banging and clanging in the kitchen. I went into the kitchen and Maggie was bustling about getting ready for breakfast service. She stopped dead in her tracks when she saw me. She instantly knew something was wrong and came over and hugged me. I cried even more.

"Maggie, I have to leave. Right now. Is there a train I can take, or a cab, anything?" I asked.

"Oh dear, are ye sure ye want to go right now?" she asked.

"Yes, please…. I need to go," as I cried even harder.

Callum came into the room and had obviously overheard everything. "I'll take ye wherever ye want to go, love," he said. I nodded at him with appreciation and followed him to the foyer. We grabbed my bags and headed outside to his truck.

"Are ye sure ye don't want to say goodbye to Mr. Strickland, dear?" he asked. "He looked desperate and upset last night when he came in after ye."

"No," I said a little too sharply. I softened, and said, "I just need to go, Callum." He nodded in return and loaded my luggage up and started the truck. Callum took me to the train station and helped me buy a ticket back to Edinburgh. I went directly to the airport and didn't even go to my apartment. I just wanted to go home immediately.

I reached the airport at about 5:00am and went straight to the ticket counter to check my bags. I had booked a flight on American Airlines on the app, so the ticket agent printed my boarding pass and handed it to me. My flight was leaving at about 9:00am so I had some time to kill. I got through security and went to my gate to wait. I got some coffee, kicked my feet up on my carryon, put my earbuds in, and closed my eyes. I just had to get home. I needed to get home. I needed to get away.

My phone rang in my ears at about 6:30. It was Sam. I didn't answer. He had probably just discovered that I was gone and was trying to find me. I couldn't talk to him. I felt like I was being irrational, but I just couldn't bring myself to speak to him. Then he texted. "Krista, please call me. Please talk to me. I'm begging. Don't go." I didn't respond. My heart was breaking and I wasn't sure if I was hurting more for letting Sam go, or because he hurt me. He wasn't going to tell me. I just kept thinking about it. I kept going back to that in my head. He didn't tell me when he knew. Was he going to tell me? Or just hope that I never found out?

The next few hours dragged by and I became more and more anxious to get on that plane and go home. I cried in the airport and people were looking at me. I went to the restroom and tried to clean up my face and pull myself together. After what seemed like forever, they were finally calling to board my flight. I was in the last boarding group, but the sweet gate agent had seen me crying and told me she would put me in the first group. I was so grateful for the kind people in the world. When I got to the desk to scan my boarding pass and show my passport, she leaned over and whispered to me, "I upgraded you to first class. You're in 1A." I looked at her astonished and then with tears welling up again.

"Thank you. You have no idea how much that means to me," I said.

"It's no problem. You seem like you could use a break right now. It's the least I can do," she replied. She patted me on the shoulder and handed me my amended boarding pass. I walked down the jet bridge and came face to face with the flight attendant that was at the door directing people where to go. When she saw me, she smiled with compassion and I had the feeling she had been told about me. She directed me to my seat personally and made sure I was comfortable. Soon after the flight took off, she came to me and asked if I wanted something to drink.

"A whisky on the rocks, please, " I responded. She returned almost instantly with the drink. I downed the drink all in one go. It nearly burned me in two, but the warmth and alcohol settled me and I lay down to let sleep keep me. I woke up some time later to the sound of the seatbelt sign dinging. I looked at my phone and six hours had gone by. I couldn't believe it. I never sleep this long on a plane. My body and mind were exhausted. And, I felt like I was reliving grief on a plane all over again. I had about 10 missed calls and texts from Sam. I didn't listen to the voicemails and I didn't read the texts. I wasn't interested in what he had to say at the moment. He had his chance to say those things and he chose not to take it. The hurt was beginning to turn into all anger.

While in flight, I took the opportunity to email Erick Eden. I told him that I either needed a leave of absence effective immediately, or I would submit my letter of resignation if he preferred. I explained that I had gone back to the states and was unsure of when I would return. I hit send and I almost immediately received a response.

"Mrs. Andrews, I'm sorry that you are struggling and I hope that everything is okay. If there is anything I can do for you, please don't hesitate to ask. If it's okay with you, I would like you to take a leave of absence rather than resign. I would hate to lose you and I'm hopeful that you'll return to the company soon. Please keep in touch about your plans. Sincerely, Erick" He is such a good man and I am so grateful for his kindness at this moment.

The plane landed in Dallas later that evening. I had texted my dad and asked if he could pick me up from the airport. Dad texted me right after my plane landed and said he would meet me at the baggage claim. Dad greeted me with a long hug, compassion in his eyes, and no questions. It was just what I needed at that moment. We drove home in basic silence and dad carried my luggage in for me. Mom was waiting for us in the kitchen and she had dinner on the table. We ate in silence for a few minutes and then I decided it wasn't fair to not give them any explanation and make them worry. I began to tell the story and the tears returned instantly. Mom placed her hand over mine when I struggled to continue my story. She said, "Krista, we know what happened." I looked at her surprised and then looked at my dad. He looked at mom and then back to me.

"Sam called us, Krista. He told us what happened. Actually, he told us everything. All of it," dad said.

"You talked to him?" I asked with heat in my voice. How dare he call my parents and talk to them. I was so furious.

"Yes, and you should too. I know you're mad and hurt, but you need to hear him out" dad replied sharply. I looked at his face and I could tell that he wasn't going to put up with my anger and sassy tone. "He's devastated. I think you need to try to hear him and see this from his perspective. If you did, you would feel differently," dad continued. Dad seemed certain that I would see it a different way, but I just couldn't imagine that. We finished our dinner and then I went to shower.

I crawled in bed that night and reflected on what my dad said. Dad generally was a quiet man and didn't say things unless he knew them to be true or he was absolutely convinced they were the truth. For him to be so direct and stern with me regarding Sam was unsettling. It made me start to question what they had talked about. I decided to read Sam's texts to me.

Text at 11:18am "Krista, I didn't know anything until the day of our hike. As you told the details, I began to realize that you were talking about my accident. I didn't want to say anything because I felt like you just needed to talk about it for yourself. You said you hadn't discussed it with anyone until then, so I didn't want to interrupt what was obviously a healing time for you."

Text at 11:40am "I'm so sorry I didn't tell you. I was struggling with dealing with it myself. I've had so much grief since the accident because I felt guilty and responsible."

Text at 12:31pm "It was my fault. I couldn't save him. I tried, but I couldn't get him out."

Text at 2:12pm "Please forgive me."

Text at 3:42pm "I love you."

Oh my gosh….the pain was worse now. I couldn't stop crying and my stomach hurt from the last 24 hours. I cried myself to sleep again.

The next morning I woke up to the smell of coffee, bacon and eggs. I put on my robe and slippers and made my way out into the kitchen where mom was slaving away at breakfast. She smiled when she saw me enter the room and immediately poured a cup of coffee. Then, she added her own homemade creamer to it and handed it to me. I sat on the barstool at the kitchen island and sipped the coffee while mom finished cooking. Once it was ready, she made two plates and slid one over to me with a fork and napkin. Not a word had been spoken, but we didn't need words. She was supporting me and giving me her love without the words.

About halfway through the plate, I put my fork down and looked over at mom. "I'm sorry for all of this. Thank you for always taking care of me," I said.

"Oh honey…you don't need to be sorry, and I'll always take care of you," mom said sweetly as she swept a strand of my hair behind my ear.

"I read some of Sam's texts last night, " I said. "He sounds broken," I added. My mom looked at me with knowing eyes and nodded her agreement. "Did you talk to him?" I asked her.

"No, but I heard him. He was on speaker when your dad spoke with him," she said. "Krista, he's devastated. Not only is he hurting that he's lost you, he's hurting FOR you, and he's still traumatized about the accident. He feels responsible for all of it. He's carrying a burden that no one person should have to carry, and it's going to destroy him. You have to help him, Krista."

After hearing my mom's perspective, I realized that it had been unfair of me not to even give Sam a chance to explain. I just ran away and blamed him for all of it. I landed all my grief squarely on his shoulders and he was already carrying the weight of my husband's death on those shoulders. It turned out that Sam needed me more than I needed him. And I wasn't there for him. I left him to grieve it all.

"I'm a horrible person," I whispered as I rested my forehead on my hand.

Twenty

Two weeks went by and I hadn't heard from Sam. I picked up my phone to text or call him so many times, but each time my stubbornness and hurt heart got the best of me and I just couldn't make myself do it. I was so conflicted. Sam hadn't tried to reach out again, either. I read his last text over and over. "I love you" registered in my heart, but my brain couldn't get past all that had happened. Honestly, I think I'm just so overwhelmed by the whole situation that I'm paralyzed and can't take action.

I'd spent the last two weeks mostly moping around my parents 'house despite their efforts to get me up and moving. My mom was very patient with me, but I could tell my dad was starting to wear thin. He wasn't the kind of person to sit around sulking about a problem. He believed it was better to tackle it head on and get it resolved. I knew he was right, but I just couldn't force myself to do anything. I was so depressed. Probably worse than I had been right after Michael's death. I felt like I was grieving two losses now.

Now, I'm lying in bed and it's 10:00 in the morning. I hadn't even dragged myself out of bed for coffee today. I know I'm depressed when I don't even want to get up for coffee. I reached over and grabbed my laptop and opened it up. The tabs on my screen looked like the thoughts in my head lately. Way too many open at the same time. I clicked into my email and sifted through all the junk. I landed on the message... containing Michael's autopsy report. To punish myself further, I opened the PDF file and began reading again. This time, I felt like there was a new light on what was inside this file. This time, I was reading it while envisioning Michael and Sam. I was creating my own movie in my head of what had happened. I toggled back and forth between the police report, which I had scanned and saved on my computer, to the autopsy report. I was putting as many pieces together as I could. What I really needed to do was talk to Sam. He was there and could tell me everything that happened, but I hadn't allowed him to do that…..yet.

The tears came again. I was so tired of crying, but every time I thought about this horrible situation, the tears returned. A knock at my door came and my mom said, "Krista, can I come in?"

"Yes," I replied as I began to sit up in bed and brush my hair out of my face.

"Honey, how are you?" she asked as she entered my room carrying a cup of coffee. She could clearly see that I'd been crying again and she gave me the most pitiful look of sadness. This had to be hard for her to watch me suffer through so much pain. I assumed no mother would want to watch their child be in pain for so long.

"I'm ok," I said as I wiped my face and took the cup from her with as much of a smile as I could muster. I confessed to her that I had been reading back through the police report and autopsy and putting pieces together.

"Krista. Enough is enough," my mom said. I was surprised that she sounded so impatient. I must have been looking at her with a shocked expression on my face because she continued. "You've been moping around here for two weeks and you haven't even talked to Sam. You owe it to Sam and yourself to have a conversation. You're not going to be able to move on if you don't."

My surprise was all over my face and I didn't quite know how to respond. This was very unlike my mom to voice frustration and be so direct. My dad....yes. But not my mom. It must be serious if she's losing her patience with me.

After a long pause between us, I said, "you're right."
'I have to talk to him." "I'm just so angry that he didn't tell
me when he knew. I feel foolish and humiliated," I said.

"Krista, I get it," my mom said. "But you have to try to
see it from Sam's perspective. He was trying to protect you
from more pain. And he was doing that BECAUSE he loves
you," mom explained.

She was right and I knew it. I had to suck it up and
call Sam. I decided to get up, take a shower, get dressed and
then I would call Sam. it would be close to 5:00pm there
once I got dressed so I might catch him after work so we
could talk.

I spent the next couple of hours getting ready. I
showered, put on real clothes, did my makeup, and curled
my hair for the first time in nearly three weeks. I felt much
better after all that, but I was still anxious about the phone
call. What was I going to say? How was I going to start?
Did Sam even still want to talk to me? There were so many
thoughts swimming in my head and I was becoming more
anxious by the second. I decided that I just needed to rip the
bandaid off and do it.

I picked up my phone, took a deep breath to try to calm
my nerves, and found Sam's number in my favorites. I
clicked on his name and the call began. It rang three times

and I was just about to give up and hang up, when Sam finally answered. "Krista…" he said with a desperate question sound in his voice.

"Hi Sam," I responded.

"Hi," he said. "How are you?" he asked.

A long pause stopped me from responding right away to that question. How was I? I didn't really know how to answer that question. I didn't really know how I was. Lost? Confused? Tired? Hurt? Missing him? All of the above?

Finally, I responded with "I'm fine. How are you doing?"

I could hear Sam waiting with bated breath and then releasing it once I responded. He said, "I'm doing okay. But I miss you. Thank you for calling."

"Are you at work right now," I asked.

"No, I just left work and I'm driving," he said.

"Are you working at one of the sites? "I asked.

"Yes, actually we've just finished up both sites and I was doing the final walk-throughs today," Sam said.

"Really? They're done?" I asked.

"Yeah and they look great," Sam said. "I wish you could see them. You'd be so proud of how they turned out," he added.

"Oh wow. That's kind of bittersweet," I said. "We put so much time and work into those projects. It's almost sad that they're done. It's like I'm attached to them." I chuckled and added, "I know that sounds dumb."

"Not at all," Sam replied. "I know exactly what you mean. I feel the same way."

There was another long, awkward pause between us and I could feel the pressure mounting.

"Look, Sam......I think we need to talk about what happened," I said.

"Okay," he said. "Where do you want to start?" he asked.

"Well, I think maybe you should do all the talking. I'd like to hear you tell me what happened at the accident. I want to hear your perspective and then we can go from there," I said.

Sam took a deep breath, and said 'Okay, I'll start from the beginning."

"The day of the accident, I was driving after work. I had been in Dallas for a few weeks on a job placement and it really hadn't been going that well. It was a stressful job and I was working with a company that was really difficult to deal with. I had no destination in mind. I didn't even really know where I was going. I left work that day and I was so frustrated that I decided I needed to get out of the city and just drive to clear my mind. That's the kicker of it all for me. I was in the wrong place at the wrong time, or the right place at the right time, depending on how you look at it. But it was a complete coincidence. I wouldn't have normally been there. Of course, as you know, it was February so the daylight was already fading and the sun was setting. It was cold and there had been ice on the roads for several days before. The main roads and highways were clear, but there were still spots that could be slick. About 45 minutes out of the city, I was traveling behind several cars and one of the cars hit a slick spot just before a bridge going over a small river or stream. Whatever you want to call it.

I was several cars back from it, but I could see what was happening up ahead. The small car hit the slick spot and started sliding. The back end of the car began fishtailing and the driver was obviously out of control. The driver hit the brakes because the tail lights came on and then they started sliding more, but now they were headed off the road and more out of control. We all slowed down and I watched the small car continue to slide off the road to the right and started going down the embankment toward the water. I think it was even slicker off the road and the car was careening ahead. There was no stopping it. At this point, as if in slow motion, the rest of the cars around me slowed to a stop and pulled over. There were about four or five other cars. Michael was one of them."

Sam stopped talking for a moment as if he were trying to collect his thoughts. Then he continued. "A couple of the cars were driven by women and they got out of their cars at the same time as Michael and I. I remember walking and running down to the water's edge as quickly as possible and Michael was ahead of me. I shouted up the embankment to one of the women and shouted for her to call 911. She got on her phone immediately and started calling. I followed Michael into the icy water after the car. The rear end of the car was slightly sticking up out of the water, but the front and most of the rest of the car was completely submerged in the water. Michael stopped when his feet hit the water and turned around and looked at me. He had already made a quick assessment and asked me to go to the passenger side while he went to the driver's side. We both went in. The water was freezing, Krista. Within seconds, my hands and feet were so cold that I could barely move my fingers.. When I got to chest high in the water it took my breath away. It was so cold. I went under to reach the door and try to see inside the car. The water was murky and churned up from the impact, so it was cloudy and difficult to see. I could see a girl in the passenger seat. The look of sheer terror in her eyes is something I'll never forget."

Saml paused again and I could hear the pain in his voice. He was struggling to tell the story again. I could tell that he never wanted to tell this story, but he was doing it out of love for me.

His voice trembled as he continued, 'I went for the door handle and it managed to crack it. I felt the door release, but I couldn't pull it open. The pressure of the water held it in place. I motioned to the girl to help push the door open with her arms and legs. The water was pouring into the car and rising quickly up to her chest. She started to panic and cry.. I was trying to talk her through it and keep her calm, but I was panicking too. She was pushing and I was pulling, but we couldn't get the door open. I went back up to get air and pulled myself back to the water's edge. When I came out, I saw that Michael had gone back to his truck and was running back down the embankment with a crow bar. He ran back down and into the water, diving back down to the driver's side. I quickly looked around and luckily found a piece of rebar lying in the grass. I grabbed it and went back down to the passenger side. The girl was holding her breath now completely submerged under water and looking like she was going to pass out any second. Bubbles were floating up from her nose. She couldn't help me anymore. I knew I had only seconds to act, so I reared back and stabbed as hard as I could at the window. It shattered. I came back up briefly for a breath and then went back down. I used my feet to push the window in. The girl had gotten her seat belt off thankfully, so I grabbed under her arms and pulled as hard as I could. She was limp. Pulling her out, against the pressure of the water, and through the narrow opening of the jagged window was all I could do. I finally got her out, and it took me what felt like forever to get her up out of the water. I dragged her to the edge and by that time other bystanders were coming down to help. An older man and woman helped drag her body up on the grass and I crawled out of the water. The woman said she was a nurse and she immediately started doing CPR. I looked around to see if Michael had come out. I didn't see him or the driver and I asked the other bystanders if they had come out. They all said no, so I went back in. I dove down into the water and I could see the girl still in the car. Michael had gotten the window broken out and the door semi-open. His upper body was through the window and into the car, but he seemed to be wedged somehow and was struggling to readjust. Blood was everywhere. He hadn't gotten the window fully broken out and it was cutting him. He was struggling and tired. His movements were slow and I could see his face starting to slack and his eyes close.

The girl was already unconscious, so I wedged my feet against the car and pulled the door open as much as I could. Even with Michael half way through the door window, I grabbed her and pulled her out. Her body got scraped and it tore her clothes, but I pulled with everything I had just to get her out. I got her up out of the water and one of the firemen was in the water to help me. I could see the emergency vehicles and lights flashing all around me. It was close to dark now. He took her and dragged her up onto the grass. I was so tired and exhausted.I took a couple of seconds to catch my breath, and then sucked in another big breath and then went back down. Michael was still stuck in the window."

Sam stopped talking and I could hear him sobbing. I was crying too. Tears streamed down my face, but I was trying so hard not to let him hear me crying. I didn't want to make him feel worse. We sat there in silence on the phone for a long while as he tried to regain his composure enough to continue. This was so painful for him. My heart was breaking for him.

Sam finally went on, "He was limp, Krista. He had gone unconscious. I frantically used my hands to push out more of the glass around his trunk. My hands were getting all cut up, but I just kept pushing. The next thing I knew, there were more arms and hands to help. I looked over and it was one of the firemen trying to help get Michael free. He was pushing the glass too. I grabbed Michael around his sides, up under his arms, and locked my hands in front of him and started pulling as hard as I could. At that point, I stopped worrying about hurting him and just pulled as hard as possible. We finally got him free and pulled him out of the window. The fireman took him and pushed him up out of the water. I came up right after him and gasped for air. I coughed and sputtered trying to get my breath while the fireman rolled Michael onto his back. He put Michael's head on his shoulder and leaned him back onto his chest as he floated him up and out of the water. Other firemen and police officers were there to help pull him out. The medics and firemen immediately began assessing. There was no pulse and Michael wasn't breathing, Krista."

Sam was crying and not even trying to control it anymore. I was doing my best to hold in my sobs. 'The medics started CPR, loaded him onto a backboard, and hooked him up to an AED. They shocked him and no pulse returned so they continued CPR. They loaded him onto the stretcher and one medic climbed on top of Michael and he continued to do CPR while the others loaded him into the ambulance. They closed the doors and took him off to the hospital. That was the last time I saw him," Sam said. "They took me to the hospital to get checked out and have my hands bandaged. I found out later that Michael had not survived," Sam said.

After a few minutes of crying and deep breaths from both of us, Sam said, "I'm sorry Krista. I couldn't save him."

It took me forever to get enough composure to respond. "I know, Sam. But you did everything you could to try. I know that. This is not your fault. You helped him save those two girls. And you got him out of that car. You did your absolute best, and I know that without a shadow of a doubt," I said.

Sam continued to cry, but he was trying so hard to be strong. Thankfully, he had pulled over and parked so he wasn't driving. We sat on the phone with each other in silence for a long time. We were both emotionally exhausted.

"I'm sorry I didn't tell you right away when I knew," Sam said after a long few minutes. "I was struggling with how to tell you, and I didn't want to lose you. But that happened anyway, so I should've just told you. I'm so sorry," Sam said again.

"It's okay, Sam," I replied. "I understand now why you didn't tell me. Both of our worlds had been destroyed and you didn't want to have to tell me that. I get it. I'm not going to forgive you because you don't require forgiveness. I'm sorry you've had to go through all this too," I said.

Sam and I ended our call that day with forgiveness and sorrow for each other. We didn't make plans to talk or see each other. I didn't know what would happen between us next…if anything. But, at least we both had the truth between us and could start to heal.

Twenty-One

The dreaded day had come. February 8th. It had been exactly one year since Michael's death. I had slept fitfully with dreams of both him and Sam. I awoke at just before six in the morning. My dreams consisted of a hodgepodge of a made-up movie in my head of the accident, and also good memories that I had with both of them. But, each of those good memories would turn bad along the way in the dream. It was as if my subconscious was torturing me.

I rubbed the sleep from my face and struggled to shake the dread from my mind. I decided that I needed to just get up and get my day started. My goal was to stay as busy as humanly possible to get through this day. First step.....coffee. I put on my warm robe and slippers because the house was chilly. When I turned the corner from the hallway into the main living space, I could see that my mom was already up and sitting at the kitchen island sipping her coffee. She heard my light footsteps like only a mother could, and she turned to greet me with a smile. She got up and immediately began pouring me a cup of coffee and adding her homemade creamer. I slid into the barstool next to hers and she eased my cup over to me without saying a word. She returned to her seat next to me and we sat there in silence for a long moment.

"The firsts are always the worst, 'mom finally said. I looked over at her with a knowing expression and took a long sip of the warm coffee. It went down and filled my soul with something I desperately needed today. "You know….. I lost someone once. Pretty tragically actually," mom said and looked over at me.

"Really?" I asked. I knew she had lost both her parents, but they both died basically of old age so I didn't think she was talking about them. "Yes, I lost the man I was engaged to before your dad," she explained. I looked at her with a puzzled look and raised eyebrow. She chuckled and said, "Yes, I was engaged before your dad. I just don't really talk about it because it's well in the past. But, I loved him very much. Much like Michael, he was killed in a car wreck about three months before our wedding."

"Oh mom," I responded as I laid my hand on hers. "I'm so sorry. I had no idea. That must have been horrible for you," I added.

"Yes, it was. It was the worst time of my life. I was devastated. Much like you," she replied. "It was not only a loss of the person I loved, but a loss of a life I had planned. We had planned. It nearly killed me to be honest. I wasn't sure I could recover. And there were some days.....many days....I wasn't sure I wanted to," Mom added. The sadness on my face only reflected the sadness in her eyes. We sat again in silence for a long few minutes. I wasn't sure what to say. If I needed to say anything. Finally, mom spoke again and said, "But I did recover. I met your dad, and he helped me recover. Not only did I find a friend in him, and fall in love with him, but he helped me heal. I've always told him that he saved me from my own grief, 'mom added.

"Mom, I had no idea. I'm so, so sorry," I said as I gave her a hug.

"It's ok honey. I appreciate that. I'm just telling you because I've been where you are to some degree. And what I can tell you is that you will get past this. You will be able to move on. It's ok to move on. And it's ok to be in love again," Mom said. Tears filled my eyes and spilled over before I could stop them. I wiped them from my face, but they fell faster than I could keep up with, and then I thought it was dumb to expect that I wouldn't cry today. May as well do it now, I figured.

Mom hugged me and rubbed my back as I cried.

"Krista, have you talked to Sam any more since your conversation with him?" mom asked.

"No, I haven't communicated with him at all since then. And he hasn't tried to reach out to me either. I suspect he's probably just trying to give me some space. Which shows just exactly the type of person he is. He's always thinking of others and what they need rather than himself," I said. The truth is that I just couldn't bring myself to talk to him. I don't know why. I had basically cleared Sam of any wrong-doing in my head, but there was a part of me that just couldn't reengage with him right now even though I knew he probably needed that from me. I was being selfish.

"You need to talk to him. You need to see him," mom said. "Not for him, but for you. You need him. He'll help you heal….you just don't know it," she said.

I looked at my mom and searched her face and eyes for the longest time. I was trying to work out in my head what she was telling me. Then it hit me. She's right. Sam had already healed me in so many ways. He had accepted me as a business colleague, a friend, and a lover. Despite my heavy burdens, sorrow, and the baggage that comes with tragic loss, he had been there for me. He was steady and let our relationship develop slowly with no pressure on me at all. He had been guiding me to healing for the last eight months. I reflected on what those eight months could have looked like without him, and it was bleak. I could have been stuck in my grief like I was those first three or four months, but he had pulled me out. And here I was.....back in the grief without him. I knew at that moment I needed to get back to Scotland.

The rest of the day was not so bad. After coffee with mom, I went to the gym in town to get a workout in. It was too cold to run or walk outside, so the gym would have to do. Later, after I showered and dressed, mom and I drove to the cemetery to visit Michael's grave. I took some fresh flowers and laid them next to his headstone. The sight of seeing his headstone with his dates of birth and death was so hard. There was such a finality to death and seeing that date etched into stone was gut-wrenching. Mom patted me on the shoulder and told me to take my time. She turned and headed back to the car. I suppose she felt like I needed some time to myself.

I stayed there looking at Michael's gravesite and thinking back on our memories together. All the memories flooded at once and it was like watching a reel with flashes and clips of different parts of our life together. The good times and the bad. Some of those memories made me smile and laugh. Others made me sad and I felt a longing in the pit of my stomach that I wasn't sure would ever go away. I sobbed into my hands as I rested my face in my palms.

Finally, I felt like I just needed to say some things to Michael, so I began talking. I didn't care who saw me or what they thought. I just needed to say some last words to him.

"I miss you so much," I said as I continued to sob. "I'm so incredibly angry that you left me, but at the same time I'm incredibly proud of you for saving those two girls. That's exactly the person I married and I can't blame you for that. I'm struggling, Michael. I'm struggling because I met someone. And he's good. He's good for me. But I found out recently that he was there with you when you died. He tried to save you, but couldn't." I cried more and more, and my whole body was shaking. "I mean come on!" I screamed out. "What are the chances that I would fall in love with the man that tried to save your life?" I pleaded in anguish. "That can't just be a coincidence, can it?" I questioned as if Michael was going to respond to me. "No, I don't think that's a coincidence at all. I think God brought us together to help heal us both," I added in a whisper.

I wiped my face once again and did my best to stop the tears. I rose slowly and stood with my hands wrapped around myself to stay warm. "I love you, Michael. I suspect that I always will. But I also know that I need to move on and I know you would want me to." I took one deep, cleansing breath, looked up to the sky, and then back to Michael's headstone. "Goodbye my love," I said and I turned and walked away.

I got in the car and my mom gave me a sympathetic look and just waited for me to tell her what I wanted to do next. "Can we please have some fun today?" I asked. "I just can't be sad anymore," I told her. She put the car in drive and we were off to lunch and shopping. It was just what I needed.

The next couple of weeks were filled with busy tasks. Mom and I decided to go through all my storage stuff and get rid of Michael's things. We gave family, especially Michael's parents, first dibs on going through his things to see what they wanted. I also set aside a few things that were special to me, and then we donated the rest of it. It took us nearly a full week just to do that, but I was relieved once it was done. Then I spent a few days working with the realtor on the sale of our house. We had received an offer just a few days after listing it and they offered just below asking. I accepted the offer right away and we were scheduled to close in two days. After the closing of that property, all things Michael and Krista would be done. I was extremely sad at that prospect, but somewhat relieved too. I just couldn't keep having that hanging over my head. It was time to move on.

After the closing of the property, I had planned to fly back to Scotland. I emailed Mr. Eden, and asked if I could return to my job and told him that I would be back in the UK by the end of February. He responded to my email right away as he always does, and said that they would be so glad to have me back. After emailing back and forth with him a couple of times, he said I should return to the office on March 2nd. I assumed we were between projects with the restoration sites and perhaps we would spend a few days in the office before returning to the new sites.

Mom and Dad drove me to the airport on Thursday afternoon and my flight was scheduled to leave at around 5:00pm for the overnight flight. I would land in Edinburgh at about 8:00 in the morning on Friday. That would give me the weekend to get settled back into the UK life before returning to work. Mom and dad parked in the parking garage of the airport so they could walk me in and help me with my luggage. I brought several pieces of luggage with all my remaining clothes, so I would have to check (and pay for) extra bags this time. I wasn't sure how I was going to manage all that luggage when I landed, but I figured I'd deal with it when I got there. After all my bags were checked and I had my boarding pass, I turned to Mom and Dad. I could tell they were a little sad to see me go again, but I knew they supported me.

We hugged for several minutes and they wished me well. "Please let us know when you land and when you make it to your apartment," Mom requested.

"Sure, no problem," I replied.

"Krista, go be happy with Sam," my dad said. "You both deserve happiness." He smiled at me and hugged me one more time before letting go.

I went through security, which wasn't too bad since I had TSA PreCheck. I found my gate and decided to sit and scroll for a while on my phone. I browsed social media for a while, then read my book, got up and walked around some, and then decided that I would text Sam. I hadn't reached out to him, nor he to me, and I wanted to connect with him before returning to work on Monday. I figured Mr. Eden probably told him I was coming back, so I was hoping to speak with him before walking into work. I didn't want our first conversation to be in front of everyone

"Hey Sam. I hope you're doing well. I'm sorry I haven't texted or called, but I was hoping we could talk if you have a minute." It was around 9:30 at night in Scotland so he might already be asleep and won't respond until in the morning. I put my phone down and continued to read until my flight left.

Once again I booked a first class ticket to Edinburgh with the proceeds from our house sale. I settled into my seat and recalled my first flight over and how grief-stricken I was. I was relieved not to be feeling that level of despair now. One can only handle so much of that before going crazy. I watched some TV as they served dinner, and then decided to head upstairs again to the bar like last time. Mostly just to walk around and stretch my legs. Reaching the top of the curved stairs brought back memories that that was the first time I had seen Sam. I just didn't know it was him at the time. I remember the way he spoke with the bartender, his dark hair, dark eyelashes, hazel eyes, and the crinkle of his eyes when he smiles. I went to the restroom and then approached the bar. The bartender, not Randy this time, asked what I wanted. I ordered a glass of wine this time. It's funny the choices you make when you're in the throes of grief or not. The last time I was at this bar, I felt like the searing pain of burning whisky was the only thing that could work to dull my senses. Now, in much less pain, I'm ordering a glass of wine just to relax.

The flight was good and I actually slept through most of it. When I awoke, our flight path monitor said we would be reaching our destination within an hour. Wow. I really did sleep well on this flight. That's the best kind of flight. One you basically sleep through. When we landed, I turned my phone off and back on expecting to see a response from Sam. There was no response which struck me as odd.

I was kind of surprised he hadn't responded. It's 8:12 am here in Scotland and I know he's probably been up for at least a couple of hours. He's an early riser and likes to get his workout in before work. Maybe he just got busy and I'll hear from him later.

The next couple of hours were pretty hectic anyway. Once I was off the plane and had collected all four of my very large, and heavy, suitcases from the baggage claim, I had to roll them outside to find transportation to my apartment. Rolling four large suitcases while carrying a backpack proved to be a little tricky. I had to go slow and stop several times to readjust when one suitcase decided to go wonky. I finally made it outside the airport and opened my Uber app to order a ride. I put in the comments that I needed enough space for lots of luggage. It connected me with a driver about sixteen minutes away. So I sat on a nearby bench while I waited. I took the opportunity to text my parents to let them know I had landed safely. Still no text from Sam though.

Nearly an hour later, my Uber driver pulled up to my apartment building. He was very kind and helped me get all my luggage out of the car. I rolled it all into the building while he unloaded it. I tipped him well and he headed off for his next ride. It took me nearly twenty minutes hauling each one of the bags up the stairs. I was huffing and puffing, and my legs were burning by the time I got them all in the door. I immediately plopped down on the couch and tried to catch my breath. My apartment was just as I had left it, and I was truly glad to be home. Then I thought "Wow… you actually think of this as home now."

I spent the weekend cleaning my apartment, sorting through clothes, getting organized, and did some shopping to prepare. I hadn't heard from Sam at all. I was really perplexed and kept checking my phone thinking maybe my text hadn't gone through. By Sunday morning, I tried to call him. He didn't answer and I left a brief voicemail asking him to return my call. No response. I guess Monday morning at work was going to be interesting. Maybe he was mad at me? Perhaps he preferred to talk in person? Who knows….. I couldn't figure out what was going on.

I went to the pub Sunday night to see Rachel. I hadn't seen her in a while, so I wanted to check in with her. She was ecstatic to see me and was able to get off so we could have dinner together and catch up. I filled her in on all that had transpired. I told her I was nervous about seeing Sam at work in the morning, and that he wasn't returning texts or calls. She found that strange too, but tried to reassure me that everything would be ok. We spent about 4 hours catching up and then by about 9:00pm I decided I really needed to get home and get in bed. Going back to work and getting up early in the morning was going to be hard. Rachel and I said goodbye and promised to get together again very soon. I took a cab home and got ready for bed.

I slept well even though I went to sleep thinking about Sam and what was going on with him. I had so much anxiety and trepidation about seeing him and facing our demons. I basically just wanted to hurry up and get to work to get it over with. I woke up to my alarm the next morning at 5:00 and went to the gym. I needed to get back into that habit, so no time like the present to start. On the way home, it hit me that I would need to call for a cab or Uber since Sam wasn't going to come pick me up like I had been used to. Thinking of him nagged at my gut and I couldn't help but feel anxious.

I was ready by 7:15 a.m and scheduled an Uber ride. I went downstairs and stood on the sidewalk to wait for my driver. He was there within a couple of minutes and I slid into the back seat with my purse and work bag. I had dressed sharply today because I wanted to make a good first impression. Well.....a second impression I guess. I hadn't seen Sam either and I wanted to look my best for him as well. I had dressed in a navy blue pantsuit with a tailored vest and jacket that fit me perfectly. I wore nude sling-back block heels that were comfortable, but chic. My hair was curled with a nice blow-out look and my makeup was on point. I looked the best I could. As I watched the city go by out the window of the car, I felt nervous. I had butterflies in my stomach at the thought of seeing Sam and talking to him. Part of it was a good excitement, and the other part was sheer nerves about what had happened between us.

The car pulled to a stop in front of the steps to Eden & Associates. I paid and tipped the driver through my app and then eased out of the car. I took a deep breath and went in the door. Allison looked up from her desk and immediately gave me a huge smile. She got up and walked over to give me a hug. She welcomed me back; literally with open arms.

After speaking for just a few minutes, Allison told me Mr. Eden was waiting for me at the top of the stairs and to go on up. I walked up and met him. He greeted me with a hug also.

"Mrs. Andrews, I'm so glad you have returned," he said.

"Oh I'm glad to be back too. Thank you so much for understanding and allowing me the time off," I replied.

"Yes, well, it seems you've had a lot on your plate really," Mr. Eden said.

Then Mr. Eden said, "Listen, Mrs. Andrews, there have been some changes here while you've been away. Uhh, I have moved you to another office that adjoins Mrs. Graham's office." He told me this information while he simultaneously ushered me toward my new office. I was more than a little confused about what was going on. When we got to my new space, Mr. Eden introduced me to one of the other associates. His name is Mr. Murray and he's an older gentleman who always wore a smile and tweed.

"You'll be working with Mr. Murray starting today and if you have any questions you can ask Mrs. Graham," Mr. Eden said.

I know for a fact that my face was stunned. I'm certain that I had the most puzzled look and was searching for answers to questions I hadn't expressed yet. Mr. Eden could see that I didn't have any idea what was going on. He led me to his office and closed the door. On the way, I could see Mrs. Graham looked at me with pity and sadness. Mr. Eden turned to me and said, "Mrs. Andrews. Mr. Strickland no longer works here if that's what you're wondering. I had assumed that you knew that given your...ehh... relationship. But it's clear to me now that you didn't know anything about him leaving."

"No," I said in a whisper. "I, uh....didn't know that Sam no longer worked here," I replied as I looked down at the floor. I was struggling with what I had just heard. I didn't know what to say. I didn't even know what to ask.

Mr. Eden could see that I was stunned and hurt. He proceeded to tell me, "Sam turned in his resignation without notice about a month ago." I looked into Mr. Eden's kind eyes and searched for a reason.

"Did he say why he was leaving? Or where he was going?" I pleaded.

"No, Mrs. Andrews. I'm sorry, he didn't. We were all shocked too. And saddened because he was an asset and friend to us here. We hated to lose him. He turned in his resignation on my desk late one evening while I wasn't here. He never came back. He didn't leave a forwarding address or anything. I've tried calling and texting him, but I haven't received a response. I even tried going to his flat, but apparently he moved out," Mr. Eden explained.

I sat down at my desk before my legs gave out from underneath me. I was in shock. I felt like my heart had been ripped out of my chest. My brain shut down and all I could hear were muffled voices. I felt like I was in a vacuum and couldn't clear my thoughts. Sam was gone and I had no idea where, or why he left.

Twenty-Two

Mr. Eden put his hand on my shoulder and patted me. He clearly felt sorry for me but didn't know what to say or how to console me. He gave me a sympathetic look and then left my office to give me time to process. My head was spinning and my thoughts were running wild. Where was he? Was he okay? Why would he just leave and not tell anyone where he was going? Was this my fault?

Of course it was my fault. I hadn't supported him in this whole situation. I had only placed blame and made him feel worse about what happened. All because I was angry and couldn't forgive him for not telling me immediately when he knew how we were connected. Why had I been so stubborn? Why couldn't I have seen his perspective and why he wouldn't want to tell me right away. He needed time to process and figure it out. It was complex and he was just trying to give himself time to navigate it properly. But, I was mad and quick to judge. I was so stupid. I had forsaken Sam, and now I couldn't even do anything about it because he was gone.

After about 20 minutes of trying to collect myself, I tried to refocus and get myself organized. I had to get it together and make it through this workday. I couldn't do anything about Sam right now, so I needed to focus on what I could do at work. I got up and walked into Mr. Murray's office and lightly knocked on his door. He looked up from his desk and smiled as he motioned for me to come in.

"Mr. Murray, I just wanted to apologize for our introduction earlier. I was more than a little stunned by the news of Mr. Strickland's leaving and I didn't even shake your hand," I said as I reached toward him with an outstretched hand.

Mr. Murray shook my hand while smiling back at me with compassion in his eyes. "It's no 'a problem, dear. It's very nice to meet you," he continued. "We'll be working closely together Mrs. Andrews as I have resumed operations for the project that you and Mr. Strickland had been working on. The first two sites were completed successfully and we have now started on the other two sites. My plan is to leave you here at the office for the next month so that you can settle back into work life. Not to mention, I haven't had an assistant in a long time and work here has fallen significantly behind, so I'm counting on you to help me get caught up. There's a load of filing, organization, and financials to get together. Mr. Eden and Mrs. Graham have assured me you're a whiz at getting organized and taking care of those things. I also have a very long list of personal tasks that I would like you to help me accomplish since I'll be on-site for one of the projects starting next week. Once you have gotten everything together here, I'm going to send you to the other site to the operations manager. You'll essentially be in charge there, Mrs. Andrews."

My eyes were probably big and I know I looked a little surprised by that information. I was kind of taken back that they would leave the whole project in my hands. That was a lot of responsibility. Mr. Murray could read the thoughts on my face apparently because he said, "I've been assured that you are more than capable of this job, Mrs. Andrews. I saw what you did on the other two sites and everyone here has done nothing but sing your praises. You may not think so, but you are the perfect person for this job and I have full faith in you."

He waited for just a few seconds and then added, "Do you have any questions?"

I looked up at him and finally said,"No sir. I don't have any questions right now. But, I do have a request," I added.

He looked at me with a quizzical look and asked, "What't that, dear?"

"Please call me Krista. Mrs. Andrews is my mother," I said as I smiled.

Mr. Murray chuckled and said,"I understand. Krista it is then. So long as you call me Lochlan."

I smiled in understanding and nodded my approval. Lochlan seemed a much smarter name than I had given him credit for. I had always assumed that Mr. Murray was a sort of nerdy introvert, but he was proving to be much more adept than my initial judgement had given him credit. Goes to show, you should never judge a book by its cover. Mr. Murray was already proving to be a great boss. He was being kind, compassionate, stating his expectations, and communicating well. It wouldn't be like working with Sam, but I think this was going to be okay.

The thought of Sam made me sad again and I quickly decided that I had to shove him out of my thoughts or I would never make it through this day. After talking a little more with Mr. Murray, I returned to my office to get started on all that was in front of me. The desk was a mess with stacks of files and loose papers everywhere. I immediately made a plan to spend today working on organizing and filing. I got busy sorting and trying to make heads or tails of everything. Just as I had done when I first started here, I spent a ton of time reading through documents and files so that I would know how to even file them. It also helped me get up-to-date on the projects that Mr. Murray had been involved with. After a while, I heard a light knock on my door and I looked up to find Mr. Graham standing in the doorway. I was sitting on the floor with my legs crossed and surrounded by files and papers.

Mrs. Graham said, "Krista, it's time for lunch dear. Come keep me company."

"What time is it?" I asked because there wasn't a clock in my office and my phone was out of my reach on the desk.

"It's nearly 1:30 love. You've been working for hours. You need a break," she said.

I guess I had zoned out in the work. Which was exactly what my brain needed to keep me from thinking about Sam. I got up off the floor and tried to wipe the wrinkles from my slacks and rearrange my blouse. I slipped my heels back on and ran my fingers through my hair. "Okay, let's go eat. Suddenly, I'm starving," I said as I smiled at Mrs. Graham.

We went to the break room and got our lunch bags out of the fridge. I had brought a random, hodgepodge assortment of boiled eggs, cottage cheese, turkey and a small salad. Mrs. Graham pulled out what looked like a delicious shepherd's pie that she had probably made from scratch. She popped it in the microwave and the aroma came to life and filled the break room with the most savory smell. It made my lunch look a whole lot less appetizing. Mrs. Graham took a seat beside me at the table and we settled into quietly eating our lunches. After about five, she couldn't take the silence any longer and said, "Ok dear. Tell me about it."

I gave her a sideways glance with a sad smile on my face. My shoulders slumped and tears welled up in my eyes before I could even start to talk. She could see the hurt on my face and placed her hand on mine. "I'm sorry you're hurting, love," she said. "What can I do for you?"

"Nothing...nothing. I don't even know what to do for myself," I said as I shook my head. I looked up into Mrs. Graham's eyes. She was so kind and I could tell she truly felt sorry for me and wanted to help. I decided that telling her the whole story would probably help. She wasn't going to be able to solve this problem for me, but confiding in someone might help me vent it. It was a better option than holding it all inside. So, I began. I told her the whole story.

Start to finish. I told her about how Michael died and the accident. I told her about the startling revelation that Sam had been involved and tried to save his life. I told her how Sam and I had fallen in love and about when he realized our connection. Then I told her about the night that I knew something was wrong and I forced it out of him and he told me that he had been the one to help Michael. I explained what had happened between us over the last several weeks and our phone conversation where he explained everything that happened at that accident site. I told her everything.

Mrs. Graham had listened intently the whole time and hadn't said a word. She didn't ask any questions and didn't interject a single time. She just listened and let me purge every bit of it. When I was finally done, I stopped and took a deep breath and exhaled. Then we continued to sit in silence for what felt like forever.

Finally, Mrs. Graham said, "It's clear you love him. And I'm positive he loves you too."

"I pushed him away. All out of anger. Anger that wasn't really with him. It was more anger at the crappy situation. And now... now I don't know where he is. He's not responding to my texts or phone calls. I don't have any way of figuring out where he might have gone," I said in desperation as tears fell freely from my eyes. I sat forward with my elbows on the table and covered my face with my hands as I sobbed. Mrs. Graham leaned over and wrapped me up in her arms holding me for a long while as I cried.

I finally stopped the tears and wiped them away. I tried to clean up my face as she handed me a box of tissues. I wasn't hungry anymore, so I started packing my lunch back into my lunch bag. I looked at my phone and the time was 2:30. It was time to get back to work.

As I cleaned up the table and collected my food, Mrs. Graham stopped me and said,"I have faith that this will work out. You'll find him. Or he'll find you. When the time is right and you have both healed, you will find each other again. My heart tells me it will be so, love."

I half smiled back at her with part hope and part doubt. I wanted to believe as much as she did, but I just couldn't see how this was going to be resolved if I couldn't even see or talk to Sam. I finished packing up my stuff from lunch and slung my bag over my shoulder. I headed back to my office and continued my work. After what I assumed had been a few hours went by, I checked my phone to see what time it was. The office had become very quiet. It was 6:15 in the evening. No wonder the office was quiet. Everyone had left and gone home. I guess they all decided to just leave me be. That was probably for the best. I wasn't very good company today. I had made a lot of headway though. The office was almost completely organized and everything was filed neatly away in the filing cabinets with labels.

I packed up my belongings and decided to head home. I turned out all the lights and walked through the office to make sure no one else was still here. I headed downstairs and checked the kitchen and living area to see if there was any sign of anyone. It was eerily quiet and dark. I had ordered an Uber ride while I was packing up my stuff, so I checked my phone to see how far away they were. The app said two minutes away, so I quickly got out my keys and locked the front door behind me. I had never closed up the office before, so I was hoping there wasn't something else I was supposed to do. Surely turning the lights off and locking the door would suffice.

The Uber arrived just as I was turning from the door and walking down the front steps. The same steps I had sat on a few months ago when Sam and I had a turning point conversation about our relationship. I smiled at that memory, but was instantly gut-wrenched that he wasn't here. The ride home was quick and I was in my apartment within about 20 minutes. I heated up some leftovers for dinner, but I really wasn't that hungry. I didn't have much of an appetite. I was love-sick. Life in Scotland didn't have the same excitement or appeal as it did when I first moved here. I was lonely and heart-broken all over again.

The next few weeks went by with each day looking the same as the day before. Life was pretty monotonous. Work was busy and I was able to get a ton done. More than Mr. Murray had really expected I think. He was on the job site and would call and email to check on my progress. He always seemed surprised at the amount I had accomplished. He would call with more tasks that needed to be taken care of, but I almost always was a step ahead of him. Having worked with Sam and on those job sites, I knew what to anticipate and what he would need done without him having to ask.

Life at home for those four weeks had been painful. I had to force myself to continue a routine to keep from falling into depression. I hauled myself out of bed every morning and went to the gym. I tried to make it a point to plan something after work at least once a week with coworkers or Rachel. The weekends were excruciating. Rachel often wasn't available because of her job or her new love; which I understood. But, it sure made me lonelier to be on my own for two days. I spent a lot of time just walking around, sightseeing, shopping, hiking, and whatever else I could do to keep myself occupied.

Mr. Murray called on Wednesday afternoon and said that he would be sending me to one of the job sites next week. But first, he wanted me to meet him in London for a business meeting for a new project. It would be similar to the one I went to with Sam to land the current account. Mr. Murray had obviously heard from Mrs. Graham and Mr. Eden that I could be a very useful tool in those meetings, so he wanted me there. That meant that I would need to take a train from Edinburgh to London which is about a four to four- to five-hour trip. I got on my train app and booked a Liner trip. Mr. Eden had come in shortly after I spoke with Mr. Murray and handed me a company credit card. He told me that the card was for me to keep and use on all company expenses including travel, food, hotel, etc. So, I used that card to book my journey. I was kind of looking forward to traveling by train so I could see the countryside and get some reading done.

On Thursday, I left work a little early so I could get home to do laundry and pack. Friday morning I went to the gym and came back home to shower and head to the train station. Just as I expected, the train ride was nice. The scenery was great and it gave me time to just read and sit and think. Of course, I spent a lot of time thinking about Sam and how I should have handled that differently. But at this point, I was starting to let go of that sadness. There just wasn't anything I could do about it. I had tried about three more times to contact Sam. I texted, called and left a message, and even emailed. There was no response to any of those attempts, so I had finally decided that I had to let it go and move on. I needed to heal. Again.

The train finally arrived around 3 p.m. at King's Cross station in London. I collected my luggage and bags and made my way off the train and onto the platform. I basically followed the crowd through the station and out the exit to the street side. Then, I grabbed a taxi to head toward my hotel which was located in the Soho area of London. The cab ride was about 15 minutes with traffic and I arrived at the Courthouse Hotel just in time for check-in. As soon as I arrived and checked in, I texted Mr. Murray to let him know I was there. He instantly replied and let me know that we had a scheduled dinner with the associates of the Canal and River Trust to discuss several projects for restoration of bridges throughout England. He asked that I meet him in the lobby bar at 5:30 and we would walk to a nearby restaurant for which I had made reservations for 6:30 p.m.

Once inside my room, I quickly unpacked and got out my dress for this evening to let it free itself of wrinkles while I showered and got ready. I had purchased a new dress that was a deep navy color with long sleeves. It was a straight-fitting option that fell just below the knees. The upper part of the bodice was made of a sheer material with embroidered flower-type designs all along the chest, neck and arms. The neckline was a mock neck and I felt like it was a good cut to accentuate my neck, shoulders, and long arms. The navy color, against my dark hair, helped to pull out the blue of my eyes. I had paired the dress with my nude heels to give it an even classier look. Overall, I felt confident and beautiful in the ensemble. It was upscale, appropriate for a business dinner, and exuded class.

Mr. Murray and I arrived at the restaurant at 6 and the host ushered us to our table. After being seated, we ordered water for the table and Mr. Murray proceeded to order a bottle of red wine without asking what I wanted. He gave no indication of concern about what I would want to drink. I was surprised that he wouldn't ask me what I wanted, and just took control and ordered for everyone. He had not previously struck me as the type to take control or be that confident, but I was learning more and more that people can't be judged based on their facade.

We chatted as we waited and I tried to quiz him as much as possible about the project and what he was hoping to accomplish with this meeting. He discussed his plan and obstacles he anticipated, helping me understand the objective of the dinner. At exactly 6:30, the usher arrived at our table escorting two gentlemen. We stood and introduced ourselves and sat back down.. We spent the next several minutes making small talk, getting acquainted and ordering. Once our food was ordered, we got down to business. The director of Canal and River Trust was Mr. Hodges and his associate was the chief financial officer, Mr. Henning. The men immediately began specifics of what they wanted out of the project and their expectations. They discussed the objectives, financial constraints, and a general timeline for the project. Mr. Hodges seemed pleased with how the conversation was going so far. He appeared satisfied with Mr. Murray's responses to his questions and concerns, but his next question was more specific to how the projects would be managed. At this, Mr. Murray angled toward me and said to Mr. Hodges, "I'm going to let Mrs. Andrews explain the nature of management. She has recent experience with management of site projects that were very similar to what we're discussing. I think she can better answer your questions."

Suddenly, I was in the spotlight, and a ripple of nerves rushed through me. Still, the company and Mr. Murray was depending on me to help seal this deal, so I straightened up, put on my best poker face and began explaining my part in management of each site and the daily operations. As confidently and concisely as I could, I walked them through the anticipated needs, crew hiring, site requirements, permits, accommodations, and all other potential needs of the project to keep it on a tight timeline. I could tell by Mr. Hodges 'and Mr. Henning's expression that they were becoming increasingly and more convinced and reassured that Eden & Associates was the right firm for this project. I gave as much information as I possibly could to alleviate any concerns. Their nods and focused attention told me I was answering questions that were in their heads or that they had—and even some they hadn't thought to ask yet. After I completed a synopsis as thoroughly as I could, I paused and asked them if they had any questions or if there was anything else I could clarify.

Both men thought for a moment and looked toward each other with questioning looks. Mr. Hodges then said, "Mrs. Andrews you've done a very good job explaining and answering our questions. I'm quite satisfied with your outline of the project and you clearly have detailed knowledge of what to expect. But, I do have one question. And, I want to apologize in advance as I don't wish to offend you."

I raised my eyebrows and looked back at Mr. Hodges with intensity. "Go on then," I responded; encouraging him to ask his question.

"Well, I don't mean to imply that you are incapable of such a project, but I would like to know how your previous projects have gone, being a woman in charge. Do the crews respond well to you?" he asked. I couldn't say I really blamed him for having such a question. It's a valid concern, but the fact that it even has to be a concern caused a fire inside me.

I took a moment to consider his question and smirked as I looked up from the table to meet his eyes. "For the most part, the crews and project subcontractors I've worked with have all been wonderfully receptive to my instruction. I do my best to be diplomatic and respectful of their knowledge and skills, and that has been reciprocated to me." I looked down at my hands on the table pondering what to say next. When I looked back up at the gentlemen who were watching me intently, I continued, "There was only one incident of insubordination on our last project, but that situation was handled swiftly by the appropriate authorities. We were able to proceed with the project without delay, and the rest of the project was completed on budget and within the timeline."

I left it there with no further details about what had happened. I just wanted them to know that it had been handled and that it hadn't hindered me from doing my job. I could tell the two men had more questions, but they did not probe further....thank goodness.

At the conclusion of our meeting, we all stood to say our goodbyes. Mr. Murray and Mr. Hodges shook hands and the two had come to an agreement. Mr. Hodges said our office would be receiving a contract to be signed by Monday morning. We all shook hands at that point and the two gentlemen left. After they had walked out of earshot, Mr. Murray looked at me and said, "Krista, thank you. You did an excellent job of reassuring them on what to expect. I'm certain you helped to seal this deal and I appreciate you."

"Oh you're very welcome Mr. Murray. I'm so glad I could be helpful," I replied. Then, as he proceeded to pay the bill, I excused myself to the restroom before we walked back toward the hotel. It was only about 3 blocks away, but I figured I needed to go now rather than wait. I walked from the table and headed to the back of the restaurant. After washing my hands, I checked myself in the mirror. I pulled out my brush and freshened up my hair, and then added a bit of powder and lipstick. I don't know why I was worried about my looks since we were headed back to the hotel, but

I just couldn't walk out looking unkempt. I walked out of the restroom and toward our table which was located just past the bar. I was busy placing my compact back into my purse and looking down as I walked. As I looked up, my eyes saw something that my mind didn't immediately register. I did a double take to make sure I was seeing what I thought I was seeing. I stopped dead in my tracks and my breath hitched in that moment. At the same time, a familiar face found mine. There, across the bar, looking back at me. It was Sam.

Twenty-Three

I sucked in an audible breath as I came to a stop about twenty feet away from Sam. I couldn't believe he was here. My head started swimming with thoughts wondering why he was here, what he was doing, and illogically questioning how he knew I was here. As if he were here just for me. He had been talking to another man as they were standing near a table, but he abruptly stopped talking when his eyes met mine. We both stood for a long moment just piercing each other with looks so deep it was uncomfortable, but we couldn't seem to break our gazes. Finally, Sam broke the look and turned back to the man he was speaking to and resumed talking. They began shaking hands, but I took his return to his conversation as a sign that Sam did not want to see me or talk to me. Instantly, a rush of heat and humiliation washed over me and I looked down toward the floor and headed for the front door walking right past Mr. Murray and our table. I could see out of the corner of my eye that Mr. Murray was confused and rose to follow me out.

I reached the door of the restaurant that led out to the street just as I was about to combust from holding my breath. I rushed out onto the sidewalk, into the fresh cool air, and finally sucked in air and blew it out slowly trying to regain my composure. My eyes were stinging with tears that threatened to fall any second. I was crushed that Sam made it evident he didn't want to speak to me. A single tear escaped my eye and I quickly wiped it away before anyone could see that something was wrong. Mr. Murray quickly appeared just behind me on the sidewalk and asked if I was ok. I assured him that I was fine and encouraged him to go on without me. I did my best to convince him that I just wanted to walk back to the hotel alone as I was going to stop at the pharmacy for some headache medicine. Somehow, I convinced him to leave me alone and he headed back in the direction of the hotel.

I turned and began to walk in the opposite direction. I didn't know where I was going. I just needed to get away and walk. I got about two blocks away from the restaurant and I felt a hand reach for mine from behind me. "Krista," I heard as his hand slowed me and I turned to look. It was Sam. He had obviously run out of the restaurant as he was breathing hard, and tracked me down. I glanced at our hands touching and then looked up into his eyes. They were soft, kind, and almost pleading. Different than they had been about 3 minutes ago.

I waited. I waited for Sam to speak and say something, but he was obviously struggling with what to say. He clearly wanted to talk, and see me, but he wasn't saying anything. So I began, "I tried to call, text, and email you multiple times. You just left without a word." He didn't respond other than to look down at the ground with a shameful or remorseful look on his face. But, he didn't let go of my hand. So, I waited longer. I wasn't going to help him anymore. He had to do some of the talking and explaining.

After longer than I thought possible without a word, I turned to walk away and he pulled at me and said, "Please don't go."

"If you want me to stay here with you, then you need to start explaining. Or say something at least," I said with as much compassion and kindness in my voice as I could muster at the moment. Man, my emotions were all over the place. I was feeling humiliation, love, desire, anger, and shame all at the same time.

"I'm sorry," Sam said. 'I'm sorry for leaving and not saying anything. I'm sorry for……everything. I thought it would be better if I just removed myself from your life."

"Well, it wasn't better. Not at all," I replied quietly.

We both looked at each other and then away, but we continued to hold hands.

"Sam," I turned back to him and looked into his eyes. "I'm sorry for blaming you. And being so angry with you. I shouldn't have blamed you for anything. You did absolutely nothing wrong. I was just angry and hurt all over again," I said as tears welled in my eyes again. My voice cracked as I continued, "and I took it out on you. I'll forever be sorry for how I made you feel."

Sam squeezed my hand as he watched tears fall and roll down my cheeks. He had a pained look on his face and he stepped closer to me. He now had tears in his eyes and his jaw was tense like he was trying so hard to hold them back. I couldn't take it anymore. I dropped his hand, stepped into him, and reached my arms up and around his neck. I pulled him in with all the strength I had and hugged him as tightly as possible. The fear of him not reciprocating didn't last long as he returned my hug by wrapping his arms around my waist and holding me close. I could hear our hearts beating wildly, and I could feel his rasped breathing against my neck. We held each other for so long without saying another word. We just stood there, on the sidewalk, with people flitting around us. The world went by as we held each other in silence. Everything we needed to say to each other was being said in silence. I forgave him, and he forgave me, all in one long embrace.

Sam finally broke the embrace and stepped back just slightly to look at my face. He reached up and caressed my face with his hand. He looked into my watery eyes and said, "I love you, Krista."

Relief washed over me, and for the first time in probably two months I felt like I could take a deep cleansing breath. I leaned my forehead against his and said, "I love you too."

"Can we go somewhere to talk?" Sam asked.

I smiled in return and sarcastically replied, "You don't want to continue our drama here on the sidewalk in London?"

"Not really," Sam said with a smirk.

I grinned and said, "Yes, let's go to my hotel. It's just a few blocks from here."

Sam and I walked hand in hand back to my hotel. When we arrived at the hotel, we went to the hotel lounge and found a table in the back away from all the other people so we could have some privacy. The bartender came over and took our drink orders and returned with drinks in no time. Sam and I sipped our drinks in silence for a few moments, and then he broke the silence.

"I feel like I need to explain," he said. I waited to hear what he had to say. It didn't really matter to me anymore, because I had already forgiven him, but I sensed he felt like he needed to clear the air and lay everything out on the table. "I thought I had hurt you by not telling you when I knew about my involvement with Michael's death. I feel responsible for his death, and like I have contributed to more pain for you. I didn't want to be that person to you. You deserve to not hurt anymore, so I figured I would take myself out of the equation. I knew that would hurt you more momentarily, but I thought you would get over me and ultimately be happier," Sam explained.

I looked at him with sadness on my face. I was heart-broken that I had made him feel or think those things because they weren't true. I was never going to be happier without him. I loved him and needed him. "Sam," I whispered. Raising my eyes to him I continued, "I'm so truly sorry. I know beyond a shadow of doubt that you did everything you could to save Michael. You did more than most people would have, and for that I will be eternally thankful. As for you leaving, I get it. I can see your perspective and why you would think that. You were wrong….but I can understand it," I said.

Sam scooted his chair closer to mine and moved in toward me. Without a single care about who or what was going on around us, Sam leaned over and asked, "Can I kiss you?"

"Please," I said and he had his lips on mine before I finished the word. It was gentle, soft, and slow. So much love was in that kiss. Sam released the kiss and we paused within inches of each other for just a moment before I returned the kiss. This time, the gentleness turned into need and desperation from both of us.

After deciding we should probably get control of our senses, Sam and I sat back in our chairs and began to talk. We held hands and talked for at least an hour. We went through everything. We talked about all the feelings, all the hurt, all the things that had happened over the last several weeks. We both shared our thoughts and feelings through every moment, and we truly listened to each other's perspectives. We talked about his new job in London. He was working for Arup as a refurbishment structural engineering consultant. Sam explained that he was currently on a 16 week assignment in London to refurbish the

Sainsbury National Gallery in Trafalgar Square. The assignment was only the design stage of the project, but he wouldn't be involved in the actual refurbishment like he had been with Eden and Associates. He had just completed week two of the project and said that he was really enjoying this pre-planning part of the project. Sam explained that's who he had been meeting with at dinner. The other man was another consultant on the job and they had met to review the current design plans and to get on the same page with their ideas. That's why he had returned to that conversation and not said anything to me in the restaurant. He didn't feel like he knew the man well enough to abandon their conversation abruptly, so he was trying to wrap it up as quickly as possible.

Of course he was. Because it was Sam, and he's always aware of others 'feelings. He's always doing everything he can to make everyone else feel good. It had nothing to do with me at all. I should have known, but I was so insecure that he didn't want me any more that I jumped to conclusions.

After another hour had gone by, the bartender came over and said they would be closing soon. He placed the check on our table and Sam immediately grabbed it before I could even make a move. He paid the bartender and thanked him.   We collected our things and stood from the table to walk out of the lounge.

"Will you walk me to my room?" I asked Sam.

"Of course," he returned without hesitation. We rode the lift to my floor and headed down the hall to my room on the fifth floor. I unlocked the door and pushed my way inside. I turned as I held the door open and Sam remained at the threshold of the door.

"Don't you want to come in?" I asked him.

"Desperately," he replied. "But I don't think I should be in a hotel room with you right now, " he said.

I smiled and said, "Surely we can control ourselves."

"You might be able to. I'm less convinced I'll be able to," Sam returned with heat in his eyes.

The desire between us was obvious, and I was feeling weak as well. Maybe he was right. We couldn't be trusted right now. So, I stepped back toward the door and gave Sam a hug. He leaned in and kissed me sweetly. Then he asked, "How long are you in London? Can I see you again?"

"I'm here through Monday. I'll leave on Tuesday morning to take the train to Bristol for a project that Mr. Murray has me overseeing for the next few months," I replied. Sam's face fell and I could see the disappointment in him that we would be separated for so long.

"Are you free tomorrow?" he asked.

"Yes, I have a planning meeting with Mr. Murray and the execs on this project in Bristol tomorrow morning from 8:00 to about noon, but I should be free after that," I responded. "What do you have in mind?" I quizzed him.

"I'm not sure yet. I just know that I want to spend the day with you," Sam said.

I replied with a grin and said, "Let's meet for lunch and then we'll go from there."

Sam said he would pick me up here outside the hotel at noon. We said our goodbyes with another kiss and hug. Sam turned and walked back toward the lift as I watched him go. I closed the door and leaned back against it. I was sad to see him go. I wanted him to stay, but I knew we wouldn't be able to control ourselves if he stayed. We wanted each other too bad. I wouldn't be able to stay true to my values if he stayed. I was too in love.

I slept like a rock that night and woke the next morning with absolute giddiness about seeing Sam later in the day. I showered, got dressed and headed downstairs to grab a coffee before my meeting with Mr. Murray and the execs. I had reserved a small conference room here in the hotel for us to meet. We spent the morning poring over the plans for the project in Bristol and laying out all the design steps and needs. The morning flew by and around 11:30 we were done. We were all feeling good and pretty confident about the expectations of the project. I texted Sam to let him know that I was going to change into something more casual and then I would be waiting for him outside the hotel within about 15 minutes. He responded immediately with, "I'm here already. Waiting outside. See you soon." Apparently, he was more giddy than I was.

As I stepped outside the hotel, I looked to my left and then to my right. I spotted Sam smiling back at me and walking toward me. He reached me and pulled me in for a hug like he hadn't seen me in years. "I hope you're not starving," he said. We've got a little drive ahead of us before lunch."

"Oh really?" I said surprised. "What have you got up your sleeve?" I asked.

"We're heading to the Cotswolds," Sam replied.

Now, I was even more giddy. I had always wanted to visit the Cotswolds. I had seen pictures of how quaint the villages were and I couldn't wait to get there. Sam ushered me to his car that was parked nearby. He opened the door and I slid inside and settled. Sam had become a pro at navigating traffic in the UK. He swiftly drove us out of the heart of London and onto the motorway. It was a beautiful day out. The sun was shining with intermittent cloud coverage. It was still chilly out, but it wasn't raining and when the sun popped out, it was downright gorgeous.

We spent the drive talking and catching up. I told him about my trip to the states, selling my house, getting rid of Michael's belongings, and returning to Edinburgh. He told me about moving to London and finding his current job. Then the conversation moved on to all kinds of other things. Our hopes, dreams, the future. The conversation very quickly headed in the direction of our future together.

"Krista, can you see yourself marrying again?" Sam asked, looking over at me with a serious expression..

"Yes, I can," I replied as I returned his gaze. He squeezed my hand, smiled, and returned his focus to the road. We spent the day having lunch in Bourton on the Water and strolling along its whimsical streets and popping in shops. It was a wonderful day with good food, good sights, and the best company I could ask for. Our drive back to London at dusk was beautiful. I only felt slightly bad for getting sleepy and nodding off while leaving Sam on his own to navigate our way back by himself.

As we arrived back in the city, I awoke and looked around to see where we were. Sam said, "Good morning" jokingly as I rubbed my eyes.

"I'm sorry I fell asleep on you," I said.

"No worries. I'm glad you could rest, " he replied. Then Sam said, "Would you mind coming to my flat? I'd like to make you dinner and we can just relax. Maybe watch a movie together or just hang out?"

"Yes, that sounds perfect," I said.

We spent the evening just relaxing and being together. It was wonderful. We worked so well together and it felt so comfortable. Dinner was really good and I was thrilled to learn Sam could cook so well. After dinner, we settled onto the couch and watched a movie together as we held hands and snuggled under a blanket.

Once the movie was over, I sat up and said, "Well, it's late. I should probably get back to my hotel."

Sam looked at me with a pause and said, "Will you stay with me tonight?"

I looked at him with both longing and hesitancy. I wanted to, but it was dangerous. We both desired more with each other and I knew it. We both knew it.

"I promise to be good," Sam said. "Nothing will happen that you don't want to happen," he continued.

"That's the problem," I whispered. "I want you and I'm afraid I'll break my own rule."

"How about if I sleep on the couch and you can sleep in my bed?" he asked. "I just want you here with me," Sam said.

"Ok," I said. He smiled as if he had won the blue-ribbon prize at the county fair. Sam tucked me into his bed and made sure I had everything I needed. He kissed me on the forehead, and went out to the living area to settle on the couch. I must have fallen asleep instantly because when I woke, I felt like I had only been asleep for about an hour. But the smell of bacon, eggs, and coffee told me that morning had arrived. I looked over at my phone and it read 7:30. Lazily, I stretched and managed to pull myself out of bed. I went to the bathroom to run my hands through my hair and brush my teeth. Sam had put out an extra toothbrush for me.

Then I wandered into the kitchen and living area to find Sam. He was busy cooking the eggs in a pan on the stove while the bacon was cooking in the oven. It smelled heavenly and my stomach grumbled in desperation for some food. Sam looked up and smiled briefly, but his smile fell to an intense look almost instantly as he looked at me. It dawned on me this was a look of desire, and I realized that I was in one of his t-shirts and my panties….and nothing else. I should have put my clothes back on. Sam looked away quickly and went back to frying the eggs as I saddled myself onto the bar stool.

"Good morning," he said as he busied himself.

"Good morning," I returned.

"Did you sleep okay? Would you like some coffee?" Sam asked.

"Yes, I slept so well. Like a rock apparently," I responded. "I would love some coffee, but I can get it myself," I said as I slid right back off the chair and headed toward the coffee machine. I grabbed a cup and filled it with coffee. Then I scooted past Sam to see if there was some creamer in the fridge. I was skeptical since Sam doesn't drink creamer, but when I opened the door there was the creamer. He had obviously gotten it this morning just for me because it was brand new and unopened. It made me smile and I turned to Sam and said, "thank you for the creamer" as I smiled at him.

Sam looked at me and returned my smile. I approached him and reached up on my tiptoes, and gave him a soft kiss. His hands were full holding the pan handle in one hand and the spatula in the other. When I pulled back from the quick kiss, heat spread to his eyes. He dropped both items on the stovetop and quickly spun to scoop me up. He wrapped his arms around my waist and I wrapped mine up around his neck. He kissed me passionately and his right arm dropped down to my backside and slid down my exposed leg. Then he slid his hand up under the t-shirt and up to my bare waist. He rested there for just a moment as our kiss deepened. Then his hand continued its journey up along my ribcage and his thumb grazed my side ever so slightly. My breath caught and I pulled back. The desire between us was palpable and was just about to get out of control. Sam broke our kiss and pulled back.

"I'm sorry," he said breathlessly. 'I just want you so bad," he continued.

I let out a sigh and said, "I know the feeling," as I smiled up at him. We both stood back from each other and fought to regain our composure and keep ourselves in check. Sam returned to cooking and soon after that we sat at the bar top and ate our breakfast together.

Sam drove me back to my hotel in the early afternoon after we had spent a lazy morning together. He walked me to my room once again and then asked, "Can we plan to try to see each other? I don't mind driving to see you on the weekends if you're willing."

"Of course. I would love that," I responded. "Do you have anything planned for next weekend?" I asked.

"Just coming to see you," he replied with a grin.

I grinned in return and said, "perfect." We gave each other a long hug and I could feel that neither of us wanted to let go. We wanted to stay that way forever and the thought of being apart at all was devastating to both of us. But, we finally broke our embrace and said goodbye. Watching Sam walk down the hall to the lift was excruciating. I've never wanted to quit my job and just follow someone else around so badly in all my life. My heart was already hurting and he wasn't even out of sight yet. Just as he got to the lift and pushed the button, he turned back to look at me. Our eyes locked as we smiled at each other. The love between us was real. Sam stepped onto the lift and gave me a sad little wave as the doors closed. I blew out a breath and shut my door. I already couldn't wait for the week to go by so I could see him again.

Twenty-Four

Monday morning came quickly and I was rushing out the door of the hotel to catch the train to Bristol. I frantically pushed my suitcase on its wheels while I carried my backpack, crossbody bag, and my work bag all strapped to me. The train station was about a 15 minute walk from my hotel so I had planned to just walk, but I was now regretting my decision. It was frigidly cold today and there was a light, blowing mist falling which made things pretty miserable. I could hail a cab, but at this point I was only a few minutes away so it seemed ridiculous to get a cab now for just a few blocks. I decided I could suck it up, man up a little, and tough it out. I wouldn't melt and a little cold rain never hurt anyone.

By the time I reached the train station, my hair was completely soaked. Thank goodness I didn't have any immediate business meetings today because I would definitely look like a drowned rat by the time I got there. I went into the station and checked the boards so I could figure out which platform I needed to be on. I had my ticket QR code on my phone, and once I reached the correct platform, I scanned it to get through the turnstile kiosk. The overhead announcements indicated that my train was due to depart in 3 minutes. Oh crap. Talk about cutting it close. I hurriedly walked at a fast pace to get to the correct train car and hoisted my suitcase up as quickly as I could. The train car had luggage racks located at both ends of the car so I put my suitcase up and headed toward the center of the car to find my seat. I had reserved a seat at a table so that I could get a little work done on the trip. I placed my backpack in the overhead rack and settled into my seat by the window. I was already exhausted and this day had just begun. I swore to myself I would never be rushed for time ever again. It's just way too stressful not to leave yourself enough time.

The train ride was supposed to be about an hour and fifteen or twenty minutes, so I decided to get out my laptop and check my emails. I also had some bookkeeping to catch up on as well, so that kept me occupied for the entirety of the trip. I occasionally looked up and stared out the window to catch the beautiful landscape as it scrolled by. Even though it was a cold, blustery, grey day in the English countryside, it was still beautiful and new to me.

The train arrived right on time and I collected my things as efficiently as possible. Thankfully, a kind older gentleman offered to help me get my suitcase down from the luggage bin and down the train car steps. I was really grateful because I had been dreading that the whole ride. Once I was off the train, I meandered my way through the station in Bristol and out to catch a cab. Thankfully, there were several cabs lined up outside the station, so I settled into one of them and told the driver the address to my home away from home for a while. It was a small efficiency type flat, but it offered everything I needed for the next few months. The kitchen was tiny with only two burners on the stovetop, but it was enough for me. I wasn't much of a big cook anyway, and let's face it....I ate out most of the time anyway. The full-sized bed was in the middle of the living space like a hotel room, so moving around a lot was not really an option. However, it did have the cutest little balcony overlooking the city with a tiny bistro table and two chairs. I could already envision myself sitting out there in the morning sipping my hot coffee and taking in the sights. The flat actually overlooked a very nice, and expansive park. Looking out the window of the balcony right now, there weren't a ton of people at the park, but it was about 11:00am on a Monday morning, so it probably wasn't peak time for park-goers.

I had already caught up on emails and bookkeeping for the business and I didn't have any meetings until tomorrow, so I decided that I would spend the day scouting out the city of Bristol. Thankfully, it wasn't raining here in the city as it had been in London, but it was still cold and grey. I bundled up with my coat, scarf, and gloves and headed out the door to have a look around. I had sort of searched Google maps of Bristol and kind of knew the general direction I wanted to go. Within just about two and half blocks, I found a quaint little coffee shop that literally pulled me inside. The smell was heavenly as I entered their door. The shop was small, but the character of it was picturesque. The wooden floors were creaky, the plaster walls had worn areas that exposed old brick, and the woodwork had been painted a deep rust color that made it feel like Autumn. I took a seat at one of the smallest two-top tables and the barista came and asked what I would like. I ordered a latte as I almost always did and he brought it back within just a couple of minutes. I sat, in peace, and enjoyed my coffee while watching the people pass by on the street. It reminded me of that first coffee shop I had found in Edinburgh when I first moved to Scotland. The thought of that time made me realize just how far I had come. That was a time of depression, sadness, grief, and utter sorrow that I was trying to work through by pushing myself into a new adventure. The hurt in my heart flickered for just a moment as I remembered what those days felt like. I was so grateful to be past that time of my life.

Once I finished my coffee, I thanked the barista on my way out the door. He smiled and wished me a good day, and I decided that this place was going to be my new go-to coffee spot while here in Bristol. I continued my walk at a leisurely pace and took in all the sights. I tried to make note of the street names so I could become familiar with the area around me. I passed restaurants and tried to commit them to memory for the future. I came across several little shops and I stopped in several of them to have a look around. Most of the shop keepers were friendly enough, and I even bought a new pair of "wellies" to wear on the job site for work.

Soon enough I realized that it was late afternoon and I hadn't had anything to eat all day. I had simply been too busy and rushed; not to mention that I had basically filled my tank with coffee and caffeine to keep me going. So, I continued to walk until I came across a small pub that looked appealing. I read the menu outside on the wall near the door and decided this place would do just fine. I entered and was immediately greeted by a waitress who told me to take a seat wherever I liked, so I sat at a small table by the window. She brought me a menu and took my drink order. In typical fashion, I couldn't resist ordering the fish 'n chips, but I told her she could leave the mashed peas in the kitchen. I love green peas, but mashed up was not my cup of tea.

Lunch was lovely and tasty. I mentally added this pub to my list of places to return before heading out the door. I walked back in the direction I had come as I figured it was probably time to go home. Along the way, I stopped at a cute little book shop and got a new book, and then I stopped in a small Tesco to grab some bottled water, snacks, coffee, and creamer before returning to my flat. Luckily it was pretty close to my flat so I didn't have to carry all that very far.

I spent the rest of the late afternoon and evening just relaxing and watching tv. I read a little of my new book as I tucked myself into bed early in the night. Just after 8:30 I heard my phone ding and I picked it up to find a text from Sam. "Hey there. Hope you made it to Bristol safely. Miss you already. Can't wait for the weekend to see you again. Could I come Friday evening?"

My heart did a flip flop of excitement just hearing from him and hearing how excited he was to see me. I responded immediately with, "Hi. Yes, I made it safely. Train ride was fun. I explored a little today. I miss you too. Of course you can come Friday. I will get off at 5 so maybe we can meet for dinner?'

"Sounds perfect. I hope your week on your new job site goes well. Love you. Sleep well," Sam replied.

After I responded one more time and told Sam I loved him too, we ended our exchange and I settled down to sleep. I laid my book on the nightstand and clicked off the lamp. I nestled my head on the pillow and watched the moonlight start to seep into the room. My mind remained on Sam and our short conversation. My heart was happy, but I missed him and was suddenly very sad we would be mostly apart for the next few months. I wished that we could work together as we previously had. I longed to return to Edinburgh and work in the office next to him, and ride to and from work with him everyday, and spend the weekends eating out and going on hikes together.

None of that could happen now and I felt completely responsible for that outcome. If I hadn't overreacted and punished him, we wouldn't be separated now. I felt so guilty for the chain reaction I had caused. But, there was nothing I could do about it now. We had to make the best of what we had. I was just grateful that Sam still wanted me, and that we had run into each other in London. That was completely dependent on fate. I was suddenly exhausted and my eyes felt heavy. I went to sleep thinking of Sam. I couldn't wait to see him in a few days.

I awoke the next morning at about 5:00am. I put on my running clothes and shoes and headed out the door. I had found a nice running path nearby and decided that would be my daily exercise until I found a good gym to go to. Running in the current weather was going to be brutal. It was still very wintery despite being the month of April and we had had snow multiple times. I wasn't much for running outside even under the best conditions, but definitely not when it's cold, rainy, and snowy. So, finding a gym was going to be high on my priority list. I bundled up and got my run in. I went about 3 miles before returning to my flat. I was frozen on the outside, and hot on the inside. The warmth of my flat was very welcome and a hot shower was at the top of my to-do list.

I got ready and dressed as warmly and professionally as possible. I had a meeting near the job site first thing this morning with the project coordinators and associates from the Canal River and Trust organization. We would be going over the first steps of getting the project site organized and up and running. I took my backpack with warm, casual clothes and my new wellies for the actual site. I put on my black pants suit and black block heels. My hair looked good and I did a full face of makeup. I quickly headed out the door and went down to meet the Uber I had arranged. The driver jumped into traffic quickly and said the drive to our meeting place would be about 20 minutes. I asked if we could stop at a coffee shop, too, along the way, and told him I would buy him a coffee if he would be willing to stop. He smiled at me with a big grin in the rearview mirror and agreed heartily. He stopped after about 5 minutes of driving right in front of a coffee shop that he recommended and I ran inside to get the coffees. As promised, he waited for me and seemed genuinely happy to have a free coffee for his driving time this morning. Then we set off to our destination.

We arrived at one of the offices of Canal River and Trust where we were scheduled to have our meeting. I entered the door and the receptionist was immediately to my left when I came through the door. She greeted me with obligatory pleasantries, but didn't appear to be truly friendly. She came across as slightly bothered and snooty to be honest. It made me wonder if the rest of the company was like this. In my experience, the front person or face that you see when you first enter a company is generally reflective of the overall demeanor of the bosses. It's usually a trickle-down effect. I made note of this and decided to be cautious in my interactions with the executives. I needed to be on guard and on my A game. I put my shoulders back and decided that complete confidence needed to be evident in my body language and facial expressions.

Ms. Snooty pants ushered me into a large conference room and motioned to a chair for me to take a seat. She asked if I wanted something to drink, but I could tell she had no interest in actually providing anything for me. She was simply required to ask. So, in an effort to make her work a little harder, I requested a coffee with cream and sugar and a bottle of water. She obliged, but was definitely annoyed that I didn't say no. I snickered to myself as she left the room and the door closed behind her. Geez...Some people are so miserable. It must be hard to be that grumpy.

After about 10 minutes, the executives finally came into the conference room and began introducing themselves. I stood to greet them and shook each of their hands with confidence and a firm hand shake. No limp noodle handshakes from me. I needed them to feel confident in my abilities right away. I needed every single thing I did and said to exude strength. I sat down after our introductions and didn't wait for them. I wanted it to feel like this was my meeting; not theirs. I immediately jumped into the meat of the meeting by letting them know I was eager to get started. I laid out the project plans and details step by step. I especially focused on my tasks and timeline during this first week in the hopes that a detailed account of my plans would help alleviate any concerns they might have. This plan appeared to be working because I could tell by their body language they were receptive to my information. They were nodding their heads in agreement and I could visibly see their shoulders and faces relax after a few minutes. The head guy interjected and asked me some clarifying questions here and there, but the others remained quiet the whole time. I suspect they were "filler" suits meant to intimidate and try to snuff out whether I was up to the job. I'm sure they all still had their doubts about a woman leading the charge.

However, after all the concerns and questions had been addressed, they all seemed content with the project plans I had laid out. No more questions were asked, and everyone began standing to shake hands again and make their departure. I assured them I would stay in contact about the project needs, progress, and timeline. They seemed positively responsive and filed out of the room. The head exec thanked me for my time and told me to be sure and let him know if I needed anything. He also said I could reach out to Ms. Banks, his assistant, if I needed anything else. He nodded toward Ms. Banks which turned out to be Ms. Snooty pants. I thought to myself, "yeah right. I wouldn't ask her for anything if my life depended on it. She'll be the opposite of helpful." But, I just nodded and smiled graciously as we exited the conference room.

Outside their office, I waited on the sidewalk for my Uber to arrive. I could have waited inside where it was warm, but that would have meant being in the same space as Ms. Banks for longer and that didn't seem like a good option to me. So freezing outside it was. The drive to the job site was about 25 minutes, so I enjoyed the sights of the city on the way. This job was really a compilation of several small jobs on various bridge reinforcements around Bristol stemming from the River Avon that fingered its way into the city. As I understood it, there were multiple historic bridges of varying sizes that required restoration and reinforcement and that was our mission. So, we were starting on the first of about 5 bridges today. The driver arrived on site and I thanked him and got out of the car. I was immediately met by the foreman of the crew that Eden and Associates had hired to complete these jobs. He greeted me with a handshake and introduced himself as Jaime St. Clair.

He was a giant, brute of a man with a firm handshake himself, but his face lit up when he spoke and he had a twinkle in his eyes that made me relax. His eyes crinkled when he smiled, and that smile was big and contagious. He seemed like a big 'ole giant teddy bear. His crew consisted of about 50 men from what I could tell. They were all standing around talking with one another as they sat on their large pieces of equipment and machinery. I was so grateful that Mr. Murray had taken care of hiring the crew and foreman prior to the job. This particular crew was experienced in bridge work and they had their own equipment. Mr. Murray had said they were pricey, but he couldn't pass up their knowledge, skills, and experience. I was really grateful for that too. That probably meant my job was going to be a lot easier.

Mr. St. Clair and I agreed that we needed to have a quick meeting, look over the plans, and get on the same game plan. I told him I was eager to get started, but I just needed a few minutes to change into more appropriate site attire. He laughed and agreed that might be a good plan, so I quickly used one of the porta potties I had delivered to the site. Changing in there was challenging, but I got the job done and met Mr. St. Clair back at the site tent. We sat down and I rolled out the project blueprint for us to look at together. Mr. St. Clair seemed pretty knowledgeable about what needed to be done first, so it didn't take long for us to get on the same page. Once we were done with that, I asked if his crew had had breakfast. He said they had, so I assured him that I would get lunch here for them by noon. I told him I would be working at the tent and he should come get me or call me if he needed anything. We exchanged phone numbers and he set off across the way toward his men. I could hear and see him gathering his crew for a meeting. He quickly seemed to organize them into subgroups with instructions on what to do and the men immediately jumped into action. You could tell they had done this many times and worked well as a cohesive team. The nerves inside me were beginning to settle as I could tell they were going to make this as seamless as possible.

While they worked, I responded to emails, got lunch ordered and on the way, called to make sure their accommodations were confirmed, and called and ordered a few more on site facilities. We were going to need more tents for breaks, porta potties, snacks, first aid gear, and propane heaters. It was frigid out here and these men (and I) were going to need somewhere to knock the chill off.

Lunch arrived at about 11:45 and I quickly jumped in to set up tables and chairs and get the food ready for them to go through the line. I texted Mr. St. Clair and told him lunch was ready and currently hot, so they needed to come to the tent. I could hear the machinery slow down and shut off and soon heard a group of voices headed toward the tent. The men entered the tent and I could tell they were impressed. I don't think they were used to having such good conditions for their lunch breaks. I got the feeling they were used to cold sandwiches that they had to eat standing up in the weather. The tent was large, fully enclosed from the weather, and warm from the large propane heaters. The food was buffet style and hot. The men quickly filled their paper plates and sat at the tables to dig in. The mood was light and jovial. They were eating, talking, and laughing. I stayed near the food to make sure I could replace items if certain things ran low. Then I began walking around and offering bottles of water to the crew. They were very thankful and complimentary.

Mr. St. Clair approached me and said, "I just want to thank you for such great accommodations. The men aren't used to conditions this nice and I can tell they appreciate it. You've done a wonderful job, Mrs. Andrews."

"Please, call me Krista. And I'm so glad they're enjoying the lunch. I want these site projects to go smoothly and I want you and your crew to be treated well," I responded. He smiled at me with gratitude as he nodded his appreciation and returned to sit with his men. I appreciated the fact that he seemed to have such a great relationship with his crew. I think that's a true testament of a great leader. By 12:30, and without a word said, all the men got up from the tables and started cleaning up. They threw their trash away and headed back out to the work site. I was amazed. No one said a word to them. Mr. St. Clair didn't announce that it was time to get back to work. They just seemed to know and collectively left together.

The rest of the day flew by and the men stopped working at about 5:30. Mr. St. Clair thanked me again for everything and told me they would see me first thing in the morning. It had been a great day with lots of progress already. I was so tired and so relieved. After today, I knew the rest of this project was going to go smoothly. I packed up my things and slung my bags over my shoulder just as my driver arrived to pick me up. The company had arranged for me to have a private driver each morning and evening, so I hopped in the car and headed back toward my flat. Dinner was a microwaved meal, and then I went straight to bed. I was tired, but it had been a wonderful first day.

Twenty-Five

T his week went by fast and slow all at the same time. Work went by quickly because the work site had been so busy. But, waiting for Friday to finally get here so that I could see Sam seemed to take forever. The crew made exceptional progress in just a few short days and I was convinced they would blow our timeline out of the water if they worked that fast the whole time. They were a pricey crew, but man were they worth every penny. They worked fast and efficiently, and they were just a great group of men. They were respectful and appreciative of everything.

Friday had finally arrived and all I could do was think about seeing Sam. He texted early this morning and said, "Good morning beautiful. Can't wait to see you tonight. I'll be there by 6." I was absolutely as giddy as a schoolgirl. I packed my backpack with a change of clothes, my makeup, and things to help me freshen up after work so I could meet him at the restaurant. I made reservations at one of the places in the heart of Bristol that a local at my favorite coffee shop recommended.

The day went by quickly and we were so busy. The crew was hard at work and Mr. St. Clair and I had to work out some issues that popped up. We had to come up with some solutions that would alter the plans slightly, so I had to be in contact quite a bit with Mr. Murray about the change of plans. I had been on the phone a ton today with him going back and forth trying to solve issues between the blueprint plans and reality. I was quickly learning that just because something had been planned out in a blueprint draft didn't mean that's exactly how it was going to be once you dug into the work site. Adjustments had to be made, so I was essentially the mediator between the work crew and the engineers who planned the restructuring. It required me to learn a whole new set of vocabulary and language to help mediate between the two while trying to keep emotions low. It had been a long day, but we made it work and everyone seemed happy with the new plans. The crew quickly made the necessary adjustments after Mr. St. Clair relayed the new instructions.

I was working on my laptop in the tent when I heard the machines begin to wind down and the sound of men' s voices picked up as they were walking to their vehicles. It triggered me to look at my phone and check the time. It was 5:00. "Oh shoot!.," I thought to myself. I had to get changed and get ready for dinner. It would take me at least 30 minutes to travel to the restaurant. I texted the driver and he said he was about 10 minutes out from the work site. I let him know I would be changing and needed about 20 minutes to be ready to go.

I hurriedly changed in one of the porta potties. It was definitely not ideal, but it was all I had. When I got back to the tent, I packed up all my stuff just as the driver was pulling in. I hopped into the car's back seat and decided that I could freshen up my makeup and hair in the car. I got busy freshening up with deodorant, touched up my makeup, brushed my hair and sprayed a little hairspray, then some perfume. The poor driver was probably about to choke on all my products, but he didn't show it. Once I put all my things away and settled into my seat, I took a deep breath and blew it out. I was nervous for some reason. Was it nerves? Or just excitement? Either way, I was feeling a little jazzed and had to make myself take some deep breaths to calm down.

I gave the driver the address and he entered it into his navigation app on his phone mounted on the dash of the car.

I could see that it said we were about 4 minutes away. It was 5:52. I was going to arrive just in time. We pulled up to the door of the restaurant that was on a busy street. There was nowhere to park so the driver just had to stop quickly and let me out and then he drove away. I had my backpack, work bag, and purse with me. I looked like I was going to move into the restaurant. It was not a great situation to have to haul all this into the restaurant, but it couldn't be helped. I opened the door and entered the lobby of the restaurant. The host greeted me and I told him my name for the reservation.

He said, "Ah yes, the rest of your party arrived just a few moments ago. Follow me." Oh my. Sam was here. I couldn't wait to see him. I followed behind the host as we made our way through the restaurant. It had wooden floors and my heeled boots click-clacked with every step. I felt pretty and my outfit looked good. I had chosen a pair of fancy denim jeans with a wide leg and cinched high waist. I paired it with a body-hugging long sleeve chocolate brown top with a mock neck. My brown belt and brown, pointed-toe boots matched perfectly.

We snaked our way through the restaurant and finally I could see Sam sitting at a round table booth in the back. He was looking down at his phone and didn't see me approaching until he heard the host say, "just here ma'am."

Sam looked up and smiled as he stood quickly to greet me. He took my breath away. He was so attractive and it was almost as if I had forgotten over the last week what he looked like. He was dressed in a nice button-down dark blue shirt with jeans. He looked casual, but nicely put together. He had good taste. His hair looked freshly cut and styled. It was dark, but the grey was filtering into the sides just every so slightly. His eyes pierced me as he looked at me with what seemed like love, desire, relief, excitement, and control.

I thanked the host and immediately started taking off all my bags and putting them on the floor next to the table. Sam helped me with them and once I was rid of them, I slung my arms up and around his neck and kissed him. I could feel him give back exactly the same amount of love I was showing him. His arms wrapped around me and we hugged for longer than we probably should have in the middle of a restaurant. We didn't care though. We were so glad to see each other and be together. It was like we were still making up for the time we had been apart and were still apologizing to each other for wasting time.

We finally released each other and slid into the booth. Sam had ordered water and my favorite drink which were already on the table so I took a sip of both. I took a deep breath and relaxed into the seat. I finally felt calm for the first time today. Sam grabbed my hand and said, "Rough day?"

"No, not rough. Just long and busy. Lots of problem-solving today and I finally feel like I can relax for the first time today," I said. "How was your day? Your week?" I questioned.

"Good. It's been a productive, good week at work, but I'm glad it's over. And I'm glad to be here with you," he said.

Sam and I ordered our food, and then we talked about our jobs and our days. It was so nice to rehash work problems and ideas with someone who understood. It also made me realize how much I needed that. I didn't have any friends here in Bristol. I had no one to talk to about work or just life in general and that suddenly made me feel extremely lonely and sad for myself. My days consisted of getting up early to workout, going to work all day, and then coming home and watching TV, or reading for a couple of hours, and then going to bed. Other than small chit-chat or my professional interactions with the work crew and Mr. St. Clair, I basically didn't really talk to anyone. I suddenly realized what a burden that was on my heart and psyche. I was suddenly very aware of how much I needed people in my life. I realized how much I needed Sam; how much I wanted him in my life. He was patient with me, kind, smart, and a good listener. He was everything I needed and wanted.

Sam could tell I was deep in thought and squeezed my hand to bring me back to the moment. "What's going on?" he asked. "Is everything okay?"

"Oh yeah….sorry. I just….. I don't know," I sputtered as I looked down at the table.

"Hey…..what is it?" he pressed with a worried look.

I looked back up at him and tears welled into my eyes. Sam could see the hurt on me and he instantly scooted himself closer to me on the booth to embrace me. He was worried about me.

"I'm sorry," I whispered. "I'm just being emotional, I guess."

"There's obviously something bothering you. Please tell me," Sam pleaded.

After a moment and a sigh, I said, "I just kind of realized right now how lonely I am. I don't have any friends here. I don't know anyone, and I really don't have the opportunity to talk about my daily life with anyone in person. It wasn't until just now, being here and talking with you, that I realized I need more of that in my life. I'm just lonely," I said. I was ashamed and embarrassed for being such a big baby about it. I felt like I was just being whiny

Sam hugged me and held me for a long time without saying a word. Then he finally released me and looked at me and said, "I know exactly how you feel. I feel the same way. It's hard." He continued, "Honestly, I miss you. I love talking to you and spending time with you. I never get tired of it, and I crave it now. I've been thinking about it a lot this week. I wish we could just be together......all the time."

"Me too," I said. "I wish we were at least in the same town and could share our lives together every day."

We kissed. They were sweet, single kisses that were tender and filled with so much love between us. It was obvious that we both wanted more. We wanted a life together. I realized at that moment that I wanted to marry Sam. I wanted to spend the rest of my life with him. I had spent the last ten months getting to know him, spending time with him, and falling in love with him despite our struggles and bizarre connection to one another. It was fate. And, I didn't even believe in fate. Until now.

Our food arrived at that moment, so we separated ourselves and tried to return to normalcy and enjoy our meal and time together. We continued to have good conversations and enjoyed our dinner together. We were at the restaurant for about two hours just taking our time together, talking, enjoying and sharing our food, and soaking each other in. It was so needed and good for my soul.

Sam insisted on paying the check as he always does, despite my objections and pleading to let me pay. After dinner, Sam said he would drive me to my flat, so we walked a couple of blocks to his car. I asked him if he had gotten a hotel room or where he was staying. He said, "I haven't made any arrangements yet. The company I work for has a standing reservation at The Radisson Blu Hotel. My boss told me I was welcome to use it anytime I'm in town. I told him about you working here for the next few months and that's probably where I would be for a lot of weekends." Sam smiled at me and it sent a warm feeling into my gut to know that he had talked to his boss about me. It warmed me even more to know that he was devoted to seeing me as much as possible.

As we settled into Sam's car, I gave him the address to my flat to plug into his phone and we started off. The drive to my flat was quiet. We didn't talk much, but we held hands and enjoyed taking in the sights of the city passing us by. When we arrived at my flat, Sam parked in the dedicated parking spot for this flat. I didn't need it since I don't have a car, but the flat came with a spot which is pretty unusual.

Sam quickly got out and came around to open the door for me and help me with my bags. He carried them up the stairs and I unlocked the door. We both stepped inside and Sam set my bags down near the small table. He looked around and said, " It's nice. Quaint."

"You mean tiny," I said with a laugh.

He chuckled and said, "Yeah, it's a little small, but still nice." He walked over to the balcony door and said, "your balcony is nice though. I bet you sit out there and drink your coffee in the mornings, don't you?" he asked.

I smiled at Sam and said, "You know me so well."

Sam walked over and hugged me. He said, "I guess I better be going. What do you want to do tomorrow? Do you want me to pick you up in the morning and we can go find some trouble to get into?" he asked with a wink.

"Well, the first thing I want is for you to stay with me tonight. So we can wake up together in the morning," I said. I looked up into his eyes and waited to see his response to that bid. His response was that of immediate lust and confliction at the same time. I could tell he desperately wanted to stay, but he was struggling with the idea of staying with me and managing to control his desires. Keeping our physical relationship in check was proving to be more and more difficult. We connected so deeply in every other way and our desire to be physically intimate was increasing by the day. Sam was clearly determined to respect my wishes regarding physical intimacy. To be honest, it was getting difficult for me to resist as well, but I really wanted to be near him tonight.

Sam blew out a breath and said, "Ok, I'll sleep on the couch. Let me go down and get my bag out of my car." While he went down to the car, I poured us each a drink. I bought Sam his favorite beer and I had my favorite gin drink. I lit a candle in the living room and also lit the one on the small bistro table on the balcony. I grabbed a blanket, wrapped myself into it, and went out onto the balcony with our drinks. Sam came back in with his bags and locked the door behind him. He found me on the balcony and poked his head out. "What are you doing out here?" he asked.

"I just thought we could enjoy a nightcap out here and enjoy the nighttime scenery of the city for a while," I said. He smiled and grabbed his jacket to join me on the balcony. We sat and talked while we sipped our drinks. He pulled his chair close to mine and I snuggled into him while he put his arm around me. I pulled my blanket over us both and settled in to feel the warmth of his body beside me. We enjoyed the sounds of the city, talking with each other, and hanging out. It seemed we never ran out of things to talk about.

The signs of spring were just beginning to show in subtle ways. It was still cold and chilly out, but there were beginning to be more days with some sunshine and springtime flowers blooming in the countryside. It felt fresh and like newness was on the horizon. Like life was going to be refreshed, and I felt joy at the mere thought of moving forward in life. With Sam.

After about an hour on the balcony, I was frozen to the bone and decided going inside was necessary before my fingers snapped in two. I blew out the candle and Sam grabbed our glasses to take them inside. I headed to the bathroom to get ready for bed. I put on my black silk shorts pajamas set. I couldn't stand sleeping in long pajamas or thick material no matter how cold it got at night. I just felt claustrophobic in those types of pajamas, but I loved using shorts sets. This pair was black with a top that had short sleeves and buttoned down the front. The shorts and the top were trimmed with light pink piping that gave them a feminine appeal. I brushed my teeth, took off my makeup, and did my 10-step skincare routine that I was convinced was going to keep me looking young forever. Then I brushed through my hair and turned off the bathroom light and walked back out. Sam was in the living room unfolding a blanket and placing it on the couch. He had already stolen a pillow off my bed to use on the couch.

"Sam," I called to stop and get his attention. He turned to look at me. "I want you to sleep with me. In my bed," I said.

"Krista.....I want to. Desperately. But I'm not sure that's a good idea if you want to keep my hands off you," he replied. He said it with intensity but a slight smile to lighten the moment.

"I know it's hard. For both of us. And, I really appreciate you respecting my wishes on that front. But, I just want to lay next to you. To not feel lonely. I want to feel your body and warmth next to me. I want to wake up feeling safe and secure next to you," I added with a longing look on my face.

Sam walked over and slid his hands down my arms to my hands and then laced his fingers with mine. He looked down at my face and said, "Ok. I'll do my best to be good." I smiled up in return, happy that I had convinced him.

I turned off the bedroom light so that only my bedside lamp was illuminating the room. I slipped into bed and under the heavy blankets. I was freezing to death and couldn't seem to warm up. Sam showered and came into the bedroom once he was done. He looked mouth wateringly good. He was wearing a pair of black shorts and a T-shirt. His hair was still wet from his shower and I could smell his body wash on him as he slipped under the covers on his side of the bed. My mouth went dry. Then I wondered… what in the world I was thinking. This was going to be just as hard for me as it would be for him. I wanted him. I smiled at Sam as he settled under the covers and adjusted his pillow.

I turned off the bedside lamp and we lay there in silence for a few moments. Then Sam started making small talk. It kind of broke the tension and helped us both relax. We talked about our childhood. Sam said he remembered that his childhood room had glow in the dark stars on the ceiling that his mom had put up there. When he couldn't sleep or settle down, he would look at those stars and count them. Kind of like counting sheep and he could always go to sleep. I told him that I had a similar thing when I was a kid. My mom had gotten me a kind of stargazer lamp that rotated the stars around the room, and I would watch that until my eyelids grew heavy.

I shuddered as we talked and tried to bring the blankets up around myself because I was still cold. Sam could feel me shaking and asked, "Are you cold?"

"Yes, I'm sorry. I'm shaking. I can't seem to get warm. Maybe sitting outside for an hour wasn't a good idea," I scoffed.

Sam immediately rolled toward me and slid over next to me. He reached his arm around me and pulled me close to him. He wrapped his leg over my legs and nestled his face into my neck. I could feel his body heat and it instantly felt wonderful and warm. He was like a furnace. At first, I was stiff and didn't want to move, but then I couldn't help myself. I felt my body relax and lean into him. I took a deep breath and smelled his scent. Heavenly. We lay there in silence and I could feel and hear Sam's breathing begin to deepen. His breaths became longer and heavier. I could feel his body weight become heavier against me. He was relaxing and falling asleep. I turned my body into him slightly so that I was facing him more and I wrapped my arm around his waist. I reached up and stroked his hair and petted him until my eyes became heavy. Sleep was pulling me under too. I felt the safest, most loved, and most comfortable I had been in over a year. Nothing was better than this feeling right now. I wanted it to last forever.

Twenty-Six

I woke the next morning to the sun streaming in through the window. I was faced toward the window and away from Sam. We were no longer snuggled together and I wondered at what point we had let go of each other. I rolled over to see if Sam was still in bed. He was lying flat on his back, but turned his head in my direction and sleepily opened his eyes. I smiled at him and stretched out my arm to touch him with my hand. "Good morning," he said quietly.

"Morning," I returned. "Did you sleep okay?" I asked.

"Like a rock," he replied as he grinned at me.

"I'm so glad," I whispered. I scooted over to him and nestled into his side as he wrapped his arm around me and kissed my forehead. "What do you want to do today?" I asked.

"This," he said. Sam lifted up onto his elbow so that he was over me and looking down. He looked into my eyes for a long moment and then leaned down and kissed me. It wasn't a sweet, tender kiss. It was a heated kiss that was dangerous and delicious. I could feel my body reacting to his kiss and touch. I gave back what he was giving and both of our breathing became ragged. We explored each other for a long time, and then Sam finally pulled away. We were both short of breath and a wildness was present in both of our eyes as we stared at one another. "I don't want to, but we have to stop," Sam said. "I'm about to reach a point of no return," he continued.

I nodded in agreement and Sam moved off of me. He got up and went to the bathroom while I got out of bed. I slipped on my robe and headed straight to my tiny kitchen to start the coffee. By the time Sam was out of the shower, I had his coffee waiting for him. Again he was freshly showered and smelling good. As he entered the living area and took his coffee, he thanked me and sat down on the couch. "You sure take a lot of showers," I said teasingly.

"I had to have a cold one this morning," he replied , giving me

a joking look back.

I chuckled and asked, "How would you feel about a hike this morning?"

"Sounds good to me," Sam returned. We sat and enjoyed our coffee together for the next forty-five minutes or so and then I finally got up and got dressed. It was sunny, but chilly out this morning, so I put on my fleece-lined leggings, a long-sleeve running shirt, and a quarter-zip tight running jacket. I pulled my hair into a ponytail and put on an ear-warmer headband. Sam, too, was prepared with his sweatshirt. and jogging pants. We both took rain jackets and a backpack with an extra change of clothes in case we decided to stay at the B&B that night. We were going to play it by ear and see what we felt like doing. We hopped into Sam's car and headed to Somerset. It was about a 40-minute drive and we decided that a visit to Cheddar Gorge was in order. We were excited to see the cliffs and caves this unique place had to offer. The sun was shining and it was a beautiful day for an adventure together. On our way, I got online on my phone and purchased tickets to the landmark.

Once we arrived and parked, we got a map of the area that showed the available trails and how to get to the cliffs. Sam and I had a wonderful day of hiking, taking in the sights, talking, and enjoying our day together. At around 4:30, we decided we would drive back to Bristol rather than stay the night. The B&B was pricey and we didn't feel like it was really worth it to stay when it wasn't that far from Bristol. So, we drove back and decided to go to dinner. First, we went back to my flat to shower and change. We were both sweaty and feeling a little gross, so cleaning up for dinner was in order.

While I was finishing getting ready, Sam found a restaurant with good reviews online. It was only about five blocks from my flat, so we decided to walk. Dinner was lovely and we both devoured our meals. A day of hiking had depleted our calories so we were ravenous. By the time we were finished, we were both looking and feeling a little tired. It had been a great day full of adventure and we were pooped. We walked back to my flat hand-in-hand. We strolled slowly and were in no rush to do anything but enjoy one another.

Sam once again stayed the night with me. The next morning we slept in and then had coffee together. At around noon, Sam reluctantly said that he probably needed to get back to London as he had some work to do to get prepared for his early Monday morning meetings. I nodded in agreement and said that I also had some things to get done. We stood in the doorway to my flat and held each other for the longest time. We didn't want to let go. We wanted to stay together all the time, but knew that wasn't possible right now. Sam finally broke our seal and I was thankful he did it because I couldn't bring myself to do it. As we were saying goodbye, I asked, "What if I come to London next weekend? Would that be okay?"

A smile slowly spread across Sam's face as he replied, "I would love that."

I returned the smile and said, "Great. I'll catch the train Friday evening after work. It might be kind of later when I get there. I'll leave work at five, come home and pack, and then get the train. It'll be an hour-and-twenty-minute ride. What stop should I get off at? I asked.

"You'll get off the train at Paddington and then take the tube from there to Piccadilly Circus" Sam said. "The tube ride is only about 10 minutes. I'll meet you outside the tube station at Piccadilly and walk with you to my flat. It's only a couple of blocks away."

"It's a date," I said as I kissed him goodbye. I watched Sam head down the stairs and disappear onto the street. My heart hurt at watching him go even though I knew I would see him in just a few days. It still hurts though. I didn't want to let him go. Ever. I decided I needed to keep myself busy the rest of the day so I wouldn't feel depressed with missing him. I changed into my workout clothes and headed out to the gym. I found a small gym about four blocks from my flat. It had good hours and was open seven days a week, which is kind of atypical for the UK. Businesses are not usually as accessible here as they are in the U.S., so I was excited to find a place that still felt small, had a good variety of weights and machines, and had good hours. The owners were a youngish couple in their thirties. They had been very friendly and warm when I went in to ask questions. The wife gave me a tour and answered all my questions eagerly. They even agreed to give me a prorated, month-to-month fee since I wouldn't be in Bristol for a long time.

I walked to the gym, did a really good workout, and then jogged back to my flat. By the time I got home, my sadness had subsided and I was busy getting laundry done and getting ready for my work week. Later that night I spent about an hour on the phone with my parents catching up and telling them all about my current job project and mine and Sam's status. They seemed genuinely relieved and happy that Sam and I had worked things out. My mom felt like us running into each other in London was fate, and a sign that we were meant to be together. I can't say that I disagree with her. I don't normally think like that, but this time was different.

I awoke the next morning at about 5am and went to the gym. My workout was fast, but power packed. Back at home, I showered and dressed quickly and my driver arrived at about 7:30 to take me to the work site. The day went by smoothly considering it was a Monday. There were very few problems to sort out that day and the crew was working at an unbelievable pace. Mr. St. Clair and I discussed the progress and he was almost certain they might be finished by the end of the next week. That would be nearly three weeks earlier than had been planned, and then they would be able to start on the next site. The second site was still in Bristol, so I was still stuck here for a while longer, but I was thrilled at the thought of wrapping up the whole project much faster than had been expected.

The days of the week went by fast and before I knew it, Friday was here. I woke that morning with absolute school-girl giddiness and butterflies in my stomach at the thought of going to see Sam this weekend.

I got up extra early this morning so that I could get my workout in and get myself packed for the weekend. I decided that I could just take my bags with me to the site and then have my driver deliver me straight to the train station after work instead of going home. That would help me not get there so late. I was more than a little nervous about traveling by myself on the train and tube late at night.

The day flew by. I was busy all day with emails, phone calls, bookkeeping, problem-solving with Mr. St. Clair, and Zoom meetings. Before I knew it, it was 5:30 and my driver was waiting on me. I grabbed my bags and piled into the car. I asked if he wouldn't mind finding a place for me to use the restroom so I could change clothes and grab a quick bite to eat to take with me on the train. He agreed and said he knew just the place.

After making a short pit stop at the cutest little sandwich shop for a bite, the driver dropped me off at the train station and I boarded the train to London. After rushing to make the 6:30 train, I settled into a seat to enjoy the ride. I pulled out my sandwich and drink and scarfed down my meal. I hadn't eaten really much of anything all day. Lunch time was kind of crazy today because the catering services arrived late and with the wrong order, so I spent the lunch hour sorting through that mess to make sure the crew were fed and just forgot to really feed myself. After eating, I pulled out my book and enjoyed some reading to pass the time.

We finally arrived at Picadilly station and I managed to get off the train with all my bags. As I exited the station, I found my way to the tube and got on the next one without much difficulty. I always have some anxiety about getting on the right one, but this seemed about as easy as it could be. The ride was short and when I got off and made my way up the stairs, I saw Sam standing right at the top of the stairs. What a breath of fresh air he was. I can't even describe the feeling of relief I had come over me when I saw him. It was like I hadn't breathed all week and now I could finally relax.

Sam scooped me up into a hug as if we hadn't seen each other in years. I hugged back and the feel of his warm, strong body against mine was instantly reassuring and made me feel like I was home. There was something about this man that just filled my cup to be near him. I could feel his strength and felt safe when I was with him. Not just that I was physically safe, but like my mind, spirit, and emotional well-being were safe too.

Sam grabbed my bags to carry in one hand and grabbed my hand with his other hand and led me down the busy sidewalk toward his hotel. It wasn't far at all and the hustle and bustle of the city around us was alive and electric on this Friday night. We entered Sam's hotel and it was a beautiful hotel in the heart of Soho. We walked through the lobby and headed straight for the lifts. Once inside the lift and the doors closed shut, Sam grabbed me up for a heated kiss. There was no holding back with this kiss. Our bodies were humming for each other. My mind went fuzzy and the rest of the world fell away. All the stress and worry of the week melted away. I could feel my body sink into him and I wrapped my arms around him. My hand went up to his neck and then I threaded my hand through his hair where the waves grazed the back of his neck. This motion caused Sam to groan and squeeze me even tighter. The next thing I heard was the ding of the lift as it arrived on our floor and the door slid open.

Sam and I finally pulled apart and came back to reality. We pulled ourselves together and hauled my bags off the lift. I followed Sam down the long hallway toward his room at the end of the hall. He unlocked the door with his keycard and pushed the door open as he motioned to me to enter. I went in and he followed me through with all my bags. It was a beautiful suite with a separate mini kitchen and living area. The bedroom and bathroom were located off the main area and there was a large king bed. The room had a great view of the street which showed off the city life going on down below.

Sam put my stuff down and asked me if I was hungry. I told him that I had already eaten a sandwich on the train. He said he had already eaten dinner too since he figured I would be getting in kind of late. It was about 8:15 by this time and Sam asked if I wanted to do anything or stay in. I told him I would be up for getting a drink if he was, so we agreed to go down to the hotel lounge for a cocktail. I freshened up in the bathroom by touching up my makeup, brushing my hair and spraying on some perfume. We headed downstairs and sat in the lounge for a couple of hours just catching up on our week, talking, and enjoying each other's company. It was a great end to a busy week.

The next morning, Sam and I woke kind of late. The sun was streaming in through the window and I looked over at my phone to see that it was about 8:30. We had slept in the same bed again and were managing to keep our physical relationship in check. But, I had to admit it was getting harder and harder to do. In my head I was thinking, we're going to have to get married so we can move this part of our relationship along. I kept that thought to myself because I wasn't sure how Sam felt about marriage. He had asked me if I would ever marry again and seemed pleased to know that I was open to that idea. However, he never mentioned it or said anything alluding to him wanting to get married. I really didn't know what direction we were headed and I was afraid to bring it up. I certainly didn't want to rush him into marriage.

We got up shortly after that and Sam had coffee delivered to the room. Then, he told me I needed to get dressed because he was taking me sightseeing today. I was actually pretty excited about that because I hadn't spent any time in London doing touristy things and I had really wanted to. We spent the day walking all over London. We hit as many tourist spots as we possibly could. Sam had gotten tickets to the Eye and The Tower of London. We also went to Westminster Abbey and on a river cruise. We then went to the Borough market and did some shopping. At about 5:30 we went back to the hotel to change and then go to dinner. Sam had made reservations at a fantastic restaurant in Soho. I was exhausted, but it had been the best day. We enjoyed the sights in London, and we enjoyed each other. We had been inseparable the whole day. We barely even let go of each other's hand all day.

On Sunday morning, we woke up and Sam took me to a lovely breakfast a few blocks from the hotel. We walked there and back. The weather was chilly, but the sun was shining so it was pretty pleasant. Then we went to Harrod's to look around. I was amazed at the size of the store and all they had to offer. We soaked in the day and squeezed in all we could before I had to get back on the train and head back to Bristol. The weekend had flown by so fast and our time together was never enough.

With each time I had to leave Sam, it got harder and harder. The sadness of not being together sunk deep into my bones. I hated this. Sam seemed equally sad about it. Then Sam said words I didn't want to hear. "I won't be able to see you next weekend. I have to go to Oxford on Thursday evening for a business trip. I will be there until Saturday and my last meeting that day is at 3:00, so I won't be back in London until later in the evening."

The disappointment was crushing. The thought of going two weeks without seeing him was awful. I hugged him tightly and we just held each other for a long while. I sighed finally and said, "Well, I guess I'll see you in a couple of weeks then." Sam smiled sadly as he tucked my hair behind my ear and kissed me again.

He went with me on the tube to get to the train station this time. He walked me and my bags to the train and helped me find my platform. We kissed and hugged goodbye and then I hauled myself and my stuff onto the train. I waved to him out the window once I had taken my seat. He smiled and waved back. Then, he turned and walked out of the station. I watched him walk out of sight and my heart absolutely hurt. Two weeks was going to be a long time without seeing this man I was in love with.

Twenty-Seven

Two weeks went by as slowly as humanly possible. Sam and I talked on the phone and texted each other as much as possible, but it wasn't good enough in my mind. I craved him. He seemed to feel the same about me, but he never really said it. That was one thing that was starting to bother me a little. Sam never really alluded to our future together. I didn't know if he didn't say anything because he didn't want to scare me off, or if he just really didn't feel the same about a future together. I didn't really know where I stood with him. He acted like he loved me, and he told me he loved me, but he didn't talk about a future together. I was starting to have some doubt in my mind about where we were headed. The time apart didn't help. When I wasn't with him, I couldn't gauge where we were in our relationship. We were no longer together every day like we had been when we worked together, so I couldn't get any kind of reinforcement about how he felt. It was starting to feel like a slippery slope.

On Tuesday of the second week, Sam wanted to know if he could come to Bristol for the weekend. I was excited that he wanted to make plans to come and told him he absolutely could. However, Mr. Murray called me later that afternoon and said he would be coming to Bristol on Friday and we would be meeting with the execs of the Canal and River Trust company to go over our progress and next steps with them on Saturday. After the meeting, we would be spending the rest of the day on the second site going over the plans and preparing for the second site project. So basically, I was going to be working most of the weekend.

While I was waiting for my driver to arrive around 5:30, I called Sam. He answered with, "Hey there beautiful." The sound of his voice made butterflies swirl in my stomach.

"Hi Sam. How are you?" I responded with a smile on my face.

"Good. I'm just getting off work and heading to the gym." he answered. "How are you?"

"I"m fine, but I have some bad news," I replied.

"Oh yeah.....what's that?" he quizzed.

"I"m not going to be able to have you this weekend. Turns out I'm going to be working basically the whole weekend," I told him. I went on to explain what my schedule would be and we both decided that Sam coming to visit would be a waste as we wouldn't be able to spend much time together. We were both disappointed, but we understood that's just how it is. We agreed that Sam would come the following weekend instead. Three weeks without seeing him. It felt like forever.

Friday arrived and I was busy with Mr. Murray and our meeting with the execs from Canal River and Trust. We spent the next two days in meetings for project planning, budgeting, and making edits to the blueprints. We finalized everything by late Saturday afternoon and then went to dinner that night. I spent Sunday basically sleeping and doing laundry. I was exhausted. It had been a long week and I had put in about 80 hours when it was all said and done. I had not really talked to any of my family or Sam much at all the whole week. I had just been too busy. When I wasn't working, I was sleeping. Sam and I texted back and forth a couple of times just to check in, but they were short "proof of life" kind of texts and nothing very substantial.

I was really missing Sam, but I was also so tired that I just couldn't put much thought into missing him. Or anyone for that matter. It occurred to me just then, that I hadn't thought of Michael in quite a while. In fact, I couldn't remember the last time I had thought of him. That made me sad. It had been about 14 months since Michael passed and I was already at the point that I no longer thought of him every day. In one way, that meant I was moving on with my life; which I needed to do for my own sake. In another way, I was shocked that I had reached that point as quickly as I had. If you had told me when Michael first died that I wouldn't think of him every day a year from then, I would have called you a liar and fool. There's no way. And yet, here I was. I was moving on and leaving him in my past.

I took a long, much needed nap on Sunday and when I woke up, I saw that I had missed a couple of calls from Sam. I called him back and he answered right away.

"Hey Krista, how are you?" he answered.

"I'm good. I'm sorry I missed your calls. I just woke up from a long nap, " I responded.

"Well, that's good. I'm sure you needed it. You must be exhausted. You've worked a ton the last couple of weeks," Sam added.

"Yes. And I can't believe I have to go back to work tomorrow. I feel like I was just there," I said.

"I hope the firm is compensating you well for all your time," Sam said.

"Funny you mentioned that…" I started. "Mr. Eden called me on Thursday and said he was giving me a raise. He bumped my salary significantly actually. I was pretty surprised," I told him.

"I'm not surprised," Sam said. "He needed to give you a raise. You do way more than just an assistant. They couldn't do those projects without you," Sam said.

"That's nice of you to say," I replied. "I hope I'm doing a good job. I've certainly learned a ton with this job," I added. "Anyway…enough about me. How are you?" I asked.

"I'm good. I also had a busy week, but thankfully I didn't have to work quite as much as you did. I do have some news though," Sam said with reluctance in his voice.

"Oh yeah? That sounds ominous," I responded.

"Well, unfortunately it's my turn to work this weekend. I have a meeting Saturday morning that will last until probably 11:00, and then I have to fly out Sunday afternoon. My company is sending me to Berlin for a couple of days to meet with a company about a restoration project there. I'll leave Sunday and be back by Wednesday. But, that probably means seeing each other for the weekend won't be possible. If I came to Bristol on Saturday afternoon, I would have to leave early Sunday morning to make it back in time for my flight," Sam said.

My heart sank. Four weeks of not seeing each other. This was seriously putting a strain on our relationship. There was no way it couldn't. Time apart during a budding relationship, especially one as unique as ours, would be a difficult obstacle to overcome.

"Oh man," I said as I sighed heavily. "I know we both have jobs to do, but I'm pretty disappointed to hear that," I told him.

"Yeah, me too. I was really looking forward to seeing you," Sam said.

"Do you think we could maybe plan some time off together? Like maybe we could both take off a couple of days from work and have an extended weekend away together?" I asked Sam.

"Absolutely," he said. "That's a great idea," he added. "I can do the weekend after next if you can," Sam said.

"I'll check with Mr. Eden and Mr. Murray to see if they're agreeable to that. I'll let you know," I replied.

Sam and I talked for another thirty minutes or so before wishing each other a good week and saying goodbye. Everything about our conversation implied that Sam was all about me and loved me. I was so eager to move our relationship to the next level. I was dying for Sam to ask me to marry him, but he didn't seem ready to move it forward. Perhaps he was just trying to move cautiously for my sake because he didn't want to rush me, but I honestly just wanted him forever. For some reason, I was feeling so unsure and insecure about where we stood. I couldn't tell if it was just the distance and time apart ruling my thoughts, or if there was really something to worry about. Nevertheless, we ended our call and Sam said he would text me tomorrow.

The week went by as usual. Busy. Sam and I had texted back and forth quite a bit and each conversation got longer and longer. Mainly instigated by him. He told me how much he missed me and we had solidified our long weekend get-away plans together. We had decided to visit the Isle of Skye. Neither of us had ever been and it's something we wanted to see. I booked a cute little Air B&B that had excellent reviews and a great location. Other than that, we really didn't make many plans for our trip. We just wanted to hike, scout around, and hang out. We were both tired from our jobs too, so a little relaxation free from planning and schedules sounded lovely to both of us. The plan was for Sam to drive to Bristol after work on Thursday and then we would get up early on Friday and drive to the Isle of Skye. We were staying for 3 nights, and we were looking forward to the drive as the landscape was sure to be spectacular.

In the meantime, I was still pouting that I had to wait four weeks to see Sam. Just then, I concocted a far-fetched plan in my head. I just couldn't wait another week and a half to see Sam, so I thought I might sneak over to London this weekend and surprise him. He had to work part of the day on Saturday, but if I took the train over early Saturday morning, we could at least spend the rest of the day and night together before he had to leave on Sunday. It would be a risk, but a great surprise if I could pull it off. I had to hope and pray he didn't have anything else going Saturday night. So, I decided in my head that a trip to London was what I needed. I needed to get out of Bristol for a minute. Work was sucking up my whole soul. I figured I could probably do some great shopping while I was in London too.

Sam and I had several text conversations for the rest of the week and I tried really hard to silently investigate what he had planned. As far as I could tell, he didn't have anything going on. Saturday morning, I got up super early and took a cab to the train station. My train left at around 7:00am and the ride was the usual hour and twenty minutes to London. I followed exactly the same route as I previously had when I came to visit last. Once I was near Sam's neighborhood, I suddenly felt very unsure about this whole plan. I was starting to seriously doubt my impulsive decision to surprise Sam and just show up. What if he was busy? Or what if he had more meetings that came up that he didn't tell me about because he didn't think it was necessary? What if this was a complete waste of time? What if Sam hates surprises and wasn't happy about my popping in on him? At this moment, I was wishing I had just stayed in Bristol, gotten some rest, and had been patient.

Sam's hotel was only about two blocks away so I decided to just go there first to see if the hotel would allow me to leave my bags there while I did some shopping. It was about 9:00 in the morning by this time and I knew Sam would be in a meeting until at least 11:00am, so I had some time to kill. There were plenty of shops around to keep me busy for a couple of hours. The front desk associate at Sam's hotel was very gracious and accommodating. I explained who I was and what I was doing there. They were very sweet about letting me leave my luggage there for a while, so I headed back out onto the sidewalk to decide what my first stop would be. Located diagonally across the street from the hotel was a Starbuck's so I decided that more coffee was definitely required. Especially since I had gotten up so early this morning and was running on very little sleep and energy at the moment.

After standing in line for my coffee for about twenty minutes, I grabbed the cup of steaming caramel latte and let it warm my hands. I sat at a small table and took a few sips before deciding to walk down the sidewalk to see what shops were open. The first one I ducked into was a bookstore. I could never resist a bookstore. I didn't need a book because I had several at home that I hadn't even read yet. But, I just loved the feel and smell of a bookstore and usually wound up buying another book every time I walked past one. I browsed around the store for a while and surprisingly was able to leave the store and all the books there this time.

Back out on the street, things were starting to get busy. More people were milling about and the traffic was starting to come alive as well. There was always something thrilling about watching a big city come to life with the buzz of activity. I walked a few blocks and ducked in and out of several little shops. I didn't leave empty-handed either. I found some new boots, tennis shoes, and a couple pairs of pants for work that I just couldn't live without. Then I saw the ultimate motherload. Sephora was just up ahead and I knew immediately that my new pay raise was about to be put to good use. I eagerly bolted inside and grabbed a hand basket. I was ready, willing, and able to fill that sucker up on beauty products. It has really been a long time since I had spent any money on that type of thing. I had been surviving on drugstore products, but now it was time to reload my inventory.

After about 45 minutes, and nearly $300, I decided I needed to wrap up my love affair with Sephora and get out of there before I went into debt. I wrapped myself back up in my coat and headed back out onto the street. It was April, but the weather was still pretty chilly out. I was ready for it to warm up. That was something I really missed about the U.S. More sunshine and more warmth. I looked at my phone and saw that it was nearly 11:00 on the dot. I decided to text Sam a vague message to see what he was up to. I thought maybe I could get a sense of where he was in his day.

"Hey good-looking. How's your day going?" I texted him.

Just as I sent the text, I looked up to watch where I was going on the sidewalk. I didn't want to be one of those people looking down at their phones while they're walking. As I did, I did a double-take and saw Sam up ahead on the sidewalk about 40 yards away. My heart jumped at the sight of him and I couldn't believe my luck that I would just run into him on the street. What a great surprise this was going to be. I watched him as I approached and I saw him check his phone. Probably my text; which was going to work out perfectly. He appeared to read the text and then put the phone back in his pocket. He didn't respond.

My face dropped a little and I was curious as to why he didn't respond. I continued to watch Sam among the crowd of people on the sidewalk. As I continued to walk, I saw Sam turn back toward the building and talk to someone, but I couldn't see who it was. I figured it was probably someone from his meeting and that's probably why he didn't respond to my text. However, as I got closer and a couple of people moved out of my sight-line, I could see that Sam was talking to a young girl. She was not dressed in business attire. In fact, she was dressed casually, like me.

I stopped walking and moved myself to the side of the sidewalk close to one of the storefronts so I could observe and not be in everyone's way. I continued to watch Sam and the girl. Their exchange was different. It wasn't business. Sam had his hands in his pockets as he spoke to her. She used her hands as she spoke to him and their faces had emotion on them that wouldn't be typical of a business exchange. This was someone that he knew personally. Then, Sam took one of his hands out of his pants pocket and reached up to squeeze the girl's arm near her shoulder. He squeezed it affectionately and then ran his hand up and down her arm as if he were warming her in a loving way. She turned her face toward my direction for just a moment and I could see that she had tears in her eyes. Then she looked back at Sam's face and then looked down. Then, Sam stepped into her and wrapped his arms around her in a full embrace. They stood there holding each other for what seemed like several minutes. Sam was rubbing her back as they hugged.

I couldn't believe what I was seeing. He clearly had a relationship with this woman. This was personal. My heart absolutely dropped into my stomach and I was broken in the blink of an eye. This is why Sam couldn't come to Bristol to see me. He had another relationship going. He probably hadn't figured out how to break it off with me yet, and just lied to buy more time.

Tears welled in my eyes and I just stood there watching them. I couldn't even move. I was devastated and heartbroken. My whole happiness had come to an abrupt halt in the matter of minutes. Again. Sam released her from the embrace and stepped back as he slid his hand down her arm. Just as he had done to me so many times. As he did so, he turned and looked down the street in my direction. Suddenly, his eyes made contact with mine. He saw me and a look of realization came across his face. First it was a smile, but that faded instantly as he saw my face. It was like it dawned on him that I had seen him with her. He knew that I knew.

My face flushed with heat and shame. I didn't want him to see me and I didn't want to engage with him. I wanted to run away. So, that's what I did. I turned and walked the other direction as quickly as I could. I thought I heard Sam yell my name, but I couldn't be sure if I actually heard it or if my brain wanted to hear him calling after me. Nevertheless, I kept walking as fast as I could. I sped up to a quick step and half jog as my mind raced with sheer panic. I had to get away. I didn't want to see him, I didn't want to face him or hear anything he had to say. It would all just be horrible excuses and I didn't want them.

I rushed down the sidewalk, weaving in and around all the people. I got back to Sam's hotel and went straight to the same desk clerk who had so graciously stowed my bags. I asked him for my bags and told him it was urgent that I get them quickly. I had a train to catch and I was late. He obliged and retrieved my luggage quickly. I hurried out of the hotel back onto the sidewalk. There was a line of cabs waiting on the street and I approached the first one nearest to me and asked if he could take me to the train station. He agreed and he helped me get my largest bag into the back of the car. He slammed the trunk shut and I opened the cab door to get into the back of the car. The cabbie was already in and ready to go. Just as I was about to step in the car, I heard Sam yell my name. I turned as I was stepping into the car and met his eyes with mine. He looked desperate and troubled. He was running toward me. More tears fell from my eyes and I slid into the back seat and slammed the door. I asked the driver to go quickly. Just as we were pulling away from the curb, Sam reached the car and put his hands on the back door window. "Krista," he yelled. "Please, don't go. Let me explain," Sam shouted to me through the window. His face looked pained, but I knew that was just the desperation of someone who got caught.

The cab driver hesitated and looked at me to see what I wanted to do. "Drive please," I replied as I watched Sam's face while we pulled away. My world was shattered. I could hardly breathe and I couldn't believe that this was where I was in my life. Hurt and grieving again.

Twenty-Eight

I ignored my phone until I was back on the train headed back to Bristol. It had been blowing up and I knew it was Sam. I chose not to look until I was settled into my seat and on our way. I pulled out my phone and saw that I had missed about 10 texts and 3 calls from him. I couldn't really understand why he was so desperate to talk to me, only to tell me that he was sorry for having another relationship going. I figured he would be glad it was out in the open and over with. Why would he care what I thought now? I clicked my phone off and decided that I couldn't handle reading all the excuses and apologies right now. I didn't want to hear them. They wouldn't matter. They wouldn't take the hurt and betrayal away.

I put my phone away in my coat pocket, leaned my head back against my seat, closed my eyes, and wished for a way to move past this quickly. Then, I started reliving all of our moments together. Searching for the signs of betrayal and disinterest. When did it go wrong? When had he found someone else? How did I miss it?

The trip back to Bristol and to my flat was the longest of my life for some reason. I walked into my flat around 3:00 that afternoon and just dropped everything. I crawled into my bed with all my clothes on, pulled the covers over my head, and cried myself to sleep. When I woke, it was dark outside. I looked at my phone and saw that it was about 7pm. I had missed more texts and calls from Sam. I still didn't want to read them, so I cleared them off my screen to avoid seeing the notifications. I pulled myself out of bed and went to my kitchen to scrounge for something to eat. I hadn't eaten all day. I was living on coffee and sorrow. I filled my belly with chips and dip; one of my favorite girl dinners. Then I went to take a shower to wash off the pain of today.

More crying ensued in the shower. I sat on the shower bench letting the hot water try to soothe me until it basically ran out of hot water. My skin was like a raisin by the time I got out. I dried off slowly and did my skincare routine with my new products from Sephora. Although, it wasn't nearly as exciting or gratifying as I thought it was going to be. Back out in the living area, I made myself a cup of hot tea and sipped on it while watching some tv mindlessly. Finally, I gave up and went back to bed. Luckily, sleep found me quickly and I drifted off without crying.

Sunday morning I woke to more texts from Sam. Before I could clear them off my screen, I read the last one. "Krista, I love you. Please call me." How could he say he loves me and be having an affair at the same time? Why? I couldn't believe this was happening. This wasn't the Sam I thought I knew. I threw the phone down into the bed covers out of frustration and left it there. I got up and went to the kitchen to make my coffee. From there, I began to form a plan.

My heart was crushed, but my brain refused to struggle through grief again. I couldn't do it. There was only so much heart-break I could put up with before my mindset hardened and I decided to just move on. It's probably what a good therapist would call avoidance and compartmentalizing, but it's what I needed to do to cope. I decided, in that moment standing there sipping my coffee, that I would protect myself from any more hurt.

I picked up my phone and I called Mr. Eden. It was certainly unorthodox to call your boss on a Sunday morning. Especially to tell him, or ask him rather, what I was about to ask. He answered the phone after a couple of rings and said hello to me.

"Good morning, Mr. Eden," I responded. "I'm sorry to bother you on a Sunday morning, but there's something I need to talk to you about," I continued.

"Of course, Krista. What is it?" he replied kindly.

I proceeded to dump the whole story on Mr. Eden. He was probably overwhelmed and stunned that I was sharing all this information. To be honest, as I was explaining the situation, I started to doubt whether telling him everything had been the best idea. In my mind, I felt like telling him about my personal life and current situation with my love interest felt completely unprofessional, but I didn't know what else to do short of quitting my job. Once I was done telling him everything, I told Mr. Eden that I wanted to keep my job, but I really wanted to be relocated immediately. I didn't want Sam to be able to find me, and I certainly didn't want to risk running into him again.

After listening quietly for several long minutes, Mr. Eden said, "Krista, I'm really sorry that you're going through all of this. But, are you absolutely certain that Sam is seeing someone else? He doesn't strike me as the type to do something like that. He seemed like such a loyal person."

"Well, yeah.... I thought so too. I mean I didn't stick around to hear his story, but it was very clear that it wasn't a professional relationship. I mean they were hugging and touching each other in a way that professionals, or even friends, wouldn't do," I responded.

"Ok, well, if it's what you really want, we can relocate you immediately. I actually have a project starting this week, but it's pretty far away and you'd be there for at least a couple of months," Mr. Eden said.

"That sounds good," I replied. "Where is it?" I asked.

"It's in Inverness. Right off of Loch Ness actually," Mr. Eden added. We have a couple of structural rehabs going on with the bridges around the loch that you would be in charge of. I have to warn you though, the accommodations are a bit different. We have an elderly couple that live right on the loch and our company essentially uses them like a bread and breakfast type of lodging. They house our crew members from time to time. I think you'll love them. They're a very sweet couple who will make sure you are well taken care of. Their names are Dougal and Fiona McLeod," he told me.

The idea of staying with other people wasn't that appealing to me at the moment because I just wanted to be alone and sulk, but it was better than staying where I was. I couldn't stay in Bristol and I couldn't go back to Edinburgh. I didn't want to be anywhere Sam could track me down and I didn't want to be in a city like London where I could run into him. I certainly didn't want to run into him and his new love interest either. The thought of him being with another woman made my stomach turn. The hurt was fresh and seared through me like a hot iron. I was still astonished this was happening. I thought I could trust Sam. I thought he was solid and dependable to do the right thing. I was absolutely blindsided.

Mr. Eden told me that he would send a driver to my flat tomorrow morning and they would drive me to Inverness. It would be nearly a 9 hour drive so the driver would pick me up in the morning around 7am. He told me that I needed to pack up all my belongings and be ready to go first thing in the morning. Even though he was being very accommodating to me, I could tell he didn't quite buy into the whole story and was skeptical about whether Sam had had an affair. I didn't need him to believe it though. I just needed him to help me get away. Graciously, he made it happen.

I spent the rest of the day doing laundry and packing up my bags. I tried to stay as busy as possible to take my mind off of leaving and the betrayal. But, deep down in my core, I was devastated. I truly loved Sam and had thought that we would likely wind up getting married sometime in the future. Now that dream and hope was leveled. It felt so off to me. Like I was living in some alternate universe and was watching my life unfold from the outside looking in. I replayed seeing him with her over and over in my head. She was so young. I was surprised he would go for someone so young. I shook my head to rid myself of the thought and continued to keep myself busy.

I slept fitfully that night and tossed and turned. I had dreams of Michael's death and seeing Sam with another woman. All of the things that could haunt me came in one night of terrible dreams. Around 4am, I finally decided to just get up and start my day. Sleep wasn't going to happen, so I put on my workout clothes and went for a jog. When I got back to the flat, I had some coffee, showered and got dressed, and packed up the last of my things. While I waited for the driver to come, I texted my mom to let her know I was headed to Inverness. I didn't tell her anything about Sam because I didn't want to go into that, so I just told her it was for work and left it at that.

My driver arrived right on time and he helped me lug all of my bags down to the car. He had a large van so all of my bags fit well and there was plenty of room to stretch out for our long drive. The day proceeded along and I actually spent quite a bit of the time checking emails, doing some work, and sleeping. The driver was from the highlands of

Scotland, so he knew all the best stops for restroom breaks and food. We even stopped a few times just to stretch our legs and take in the views of the Scottish countryside. It's a beautiful country. I was grateful to be seeing it, but sad that I was doing it alone and under my current circumstances.

By about 5pm, we arrived at Loch Ness and reached the McLeod's home shortly after. It was a beautiful house located near the loch with the most gorgeous views. I could tell right away that my heart and mind would be healed here. They both greeted us as the driver pulled the van up the drive and parked near the side of the house. Mr. McLeod was sitting on the porch and stood once he saw the van. Mrs. McLeod came out the screen door with a smile on her face as she wiped her hands on her apron as if she'd been cooking. They both treaded down the porch steps and introduced themselves as I exited the van. The driver and Mr. McLeod proceeded to grab all my bags from the van and haul them into the house. Mrs. McLeod introduced herself and pulled me in for a hug as if she were my grandmother and we were being reunited after many years apart. At first I felt awkward, but something about her hug made me melt and relax. I think I needed a hug and just didn't know it. She had the sweetest demeanor and instantly made me feel at home. She was a semi-plump woman probably in her late

60's or early 70's if I had to guess. She had silver hair that was thick and pulled back into a low bun. She had crystal blue eyes that literally twinkled when she spoke and smiled. Her face was sunkissed and the corners of her eyes wrinkled, but it almost made her more beautiful because of her contagious smile.

We made our way into the house, and I was immediately accosted with the smell of delicious food wafting through the air. It smelled of soul-lifting soup and freshly baked bread. I had no idea if that's what it was, but it sure smelled good. Mr. McLeod had taken all my bags to my room and he was tipping the driver when we entered the house. The driver smiled and nodded his head at me. He bid me farewell and I thanked him for his time. He responded in kind and quickly left out the side door and headed back to his van.

Mr. McLeod said, "Well then lassie. You must be starved and exhausted after a long day of travel."

I nodded and said, "Yes, I'm a little tired, but it was a beautiful drive."

He grinned at me and motioned for me to sit at the table as he pulled out a chair. I sat and had a cup of tea in front of me faster than I could have imagined possible. Mr. McLeod sat at the table with me while Mrs. McLeod continued with whatever she was doing in the kitchen. Mr. McLeod was also a slightly plump man who had on a long-sleeve flannel shirt, work pants, and suspenders. His hair was cut short and fully grey just like his wife's. He too had a sun-kissed face with wrinkles lining the outer corners of his eyes. His eyebrows were the same grey color and were very bushy. He smelled of pipe smoke which I hadn't smelled in years. It made me melancholy because it reminded me of my grandfather who had passed away long ago.

Mrs. McLeod brought over two large bowls of steaming soup and a platter of freshly baked bread. I nailed it. She said it was stew that she had been working on all day. It smelled wonderful. She also put out butter to put on the bread. Mr. McLeod dove right in and started buttering his bread and passed me the bread platter to offer me a slice. I followed suit and prepared my bread as Mrs. McLeod brought her own bowl of stew to the table and sat beside me. I was sitting at the head of the table and they were each sitting beside me. I sort of felt like I was in the hot seat as they began to ask me questions about myself.

We continued to talk and share information about ourselves as we ate. When we were done eating, Mrs. McLeod stood from the table and started to clean the dishes off and carry them to the sink. I jumped up and started to help. "I'd like to help you with the dishes, Mrs. McLeod," I said.

"Call me Fiona, dear," she said.

"And you can call me Dougal," Mr. McLeod interjected from the table.

I smile at them both and say, "Well, you can call me Krista."

We continued our chit chat while Fiona and I did the dishes and cleaned up the kitchen. After that was done, Fiona saw me stifle a yawn and said, "Och, dear, you're exhausted. Let's get you to your room, love."

I followed gladly and was so happy with the room they put me in. It was a large room with a huge window that overlooked the loch. It had a padded window seat next to it where you could sit and stare out over the loch. The sun was low in the sky and the colors reflecting off the loch were astonishing. It seemed so peaceful here. My bed was a large, four-poster queen bed that sat high up off the floor. It looked like something royalty would sleep in. There were two nightstands and two chairs with a small table situated in between them just in front of a fireplace. It was exactly what you would conjure in your head if you thought of a Scottish castle.

Fiona insisted on turning down the bed for me and she showed me where the fresh towels were in my private ensuite bath. The bathroom had a stand up shower and a claw foot soaking tub. It was all decorated in quintessential Scottish finishes of plaid and mahogany wood. It was a dream and I felt so grateful to get to stay here. They were lovely people and I felt like I was going to be able to mend my heart here. I needed them and their love more than they knew.

Soon after Fiona wished me a goodnight, I unpacked my bags and then showered. I felt like a new person after my shower, and it was nice to wash off the day of travel. I got into the large bed and settled in under the plush covers that smelled of fresh linen laundry soap. I felt my body relax for what felt like the first time in several days. My eyelids grew heavy almost instantly and I closed them hoping for a restful night sleep.

Twenty-Nine

I awoke the next morning to a text message from Sam. I still had not read any of his texts other than the one saying he loved me. This time when I looked at my phone screen, the beginning of the text said, "It's not what you think. Please let me…." and I couldn't see the rest. Part of me wanted to click into the text to see the whole message. But another part of me didn't want to risk getting sucked into his excuses and be hurt more. I mean…what could he possibly say that would change the fact that he was seeing someone else? My mind flashed again to seeing them there on the sidewalk. The way he stroked her arm with his hand. The way he was looking at her; the emotion on his face was clearly love. Or at least endearment. It was something. Something meaningful. A look he had given me before. That's why I knew it was more than just a friend. How could he possibly explain that away?

Before I knew it, tears welled in my eyes and my heart was wrenched thinking about him and his betrayal. At that moment, I decided to do something I had struggled to pull the trigger on until then. I went in and blocked Sam's number. I didn't want to keep putting myself through this torture. I wanted to be free of the heartache. I needed to move forward and preserve my sanity, so severing communication with Sam was the only way I could foresee doing that. I put my phone down on the nightstand, took a deep breath, wiped away the tears from my face and decided to get up and get moving. I needed to run. I needed to get out some of my anger and emotion.

I quickly dressed in my running leggings, a sweatshirt, and my tennis shoes. I brushed my teeth and pulled my hair up into a ponytail, and then headed downstairs. Halfway down the stairs I could smell the deliciousness of coffee and bacon wafting through the house. I went to the kitchen where I knew I would find Fiona, and sure enough she was there hustling up a huge breakfast. She greeted me with a bright, warm smile that melted my heart. Fiona asked, "Good morning. Did ye sleep well, lass?" Her Scottish accent thrilled me to no end and made me feel at home.

"Yes, actually. Better than I have in several nights. That bed is so comfortable," I replied with a smile.

"That's great, love. Would ye care for some coffee or tea this morning?" Fiona asked.

"Yes, definitely, but I'd like to maybe go for a run first. Is there somewhere safe to get a jog in around here? Or a gym I could go to?" I asked.

"Oh yes, dear. There's actually a lovely trail that follows the edge of the loch. The head of the trail is just there," as she pointed out the window toward an opening on the opposite side of the driveway. "There is a gym fairly close to here in the little loch village. I've never been there, but some of our other guests have reported that it's nice. It's a little less than half a kilometer from here. Most of our guests just walk or jog there up the same road ye came in on," Fiona explained.

"Wonderful," I said. "I'm going to take a jog outside for today, and then I'll head to that gym later and see what I have to do to attend there during my stay," I added.

"Sounds lovely, dear. Be safe, and I'll have yer coffee waiting when yer back," Fiona said lovingly. I truly felt taken care of, and hadn't realized until now how much I needed that feeling. As I headed out the door and onto the porch, I was greeted by Dougal and about five other men all dressed as if they were ready to work outdoors. They were all friendly and greeted me with head nods and smiles as they went inside. I assumed they were about to be fed by Fiona, hence the hustle and bustle in the kitchen with the large spread of breakfast.

The air was chilly and my breath fogged out of my mouth instantly. The cold air hit my lungs and it stung a little, but in a good way. It made me feel alive and invigorated. I was going to have to really move to stay warm, so that was inspiring to me to get going. I set up my run app, put in my earbud, turned on my music and set off on the trail. It was a great trail that was wide enough for walkers, runners, and bikers. The view of the loch was absolutely stunning and the sun was shining this morning. I settled into a nice pace as I jogged and my mind was occupied with music, the sites, and just generally thinking about the state of my life. I was certainly not where I thought I would be at this point in my life. I thought I would be married to Michael and living in Texas. I had planned out our life together, prepared our home together, and now none of that was reality. I had never dreamed that I would end up alone, in a different country, at a totally different job, and trudging through grief over and over. My thoughts were starting to suffocate me, so I decided to clear my mind and speed up my pace. I was going to run the depression right out of myself.

I got back to the house about an hour later. I had enjoyed a good three mile jog and walked for several more minutes just enjoying the fresh air and the view. I had decided during my run that I needed to take advantage of the opportunities in front of me and enjoy where I was. Both literally and figuratively. My life wasn't where I had expected it to be, but I had a chance to explore and soak in something that not everyone had. So, I was going to make the best of it.

I skipped up the steps of the porch and went into the house through the screen door. It squeaked as I opened it and that alerted Fiona to my presence. She smiled and asked how my run was, and I told her it had been like good medicine to my soul. I sat at the table that was located in the heart of the kitchen, and from what I could tell, this was pretty much where they ate all the time. It was quaint and felt so homey. They had a formal dining room I had seen when going to my room, but it seems that's reserved for special occasions. Fiona brought me a cup of hot coffee and placed an array of cream, sugar, fudge, honey, and cinnamon on the table for me to choose how to dress my coffee. I doctored my coffee and I smirked as I thought about how

Michael always said my coffee was more sugar with a side of coffee. I liked it "taupe" colored.

Fiona sat down in the chair beside me with a cup of tea. I think it was the first time she had sat all morning after slaving away in the kitchen. Actually, it struck me that it seemed like she had been waiting for me to get back to sit and be still with me. We both settled into our chairs and sipped our tea and coffee as we chatted. Fiona was an inquisitive woman and asked me questions about my life. She didn't strike me as nosey, just curious to know where I was from and how I got here. I told her as much as I felt comfortable, and shared that my husband had passed. I could tell that affected her deeply as she placed her hand on top of mine as if to show her love and compassion for me. I didn't tell her about Sam. I didn't want to talk about that, but I think she sensed that I was purposefully leaving things out. I wasn't sure how much she knew and what Mr. Eden might have told them before my arrival. I'm sure he had to explain something when he wanted them to house me in a hurry, but I couldn't imagine that he gave them any specific details. Fiona didn't push me for more information though. She was content to let me tell what I wanted to at my own pace.

After another hour of drinking coffee and chatting, I decided that I needed to get started with taking care of business. I was supposed to go visit the work site today and meet the crew, but wouldn't officially start until tomorrow morning. I headed upstairs to shower and get ready. Dougal agreed to drive me to the gym and then on to my worksite for my meeting. He said that he would be driving me each day to the worksite and back, and gave me his cell phone number so that I could stay in contact with him whenever I needed a ride. I felt bad that he was having to chauffeur me everywhere, but he assured me that was part of the deal with them housing guests. That's what was arranged between them and Eden & Associates, and that I wasn't to hesitate to ask anytime I needed a ride for any reason.

We first stopped at the gym in the little village. I didn't really know what to expect considering how small the town was. I was kind of expecting the gym to be small with maybe two treadmills and a weightbench, but surprisingly it was a pretty good size with lots of options. They even had a sauna and showers. It was a really nice facility that was modern and clean. And even better, there was a lovely little coffee shop right next door. The owner of the gym was working behind the desk as I entered. Dougal went in with me and introduced me to the owner, Liam. He was a nice man who was probably in his forties, and not surprisingly, looked pretty fit. Dougal told Liam that I would be staying with them for the next few months and would need a short-term membership to the gym. Liam responded quickly with, "Of course. We'll get you signed up right away." He handed me a clipboard with some typical paperwork to fill out. Once I was done with that, he handed me a key fob that would give me access to the gym 24 hours a day. My membership would be on a month-to-month basis and would cost 25 pound per month. I was astonished at the price being so low on a month-to-month basis, and happily signed the contract. After thanking Liam for his help, Dougal and I hopped back into his car and headed toward the work site. It was about a 20 minute drive and Dougal spent that time explaining the area and telling me all about my surroundings. He knew more than I expected him to know about the work sites I would be on for the bridges.

When we arrived at the site, there were a crew of men milling about seemingly setting up equipment and trying to get organized. I got out of the car and Dougal stayed in. He had agreed that he would just wait for me there. I sort of stood by the car and surveyed the activity around me, and then I saw a man in a hard hat with a roll of what I assumed were probably blue prints looking over in my direction. He stopped his conversation with one of the crew members and began walking toward me. When he was close, he greeted me with, "Good day," and stretched out his hand to shake mine. I returned the gesture and said hello.

"Hi, I'm Krista Andrews," I responded. "I'm the new work site manager," I added.

He looked slightly perplexed and said, "Yer American?"

I smiled and said, "Yes, I am."

"I'm sorry. I don't mean to be rude. I didn't know you would be American, so I'm a little surprised. Ye don't meet many female, American site managers," he said as he chuckled. "My name is Ian. We're glad to have ye."

"Well, I hope I can be helpful to you, Ian. I'll admit I'm behind the game on this project, so I don't really know what you need. Do you have time to go over the plans so we can figure out what the priorities are?" I asked.

"Of course," he replied. We walked over to one of the cars and Ian unscrolled the plans on the hood of the car. We went over the plans and anticipated phases of the project. He let me know that his crew was spending today organizing their equipment and getting everything they needed on site. Ian and I talked for a long while as I made a list of the things I would need to get organized for the site. There were currently no facilities at all, so I would need to arrange a work site tent, tables, food, water station, and more equipment that they would need for the project. I had my work cut out for me on this one and I was already behind. Ian and I wrapped up our meeting and I think he felt relieved I was there to take care of all the things needed. I, on the other hand, was feeling very overwhelmed. I was new to this area and didn't really know who to contact for all we needed. I was going to have to spend today doing some research and asking some questions. I was hoping Dougal would have some good insight to share with me.

Back in the seat of Dougal's car, I took a deep breath as he pulled out of the site parking area. He asked me how it went, and I gave him a side-eyed glance that clearly indicated my stress level. "Well, I've got my work cut out for me," I said. "To be honest, I'm a whole lot nervous about this one. They don't have most of the things they're going to need and I don't know anything about this area. I'm going to have to do some research today to find everything we'll need," I shared. Dougal looked at me with pity and then refocused his sight on the road ahead.

"Don't worry, lass. I have connections around here. I can help ye with whatever ye need," Dougal said. Somehow, it was like my dad was telling me not to worry and it made me feel so much better.

"Thank you so much," I replied. Inwardly, my anxiety level went down significantly knowing that I would have some help on this one. I was feeling really out of my depth here. These people were counting on me and they didn't know I wasn't really an expert in this area. They didn't know that I was really a pharmaceutical sales rep who had only been doing this job for less than a year. They just thought I was going to make their lives easier and get whatever they needed. Oh so much pressure.

When we got back to the McLeod's house, it was about 1:30 and Fiona was once again slaving away in the kitchen. I was beginning to wonder if she ever got to get out of the kitchen and do something different. Dougal immediately sat at the kitchen table when we entered and Fiona greeted us. "Thank you for driving me today, Dougal," I said with a smile. "I'm going to head up to my room and get started on getting organized for tomorrow," I told them.

Dougal scoffed and said, "I'll help you right after we have some lunch, lass." He pulled out the chair at the end of the table and motioned for me to sit. I was hesitant because I knew I had a ton of work to do and I was extremely anxious about getting started. "I know yer worried, but I promise we'll get it all sorted right after lunch. Ye canna work without a belly full of Fiona's food," Dougal persisted. I sighed and relented by sitting down at the table. Just as I sat, Fiona brought over two plates full of food and placed them in front of Dougal and me.

"What do you need help with, lass?" Fiona asked.

"Well, for starters, I need to figure out where I can rent a large tent, chairs, and tables to be set up on the work site. I'll also need port-a-potties. Or, uh...porta-loos as you say here in Scotland," I giggled. "I also have to get on-site lunch arranged for tomorrow," I continued as my face fell back into serious mode.

"Och, that's no 'a problem," Dougal said. "There's a local rental company in Inverness where ye can get all that equipment," he continued. "I'll call them right after lunch," Dougal said.

"Aye, dear. And I know the perfect catering company to help you with meals. There's a young widowed mother here in the village who started a catering company a couple of years ago. Her husband died leaving her with three young children. She's a wonderful cook, so she started a catering company to help support her wee family," Fiona explained. "Her name is Katherine. You'll like her because you're about the same age. She's a fine young woman. You know, come to think of it, she likes to run as well. We often see her on the trail," Fiona said.

"That's great," I said. "Perhaps we can call her after lunch as well," I added. I tried to relax and enjoy the moment and we ate Fiona's delicious lunch. I was seriously going to add some pounds on while I stayed here if I wasn't careful. I was probably going to have to do two-a-days on my workouts so I could still fit through the doors.

After lunch, Fiona started cleaning up the dishes and I got up to help her. She shooed me away and told me to start working on what I needed to do. Dougal grinned and gave me a look like "nice try." Then, Dougal got on his cell phone and put it on speaker. He called a nice gentleman named Alex, who owned the rental company he had spoken of. Dougal quickly introduced me to Alex and I explained what our project was, the company I worked for, and what we were going to need for the work site. Alex was very helpful and said he had the things we needed; including the porta-loos. I reluctantly asked how soon we could get those things to the work site thinking it would take a week or more. To my shock, Alex asked, "Would tomorrow morning around 8:00am be soon enough?"

"Um, yes! That would be perfect," I said with excitement in my voice.

Alex said, "Ok, consider it done then, lass. I'll send you an invoice if you'll text me your email address. You can pay online through the link that'll be provided in the email if that suits ye."

"Yes, that's great. Thank you so much," I replied. I was really shocked at how easy this had been.

Then Dougal asked Alex if he knew a company where we could rent some of the heavy equipment the crew needed for the job. Alex gave us the name and number of a company located just outside of Inverness. He said he had used them before for personal use and they were easy to deal with. After the call with Alex, I called the equipment company. I then did a 3-way conference call with Liam so he could explain exactly what they needed for the project. Liam was able to tell them what he needed, and I worked out the details of the rental agreement and payment over the phone.

I was astonished. In the matter of twenty minutes, we had solved some major issues. The only real obstacle left was figuring out how to feed the crew. By that time, Fiona was finished cleaning up the kitchen and she turned to the table and said, "Get your stuff, lass. We're going to pay Katherine a visit." Dougal casually tossed the car keys to Fiona and gave her a wink as he continued to sip his tea. I smiled at the exchange between the two of them and my heart was warmed by how much they had helped me.

I walked over to the table, leaned down, and gave Dougal a kiss on the cheek. "Thank you so much for your help. You have no idea how grateful I am," I said.

"Och, it's no 'a problem dear. Happy to help," Dougal said as he blushed. I smiled and followed Fiona out the screen door and down the porch steps to the car. We both got in and Fiona had to scoot the seat up to the steering wheel to reach. We set off on our way and Fiona talked about Katherine and her history on our way. Just a few minutes down the road, we reached a quaint little cottage with a sign on it that read "Katherine's Kitchen." Fiona approached the door to the cottage and knocked. The door opened and a young woman greeted us with a broad, sweet smile that made you feel welcome immediately. Fiona said hello and introduced me to Katherine. She had the brightest red hair and lightest green eyes I have ever seen. Her eyelashes were long and her nose was sprinkled with freckles. Her smile revealed beautifully straight teeth, and she had a dimple in her cheek that made her seem sweet without even knowing her.

Katherine welcomed us both warmly and invited us in. As we stepped in, I could see that this wasn't just her business, this was her home. The kitchen was to the left just as you entered the door and the living area was to the right.

The space was small, but decorated charmingly. There were no children present, but there was evidence that kids definitely lived here. Toys were piled in the corner in a large basket on the floor, and pictures of children were scattered across the room in frames to capture every age.

Katherine guided us to the kitchen where she, too, had a dining table. She asked us to have a seat and began to serve us a cup of tea. It made me wonder if all Scottish women just keep a kettle of water on at all times so they can offer tea at a moment's notice. As she poured the water over the tea in our cups, she asked about the nature of our visit. Fiona proceeded to explain that I worked for a company and we might be interested in her catering service. Fiona looked toward me to continue the thought as Katherine slid a platter of cream and sugar condiments toward us on the table. We prepared our cups of tea as I explained the company I worked for, the nature of the project, and my role. I told Katherine that I would need to have lunch and snacks provided to the crew every day for at least the next two to three months. Katherine's eyes grew wide and she said, "Two to three months?"

"Yes," I said wearily. I was afraid she thought that was too big of a job to undertake by the look on her face and tone of her voice. On the contrary though, her shocked face turned to delight as she clapped her hands together and jumped up and down.

"I'd be thrilled to help you," Katherine said excitedly. "Do you have time now to go over menus and what you would like to serve?" she asked.

"Um yes, I would love that. I'm eager to get this nailed down," I responded. Katherine sat in the chair next to me at the table and grabbed a notebook and pen that were lying on the table. She opened the notebook and began to ask me questions and took notes. I told her that we were feeding a crew of about 60 men everyday, so there needed to be a lot of food and it needed to be "man food" if she knew what I meant.

Katherine laughed, and said, "Yes, I understand exactly what you mean." We proceeded to line out the meals for this week and I just basically gave Katherine some general direction with food, but I really just wanted her to do the planning. I definitely didn't want to micromanage food menus, so I let her know that was at her discretion. She seemed very pleased with that idea.

"If you don't mind me asking, Katherine....." I started hesitantly.

"Go on then," she encouraged.

"Are you going to be able to cook and deliver this quantity of food everyday by yourself?" I asked.

"Oh no. Definitely not," she said. I looked at her with a puzzled look and she grinned teasingly and continued. "I have three employees that help me cook and deliver. I have a van and all the equipment needed to take care of jobs like this," she said reassuringly. I sighed and didn't even try to hide my relief to hear this. Katherine patted me on the shoulder and said, "Don't worry, love. I can handle it."

We finished our conversation and Katherine agreed that she would send an electronic invoice to my email. I paid her a deposit before we left, even though she tried to tell me I didn't need to do that. We worked out a deal that I would pay her on a weekly basis moving forward. She would plan all the meals and snacks and send me the menu prior to each week to review. In my head I was thinking, "I really don't care what it is. As long as a bunch of men will eat it, it's fine with me" but it seemed to make Katherine feel better to run it by me. About an hour later, we had all the details hammered out and Fiona and I were saying our goodbyes. Katherine said she would see me tomorrow, and she would be there at about 11:30 to set up the lunch meal.

Fiona and I settled into the car as we drove back toward the house. I reached over and put my hand on Fiona's arm. "Thank you," I said. "You and Dougal have spent your whole day helping me and I can't tell you how relieved I am. And how much I appreciate your help." Fiona smiled at me and patted my hand lovingly.

We arrived back at the house at around 4:00 and Dougal was splitting wood in the yard. Fiona scurried into the house to probably start another meal if I were to guess. The weather was lovely so I decided to sit in the adirondack chairs on the porch that overlooked the loch to take in the beauty for a moment. It had been a good day, and I marveled at how well two perfect strangers were taking care of me. Like I was their own. I just met them yesterday, and already they were treating me like a part of their family. It felt good. It had been too long since I felt loved and taken care of.

Thirty

I slept fitfully that night and dreamed of Sam, and Michael, and everything in between. I dreamed about this newest job site and all the things that could go wrong…. did. In my dream. I woke up at about 4:30 in the morning, which was about thirty minutes before my alarm was supposed to go off. I knew the minute I opened my eyes that there was no chance of going back to sleep, so I just decided to get up and get started. I quickly threw on my workout clothes, brushed my teeth and threw my hair up in a pony tail. I packed my work bag and a backpack with clothes to change into for the work site. My goal was to shower and get ready for work at the gym. I wasn't yet sure how I was going to get from the gym to the work site, but I figured maybe I could call an Uber or a cab. I didn't want to bother Dougal with it.

I ran down the stairs at about 4:50 and to my surprise, Fiona and Dougal were both sitting at the table in the kitchen drinking coffee. I stopped when I saw them and they both looked at me. Fiona said, "Good morning, love. Yer up early."

"Did I wake you both up? I'm sorry if I was noisy," I said apologetically.

"Don't be daft, Krista, " Dougal said. "We've been up since 4:00."

"Aye, love. We get up early every day to enjoy the quiet of the wee morning hours. Truth be told, we may have awakened ye," Fiona said.

"Oh good," I said with my hand on my heart. "I was afraid I had been too loud. I don't think you woke me up. I didn't sleep well last night. I had lots of ummm, unpleasant dreams," I told them.

"Oh I'm sorry, love," Fiona said with compassion.

"It's ok. I think I'm just anxious about today and the new work site. There are a lot of things that I need to come together seamlessly," I explained.

"I'm sure it's going to be fine, dear," Dougal added.

I smiled at their attempt to reassure and comfort me. They were such sweet people and I couldn't believe how blessed I was to be in their home and receiving their help.

"Thank you. I'm going to head to the gym before the work site. I'll see you both when I get home this evening.

I'm not sure what time that'll be. The first day on a job site is usually a long one," I told them.

Dougal jumped up and grabbed his keys. He said, "Let's get this party started."

"Oh Dougal...I hate to make you take me to the gym. I really don't mind walking there," I said.

"Nonsense," he said. "You'll do no such thing. I'm going to drive you to the gym and once yer finished there, I'll drive ye to the site," he chided.

"Are you sure, Dougal? I hate to make you chauffeur me all over the place," I said.

"I'm happy to do it. In fact, I'm looking forward to it. I'm planning to have more coffee next door while yer at the gym, so let's get a move on," he urged me.

I looked at Fiona who gave me a reassuring look, smiled, and said, "Ye better do as he says, love."

I sighed and relented as I realized I was not going to win this battle. Dougal and I slid into the car and took off down the drive. We arrived at the gym in no time because it's not very far. Maybe a half a mile at most and I reconfirmed in my head that I definitely could walk to the gym; even while carrying bags if I needed to. But, I was doubtful that Dougal was ever going to let that happen. The thought of that made me smile. I was astonished at how much he and Fiona already felt like family to me. They didn't know me at all and had only had about twenty-four hours' notice that I was even coming to stay with them, but they already made me feel like I was one of their own. It was something that my heart needed. That feeling of belonging.

Dougal parked the car in front of the gym. Before we got out of the car, Dougal gave me his cell number and told me to save it in my phone. He wanted me to text him when I was ready to head to the work site. He said he would be next door having coffee and chatting it up with the locals. I smiled and nodded in agreement, and thanked him for being so helpful. As I entered the gym, I was immediately greeted by Liam at the front desk. He said he had just gotten there and no one else was in yet so I had the place to myself. I was grateful to hear that for my first time so I could get the lay of the land while no one was watching. I put my things in one of the lockers and then went and found a treadmill.

I put in a pretty good workout with a run on the treadmill and then some heavy lifting. I think it helped to clear my mind and work out some of the anxiety I was feeling in life right now. I spent the majority of my run thinking about my dreams last night; in particular the parts about Sam. I knew why I was dreaming about Michael. That made sense to me. But, dreaming about Sam was new. It meant that I was subconsciously thinking and worrying about what had happened between us. Part of me wondered if I had handled it well. Should I have heard him out? Should I have read all those texts? Maybe I had overreacted. But, despite questioning myself on the matter, my thoughts kept going back to what I saw that day on the street. I couldn't get those images out of my head. I couldn't unsee it. And, any time I thought about that, the feeling of betrayal seared through me all over again. So much so that it almost made me sick to my stomach.

So, I pushed those thoughts down and continued to work. I refocused my efforts to what was in front of me for the day. After my workout, I used the gym locker room to shower and get ready for work. I texted Dougal at about 7:00 and told him I was close to being ready. I told him I would walk over to the coffee shop so I could grab a coffee before we left. As I walked out the door of the gym, I saw Dougal standing beside the car with two coffee cups in his hand. He smiled and handed me one of the cups. I'm guessing I looked puzzled, because he said, "I got ye a coffee. I just guessed that ye might want a fruity tooty latte based on what I've seen ye add to yer coffee at the house." He said it with so much sarcasm that I had to laugh. He wasn't wrong, but I thought it was hilarious that he had even noticed how I liked my coffee, and that he had such a strong opinion about it.

"You're the best, Dougal. Thank you," I said enthusiastically. I was really happy to be having a large cup of fru fru coffee. I took a sip of the warm latte and it thrilled me to my very core. It was exceptional and exactly what I would have ordered myself. "Mmmm, sweet morning nectar," I said as I closed my eyes to show my appreciation. Dougal rolled his eyes and chuckled at my reaction.

"Glad I could help ye, love," he said jokingly.

We settled into the car and headed off toward the work site. About twenty minutes later, we arrived around 7:30 and we were the first ones there. Dougal insisted on waiting with me until someone from the crew arrived, so we waited in the warmth of the car. At around five til eight, multiple vehicles began to pull into the site parking area. I saw Ian step out of one of the vehicles and start talking to some of the crew members and was using hand gestures to show them where to begin. Soon after that, a large truck with a trailer pulled into the site. I could tell that it was the rental company because there were porta-potties on the trailer and other equipment. Then, another large truck pulled in behind that one. Several men jumped out of those trucks and began unloading. Dougal said, "That's Alex there," as he pointed across the way. "The man in the blue shirt that's pointing," he said.

"Great," I said. "I better get over there and give them some direction. Thank you, Dougal. For everything," I said as I smiled.

"No 'a problem," he replied. "Text me about a half hour before yer ready to leave today. No matter the time," Dougal added.

"Will do," I promised him as I smiled and got out of the car. I grabbed my bags from the back seat and headed over to talk to Alex. He greeted me with a smile and a firm handshake. He was a very pleasant man and seemed eager to make my life easier. I couldn't help but like anyone who was eager to help me. Alex and I quickly outlined where everything needed to go and his men jumped into action. First, they set up the large tent. It was probably about a 20 x 40 area and even had tent walls with built-in plastic doors. I hadn't expected that. I thought it would just be a roof-type tent like we had had in the past, but Alex said they liked to use tents with walls because it rains sideways here in the highlands quite a bit. At that moment, I was even more grateful for Alex.

Soon after the tent was put up, the men began to pour tables, chairs, and propane heaters into the interior of the tent. I was ecstatic about the heaters. I hadn't even asked for those, but it seems that Alex really knew what he was doing and just brought what he thought was necessary. Of course he asked me at every turn if those decisions were okay, and I kept reassuring him that I was thrilled he had thought of those things. I truly meant it too. It was rare to find someone that uses their own brain and common sense to make life easier. While the tent and its contents were being set up, a couple of other men were unloading the port-a-potties and the equipment that Ian had needed for the work. I could see Alex and Ian discussing the equipment and getting it all worked out. I walked over to the two of them and asked if everything was okay.

"Oh yes, Mrs. Andrews. Everything is just as it should be," Ian said.

"Krista. Please," I said with a smile. He nodded with a half smile in return. "Alex, thank you so much for everything. You and your crew are exceptional. Please send me the invoice and I'll get you paid," I said.

"I actually have it already prepared for you. I'll send it to your email right now and if you agree, then I can accept an electronic payment," Alex replied.

"Even better," I said as I opened my email on my phone. I read through the invoice and was very pleased with the total. So, I followed the link and got Alex paid right then and there. We shook hands and he told me that if there was anything else I needed, to not hesitate to call him. Then he gave me his cell number just in case. Wow. I really could not believe how easy that had all been.

The crew got to work immediately and so did I. I set up inside the tent with my laptop and hotspot for wifi so I could get some accounting done and return emails. I had completely forgotten about getting water on site for the men. I got up from the tables and went out of the tent. It was chilly out and the wind was picking up. I grabbed my coat and gloves so I could walk around the site comfortably. I walked over to Ian and asked how things were going. He said everything seemed to be on track so far. I watched as the men worked and I could see that many of them had brought thermoses with water or other drinks, so they weren't completely devoid of hydration. But still, I felt like that was something that needed to be provided. I grabbed my cell phone from my back pocket and decided to call Katherine. It was about 10:30 so I was hoping I could catch her before she headed toward the site with lunch.

Katherine answered immediately and I told her that we were needing some large water jugs set up and also maybe some coffee on hand at all times. Luckily, she said she had just the thing and she would add them to the delivery today. About 45 minutes later, she pulled into the drive in her very large van. She and two other women piled out of the van and began carrying huge pans of food into the tent. I went over and greeted them and asked how I could help. Katherine handed me a couple of large pan food warmers and we got to work. She and her small crew were even more efficient than Alex's crew had been, and they had the lunch service set up in about 15 minutes. I was convinced that the Scottish people were not only exceptionally kind and giving, but they were incredibly efficient.

The rest of the day went by so fast and smoothly that I was actually done with work by 4:00. I was basically just waiting for the crew to wrap up their day. I texted Dougal at about 4:30 and let him know that I thought I would be ready by 5:00. He gave me a thumbs up emoji, which I found humorous coming from someone his age. He then texted again and said he was on his way. The crew began shutting down their equipment and organizing it to leave overnight. Ian walked over to the tent and said they would be back in the morning, but they were planning to get started a little earlier than they had today. He indicated they would likely arrive around 6:45 and get started at about 7, but he assured me that I shouldn't feel obligated to get here that early. I agreed and told him I would see him tomorrow. He, too, gave me his cell number just in case I needed to contact him.

Dougal arrived exactly 20 minutes after I texted him and I marveled at how fast he must have run out the door when I texted him. The ride back to their house was nice and Dougal peppered me with questions about my day. When we got to the house and started up the steps of the porch, I could already smell dinner wafting outside. In my mind's eye, I knew what I was going to see when I walked in. Fiona would be in the kitchen, with her apron on, hair pulled back into a low bun, and cooking up a storm. As I had expected, that was exactly the scene. Fiona greeted me with her sweet voice and smile, and asked me how my day had been. I sat at the table, as I knew was expected, and Fiona slid a cup of hot tea my way. It was already dressed the way I liked it which made me smile to myself.

The three of us sat and chatted about our days and Fiona served up one of the best meals I think I had ever had in Scotland. The food was exceptional, but the company was even better than that. As we finished our meal, and Fiona began to clear the dishes, I stood to grab my bags and head upstairs. Fiona said, "Oh Krista... I nearly forgot. A young lady came by today looking for ye," she said.

"Oh really?" I questioned. I was shocked someone would be looking for me here. No one knew I was here except maybe from work.

"Aye, love. I wrote her name and number down on a piece of paper. She was American. Said she was staying in Inverness at the Royal Highland Hotel," Fiona said. Now I was even more puzzled. It certainly wasn't someone from work if she was American. And, it couldn't be anyone from my family because they didn't even know where I was. Even my parents wouldn't know to reach me here. All they knew was that I was at a Bed and Breakfast type place near Inverness.

"Did she say what she wanted?" I quizzed Fiona.

"No, she just said it was really important that she talk to you," Fiona answered.

"What did she look like?" I probed.

"She appeared to be verra young. Maybe nineteen or twenty if I had to guess," Fiona replied.

"Hmmm." I was so perplexed. I couldn't for the life of me figure out who it could be. And what did she want with me?

I thanked Fiona for the message and headed upstairs. I threw my bags on the floor and plopped myself down on my bed. I was exhausted. It had been such a good day, and a very productive one too, but I was pooped. I was partly just relieved that everything had worked out and gotten done that needed to. I was hoping that I would sleep better tonight since I didn't have as much anxiety now. I spent the next hour or so catching up on social media, texting back and forth with my mom and dad, and then I did some reading. Then, I clicked on the tv and decided I would catch up on some of my shows I had gotten into. Just at that moment, there was a knock on my door.

"Krista," Dougal called from the hallway. I jumped up and opened the door. "There's a young woman downstairs asking to speak with ye," he said. I gave him a perplexed look and he shrugged his shoulders as he turned to go. I followed him out and down the stairs. He pointed me to the formal front living area of the house that no one ever seemed to use, but it was the official front door she had come to apparently. Dougal ushered me into the living area and then left to give us some privacy. As I entered the room, I saw a young woman with her back to me. She was standing in front of the fireplace looking at the pictures above the mantle. She had long blonde hair that was straight and fell to her mid back. She was thin and dressed in very American clothes which consisted of faded jeans, a sweatshirt, and sneakers. As I entered the room, she obviously heard my footsteps and turned toward me. When she turned, and I saw her face, I stopped dead in my tracks. It was her. It was the young woman I saw with Sam on the street in London.

Thirty-One

I was stunned and couldn't speak. I just stood there staring at her without saying a word. It was awkward and I could see she was trying to figure out what my problem was. She seemed hesitant to speak; like she was waiting for me to initiate, but I couldn't say anything. My head was swimming in thoughts ranging from "What the hell is she doing here?", "how did she find me?", and "I wonder if I can just run out of the room?" Her face looked innocent and young. She was beautiful with blue eyes shaded by long black lashes. Her eyebrows were a light brown shade that didn't match her hair or eyelashes, but somehow complimented both. Her skin tone was more olive, and she had a soft pink lip shade on. She didn't require much makeup to be beautiful. I was starting to hate her even more.

Finally, after what felt like a million minutes, she stepped forward, reached out her hand to shake mine, and said, "Hi, my name is Amy. Amy Bradford." I responded by shaking her hand, but somewhat begrudgingly.

After clearing my throat and delaying my response a little longer than I should have, I said, "I'm Krista Andrews."

"It's so nice to meet you, Mrs. Andrews," she said with a half smile.

"Umm, yes. You too," I responded as politely as I could. But in my head, I was still trying to figure out why on Earth she had shown up here to meet me.

"I know this is kind of awkward of me to show up here, but I've been trying to find you for quite some time," Amy said.

I'm certain my face went back to looking perplexed and blank as it had been about three minutes ago. What does she mean by 'quite some time? 'because it's only been about a week since I saw her with Sam. I still couldn't wrap my brain around why she would even be looking for me. How does she even know who I am? Unless Sam told her they had been discovered and she's trying to somehow make it better and smooth things over. That wasn't going to go well if that's why she's here. And why would she come see me and not Sam? Surely, if she found me, then he probably knows where I am too, right? So many jumbled thoughts were bouncing through my head.

"I'm sorry. I don't understand," I finally responded. "Why are you here?" I asked.

"Well, I uh…" the girl started. I could tell she was becoming more nervous by the second, and based upon my facial expression, was probably starting to question herself. But, to my surprise, she straightened her back and sucked in a breath to show confidence and continued. "I'm here because I just wanted to say I'm sorry," she said. She's sorry, I thought. I'm sure she is. She was busted having an affair with my boyfriend. I bet she's sorry. I didn't say a word. I stood there looking at her with a purposeful stoic expression waiting for her to elaborate.

"I, uh…., just wanted to, uh….., tell you how incredibly sorry I am about your husband," Amy continued as she stuttered along in her words. My face fell at first, and then I could feel it twisting into confusion with a knitted brow. What was she talking about? Sam? Did she think he was my husband and she's here to apologize?

I stood there for a long moment not responding to her at all. She took a step back from me and I could tell she wanted to retreat. But, she again braced herself and went on. "Mrs. Andrews, I was one of the girls your husband attempted to rescue from a car over a year ago," she said. I looked into her eyes and could now see a tremendous amount of hurt. Tears began to well in her eyes and threatened to spill over her beautiful, long black lashes. "I'm the reason your husband died," Amy continued as her voice broke and the tears rolled down her cheeks.

My mind could not register what I was hearing. My mind raced as I tried desperately to put the puzzle pieces together to process what this young woman was telling me. My ears were ringing and a fullness in my hearing came over me; like I was underwater. I could feel my face burning, but the blood draining out of it at the same time. I suddenly could only hear my heartbeat and my own breathing. My hands were shaking and I couldn't speak. I just stood there looking at her. I was in shock. My thoughts were swimming. All the events of the past week flashed in my mind and I was putting it all together. Seeing her on the street in London with Sam. She must have found him too. She wasn't having an affair with him, she was thanking him. He didn't cheat on me. Oh my gosh. What have I done?

"Are you okay, Mrs. Andrews?" Amy asked as she stepped toward me. My whole body was shaking now and I was feeling very light-headed. Like I might pass out. I wavered and lost my balance and Amy stepped even closer and grabbed me with both arms to steady me. "Here, let's sit you down," she said as she motioned to the sofa. I sat down and immediately put my head between my knees. I took deep breaths as she sat beside me and tried to comfort me. "Do you need a glass of water, or something?" she asked.

Just at that time, Fiona came into the room and rushed over to check on me. "What's the matter, dear? Are ye alright?" she pleaded. I raised my head back up and continued to take deep breaths, but I couldn't yet find my words.

Amy said, "My name is Amy Bradford, ma'am. I came here to meet Mrs. Andrews and thank her. And, well, apologize too."

"I'm Fiona," she replied. "What are ye talkin about, love?" Fiona asked.

"I'm one of the girls that Mrs. Andrews' husband rescued from a car in an icy river over a year ago," Amy responded.

I could see that Fiona was still confused. She didn't know anything about Michael's death, or Sam, or any of it. I had a long story to tell, but for the moment, I was just trying to catch my breath. Fiona rushed to get me a hot cup of tea and a glass of water. I'm sure that's all she could think to do to help me since she didn't really know what was going on. Amy sat on the sofa next to me and said, "I'm sorry to have caused you such grief today. That was never my intention," she said sweetly. I turned my head to the side and smiled at her. I reached over and grabbed her hand and squeezed it to let her know that everything was okay.

After several minutes of pampering and fussing by Fiona, I was starting to feel better and the blood was returning to my face. By this time, Dougal was in on the action too and they were all huddled around me in the living room. I finally looked around at the faces that were trained on me and decided that I needed to clear the air.

"Amy, thank you so much for finding me. It really means a lot to me to be able to meet you," I said. Tears again welled in her eyes. Then, looking at Fiona and Dougal, I began to explain. They sat quietly and listened, mostly in disbelief, at the long story of Michael, Sam, and now Amy and how their stories melded together. Hearing myself tell the tale, I could now hear how unbelievable it is that they all connected together the way they did. It was almost as if fate, or divine intervention, kept bringing us all together in the most implausible ways.

When I was done telling everything from my perspective, Amy told her side of the story. She talked about the accident and answered my questions. They were hard questions, and a heavy topic, for someone as young as she was. I felt awful for her that she had to bear such a heavy burden in her young life. To know that she was the reason a man died would be a horrible tragedy to get past. Surprisingly, Amy was very mature about the topic and spoke about how Michael had treated her and her friend that day. She gave very specific details about what he had done to comfort them as he was trying to get them out. She also talked about Sam and the things he had done to try and save all of them; including Michael.

By the end of her story, we were all in tears. Even Dougal and Fiona were feeling the heaviness of the situation. After we had discussed every detail, I realized it had been well over an hour. Amy spoke up and said, "Well, I probably should get going. I just wanted to meet you and say thank you. If it hadn't been for your husband, I would not have lived to tell this story."

I stood and wrapped my arms around her and hugged her tight. I could feel her relax into me and let go of all her tension around this moment. I pulled back and looked into her eyes. "Michael would be thrilled to know you and to know that you survived and are doing well. As am I. Thank you for finding me," I said. "I would really like to stay in touch. Could I get your cell number, maybe?" I asked. Amy seemed genuinely happy about sharing her number with me, and I got the impression that this was a big part of her healing process too.

Amy left after we all said goodbye and Dougal closed the door. I let out a big sigh and looked at both of them with relief. We all walked to the kitchen almost instinctively. As if that's the place where life gets sorted out. We sat at the table while Fiona made yet another round of tea. When Fiona obviously couldn't stand it anymore, she said, "So… what about this Sam fella?"

I raised my eyebrows and sighed again. This time with trepidation evident on my face. I began to explain to them about Sam's and my relationship and what I had seen on the street in London. I had seen Amy and had assumed he was having an affair because of the way they were talking to each other, their facial expressions, and touching each other. They had hugged, and he had stroked her arm with his hand. I could now see that it had been innocent. He was comforting her because she was probably emotional when she confronted him to thank him for saving her life. He was being the wonderful person he is, and I had made some horrible assumptions.

"Oh my gosh….," I said as I buried my face in my hands. "He's never going to forgive me." Dougal leaned over and placed his hand on my shoulder.

"He will, Krista. If he truly loves ye, he'll forgive ye," Dougal said. I looked at Dougal with tears in my eyes once again. "Have you talked to him since then," he asked. I shook my head and lowered it back into my hands.

"Don't worry, dear," Fiona said. "Just give him a call and explain everything. And then say yer sorry."

They made it sound so easy, but I knew it wasn't going to be that easy. I had been awful to Sam. I had completely cut him off and blocked his calls and texts. I left without a word and he had no idea where I had gone. I had made the most horrible assumptions and jumped to conclusions without even giving him a chance to explain. There's no way he was even going to want to talk to me at this point; much less forgive me for being so awful.

I wiped the tears from my face and told Dougal and Fiona that I just needed to go to bed. I could tell they were hurt for me and felt helpless themselves, but there was nothing they could do. I pushed in my chair and headed up the stairs after saying goodnight. I went into the bathroom and took a shower. I stood in there forever just crying and rehashing the whole, crazy story over in my head. I wasn't even sure I should try to reach out to Sam at this point. The probability of him even wanting to hear from me was very low. He most likely wouldn't return my calls or texts. That's what I would do if I were him.

I crawled into bed that night and once again cried myself to sleep. My life had become such a mess. I kept going through this cycle of grieving over one thing or another and I wasn't sure how much more of it I could take. The next morning I awoke and my first thought was that it had all been a dream. I mean all of it. Like, Michael was still alive and it had all been a horrible dream. But, once my eyes were fully opened and I looked around the room at where I was, I knew that wasn't the case. My heart sank again. I looked at my phone and it said 7:00. Holy crap! I overslept! The men would be on the work site already.

I scrambled out of bed and dressed as fast as I possibly could. I took my makeup bag with me and grabbed my work bag. I sounded like a stampede of cattle getting down the stairs and met Dougal and Fiona in the kitchen as usual. Huffing and puffing, I looked at Dougal in desperation. He grabbed his keys and said, "Let's go, love." Fiona handed me a thermos of coffee as we rushed out the door. They were always taking care of me. I was more trouble than I was worth.

I spent the 20-minute drive putting on my makeup and trying to look alive. My eyes were red and puffy, and no amount of concealer was going to hide what I had going on today. Dougal didn't say much on the way because I think he knew I was struggling to just put one foot in front of the other today. We arrived at the site to find the crew hard at work. I jumped out of the car, grabbed my stuff from the back seat, and gave Dougal a wink to indicate my gratitude to him. As I headed toward the tent, I ran into Ian who greeted me with a smile and said good morning. I returned the greeting and asked if everything was going okay today. He said all was well and the men had everything they needed. He said Katherine had arrived at the same time they did with fresh coffee, water, juice, and bagels so that made the men happy. I was so glad to hear it, but surprised she had done that because we hadn't discussed breakfast or arriving so early each day. She must have done that out of her own kindness.

Once I sat all my stuff down and got my laptop out, I called Katherine. She answered the call with a chipper "Good morning, Krista."

"Good morning, Katherine. I heard you made the work crew extra happy this morning with coffee and bagels," I said.

"Aye, they definitely seemed appreciative," she answered.

"Well, thank you for doing that. I didn't think you were going to do early morning breakfasts," I said.

"I just thought it might be a nice extra to make the crew happy and it really is no trouble at all. I'm so grateful for yer business, so I wanted to do a little extra to help," Katherine explained. "Ye really have no idea how badly I needed yer company's business over the next couple of months. It saved me. I'll be able to buy my kids 'school clothes with that extra money."

"I'm really so glad we could help each other out, Katherine," I said lovingly. She really was one of the most wonderful people I had met in a long time. And, it was nice to talk to someone my age. Secretly, I had hoped that we might become good friends while I was here. I realized at that moment that wasn't going to happen unless we had an opportunity to hang out. "Katherine, would you be available to have dinner with me sometime this week? Outside of work. You know…just to hang out?" I asked. I hoped she didn't think I was totally weird for asking.

"Oh my heavens, yes! I would love to. How about tomorrow evening? My aunt usually watches my kids on Friday nights so I can have a free evening. Would that work for you?" she asked.

"Um, yeah. That sounds great! You pick the place because I don't know anything about this area," I added. "I'll be available around 6:30 or so.

"Great," Katherine exclaimed. I'll pick you up at the McLeods 'at 6:30 and we'll go into Inverness to have dinner and see what kind of trouble we can get into."

"I can't wait," I said.

"Ok, then. I'll see you around 11:30 today with lunch on site," Katherine said.

After we hung up, I sat back in my chair and realized I had a smile on my face. I was genuinely excited about having a friend to hang out with. I put my phone down on the table and opened my laptop to check emails. The first email at the top of the list was from Erick Eden and had been forwarded. The subject line read: FW: Urgent-finding Krista. I looked at the time it was sent and it read 6:48 a.m.. I was a little shaken at the subject title with the word "urgent" in it. I couldn't imagine why he wouldn't just call me rather than forwarding an email.

I clicked open the email to read what was so urgent. "Mrs. Andrews, I hope to find you well. I have forwarded an email below that I received on your behalf. I have not responded to the email as I would like your input on how to proceed. Best regards, Erick Eden." I continued to scroll down to read the part of the email that had been forwarded.

"Dear Mr. Eden,

I hope you are doing well and business is booming. I know it's been a while since we've spoken, but I need to get straight to the point. I'm looking for Krista Andrews. As you may know, we've had a relationship over the last year or more. There was a misunderstanding between us recently and I am desperate to clear it up, but she has seemingly vanished overnight. I have tried to call and text her. I even tried going to her flats in Bristol and Edinburgh to find her, but she is nowhere to be found. I would really appreciate it if you could help me. At the very least, I would like to know that she's okay and nothing has happened to her. Respectfully, Sam Strickland "

My heart absolutely sank. Poor Sam. He must be beside himself with worry. I know he would never reach out to Mr. Eden unless he was truly feeling desperate. I immediately replied to Mr. Eden. "Good morning, Mr. Eden. Thank you so much for forwarding this email. I will handle it and reach out to Sam."

With that done, I now had to figure out how to contact Sam and what to say. Part of me was just grateful to know that he even still wanted to hear from me. So, I picked up my phone and scrolled through my contacts to find his number. When I found it, I clicked on his information and chose to send a message. That brought up all the texts he had sent to me that I had never read. I scrolled back through dozens of texts to start at the top where we last left off. I read through all of them. Some were very long and my heart was broken for not having read these sooner. Sam was crushed. He knew what I had seen on the street that day in London and he knew what it probably looked like. But, he explained every detail and continually tried to tell me the truth. I had been unwilling to even read them.

After reading through all the messages, I made myself go listen to the voicemail messages he had left. The sound of his voice was devastating. He was so hurt, and I could hear the desperation in his voice. Toward the end of the messages, I could hear the fatigue and raspy tone of Sam's voice. He was struggling and hurting. I had broken his heart.

I wiped away the tears from the corners of my eyes and looked around the work site to see if anyone had been watching me. The men were busy and definitely not paying any attention to me. I sat up straight in my chair and decided that I just needed to call Sam. I had thought originally that I would text him, but after reading all those texts and hearing his voicemails, I felt the respectful thing to do was to call him. He deserved more than a text message or an email.

I hit 'call 'on his number and quickly cleared my throat. I stood and walked around inside the tent as I waited for him to answer. I needed to move and get some of my nervous energy out. The line rang three times and then I heard the click of an answer. "Krista?" Sam asked. Oh my heart......the sound of his voice made me tear up again. To hear him was like medicine for my soul. I hadn't realized how much I needed to hear him and talk to him.

"Hi Sam," I responded quietly.

"How are you? Are you okay?" Sam asked in a panicked tone.

"I'm fine," I replied. "How are you?" I continued.

He took a deep breath and hesitated for just a moment before saying, "Well, I'm better now that I know you're okay."

There was a long pause. I really didn't know how to proceed or what to say. My thoughts were swimming and I didn't know where to begin, so after several seconds I said, "Sam, I'm sorry." He didn't respond right away. There was just silence on the other end of the line. So, I continued. "I'm sorry I didn't give you a chance to explain what I saw on the street in London. I'm sorry I didn't read and respond to your texts and phone calls. I'm sorry I blocked you. I'm sorry I made assumptions and ran away without a word." By this time, I was full-on crying and was a blubbering mess. My voice was cracking and I was struggling to get words out at this point. "I'm sorry I hurt you and made you worry," I whispered, and then I sobbed

Sam didn't respond right away. I could hear him breathing on the other end of the phone, but he didn't say anything. I just knew he was so done with me. I stopped pacing around the tent and began to nervously bite at my fingernails and cuticles while waiting for him to say something. Finally, after what felt like an eternity, Sam spoke up and said, "I'm sorry too. I'm glad to know you're okay, Krista." Then, the line went dead. I looked at my phone, put it back to my ear and said, "Hello? Hello?," but the call had ended. He had either hung up, or the call got disconnected. He didn't try to call back and he didn't text. I guess that was my answer.

Thirty-Two

I spent the rest of the day walking around in a fog. I went through the motions, but I wasn't really present. Or useful for that matter. I was heartstruck that I had let a misunderstanding guide my decisions and had caused so much pain for both Sam and me. I had ruined it all because I had been stubborn and unwilling to hear him out. What a fool I was. I deserved every bit of pain I was feeling at the moment.

Katherine brought lunch to the site today and she could tell something was bothering me. She asked several times if I was okay. I finally alluded to something being wrong, but that I didn't want to talk about it while at work. I asked her if I could explain when we went to dinner tomorrow night, and of course she graciously nodded and said, "Of course, love."

I texted Dougal at around 4:30 to come get me. When he arrived, I threw my bags in the back seat and slid into the front beside him. I gave him a tired, half smile and focused my eyes on the road as I rested my head on my hand near the window. I gazed out the window all the way back to the house and we didn't say a word. I was glad Dougal didn't drill me with questions. I just couldn't handle any more today. When we arrived at the house, I walked in and went straight up the stairs. I stopped on the 3rd step and turned back to greet Fiona. "Hi Fiona," I greeted. "I"m really tired and not hungry. I'm just going to get in bed early tonight."

"Sure, love. Whatever you need," Fiona responded lovingly. I proceeded up the stairs and went into the bathroom to draw a bath. I turned on the water to let the tub fill, and then went to build a fire in the fireplace. It was chilly in my room and I knew I would be cold getting out of the bath. Once the bath was filled, I stepped in and settled down into the tub, leaned my head back, and closed my eyes. I took a deep breath and tried to let my worries and pain evaporate into the hot water. I retraced my conversation with Sam and all I had said. I pored over every word and wondered if I should have said something differently. Ultimately, I had squandered this relationship because of my ignorance and stubbornness. No one was to blame but me, and I had to cope with the consequences of what I had done.

The next day at work was another blur. I knew I was distant and distracted, but being on site and being busy was the only thing saving me from my thoughts. I really was not in the mood to go to dinner with Katherine that night, but I didn't want to be a jerk and cancel at the last minute. So, once Dougal got us home around 5:30, I quickly showered and changed clothes. I dressed up a little, did my makeup and my hair. Looking myself over in the mirror, I realized I hadn't put much effort into myself in several days. I felt a little better already.

Katherine arrived right on time and I met her in the driveway as she pulled in. We set off toward Inverness and it was about a 30 minute drive so we had some time to chat. I asked Katherine questions about her, her children, and her business to try to get to know her and also to try to avoid having to talk about my situation. As we reached the town, Katherine navigated through the streets and found parking at a local car park near the downtown area. She said we would park and need to walk a few blocks to the restaurant where she made reservations.

After we parked and started walking, Katherine said our reservations were at a Mexican food restaurant called EscoBar. She grinned at me and said, "I know you Americans really like your Mexican food, so I thought I would try to give ye a taste of home." I nearly stopped on the sidewalk and looked at her in amazement and smiled the biggest smile I had put on my face in a long time. I was truly excited to be having Mexican food. I was even more happy to have a friend who cared that much. We kept walking as I put my arm around her shoulders and gave her a squeeze with a squeal of excitement.

Katherine and I both ordered a margarita on the rocks and began to gorge ourselves on chips, salsa, and queso. The food was already hitting my soul like it was crack cocaine. It had been so long since I had had food like back home and my mind and body needed the fix. We settled in and enjoyed our conversation in the lively restaurant that had great ambience. The food was surprisingly really good and in fact tasted like home. Admittedly, I had been skeptical about whether Scottish Highlanders could pull off good Mexican food, but they had proven me wrong.

After we were mostly done with our food, Katherine finally asked, "Okay, are you going to tell me what was going on with you yesterday?"

I chuckled as I proceeded to take another sip of my margarita in an effort to collect my thoughts. I spent the next hour telling Katherine everything. And I mean absolutely everything. I started with where I lived in Texas, told her about my marriage to Michael, how he died, about meeting Sam at work in Edinburgh, and finding out about his connection to Michael, and on and on and on. Katherine listened intently and asked questions along the way. Finally, I told her about seeing Sam on the street with the young woman, my assumptions, fleeing Bristol to come here, and everything that had happened over the last couple of days; including my conversation with Sam on the phone yesterday.

Once I was done, Katherine leaned back against the seat of the booth with her arms crossed and blew out a big breath. As if to say, 'wow that's a lot.'

"Yeah, I know," I said. "It's a wild sequence of events that are both tragic and unbelievable."

"So, ye haven't heard from him? He didn't call you back or text ye?" she asked.

I shook my head slowly and said, "Nope, not a word."

Then I leaned back on my seat and added, "I think he's probably very done with me."

Katherine lifted her eyebrows and her shoulders at the same time and said, "Ye never know, love. He may just need some time."

"Yeah, maybe. I mean I hope so, but I don't think I should count on it. I probably need to focus on moving on," I countered.

After nearly two hours at the restaurant, we paid out and decided we should probably head back home. Katherine needed to go pick up her kids from her aunt's house and get home. And to be honest, I was physically and emotionally exhausted. I was looking forward to getting into bed and sleeping in tomorrow morning. On the other hand, I was kind of dreading the weekend because I didn't have any plans and nothing to distract me from my thoughts.

The next morning I woke up as the sun shone directly into my room. The sun had not been out much lately, so this was a nice change even though it woke me prematurely. It was 7:30 in the morning, so that was pretty much sleeping in for me. I stretched in my bed and enjoyed being lazy under the covers that were so comfortable. Even though the sun was out, it was still cold in Scotland and I knew the room would be chilly once I got out of bed. I picked up my phone to check social media, read a text from my parents, and checked my emails. Then I decided to get up and run to the gym to get a workout in. I dressed and pulled my hair up as I jogged down the stairs.

As expected, Dougal and Fiona were chattering and milling about in the kitchen as they enjoyed some coffee. I decided to sit at the table and enjoy some coffee with them for a while before heading out the door. My jog to the gym wasn't far, but the cold air stung my lungs. I managed to get in a great workout that was almost free of interruption because the gym was basically empty. By 9:30 I ran back to the house and slowed to a walk up the drive. The wind had calmed and the loch looked pristine from the overlook view. My mind had been swimming with thoughts all morning during my workout and jog, but as soon as I settled into that view, my world calmed. I took a deep breath and let the sun wash over my face as I stared off across the water.

"How was yer exercise?" Fiona called out from across the drive. I turned to see that she was walking out toward me and smiling. I couldn't help but be surprised when I looked at her because for once, she wasn't in an apron. She was all cleaned up and looking like a million bucks. Her hair was down, styled, and curled nicely. She always wore it up in a low bun and I had never seen it down. It was actually beautiful with streaks of silvery grey throughout. She had on a nice pair of black slacks, black square toed boots, and a lovely bright royal blue sweater. She had on makeup too. I had always thought her face was lovely, but she looked radiant with makeup on. The black mascara on her lashes, and the contrast of the blue sweater, make the blue color of her eyes pop. Her cheeks were a pale pink blush, and she had a rosy shade of pink on her lips that complemented her cheek color. She was smiling broadly at me as she approached, no doubt amused by the look on my face as I admired her beauty. "I clean up fairly well, heh?" she said with a twinkle in her eyes.

"Yes, you sure do," I replied. I was a little ashamed at how blatant my surprise was. But, it was truly like looking at a different person. She was gorgeous. "Where are you going all gussied up?" I asked.

"Dougal and I are headed to Oban today. We have some business there and then we're going to have dinner with some family. We're planning to spend the night and then drive back tomorrow," she said.

"Oh, that sounds lovely. I hope you have a wonderful time," I replied.

"We plan to," she responded. "Krista, we would really love it if you would come with us," Fiona added. She looked me in the eyes and searched my face for a split second. She could see the refusal coming and did her best to head me off at the pass. "It's such a lovely little harbor town and you'll love it. We would really love the company on our drive. I think you'll have a great time," she said. She paused for a moment as I tried to come up with excuses not to go, and then she grabbed my hand and said, "Besides, I'm afraid ye'll starve to death while I'm gone."

I laughed out loud and consented that she might be right about that. I wasn't much of a cook and would likely just forgo eating completely rather than cook for myself. Fiona continued, "Come on, love. It'll be good for ye. Ye need to get out of the house and stay busy. A broken heart won't mend on its own," she said. I looked down at the ground and wanted her to be wrong about that, but I knew she was right.

I looked up at the loch once again, sighed deeply, and then looked back at her face and said, "How much time do I have to get ready?" She grinned widely and then hugged me tightly.

"Ye have about an hour. "We're leavin 'no later than 11:00, so ye better get a move on," she said. I smiled back at her and we both turned and headed for the house. I ran upstairs and quickly showered. I got dressed and packed an overnight bag as fast as I could, and I made it back downstairs with five minutes to spare. Fiona and Dougal were in the kitchen sitting at the table as they always were. Fiona handed me a thermos full of coffee prepared just the way I like it. She said, "I figured ye might need a little go-go juice for the road." I just loved her. She was becoming like a second mother to me, and I hadn't realized how much I needed people like that in my life right now. Dougal took my bags and went out the door to load them in the car. He had the car running and warm, so Fiona and I settled in. She insisted that I sit in the front seat with Dougal and when I protested, she said,"Ye need to see the sights of the Scottish highlands, love. I've seen it." I rolled my eyes and then smiled as I relented and followed her command. I knew I wouldn't win when it came to something Fiona thought should happen. I felt bad momentarily for making her sit in the back, but I had to admit I was truly excited to see the sights through Glencoe.

The drive was beautiful and even more special because Dougal and Fiona were able to tell stories and explain details that I wouldn't have gotten if I were traveling through the highlands on my own. They regaled me with tales of long ago and how the Scottish clans existed sometimes together, and sometimes not. It was fascinating to imagine their way of life as we navigated what used to be uninhabited land and countryside with no roads or modern conveniences. About an hour and a half into the drive, I found myself getting really sleepy. The whirlwind and emotional rollercoaster of the past week was finally catching up to me. I leaned my head back against the headrest and closed my eyes. I rested my head to the side against my hand with my elbow propped up on the door by the window. The car went quiet and Dougal turned up the radio to fill the silence. He was probably trying to keep himself awake to drive.

The next thing I knew, the car was slowing to a stop at a stoplight. My eyes opened slowly and I tried to readjust to sit myself upright to take in the sights around me. The weather had turned from sunny and bright, to grey with a light misting rain. The road wound around through a quaint little town perched at the edge of the sea. Dougal drove us along the road that bordered the harbor where boats of all types and sizes were scattered about. People were walking along the sea wall and seemingly enjoying themselves despite the cruddy weather. It seemed to allude to what an intoxicating atmosphere this little coastal town had on people. Dougal pulled the car into a grand hotel located right along the harbor with what I was sure was going to have the most stunning view. It was called the Oban Bay Hotel and it had a glass front that ran the length of the hotel along the sea. I could see chairs and tables with people sitting cozily looking out over the sights. It looked inviting already and I wasn't even inside yet.

We parked along the rear of the hotel and Dougal hopped out and began to immediately get the bags out of the back of the car. We rolled our bags to the front entrance, which was actually on the side end of all the glass windows, where we were met by a hotel worker that greeted us warmly. He appeared to be familiar with Dougal and Fiona, so I assumed this wasn't their first time to visit. This was confirmed as we approached the front desk where the staff greeted Dougal and Fiona with big smiles, warm hugs, and handshakes. I was instantly in love with this hotel with its plaid carpet and drapes, as well as rich mahogany wooden walls. There was mahogany wood everywhere. The tapestries that hung from the wall and the upholstery of the couches and chairs were exactly what my mind's eye had dreamed of for Scotland. As suspected, people were settled into large wingback arm chairs situated so that they had a spectacular view of the outside surroundings and the sea, but in a cozy room with a fireplace at each end of the long, vast array of windows. It was heavenly and I couldn't wait to be settled into one of those chairs with a glass of brandy myself. I didn't even like Brandy, but it just seemed like the right way to appreciate this ambience.

The bellman led us to our rooms, and I entered my room to find a large bed decorated in plush blue and green fabrics and pillows. There was a small window that opened up and I could see the harbor from my room. It was quintessential Scotland and felt like a dream. It was early afternoon at this point and Dougal and Fiona said to plan to be ready to join them for dinner at around 6, so I had some free time. My first order of business…..a small nap. I still felt exhausted and I just needed a little more rest, so I lay down on the bed and pulled the throw up over me. I set my phone alarm for one hour. I didn't want to sleep all afternoon because I wanted to go explore a little before dinner. I must have fallen asleep almost instantly because the next thing I knew my alarm was going off. I felt like I had slept for five minutes. I groggily pulled myself up off the bed and decided to freshen up just a bit. The weather was still obviously gross outside, so I put on my rain jacket and got out my umbrella.

I walked down the wide sidewalk that followed the sea wall toward the town. Once I was near the town, I quickly found a small coffee shop right on the corner. It seemed like a good place to refuel with caffeine and sit for people watching. I sat in the small shop at a table right next to the windows and enjoyed a large cup of hot latte as I pondered life and the life of those walking past. I did a little more walking around once the weather cleared a little. It was still grey and cloudy, but the mist and rain had subsided for the moment. The wind by the sea was ruthless though and battered me as I headed back toward the hotel.

Back in my room, I decided to get ready for dinner. Fiona told me this morning that it would be a fancier dinner and that I would probably want to wear a dress. So, I brought one of my long-sleeve black dresses that was midi-length. I paired it with my close-toed black sling-back heels and sheer black tights. I would be classy, but warm. I added makeup and contrasted my all black attire with smoky eyes and a nude colored lip. I curled my hair and tried to revive it from the rain and wind. Lastly, I added diamond earrings and a diamond tennis bracelet my parents had given me to add a little sparkle to the look. As I stepped back from the mirror to give myself a once over, I was pleased with the result; but I was also reminded of the last time I wore this dress when I helped Sam with the business dinner meeting. That had been such a wonderful time, and I was sad that time was long gone. As was our relationship. I decided to brush that feeling off and try to focus on what was in front of me and enjoy the evening.

I had no idea what to expect for the dinner plans. Dougal and Fiona had said they had business to tend to and a dinner with family, but hadn't elaborated further. I carefully navigated the long, narrow stairs that wound strangely down to the first floor. At the bottom of the stairs, I stood momentarily looking around to see if I could find Dougal or Fiona, but didn't see them anywhere. Standing there looking lost, one of the hotel staff approached me and asked if I was Mrs. Andrews. I replied, "Yes, that's me," and he said to follow him to the dining room.

He said, "Mr. and Mrs. McLeod are waiting for you." I smiled and followed behind him as we walked through an arched doorway near the front desk and headed toward the back of the hotel. Down a short hallway lined with more mahogany wood and framed pictures, the hall ended as it opened into a dining area. It seemed to be a private room with one large table and there sat Dougal and Fiona.

"Och, there ye are, love," Fiona said as she scooted her chair out and rose to greet me. She looked lovely in a dark maroon colored dress that fell to her ankles. Her hair was still nicely curled and styled neatly, and I wondered how she managed that with what I knew the weather to be outside. Dougal also rose and walked over to greet me with a hug. He, too, looked sharply dressed in a nice navy suit and maroon tie that matched Fiona's dress. They were such a darling couple and I deeply admired their relationship and love for each other.

I sat next to Fiona as we all took our seats at the table. The waiter came with water and took my drink order. Fiona and Dougal both already had a glass of wine, so I decided that would suit me as well.

"So, who's going to be joining us this evening? You said you had family here that would be at this dinner?" I questioned as I took the first sip of my red chianti.

"Oh aye, dear. Family are going to join us any minute now," Fiona said as she too took a sip.

"In fact, here they are now," Dougal said as he motioned to the doorway of the dining area and began to stand. I sat my glass down and looked over to my right toward the door. My eyes deceived me. There stood my parents with the hugest smiles on their faces. I was shocked to my very core. I could feel my mouth fall open with my jaw practically on the floor, but I couldn't do anything about it. I couldn't believe they were here. It was the very last thing on Earth I was expecting to see. I stood slowly from my chair as I watched my mom stretch her arms open wide and approach me. Her eyes were beaming with love and they were ever so slightly shiny from welling tears. My dad followed closely behind her with the biggest grin on his face. They both embraced me at the same time and we stood there and hugged for the longest time.

"I can't believe you're here," I said shakily as we continued to hug. I pulled back from the hug, looked at both of them, and then we hugged again. Once we let go of each other, I asked, "How in the world did you all pull this off?

I'm so confused," as I looked back and forth between my parents and the McLeods. They all smiled and giggled like schoolchildren that had just pulled off the biggest stunt ever.

"Well, that's where I came in," I heard from across the room. I looked around them all to see who was talking when I saw Amy standing in the doorway of the dining room. She too, was dressed nicely for dinner and had obviously been in on this whole thing. Just when I thought I couldn't be any more surprised or shocked, they upped the ante. Amy walked toward me and began to explain as I'm sure she could see the million questions on my face. "I contacted your parents after we met the other day," she said. "I gave them Mr. and Mrs. McLeod's number so they could plot and scheme together," Amy continued. "I just felt like you needed some family around right now," she said with sympathy on her face.

I walked over and hugged Amy and thanked her for being in on this wild surprise. We all laughed and rehashed how they all pulled this off as we began to seat ourselves at the dinner table. The waiters came in and took more drink orders and began to place bread baskets on the table. Of course, my dad and Dougal instantly jumped on that as they both agreed it was time to stop hugging and get to eating. Men are the same no matter what country, I thought to myself.

We laughed and conversed freely for several minutes while we sipped our wine and began enjoying each other's company. I still couldn't believe they had pulled this together. What a gamble, I thought. What if Fiona hadn't been able to convince me to come to Oban? I could have very easily refused to come on this little trip and then what? I was astonished at how this had played out. As I shook my head once again in disbelief, I saw my mother's phone light up next to me and she checked it. She was responding to a text, which was weird because she wasn't usually one to have her phone out at dinner or check her texts that religiously. My dad interrupted my thoughts and asked me how my new work site had gone this week, so I began to rehash the events of the week.

My mother then interrupted the conversation and said, "Krista." I stopped and looked at her with questioning eyes as I waited to hear what she had to say. "We have one more surprise for you this evening," she continued. I half-smiled with a quizzical look at the others around the table. Dougal and Fiona looked just as curious as I was, so I got the impression this wasn't part of the surprise they were in on. "Honey, we invited someone else to dinner this evening," my mom said. Just then she turned and looked toward the doorway. I turned my head to follow her line of sight, and that's when I saw him. It was Sam.

Thirty-Three

Sam was standing in the doorway with his eyes trained intently on me. We locked eyes and he had a look of seriousness that burned into me. He had his hands in the pants pockets of his dark gray suit. He was wearing a crisp white shirt with a dark tie that perfectly complemented the suit. He looked absolutely delicious and made my stomach flip just to see him standing there looking back at me. His gaze quickly softened into a half smile as one side of his mouth turned up and he winked at me. I tried desperately to gain composure over my continued shock this evening. Then, I audibly let out a gasp as I stood from my chair. I could feel the other eyes at the table watching us to see our reactions to each other. I began to slowly walk toward him and he began to take his hands out of his pockets and move toward me in return. His gaze went back to seriousness, but this time it spoke of intense desire and love.

I sped up my walk to him and we closed our gap within seconds.

I was suddenly completely oblivious to the watching eyes. All I could think about was wrapping my arms around Sam. Which is exactly what I did. He hugged me back with his arms around my waist and his face buried into my hair and neck. He picked me up off the floor so that my legs were dangling and continued to hug me tightly. Tears fell from my eyes. Eventually, I pulled my head back to look at his face as I whispered, "I'm so sorry. Please forgive me."

"Already done," he whispered back in my ear and then kissed me softly and pulled me tighter into a hug.

Realizing that we were giving everyone quite the show, Sam and I pulled away from each other and turned to look at our audience. My mom and Fiona had tears in their eyes. The looks of love and hope on their faces were priceless. I smiled as I looked upon the faces of people I cared about and took Sam's hand to lead him to the table. But, Sam stopped me by gently pulling back on my hand. I turned back to look at him and found Sam going down on one knee with a ring box in his other hand.

How much shock and surprise can one person handle in the span of just a few minutes? I looked at the ring and then back at Sam. My mouth was absolutely agape and there was honestly nothing I could do about it at this point. I wasn't even going to try to regain my composure.

"Krista," Sam started. "I've loved you almost from the first moment we met. We have the most unusual connection and fate seems to keep bringing us together in the most astonishing ways. I can't take away the hurt of your past, and I can't replace Michael. Nor do I want to. But, I desperately want to be a part of your future." Sam paused for just a moment and searched my eyes to see if I agreed. Then, he asked, "Krista, will you marry me?"

The amount of tears streaming down my face were almost alarming. All the pain, and all the grief I had endured were finally dissipating in this one moment of pure joy and happiness. I tried fiercely to get control of my twisted, ugly-cry face so I could respond. After a deep breath, I said, "Yes. Nothing would make me happier." A slow, giant smile spread across Sam's face and he took the ring out of the box and slid it onto my finger. He stood in one fluid motion and scooped me up into a tight hug once again.

As he hugged me, I looked toward the doorway and saw another couple standing there beaming with delighted looks on their faces. They were an older couple and the woman had her hands clasped together as if she were just as happy as the rest of our group. Sam saw where I was looking and turned to look at them as well. He smiled at them and then looked back at me and said, "I'd like you to meet my parents."

Oh my heavens. I didn't think my heart could take much more of this. Once again, I was truly stunned at the events unfolding at that moment and how all these pieces fell into place completely unbeknownst to me. The couple approached us as Sam gestured for them to come over. He introduced us all and his mom hugged me like I was the daughter she never had. She genuinely seemed so happy about this moment. Our small audience stood from their chairs and my parents rushed over to us and began congratulating us as they hugged us both. My dad shook Sam's hand and then pulled him into a hug as well. Introductions were made all around and we all fell into a comfortable hum of excited chatter about the events that had just unfolded.

We all eventually sat at the table and began to talk about how we had come together and the divine intervention that had joined us. We enjoyed each other, got to know one another, and took our time relishing in this moment. We ate, drank, laughed, and cried. There were many questions from our loved ones about Michael's death, Amy's part in this story, and Sam's incredible act of heroism that bound us all together. Sam took over and answered most of the questions to fill the group in on the timeline of events, and I just sat back and listened. I would be fascinated too if I didn't already know the story. It was truly remarkable how we fit together like a puzzle. In my mind, it was something that only God could have come up with.

I looked around the room at the faces present at the table and my mind drifted. I wondered what Michael would have thought of all of this. I think if he knew how this crazy story ended, he would be thrilled for me. He would be content knowing that I found another great love on the other side of deep despair. I had not only survived his loss and the grief that came with it, but I was given the chance to build a new life with someone who loved me just as much as he had. My heart was full and finally healed.

Epilogue

Three months later, Sam and I were boarding a plane bound for Edinburgh, Scotland from Dallas. We were standing on the jetbridge following a long line of passengers patiently waiting to get on the plane. It was about 5 o'clock in the evening and the jetbridge was hot and stuffy. Sam and I stood side-by-side with our arms around each other as we inched our way forward. We looked at each other through side glances and smiled at each other like we were teenagers in love. A week earlier, we had gotten married in Texas at my parent's house in their backyard. It was a small ceremony with only our closest family and friends, and it was perfect. Even Fiona, Dougal, Rachel, and Katherine had made the long journey across the pond to celebrate with us.

As we stood there in the line on the jetbridge, my mind flashed back to the first time I flew to Edinburgh by myself. I had stood on a similar jetbridge that was hot and stuffy, and waited to get on a similar plane. That time had been filled with suffering and sheer agony. I remembered the hurt and feeling as if my heart would never recover. I could barely put one foot in front of the other. I thought about the sweet, older couple I had been behind and how I was jealous of them and their dependence on each other. I remember wanting to just sleep so that I wouldn't have to endure it any longer. But, now ... .I didn't have to be jealous anymore. I had the same thing. I thought to myself, "Look how far I've come. Thank God." I was no longer in pain. In fact, now, I was happier than I could have imagined I could be given what I had been through.

Sam squeezed my side as if he were able to read my thoughts and felt the pain I was reflecting on. It made me wonder if he was thinking about how he felt on that flight too. He had been there. He must have been going through a terrible time too. I looked up at him and his face let me know that he was feeling it as well. We hugged and leaned our heads on each other without saying a single word.

We boarded the flight and once again I was excited that I was getting to sit in first class. Sam helped stow my carry on in the overhead bin and we settled into our pods next to each other. We were headed back to Scotland to resume our lives. Sam had quit his job and called Erick Eden to ask for his old job back. Of course, Erick gladly welcomed him back before Sam could even finish his sentence. I was excited about what the future held. Sam and I were going to have the rest of our lives to love each other and go on adventures.

At that moment, the flight attendant interrupted my thoughts and said, "Excuse me, do you need anything before we depart?" I looked up and realized I recognized the face that stared back at me. It was Kate. My goodness…how things have come full circle. Kate donned a look of recognition too. I unbuckled my seat belt and stood to face Kate. We looked at each other for a moment and I enveloped Kate in a full on hug.

"Thank you," I whispered to her. She looked back at me with questions on her face. "Thank you for taking care of me the last time we met. I was broken and newly widowed on that flight, and I needed someone to be nice to me. You treated me so kindly. I will never forget that," I said.

Kate looked over at Sam, and then looked back at me and smiled. "It seems you are not broken anymore," she replied. I agreed with a smile and returned to my seat beside my husband.

About the Author

Page Parker was born in Texas and currently resides in Oklahoma. She studied communication sciences at Texas Woman's University and has a master's degree in communication sciences and disorders. Page currently practices as a Speech-Language Pathologist, and enjoys writing when she's not working with patients. Page enjoys writing fictional romance as it's a way to escape the reality of everyday life momentarily and use her imagination for story creation. When not writing or working, Page enjoys traveling and spending time with her husband and children. Tethered Remnants is Page's first fictional novel.